UNCLE BASIL'S DEMISE

Victorian London – To Die For
Book One

Karen Dean Benson

ISBN: 979-8-88653-273-9

Published by Satin Romance
An Imprint of Melange Books, LLC
White Bear Lake, MN 55110
www.satinromance.com

Published in the United States of America.

Cover Design by Ashley Redbird Designs

Donna Marie Hoisington Parks
b. 5-2-1942
d. 6-29-2023
...she was one of life's treasures...

I have blessed friends/fans who love to read, thanks for making it so much fun to write stories for you.

Many thanks to Lauri Shappee, Linda Newmann, and fellow author/reader Karen Auriti for setting me straight on a few things writerly. And, for Charlie who never says no to me.

If you're reading this, I would love to hear what you think of my stories. Karendean.benson@gmail.com

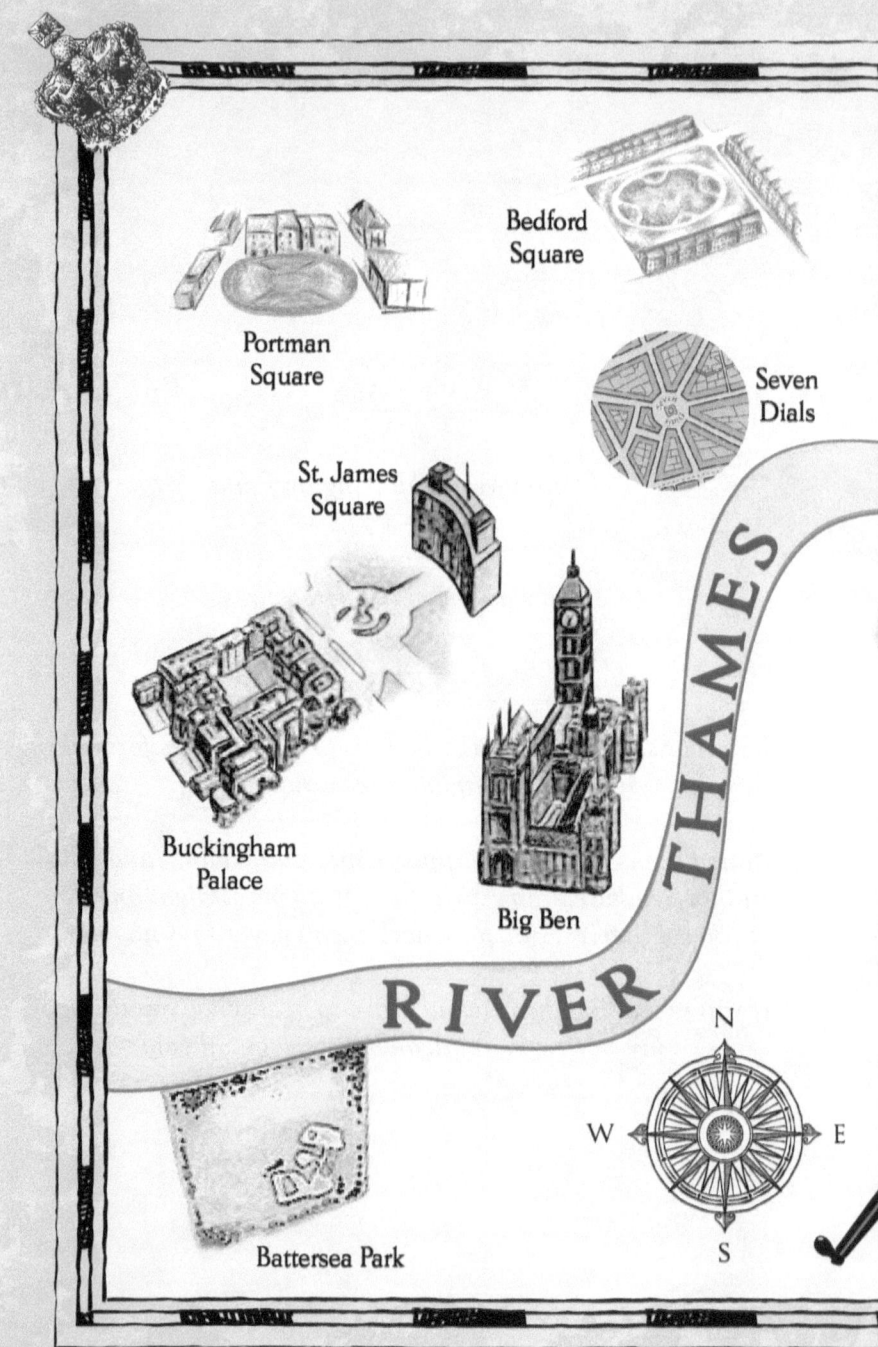

Lincoln's
Inn

Whitechapel

St. Magnus
The Martyr
Church

Pennyfields

Londen
Bridge

The Docks

Southwark

London

Chapter One

Tuesday, 11:45 p.m.
20 September 1870

I ndistinct noises penetrated Tamsin's sleep and she lifted her groggy head off the eiderdown pillow. Though muffled, the voices sounded belligerent, like an argument was occurring in her uncle's library directly below her chamber. The mahogany long-case clock in the downstairs hall chimed the Westminster third quarter.

She scrambled from the bed, shoved her arms into her robe, and swept along the corridor, down the front stairs toward the muted friction. The staff, housed in the attic, would most likely not be aroused considering their distance from the first floor.

As she entered the library, Uncle Basil reclined in his desk chair, his head resting against the leather back. His hands curved over the arms of his chair. His hazel eyes stared at the coffered ceiling seemingly deep in concentration.

She touched his shoulder. "Can I get you something?" And gently shook him. "Uncle."

Puzzled when he didn't respond, she took note of two glasses of his favorite brandy on the desk. The one nearest him nearly empty, the other untouched.

She placed her hands on his warm cheeks. It crossed her mind he might have imbibed too much, though it wasn't his usual behavior to do so.

The chill of the night air washed over her and already suspecting mischief, she spun to the hall noticing the front door ajar. Stepping over the threshold she glanced at the walk that divided the lawn. Then she pattered to the iron gate and latched it as her cursory glance swept up and down Berkley Street.

Streetlamps cast gloomy circles of light in the night's dense fog filtering through Portman Square. A hack approached, the clip-clop of the horse's hooves echoing on the cobbled street but no movement otherwise.

Returning to the library and her motionless uncle, Tamsin's panic increased. Had he suffered apoplexy?

She laid a hand on his shoulder feeling his warm strength beneath the cambric of his white shirt and noticed tiny crystals like froth on his lips.

Clutching the chair arm, her gaze swept over his distinctive features. She loved this kind man as if he were her father.

A sliver of fear crept its icy fingers along her spine circling her heart.

Someone had been here with him. Who? At this hour she supposed the business would have involved intrigue. Though retired, he had been one of The Queen's trusted men. Sweeping her palm over his forehead she brushed his thick auburn hair off his brow.

"Uncle, you need to go to bed."

Moments passed. Her hand rested on his shoulder, and she suddenly realized he wasn't breathing.

As she leaned over him his arm fell off the arm of the chair...and her heart skipped a beat.

Was he...was he ill...

He didn't respond.

His eyes hadn't closed.

Her heart clutched. No. Dear God, please. No.

She leaned over him again, her arms about him. At some point she knew he was dead, and yet her mind couldn't accept it.

Time passed. She moved backward a step or two, lifting his arm to his lap.

She glanced at the desktop, the two glasses, the low-lit lamp. She smelled the aroma of his pipe and his spicy outdoorsy scent.

He might have died of natural causes. Yet her intuition told her the liquid in the Waterford crystals killed him.

Poisoned him.

Who spent the last minutes of his life with him?

She touched his cheek, and his head rolled toward her. She caught a scream bubbling in her throat and readjusted his head against the back of the chair as his arm dropped from the armrest again. A sure sign.

He was dead.

Her heart raced and she had trouble breathing. Her legs melted like jelly. She leaned against his desk taking in the whole of his body as it appeared to be resting in the chair.

Dear God.

He...was...dead.

It was almost as if she floated above his desk and looked down on her beloved uncle as if nothing more than a horrid dream.

Cupping his face with her cold hands, she drew herself

into the truth. The numbness of the moment chipped away as the ache in her heart seeped into her mind and the hands that touched him. The knowledge they'd had their last conversation, their last laugh, never more to hug.

Could he be poisoned? The bit of froth on his lips led her to believe so.

Again, she leaned over him and touched her ear to his heart. No sound at all. Her fingers, pressing to his neck didn't detect a pulse. Her muddled brain focused on the stain of froth drying on his lips. Could it be a stroke? She reached for the glass he must have drunk from, the one nearly empty, and sniffed. Unaware if poison had a scent and equally unaware of what amber liquid it held.

She couldn't decide if the odor smelled the same in both glasses.

A new day rang in with the chime of midnight from the hall clock. She needed to send Charlie with a whistle to the corner hoping a night watchman stood nearby.

Gripping the collar on her night rail her gaze shifted as Uncle Basil's head plopped backward. Gently she swept her fingertips over his eyes closing them as she forced back a wave of pain so strong, she could have fainted. Her grip on the desk steadied her as memories of their life swam before her.

She felt she would die without him.

For certain, he had gone to his heavenly reward.

How long she hovered over him, she knew not. A sense of practicality wandered into her thinking. Breathing deeply, she needed to be strong and think.

Just yesterday he talked of his financial state and what she would have to deal with after he died. Did he know he might lose his life? Did he look into the eyes of his murderer knowing what was to come?

Nausea curdled her stomach. Gulping air, she did her

best to stifle the impulse to regurgitate. Who would murder this wonderful gentleman?

The *why* escaped her as she realized what this meant for the household, small as it was with a housekeeper, cook, and two maids. And, Charlie Bates the all-around man.

Uncle Basil had taught her to keep the household ledgers. She knew that beyond the fact she had lost her dearest and last relative, they could be in dire straits soon. She assumed his pension from Her Majesty would end with his demise. Clasping a hand over her mouth, she realized the staff would have to be let go.

She mustn't forget Uncle Basil's estranged wife, Mrs. Reynolds-Walker. She would need to be told, which meant a visit to her home. Tamsin had always found it difficult to feel any consideration toward her. She hardly knew the woman who'd spent less than a month in this house when the two had married many years earlier.

Barely six at the time, Tamsin didn't know the particulars of their separation. But maids do tittle-tattle, and she had a naughty habit of quietly listening as they gossiped. Mrs. Reynolds-Walker agreed to part as soon as he could procure a home for her.

He had also settled a yearly stipend allowing her independence. As the years sped by, she hardly saw the woman whose visits were infrequent and usually to do with a repair on her home, or her carriage. Her visits had always involved money.

Tamsin drew a palm over her uncle's forehead. She felt no regrets about Mrs. Reynolds-Walker's loss of income or home. Ironically, her prosperity would diminish along with Tamsin's household.

The great clock in the hall chimed the half-hour.

He must be at the heavenly gates by now. St. Peter would certainly rejoice when greeteing him.

The pain in her heart caused her breath to catch and she almost swooned. Her palms cupped his face, the stubble on his cheeks comforting. He still felt warm, perhaps, a bit less. Her instinct to cover him with the wrap that was slung over the easy chair in the corner seemed silly. She chided herself for the foolish thought.

And that thought forced her to consider the coming day and the maids. She glanced at the calendar on his desk. Tomorrow—well, today—a two o'clock meeting with Mr. Manchin. The two men had worked together for decades at Her Majesty's Secret Service. Her uncle retired several years ago. He'd been a Lieutenant Detective in Her Majesty's service at Scotland Yard and continued to dabble in lesser cases of murder, theft, vagrants, prostitutes, and predators. He had occasion to remind Tamsin the population on the streets of London burst with all manner of mankind.

Tamsin went to the window and pulled back the drape enough to see outside and the pale pools of light from the lamps that seemed to disappear with the thickening fog. Layers of reds and oranges would begin to color the inky sky in another hour or so.

She pulled the drape into place and took hold of herself.

For certain, she wasn't ready to let anyone know her beloved uncle was gone.

If we are to get on with living here, I must put you some-where safe--for a day or two until I can think of something better.

She pulled a large quilt from the wardrobe in her room and laid it out on the floor next to his chair then slid him onto the blanket. Folding the blanket over him she dragged him through the hall and the kitchen, thankful for the smooth oak flooring.

She knew enough about the law to realize she tampered with a crime scene. Though if he died of a stroke, it wouldn't be a crime scene. She felt deeply disturbed about her decision and was compelled to hide him. Opening the kitchen door, she tugged him down the few steps onto the damp grass then quietly closed the door.

With a sliver of moonlight intermittingly streaking the foggy night, she knew it would take every ounce of determination to get the blanket to the latched doors of the cellar; tug she must and reached for the ends of the blanket.

Tears clouded her vision as she thought how they would all get on without him. She stilled, hands on the blanket and bowed her head.

I love you so much. She swiped at the wetness on her lashes, took a deep breath and jerking on the blanket, dug in her slippers, and slowly trudged toward the latched doors one step at a time dragging his remains across the damp lawn. Thankfully the thick foggy mist covered her actions as she murmured, *I will find out what happened to you or all the times you talked to me about your work will be meaningless.*

Turning the lock over, and lifting the door, she cringed at the metallic squeak and held her breath as the deep night rustle of branches appeared normal. Satisfied she'd not awakened Charlie, she took hold of the blanket and whispered as if Uncle Basil still lived.

Forgive my bumbling.

He slid easily downward over the steps into the earthen floor, though she cringed at the disrespect to his dear self. The shifting clouds intermittently allowed a pale slice of light to guide her as she maneuvered his body toward the back of the dugout where the sharp scent of parsnips and turnips filled the air. Potatoes and carrots also mingled in the musky air. Cook Ames' makings for horseradish assailed her.

Dragging the blanket behind a store of empty crates and unused items, she tucked him into a corner where she secured the blanket about him, then placed several empty crates in such a fashion that anyone entering the space would not think to scavenge beyond. She sat for a moment and slid her hand beneath the blanket noticing the heat of his body evaporating. Her fingers swept through his thick reddish head of hair as she calmed herself. Her heart ached with the loss of him the hard realization of his death beginning to seep into her heart.

This was no time to shed tears. Not yet. He would stay alive in her heart until she solved how he died.

She couldn't help but think of the second glass of spirits. That alone gave her pause to consider murder. That and the front door and gate left open—and the little crystals of froth on his lips. Her throat tightened to think of the unsuspecting pain he must have felt if it were poison.

Closing her eyes, she prayed in the dark, whispering to her beloved uncle.

If I've learned anything from you it's resilience. I'll pursue the truth Uncle Basil, or I'm not the niece you raised.

One last look at the contents of the stone and mortar walls with the dirt floor, she felt he was secure and stepped up and out, closing and latching the doors. She kicked up her slippers in the damp grass on the walk back to the house, effectively hiding the drag marks.

Returning to the house, Tamsin cleaned any trace of having hauled a blanket down the hallway and kitchen. She hid the two glasses behind books in the library, arranging them to look normal and set the decanter on the floor behind a stack of books.

Glancing over his desktop, knowing how fastidious he'd always been about leaving his work area in precise tidiness for the next day's business, she firmed up a stack of papers.

Overcome with the tragedy, her sense of well-being shattered. How would she carry on without him? How does one pretend to be normal, when the most important part of one's life is wrenched from them?

The hall clock chimed the full Westminster Quarters and stroked the fourth hour. After one last cursory glance about the library, she scooped up the candle and climbed the stairs to her room. In the morning, it would be important to be refreshed and answer the obvious questions about his whereabouts.

Chapter Two

Westminster chimes mingled with her dream of the earth cellar, horseradish, and spiders when she gasped and sat up in bed.

Throwing the covers aside, she scrambled out of bed. Her watch noted seven a.m.

The full truth of her dream and the night whooshed at her as she fell back on the mattress, shaken with sadness and disbelief. Covering her mouth, she gasped for breath.

Her beloved uncle was gone.

Dead.

Packed away in the underground cellar as if he were cabbage.

Tearing off her night rail, she scrambled to dress quickly, ran a brush through her hair, and wound it in a bun securing it with pins. One quick glance in the mirror forced her to splash water on her face and pinch her cheeks. She looked a mess and took a deep breath reminding herself she had a role to play. No one must know what lay hidden in the cellar or her heart.

Slowly making her way toward the stairs, she heard the maids, Sally, and Evie, chattering about their chores for Tuesday. Besides the usual, in September the maids dragged the rugs outside, laid them over the back door railing, and beat them with a bat until no more dust flew in the air.

She knew they still had the back parlor and two bedrooms and—she almost fell down the last few steps—her uncle's library to air. *Oh my.*

No one must be allowed to go into his library. The thought made her weak-kneed. It should remain untouched. With heavy heart, she turned back up the stairs to her room. How will she dare look Mrs. Thistlewaite in the eye and tell her not to touch the library?

In the same moment, the housekeeper called up the stairs, "Miss Tamsin, were you on your way down? I have need to talk to you."

She gathered herself up like a soldier might, strong and forthright as possible. Considering she would be lying her way through the next several days, it would prove to be a challenging task.

Taking a deep breath, she gushed, "I forgot something, I'll be right down."

"As you please, miss."

Within a minute, she plunged her way down the stairs and greeted the housekeeper. "Yes. Sorry about that. What needs have you?"

"It's a private matter. Can we step into the parlor quick like?"

"Certainly." Tamsin walked ahead allowing the elder to follow.

Mrs. Thistlewaite's pursed lips spread into a thin line. She barely mumbled. "Mr. Walker's bed hasn't been slept in." Her chin rose a teensy trifle as if her burden of knowledge got the best of her.

Not sure if her voice would give away the lie, she offered, "Mr. Walker left last night on business. He will be gone for quite some time. He rushed at the very last minute you see. Late evening."

"Well, then. That will affect our weekly menu. And the laundry, too. It would seem I might have been made aware sooner than later."

"I take all the blame, Mrs. Thistlewaite. He received a special delivery letter late and you had already gone to bed. I didn't think it necessary to disturb you. Accept my apology, please. You work hard enough as it is to be awakened from your slumber."

The housekeeper's white cap bobbed with her acceptance of the truth. "Your breakfast will be served within minutes, miss. Will you dine in the parlor as usual?"

"Yes, thank you. Also, the carpet in the library can be skipped this time. Would you let Sally and Evie know?"

Mrs. T nodded. "They will be glad of it."

Tamsin turned toward the library and cupped the knob, taking a moment to brace herself before entering the heartbreaking scene. The air smelled faintly of whiskey or whatever liquid filled the decanter. Brandy, she remembered, that's what he enjoyed. He once explained it was fortified with wine which determined it a man's real drink. His eyes had twinkled along with his merriment.

She glanced at the cushioned mahogany chair where she found him. The leather back and seat were outlined from the weight of his body. All else looked as if he still lived and ate his breakfast in the dining room. Two strips of crisp bacon, three eggs, runny yolks, toast with marmalade, fried potatoes, and hot coffee. Ridiculously hot coffee.

She wanted this to be one of her bad dreams and nothing more. Her hand spread over her thudding heart. The ache coursed through her as if darts pelted her skin.

How could she cope with the loss of him?

How were any of them to do so?

The front bell rang and Mrs. Thistlewaite's light steps pattered down the hallway. Tamsin recognized the voice, and her nerves tensed to the point she felt faint-hearted.

The housekeeper rapped on the library door, then leaned in through the opening. "It's Mrs. Reynolds-Walker. What should I tell her?"

Without waiting to be let in, the tall woman nudged the door open almost causing Mrs. Thistlewaite to fall away as she'd been leaning on it.

Cloth flowers bobbed on the rim of Mrs. Reynolds-Walker's hat as she deliberately ignored the housekeeper and barged into the library. "Where is he? Where's he got to this early?"

The *he* she obviously referred to would be Uncle Basil. Tamsin eyed the woman. "Mr. Walker is on business and will not be receiving for a while. Several months I should think. What is it I can do for you, Mrs. Reynolds-Walker?"

The woman's gaze scraped over her as if raking up dirt. "I hardly think you can do anything for me. Where has he gone?"

Mrs. Thistlewaite tiptoed backwards closing the door behind her and managed to give Tamsin a wide-eyed stare just as it closed.

No one in this house cared for that woman. The wife that had never been a wife, is how they whispered about her. Her visits were infrequent, mayhap once a year at most. It

13

concerned Tamsin. Why of all days would she make an appearance today?

Squaring her shoulders, Tamsin forced a smile. "'Tis not your business to know my uncle's whereabouts."

Mrs. Reynolds-Walker's eyes narrowed with discontent. Tamsin could see the self-centered woman readying a nasty comment. "Nothing you are capable of handling." She stepped further into the library glancing about, making little *humph* sounds. She slowly ran a finger of her white glove over the front of his desk as she tried to read the top letter on the stack Tamsin had neatened last night—*er, more like four this morning.*

She quickly placed a book on top of the letter thus cutting short Mrs. Reynolds-Walker's obvious snooping.

Rather than make eye contact with the woman, Tamsin glanced about the room. As she did so, her gaze fell on Uncle Basil's pince-nez that must have fallen off his nose in his last moments.

It will be a miracle if his wife doesn't step on them.

The front doorbell rang. Again. Mrs. Thistlewaite's steps tip-tapped along the corridor. Tamsin wasn't up to full speed yet and with little sleep, she would soon be collapsing in a chair if she weren't careful.

She overheard Mrs. Thistlewaite in the foyer, "Good morning to you, sir. She's in the library."

The timber of Harrison Spencer's voice had already announced him to Tamsin. She didn't know if she should be relieved to see him or more concerned that Mrs. Reynolds-Walker didn't show signs of leaving. What a morning this turned out to be. If she had her way, she'd bury herself beneath a comforter and weep her sorrow.

His face lit up the moment he saw her. She knew his heart would break to learn the truth. He'd be devastated. His relationship with her uncle resembled that of a greatly respected tutor and pupil.

Uncle Basil's stories about his detective career, adventures, and misadventures were what influenced Harrison to decide on law rather than police work.

Mrs. Reynolds-Walker instantly shattered the silence in the room as she glared at the young gentleman. "And who might you be?"

That's when Harrison, about to say something to Tamsin, realized they weren't alone. He glanced in the direction of the peevish voice.

Tamsin offered, "Mr. Spencer. Mrs. Reynolds-Walker."

The woman didn't wait for Mr. Spencer to respond and snipped, "You, young lady, have yet to answer my inquiry about Mr. Walker."

"What might your inquiry have been?" She smiled woefully at him.

"Where did you say Basil has taken himself off to? I need to know his whereabouts." She brushed a gloved hand across the back of the chair and suddenly squalled. "Where is my other glove? They are my favorites."

She backed away from the desk causing quite a rattle.

Harrison glanced at the floor in front of the desk, and Tamsin followed suit looking at the floor near the door to the library and behind it, something white caught her eye. "Is this the match?"

Mrs. Reynolds-Walker snatched it from her. "Were you hiding it from me?"

"But I..."

Harrison intervened. "You should be grateful to once again have a matched pair."

She landed a starchy glare at him before snapping at Tamson, "You have yet to answer my question about where your uncle has gone."

Mrs. Reynolds-Walker irritated her to no end. She tried not to huff when answering. "I will not say where he has taken himself as I do not have his leave to announce his whereabouts. It's a shame you've come all this way without being satisfied. Is there anything else I might do for you before you leave?"

Two could play the game of stratagem, and cantankerous ill will.

Tamsin noted Harrison gave a slight bow to Mrs. Reynolds-Walker. With his two eldest sisters, he certainly knew better than to get into the middle of a hassle between them.

A moment later he started to lean down to retrieve her uncle's pince-nez on the floor when Tamsin, fully aware of what he spied, grabbed his arm to make him look at her. "I am glad you've come. Uncle Basil put a book aside for you, thinking you might like it."

With that, Tamsin glanced at Mrs. Reynolds-Walker as if to ask when she might depart.

The woman, known for her discourteous manner, acted particularly odd. Usually a harpy, though she would never have intimated such to her uncle. He did marry the woman although she never resolved the *why* of that. They certainly weren't in love and had never shared a roof, except for the first few weeks of marriage. The new Mrs. Reynolds-Walker had slept in a guest room at that time.

The woman made her way around the desk reaching for the door latch. "Oh...look there...Mr. Walker's eyeglasses. How will he manage without them, I wonder?" The smile she turned on Tamsin was fraught with calculation.

Harrison picked them up and handed them to Tamsin.

Her heart thumped; she soldiered herself. "I expect he will not miss these. He owns another pair for just this reason. How they got on the floor will remain a mystery, I imagine."

A russet-colored autumn flower in Mrs. Reynolds-Walker's hat waved in her turnabout as she stalked toward the door articulating her dissatisfaction. "It would do you a service to polish your manners, miss. Your uncle is remiss in allowing you to reign over his affairs while absent. You lack charm and courtesy when dealing with others."

Tamsin's anxiety lowered the moment that dreadful woman forcefully closed the door with her exit. She could never abide her. Mostly because she thought she knew what that woman did to her dear uncle so many years ago, and the reason they never lived together as husband and wife.

Chuckling, he said, "Well, well, Miss Tamsin. Seems you have an enemy in the camp."

Frowning, she snapped. "I've been left with more than I care to manage. My nerves have thinned. And—"

Harrison's handsome face spread into a cockney smile. "What, you cannot abide that woman? Tch, tch. I would think you in the majority if a poll were to be taken." He nodded toward the dining room. "Mrs. Thistlewaite invited me to breakfast. Considering Basil is off somewhere, there should be plenty."

Tamsin wasn't sure she could stomach anything. Simply sitting with him for a bit and pretending normalcy seemed best.

"She's being thrifty. Though your company is quite welcome."

Sipping her morning tea, she watched him devour eggs and bacon much like her uncle and allowing her a bittersweet moment to compare the two. Her eyes squinted and she quickly patted them with a napkin. "Oh, my, the tea is hot."

"You aren't eating? This is delicious. Mrs. Labady could stand to take lessons from your Cook Ames." He buttered a warm scone then pasted it with raspberry preserves.

"I'd be interested to know why you live in a boarding

home when I'm rather certain you could afford something much better and more private." She leaned in, elbows on the table, her chin resting on the knuckles of her hands.

For a moment he gave his living arrangement a thought. "Well, the location for one. It's easily accessible to my work. And I've most amenities taken care of."

"It just seems your privacy is at a minimum. Don't you have to share the washroom? I'd dislike that most of all I think."

He chuckled and set his cup on the saucer. "Living in a boarding house is a fraction of what it would be in a residence. And the cost fits within the budget I've chosen."

A forkful of egg followed his answer.

She knew he was mindful of finances, having overheard her uncle answering some of his questions from time to time. He had no idea the comfort he brought to her right now.

"As long as you live in a boarding house, you will most likely never enjoy food equal to Cook Ames." She tried not to sound wistful. "Breakfast was Uncle Basil's favorite meal of the day."

"Was? At least he's returning, don't forget. By the by, can you at least tell me where he's gone? I know how to keep a secret."

She met his hazel green eyes over the rim of her cup, knowing that lying to him would diminish their friendship. It could not be long before he found out the truth about her uncle. However, until she decided whether murder or a stroke were to blame, she couldn't tell the truth. And even then, if it were a stroke, the pension might still go away.

She busied herself slathering a scone with jam and scrambled to think of a plausible answer.

"He had an emergency wire from his plantation, Hilldale, late yesterday. There is a severe problem that his British overseer cannot solve. Luckily, he booked passage to India and boarded late last night."

Swallowing the bacon he'd just bit off, he added, "Well, that's interesting. Did the wire include the problem?"

"Not that I am aware. He took it with him. He really didn't want any fuss about anything, he just wanted to leave at once."

"If there is anything I can do in his absence that will make it easier on you, please inform me." He set his knife and fork aside, having finished eating, and patted his mouth with the napkin. "I mean it, Tamsin. I am here for you."

His sandy hair parted off center with curls at the neckline and around his ears. A lock of it flipped over his high forehead. On impulse she wondered what it would be like to comb her fingers through it, as if he were a younger brother who needed tidying up. Which was a silly thought considering he was several years older than she.

"Stop fussing over me. Tell me about your Inns party last week."

"The highlight of course made the celebration. Prince Albert appeared. He asked many interesting questions of us and prevailed upon several of us to mention our ambitions. He also asked about my father. It has to do with his archeological traipses to Egypt that mostly interested His Grace."

"Prince Albert singled you out. That ought to go a long way in getting through your pupillage."

He chuckled. "Are you saying I need assistance to pass my exams?"

"Uncle Basil thinks you'll breeze through it all. Your star shines bright in his estimation."

Their hands rested on the linen tablecloth, and she lightly patted his. "I agree with him, if anyone is ready to tackle the qualifying sessions, it will be you. You told me once that Lincoln's Inn is for the scholars."

"Ah, you throw my youthful bragging at me." His white teeth slashed with a grin. "As excited as I am to be nearing the end of my studies, I am still not entirely sure whether I lean toward family law or commercial law. It's a bugger of a decision." With his head slightly bowed, he glanced at her with the silly smile on her face and shrugged his shoulders. "Decisions, decisions."

"Uncle Basil always says, 'Follow your heart, and then your mind.'" And in that instant, pain like a bolt of lightning struck her and she gasped.

"Are you all right?"

She forced a smile and nodded.

"He does say that doesn't he? It's one of his favorite idioms." He lightly slapped the tabletop. "Well, I shan't take up any more of your time. I know how busy you must be with him gone and leaving everything to you. You are now the temporary commander of this ship."

Compelling herself to be amiability as they both pushed back from the table, she offered, "Do stop by and check in on us. I'm going to be quite lonely." She nerved herself up not to get maudlin as she spoke the truth.

"Give my regards to Mrs. Thistlewaite for the perfect way to start the day."

She walked him to the front door and slowly closed it, leaning against it as she surveyed the hall and the door to Uncle Basil's library. She'd never see him in his chair again. Ever.

A knock on the door startled her. Opening it to Harrison, who grinned at her, "You mentioned Basil had a book set aside for me?"

"Oh my, yes. How thoughtless of me. I'll get it."

She returned with *An Anatomy of Criminal Law* and handed it to him.

"I see he has marked several passages." He drew a finger

over the pieces of paper sticking out from the pages. "He puts great stock in this author. Well, thank you." His bright smile made her feel even more horrid lying about her uncle's absence.

Tamsin returned to the library and stood beside the chair her uncle last occupied. She touched the leather thinking of the moment, just hours ago, when she realized he was dead and bit her lip rather than sob her heart out. She had an urge to throw herself into his leather chair. Yet she refrained from doing so should someone observe her odd behavior.

Chapter Three

Harrison intended to flag a hack, yet his concern that Basil would leave Miss Tamsin and her household without protection surprised him. He surmised that Basil's rush to catch the ship gave him no time to plan properly. And anyone who knew Tamsin would agree about her solid independence. Yet, the household of women needed proper security.

He decided he could take a minute or two and walked toward the back of the house and seek out the next best thing. Charlie Bates, the all-inclusive stablemaster, gardener, and footman seemed quite capable of handling what he intended to ask.

Basil had mentioned not too long ago that he considered ridding himself of the horse and carriage. More so because of how impossible maneuvering their vehicle through the crowded overrun streets had become. Hailing a carriage or riding the underground tube were better choices.

Though relatively new, the rail, after extensive trials, has proven to be a feat of magnificent proportions. Skepticism slipped away like rain in a gutter as Londoners by the thousands began using the underground. With the tube operating at maximum efficiency, God forbid The Queen should be out for a ride, not a body could get through the streets what with the throngs that push and shove to get a glimpse of her equipage.

He approached the back of the home and caught Charlie Bates bending over a patch of rose bushes along the south side of the property.

"What have we here? A rose budding in September?"

With a groan, Charlie used the palm of his hand against his thigh to straighten up. "Mr. Harrison, how are you today?"

"Fine, thank you. I'm on my way out after a delightful breakfast and thought I would catch you first and mention something now that Mr. Walker is gone for a month or so."

Though the day was cloudy, Charlie drew off his woolen tam, and swiped at the few remaining strands of hair straggling down his brow. "I'd heard. Sudden like, weren't it?"

Harrison stepped gingerly across a muddy patch and neared Bates so he wouldn't have the neighborhood listening. "I understand an emergency of some sort arose. What I am concerned about and want to mention is that the women in the house are without a male should there be problem."

Charlie replaced his woolen tam, grunting as he did so. "Miss Tamsin and Mrs. Thistlewaite together would scare the *bejesus* out of any intruders I'd dare say."

A sudden grin widened Harrison's cheeks. "True enough. I just thought you could be a bit more watchful in the evenings. Perhaps have a walk about before you retire. Would that suit you?"

"Sure, as fittin', Mr. Harrison. You can count on me. 'Sides, I'd hear a ruckus. When they get riled, neither of them is quiet a'tall."

He barked a laugh at the image that came to mind. "Then

I will leave the situation in your capable hands as I bid you good day."

He made his way toward Oxford Street hoping to catch a ride. His thoughts continued to center on Basil and why he would leave Tamsin to carry on without a man in the house. No matter the rush to catch a ship, it didn't seem like him to neglect the safety of his cherished niece and the female staff.

Tamsin pushed aside the gauze curtain and peered out the parlor window. She guessed the distance from the house to the underground vault could be nearly twenty yards. Sturdy oaks and beeches spread out over the area meant to offer shade. The home had been built in the early eighteen hundreds, and the underground room at the same time. Though the house had been updated several times since, she knew the storeroom was original.

Dropping the curtain back in place, she felt the need to take care of correspondence on Uncle Basil's desk. One of them being a note to Mr. Manchin informing him Basil would not be able to meet with him today at two, and asked Evie to deliver it to his office. Then she devoted the next hour to the household accounts and felt certain they were solvent for a month or more.

With her uncle gone, Mrs. Thistlewaite agreed to whittle down the amount of food needed. Tamsin hadn't given thought of doing so until the housekeeper mentioned it herself—though her reason being the temporary absence of her uncle. Tamsin's motive was far different. How long could she keep up the running of the household as they all knew it now?

Wednesday, 10:00 a.m.
21 September 1870

The doorbell rang, and the housekeeper's light step pattered down the hall.

"It's an elder woman to see Mr. Walker. She seems a nervous sort, Miss."

"Send her in. I'll see what I can do for her."

Seconds later, a neatly dressed woman appearing to be in her sixties entered the library. "Mrs. Adele Thomson. I've come to speak with Mr. Walker about a private matter."

"Miss Morgan at your service. Please take a seat. I am pleased to meet you, Mrs. Thomson. I will be assisting you as Mr. Walker's away for a time. He instructed me to take charge of his clients in his absence. How may I help?" She sat in Uncle Basil's leather chair and felt the warmth and comfort of him. Surprisingly, it imbued her with a sense she could do this.

Taking note of Uncle Basil's degrees and awards, the woman's eyes narrowed as she perused his recognitions and laurels through the years. "When will he return?"

"It could be several months or more."

"I can't wait that long."

"I've worked with Mr. Walker for several years."

"How does your experience compare to his?"

Tamsin inhaled slowly. "His years as an honorable detective for Her Majesty's service are unparalleled. I can assure you if our work does not get results, you will not have to pay a fee."

"You speak in the plural. Are you inferring you aren't the only detective?"

Tamsin could not blame her for inquiring, yet to acknowledge she was the only person in the office would surely send her on her way. "We have been taught by the best, that I can assure you, ma'am."

Mrs. Thomson's brow eased, her skepticism fading. Tamsin quickly added, "Why exactly do you need our service? Is it a family issue, or something else?"

The woman folded her gloved hands over the satchel on her lap. "My grandson has taken me to my wits end. I've sole responsibility of the lad as his father's disappeared, and his mother went out one eve and has not been seen nor heard from since. It's me and him."

Tamsin made notes as the woman talked. "How long ago would you say?"

She tapped her chin, "Hmm, goin' on two years now."

"I need his name and age, please."

"Joshua. Joshua Zillig. He's fifteen." She fumbled with the clasp on her pocketbook and swiped at the side of her left eye with her glove.

"What is the situation with your grandson?"

"He's always a loving mite. Up until he fell in with some blokes, whom I've not met. Just the same, he's changed."

"Can you be more specific?" Tamsin noted the concern in her elderly features. Furrows in her forehead, troubled eyes. She should be enjoying peace at this time in her life.

"He refuses to go to school. He stays out to all hours of the night. I live alone and hate to lock him out. It is also hard to stay up waiting for him. Most of the time I do not see him until the next afternoon when he turns a surly eye then goes to his room and sleeps away the rest of the day."

A disconsolate sigh followed. "Then it begins all over again." Her features scrunched with sadness. Dejection perhaps or regret. Which struck Tamsin with remorse. Losing a daughter and having the care of a troubled grandson was certainly cause for despondency.

"He's throwing away his life on these lads who have led him down a wrong path. I wanted him to be so much more than what his parents aspired to."

"Can you tell me the names of the lads? Where do they live? Anything at all that you remember."

The grandmother closed her eyes and bowed her head in thought finally offering, "One night several young men gathered outside the front stoop. They were teasing and poking him, I think. Their voices carried that tone that means they are angry or challenging. Someone called him a bog trotter...a cowardly fella. A cake, they said."

Tamsin drew in a breath. A bully leader challenged her grandson.

Mrs. Thomson added, "Then the tyrant told him not to care about an old woman who refuses him his lads. As if I am the problem. I try my best. He's my grandson; all I've got left."

"Where is it you live?"

"Old Queen Street #6. It's south of..."

"I'm familiar with the area." She wasn't surprised they lived on a backstreet of old 17th century homes gone to ruin and squalor. The area was in keeping with her grandson having fallen in with a bad lot.

"How often do they meet?"

"Joshua goes out every night."

"How does he treat you?" Tamsin made notes on a pad of paper as the grandmother talked.

A faint blush colored the woman's cheeks. She fussed with the clasp on her satchel. "I'm sad to say he shows signs of bein' like his father. A mean sort who'd give the back of his hand to my daughter for nothing a'tall."

"He's been rough with you, then?" Tamsin's fingers pinched her writing tool.

Mrs. Thompson's eyes misted as she shook her head.

"No. No. Though I see the look of his father in his eyes when I try to get him to listen to reason. His father came to be a bit of a brute. I'm at my wits end Miss Morgan and have little money to pay you. He's a good lad until several weeks ago. He's all that's left of all my years on this earth."

"Would you have a likeness of him?"

Again, she shook her head. "He walks with a limp. An injury as a toddler that never healed proper."

Tamsin nodded and finished writing. "Should I suppose the father had a hand in the injury?"

Mrs. Thomson glanced sideways as if she was ashamed to look into Tamsin's eyes. "Something his father gave him for whining too much."

"I am deeply sorry to hear that. Can you tell me what exactly it is you want from us? He would not be considered a runaway as such."

The elderly woman sat straight in her chair, her chin up. "I want you to put the fear of God in him. I want him to see he's on the wrong side of the path he's chosen."

Tamsin took another deep breath and pushed her uncle's chair back. "Fair enough. I think I have sufficient information for now. We will see what we can do. Would it be convenient for you to return in three days? I hesitate to go to your home. It's better for me if Joshua doesn't know I exist. Hopefully, we will have some information for you."

She walked the elderly woman to the door and closing it, berated herself for thinking she could help with the lad. The poor grandmother, all she had in her life was her grandson and he was on the threshold of turning to a life of crime. She chided herself for thinking she could turn him about. Her uncle's death taught her there were no guarantees in this world.

An idea came to her that with some help, it might just be the making of Joshua Zillig.

First things first. She went to her uncle's closet and dug through his clothing to see what might be of use to her. In doing so, she realized how saddened she is at the loss of him. A more dapper man had yet to be seen. He carried himself handsomely and always with a pleasant face as he greeted those who sought him out. She buried her face into the tweed jacket in front of her. It smelled of his cologne.

How she wished to feel his arm around her shoulder, hugging her, or sharing some tale about someone he had run into at White's.

An hour later, dissatisfied with the few articles of clothing she deemed somewhat appropriate to conceal her identity, she needed to shop. Her uncle, six feet and stocky, and she five feet and a half inch, and slender— his clothing would not suit. She needed a costume now. She also needed boots that would fit.

Gathering up her cloak and gloves, she sought Mrs. Thistlewaite. "I'm going out for a bit."

Cook Ames, busy showing Sally how to carve out the insides of a duck, presumably the evening meal, gave a nod to Tamsin, and didn't skip a word with the maid's instruction.

Before Tamsin left the kitchen she asked, "Sally, did the note get delivered to Mr. Manchin?"

"Yes, ma'am."

"Was there a reply?"

"He thanked me is all."

The day turned decent for once and Tamsin arrived near Seven Dials at Dudley Street with a bleary sunshine not quite warming her shoulders. She picked her way through the crowd of confusion and clamor seeking men's clothing. She'd never had reason to come here and wondered how business could be carried out with such an uproar. The disorder and wrangling amongst the stall owners and prospective purchasers made her want to give up. Except she needed male trousers and a few other items that would be a better fit than her uncle's.

Elbowed and jostled, she glanced about the row of carts and tables as best she could navigate and not be swept into a crush. Somewhere in the long tangle of cobbled street the scent of spicy Indian food curled in the air, and fish on a hot pan sizzled in fat. Her stomach clenched at the curry, cumin, and fat. She took a deep breath through her mouth.

Eventually she spotted shoes dangling on their laces from a rod and elbowed her way to the front of the stall.

A thick shawled woman bent forward. "What' cha lookin' for dearie?"

"A pair of men's boots, about this size." She held up her hands indicating six or seven inches.

A big toothless smile rewarded her. "Right char, miss." She grabbed short black boots hanging from the frame of the tent and went around the front of the stall. Setting them on the cobbled street, she dug under her table and pulled out several more, giving Tamsin a variety from which to pick.

Tamsin lifted her skirt and measured the boot against the side of her own kidskin. "These should do fine. Have you a man's jacket that might fit me?"

The bleary-eyed woman cast a worn glance at Tamsin's upper torso and turned to a bag of old tweeds pulling out a jacket. In the stall next to them, the scent of curry and fish assaulted her.

Tamsin thought if she were to come across the lad in her midnight search, surely, he'd smell her before she could approach him.

An extremely tall young man waved a banner above the crowd, hawking chestnuts, walnuts, apples, and pears in a loud baritone. The crowd opened for him as he slowly made his way, wares thrown over his shoulders that he hoped to sell.

As soon as he moved on, Tamsin leaned toward the clothing stall. "I will take it. Perchance would you have pants that might fit me?" She backed up, careful she wouldn't be knocked down by the crush of traffic and opened her cape.

The seller squinted. "Yer a might thin. Ye'll be needin' a rope or belt to hold them up."

"And have you such a belt?"

The seller disappeared beneath her table digging in a container, and finally came up for air with two sets of trousers and a belt. Her hair had come loose from pins with her effort, and she drew her arm over the strands getting them out of her eyes. "Try these for size."

Tamsin held the brown tweeds in front of her and felt they would suit with the aid of a belt. Drawing it around her waist, she could make do if she punched a hole in it.

"These will do fine." She glanced about as the woman shoved her purchases in a bag.

London's misty days had let up recently accounting for the dryness of the walls and lanes of the street-seller-marketplace. She shuddered to think of picking through damp items. The marketplace could certainly be characterized as second-hand and threadbare. She was mighty pleased with herself coming here. She'd found exactly what she needed for disguise.

"Well, then I think I am done. What do I owe you?"

The fumes from the woman's pipe circled the air above her as she mentally tallied the cost of Tamsin's unique purchases.

"That'll be 5 shillings, missy," sputtered the raggedy woman.

Tamsin's heart strings tugged at her benevolent nature, and she added another shilling.

Crunching the coins with her back teeth, the seller

removed the coinage from her mouth eyeing Tamsin with suspicion. "I've a wonder what yer aboot, miss."

Tamsin pulled the string on her reticule taut and shoved it inside the pocket of her cape. "A bit of fun. A prank. Nothing more." And with that said, she scooped up the bundle and hurried on her way.

On the walk back to Berkeley she had plenty of time to think of Uncle Basil, and this idea she could make a living sleuthing for others.

Taking this upon herself to keep a roof overhead, she mumbled. Why else would I wear men's worn and smelly clothing?

Well, commonsense came to mind and she decided she might have bitten off more than she could handle.

Returning to Portman Square, Tamsin had already set out the clothing she'd purchased and opened the windows of her bedroom, then shut the door to the hall. She hoped the rank scent would dissipate within a few hours.

As her second task upon returning home was to send Harrison a note asking a favor. A big favor. One that she implored him *not* to question. She relied heavily upon their friendship and the hope that he would say yes.

It was after ten o'clock when she heard a rap at the front door and quickly opened it, slipping outside where Harrison waited for her.

"What the bloody hell?" whispered Harrison. "You smell like a refuge bin in a back alley."

Her cheeks were faintly blackened, and with her hair

tucked beneath a tam she looked like a lad dressed in men's clothing.

"Shush, you'll wake the house."

She grabbed his hand and led him down the steps, past the gate, and away from the streetlamps.

He drew back, halting in his tracks. "I will not go a step further until you tell me what in the name of God you are doing dressed like this."

"Do not blaspheme." The word *this* embodied a whole bundle of ridicule. Arms crossed, and clearly noting his glower in the weak lamplight, she proclaimed the entire problem, Joshua Zillig's situation, adding his dear grandmother's fears—all in a rush of words to get the telling over with.

She knew him to be a typically insufferable male.

He glared at her—at a loss for words. His eyes bulged with disbelief. "I'm to be your second in command as you attempt to pound common sense into a lad of fifteen. Are you out of your mind? Gangs carry knives." He fisted his walking stick shaking it in the air. "'Tis all I've got to defend us."

"Not so. I brought this." She handed up Uncle Basil's Webley Bull Dog revolver. "You are welcome to use it."

He gaped at the revolver in her hand. "In the name of the Almighty, Tamsin. What are you involved with?"

"I just told you. And, if you do not want the revolver, I'll use it."

He snatched it from her. "And shoot yourself or me in the foot? I think not." He glanced at the five-cylinder barrel and noted all the chambers fully loaded. "Who loaded this?"

She was beginning to sour over his condescending attitude. "Who else? Uncle Basil certainly didn't load it and hand it to me now, did he?"

He glared daggers at her. She'd seen that look before when she challenged him to teach her fencing and he'd refused. She'd been fourteen and taunted him to the point that he appeared quite concerned she might best him once she learned.

Her uncle saved the day by paying for lessons at the Grobel School of Fencing. Private lessons because of her sex. Through the years since, Harrison steadfastly refused to sport with her.

Chapter Four

As the bawdy sounds of life dimmed with the late hours, the market awnings folded, and the garish gin pubs tossed out the foul and slummy crowds sending them to tramp the streets in the dead of night, London prevailed in its least stately presence.

Benches in the parks were already occupied with the poor seeking a dry place to sleep off their drink. The night hovered as the fog rolled in off the river in thick blankets covering the profligates.

Tamsin and Harrison agreed to make their way toward Old Queen Street #6 and stake out Mrs. Thomson's abode.

Oddly, the thick mist allowed Tamsin a sense of security. She felt certain the lads would have taken Joshua off. She wanted to see his home and try to piece together a scenario about him. Thus far, Harrison kept his pace to hers as they stalked down Bond, crossed over Piccadilly, and circled east around St. James Park.

His voice lowered as he vented. "When this business of yours is completed, I'll see you home."

She refused to show weakness. "I'm sorry I invited you when clearly you aren't up for a brisk walk."

His words ground out of him. "Take care, Tamsin. This is no child's play you've got us into. The gangs that run the streets this time of night are to be feared. Not coddled."

Thinking of his warning, she took heed and stepped closer to him.

The bleak night with its pungent smell of rot rolling about in the heavy air made the investigation even more unpleasant. That and Harrison's grunts of rising irritation.

As they neared Old Queen's Street, he grabbed her arm slowing her gait and in hushed tones asked, "What have you in mind?"

"I'm looking for #6. It's where the grandmother lives. I want to get a lay of the land." Within seconds she pointed at the door. Nothing distinguished it from the other dwellings but the number.

Muted sounds drifted on the fog from further down the street. Harrison yanked her into the shadows. "Look over there." His chin nudged to the east. "Do you recognize the youth we are looking for?"

Five young men gathered beneath a thin light from a lamp post. Staying to the shadows, Harrison kept them about eight yards from the group.

One lad pushed another causing him to fall back as he tried to keep his balance. She made out *batty fang ye* and caustic laughter that followed the threat.

The lad that had been pushed got up off the ground and limped his way back to the group to the tune of much ridicule and chiding.

She pointed to the youngest and whispered, "I think that's the grandson. He has a bad leg."

The tallest of the bunch finished his cigarette and flicked it on the ground then approached Joshua, a bottle of something in hand. "Drink up, laddie. It'll give ye guts ta do it."

Obviously hedging, Joshua reluctantly drank part of the

liquid shuddered, and wiped his mouth with the back of his hand. A vehicle traveling at breakneck speed stirred up leaves in the gutter as the thunderous sound sent the lads scattering to get out of the way narrowly missing the crunch of the hooves and wheels.

The lad, she guessed to be Joshua spun about and hobbled into a run in the direction of where she and Harrison hid.

"Not so friggin fast, gimp leg." The tall lad reached for Joshua's arm and spun him about. They were hardly three feet from Harrison and Tamsin. "Ta be a member, ye've got ta prove yer worth. How do I ken less I test ye? So's yer gunna steal from yer grannie, punk. I'll be needin' all she's got if yer ta prove yer worth."

A loud bang sounded like something hit the cobbles and rattled into the dark night. The group of lads jumped and whooped in reaction until their bully leader yelled, "Shut yer holes."

He turned back to Joshua with a forceful clench of his chin.

Tamsin saw the calculating gleam in the bully's face as he shoved his finger into Joshua's chest. She knew from what Mrs. Thomson related about her grandson; he'd been decent until a few weeks ago. She watched him now. Scared and almost breathless. The gang leader, spittle mixed with his threat, dared Joshua to rob his grandmother.

The bully glanced at his rough audience, younger and obviously under his thrall as he egged Joshua on. He seemed to grow taller with his authoritarian threats. "We'll beat yer bloody ars if'n ye don't do as I say." He pushed his worn tam off his forehead and glanced at his mates. "Unless yer hidin' signs of a girlie in them trousers. Mebbe yer nana's little baby, wantin' yer mash, and ditty wipes."

His followers guffawed, enjoying the taunting, and belittling of Joshua.

Led on by his followers, the tall lad withdrew a knife from his belt and waved it in front of Joshua's face.

Harrison clamped on Tamsin's arm whispering for her to back up.

The bully's threat, not to be taken lightly, caused her to shiver as she realized the jeopardy in which she'd put them and was grateful for the gun he held.

The large fellow shoved his fist into Joshua's chest causing him to stumble backward against the brick wall.

Tamsin's breath caught. She ached for the lad thinking all he wanted were chums to hang with. Certainly not these vile, thieving wretches.

"If'n ye ain't here tomorrow, I'll come lookin' for ye. Mebbe I'll have ta see ta yer granny meself then." With that avowed, he coughed up spittle and hacked it somewhere near Joshua's boots.

Joshua turned and limped away.

Tamsin believed his desire to belong prevailed foremost in his mind. Or he could not show up tomorrow and face consequences from the gang of ruffians. The lad's hand fisted with frustration or fear. Mayhap he'd just as soon punch the bully. Certainly, he wouldn't come out the victor; he appeared to be at least two stones lighter and several inches shorter than the rest of the lads.

Harrison whispered in her ear. "Stay here." He shook her arm. "*Do not* follow me."

Quick as lightening he grabbed hold of Joshua's arm and pushed him toward the alley, whispering, "I'm here to help you, so don't fight me." He shoved a card at the lad. "Put this in your pocket."

Joshua glanced at him, and Harrison lowered the brim of his hat, to hide his features and with a grip on the lad's arm, approached the group. His six feet of height made him at least a head taller than any of them. He stepped into their circle, pushing Joshua into the center of ruffians.

"You gents have the wrong street corner for your business." He pushed his right hand into his pocket drawing their eyes to the outline of a gun.

The bully, arrogant as ever, stepped forward as if guarding his group. "Who says?"

Harrison smiled. "Take my word for it, pimple face." He cleverly brought attention to the bully's weakness.

He lunged at Harrison who sidestepped, turned, and kicked him in the knees all in a split second. "If you were paying attention, you would know, 'twas I who spoke."

On his back, groaning in pain, the bully didn't look so threatening. Harrison glanced at the others, noting Joshua's wide eyes and gaping mouth. The others backed off separating themselves from the bully.

Using Joshua as a target, Harrison advanced on him. "You better get the hell away from here or you're likely to get what this bloke got." He nodded to the other mates as silence fell over them. "And take this trash with you."

Suddenly the bullies sprang into the service of their leader and helped him stand. His knees couldn't take his weight and each of the lads grabbed a limb, Joshua included.

Harrison hissed, "You get out of my territory, or you'll regret we ever met."

Hidden in the alley, Tamsin peeked around the corner as she listened to the whole of it. Harrison allowed poor Joshua to stay with the gang. Fisting her hands, she was stymied, the whole purpose was to help the lad.

Harrison stood in the middle of the street watching the group scurry off. When he could no longer see them, he turned toward the alley.

Tamsin met him halfway, fury in her voice. "You let Joshua go with them. How could you be so irresponsible?"

Ignoring her, he cupped her elbow forcing her to keep up with him as they vacated Old Queen's Street. Practically running, she tried to get free of him. Once they turned the corner, he drew her into an alcove and let go of her.

She rubbed her elbow. "You made the wrong decision to allow Joshua to stay with them."

In a monotone, as if he were trying not to strangle her, Harrison reminded her, "You gave me permission." He tucked his fingers into his vest drawing out his watch. "It's half past one. I'm usually asleep at this hour."

She didn't know whether to slap him or rue the fact she felt wide awake and wouldn't sleep for hours.

Running footsteps echoed in the fog and Tamsin stepped back trying to figure out which way they were coming. The fog distorted the sound.

Suddenly, Joshua appeared out of the mist. "I want ta thank ye, sir. Ye saved me life."

"Mind your grandmother in the future. You may think her out of touch, but she has your well-being in mind and loves you."

"Aye, sir. I'll be sure ta distance meself from Billie and his gang. An, I've got yer card should a need arise."

Tamsin knew his night's sleep would be in the shelter at the backside of his grandmother's home. She had mentioned during their interview that she always locked the doors when going to bed.

Tamsin stepped forward out of the dark.

Harrison offered, "This is Miss Morgan. We work together."

She caught the sardonic slant of his mouth and would have liked to slap him. She couldn't refute his admirable handling of the situation. She'd give him that. He'd also saved

Joshua from the decision to rob his only living relative and allowed him to continue under her roof.

She felt deeply sorry for the lad's plight, thinking she could have walked in his shoes tonight if it hadn't been for Uncle Basil taking her in.

A screech and the rustling of foraging animals kept her wary. Mist on the verge of rain threatened her walk home to be a wet one. With a nod, Joshua slowly turned, lumbering past them.

Harrison took hold of her elbow and urged her forward to the street in search of a hack.

Arriving at Portman Square, he walked her to the door saying. "We need to discuss tonight, though I believe we are both tired and ready to put an end to the day."

With that he turned and dashed to the carriage as the rain began. Tamsin quietly made her way to the backyard. She heard Charlie's faint snore in the stable.

She pulled the latch on the wooden door of the cellar. It creaked open same as last night displaying brick walls and the five steps down to the earth floor. The faint light of a bleary moon aided her. Thinking it must be near two in the morning, now the second day of Uncle Basil's demise.

Bins stacked with apples, potatoes, beets, and dried fruit filled the front of the cellar. A ham and two chickens hung from the rafters. Drying spices also dangled from the rafters their scent mingling with the earthiness of the room.

Uncle Basil lay wrapped in a blanket behind the barrier she'd arranged last night. She was suddenly chilled and drew her arms about herself as she thought his life was likely taken with the sip of a drink.

Was his visitor expected? Who would have arrived so

late? The questions rolled in her mind. For some reason, she thought of the time The Queen honored him with a medal when he retired. The occasion was still vivid in her mind. Mrs. T had taken her shopping for an elegant outfit several years ago now, she'd been nineteen.

Wishing she had the power to turn back time, she stepped to the far corner where, wrapped in a blanket, he reposed. His ink-stained fingers curled slightly and lay open atop the covering. He'd been working on something at his desk the last time she saw him alive.

His face covered with the blanket, she kept it so when she sat atop a crate and set the candle on a nearby stack of burlap. Fear and sadness overcame her. The decision to hide him had begun to overwhelm her. The depth of what she'd done washed over her like nothing else she'd ever undertaken. And the loss of him weighed like a stone on her heart.

A sob almost like an animal in the forest plunged out of her. Her wrist pressed against her mouth.

Uncle Basil, please help me. Give me strength and wisdom to figure out how you died, and to carry on for the sake of those of us who do not want to lose our home.

She reached over to tuck his hand beneath the blanket. Finding it stiff and cold she lifted the cover and laid his arm across his chest. A faint, not unpleasant scent reminiscent of varnish wafted as she replaced the blanket.

Returning to the house, she made a mental note to ask the apothecary about froth on the mouth of a dead person. Or should she ask the mortician? It occurred to her she might have made a horrid mistake hiding his body.

Tamsin didn't think she could be labeled a cynic. She tried to refrain from ill will toward others. All the same, the puzzle over her uncle's death kept her recalling the two glasses of brandy, one nearly gone, the other untouched. And, of course, the front door and gate were wide open as if someone rushed away. The killer no doubt.

Someone stood on the opposite side of the desk from him in his last moments. Most likely a man. She could hardly fathom a woman alone in the night confronting her uncle and drinking. But assuredly it was their heated conversation that woke her.

Depending on whether poison or a stroke killed him, she needed to get on with an investigation into his murder and find a medical reason for his death.

Thursday, 9:00 a.m.
22 September 1870

After breakfast, Tamsin visited the local apothecary on Upper George Street. The last time she frequented the shop, Sally had needed salve for a poison-ivy rash. She never forgot the rhyme, leaves of three, let it be. This time of year, the leaves were turning and made it easier to spot the bad ones; nonetheless, the maid suffered with the rash for several weeks.

The bell tingled as she stepped into the mahogany paneled pharmacy with its many shelves of ointments and pills.

The apothecary, Mr. Fowkes, greeted her as she approached the counter. "Do I remember? Is it Miss Morgan?"

"Yes, sir. Your recall is correct. It's been at least a year I believe."

His full red beard flagged against his upper chest as he

spoke, "What can I do for you this time? Not poison ivy again, I hope?"

She smiled at his power of recall. Mrs. T always commented on it after visiting his shop. His intention surely was meant to be friendly, though it bore a smidgeon of intimidation. She felt it as she recalled Sally's severe itching. "No, sir. I have a question and think you might be the best person to ask."

He folded his beefy arms across the bib of his apron. His upper lip spread into a smile.

"I wonder, is there a poison that if drunk, would leave froth on a person's lips?"

His blue eyes widened. "It would depend upon the amount they had drunk and the poison." He unfolded his arms and placed his palms on the countertop leaning toward her.

"Hmm." She eyed him directly as several thoughts churned. "If it was the right amount to make froth, how long would it take for that person to die?"

He chewed his lower lip, not taking his eyes off her. "Again, that would depend on the poison and the amount ingested."

"If they drank half a glass of arsenic, would that be enough to cause frothing and death within a few minutes?" She stood at the counter, her hands clenching her purse. It dawned on her that he would not likely forget her questions for a very long time.

"In all probability, yes." His curiosity deepened.

Eager to leave his noticeably narrowed observation of her, she said, "Thank you for your time, Mr. Fowkes."

She turned to leave but he wasn't ready to let her go. "Who is it you plan to do away with?" He smiled in recognition of her natural curiosity.

The skirts of her cambric rustled as she turned to him

puzzling over his question. Two men who had come in off the lane glanced at her, clear interest on their faces.

She immediately responded. "I'm writing a mystery novel and thought I might use poison as part of the plot."

He slapped the countertop with his fleshy palm. "By jove, what is the title? I'll look for it in the bookstore."

Her lie forced her to play along, and she blurted, "I've tentatively titled it *The Mystery of Aunt Henrietta's Death.* I'm in the initial stages of writing. It will be a while."

"Well, you are welcome to return anytime with your questions, Miss Morgan. I fancy myself quite the patron of the arts."

"Thank you, Mr. Fowkes. I might take you up on that." She waved at him, and the door jingled as she pushed it open.

Holy heaven. A liar, a corpse hider, and a thief of her dear uncle's money. What else would she be adding to the list of wrongdoings before her investigation could be considered solved?

For a moment, when he'd asked who she planned to kill, her blood had run cold. Of course, it seemed only natural for him to be curious. She couldn't fault him for inquiring. Her uncle had marveled a time or two when she responded quickly to certain situations. He often chuckled at what he referred to as her "quick wit."

Henrietta Reynolds-Walker's image had come to her in an instant when Mr. Fowkes asked. She'd never taken to the woman in all the years they'd been acquainted, so why did her name come to mind? She hoped there wasn't a desire deep within her to see the woman vanish.

Quick wit, indeed.

As requested, Mrs. Thomson came by and paid for Tamsin's service and to thank her for most likely saving Joshua from a life of regret and likely imprisonment.

Tamsin felt as if Harrison should be given the full fee she charged. Her endeavor to earn money for the household hadn't turned out the way she envisioned so she decided to split it with him.

Chapter Five

M rs. Henrietta Reynolds-Walker's personal maid, Gertie, put the final touches to her mistress' chignon and held the mirror for her approval.

Waved off by her mistress, Gertie turned to laying out a dress named after the Princess of Wales, spreading it on the bed and smoothing out the mauve grosgrain.

Henrietta anticipated how well the gown would look on her. Mayhap even more so than when the Princess had worn a similar style at last week's Liberty Ball.

Henrietta drew the hand mirror close and gently patted moisturizer with the tip of her finger to the creases spreading out from the corner of her eyes.

Gertie had been in her employ since her marriage to Mr. Walker in 1855. At the time, Henrietta had been a young woman of twenty-one and deeply angry her parents had forced the marriage.

She peered into the mirror dabbing another small amount of cream on her forehead creased with a line of anxiety.

She had always wanted freedom from them; unfortunately, the only way she could have that was to marry. They chose Basil Walker and her refusal had caused an uproar.

What her mother and father didn't know was that her beloved, De la Croix, was in full agreement that she should marry Mr. Walker.

De la Croix was a devastatingly handsome, black haired, blue eyed, and lustful gentleman who wooed her artfully. His mere touch melted her.

At the tender age of sixteen, Henrietta allowed him the unforgettable experience of taking her virtue. She had been certain he would seek approval from her father, and they would marry and live happily ever after.

Henrietta could not have been more wrong.

By the time she was twenty-one, her father forced the marriage with Basil Walker.

They reminded her of Basil's wealth and that he had the ear of The Queen which cast him in a very favorable light.

Life went on.

Basil had been officially offered the position of First in Command of the Detective Branch, which meant mostly paperwork, meetings, and organization. In other words, taken out of the battle front of crime in London.

Basil was one of his sovereign's favorites; though he was a simple man, with a rather calm life, The Queen had mentioned on occasion, his attention to Miss Henrietta Reynolds. From the tone she used, Basil knew The Queen didn't hold her in high esteem.

When Basil began courting Henrietta, The Queen asked him about her pastimes, her interests. It amused him that she would be interested. It wasn't until many years later that Basil realized she was trying to protect him from a disastrous marriage.

Henrietta, on the other hand, considered him a bore, buried in scholarly ambitions. She wanted to be smothered but not by Mr. Walker, and certainly not with scholarly tomes.

If Basil had known about Henrietta's *other life,* he never let on.

Henrietta took refuge in the arms of Desmond, hoping he would be the prince to Cinderella, or the honorable knight in shining armor.

In truth, Mr. De la Croix came to be the opposite of a knight. Henrietta continued to be madly in love with him and didn't for a moment see him as a manipulator. She saw a man who knew what he wanted—her.

Blinded by his attention, she did his bidding, lived and breathed under his spell, and performed as he wished in all things.

Unfortunately, accepting Basil's offer of marriage became De la Croix's persistent demand.

He reminded her that their harassment would stop. And she would have freedom to live her life as she desired—in *his* arms.

He teased her about Mr. Walker saying he wasn't man enough to be a threat to what they shared. He promised her they would continue as they had been. All the while her husband's nose would be buried in work or a book.

Henrietta had thrown a tantrum. Mr. De la Croix coddled her, baited her, and finally, when all else failed, threatened her. If she did not marry Mr. Walker, he would end their affair.

His devil eyes darkened with his threat his sensuous mouth thinned into a hard line—the lips she yearned for.

She could not lose him and finally bowed to his and her father's and mother's demands.

Henrietta sulked all the way to her wedding night. She blamed Basil for the suffering forced upon her by her parents and Desmond.

Oddly, Basil didn't react when she told him she loved another—as if he somehow knew. Pragmatic and stoic when he spoke, she wondered if he even loved her or at least liked her. She felt conflicted over his calm reaction, not because she cared, rather that she considered herself a catch for any man. It never occurred to her Basil would send her away. She thought she flourished as a centerpiece of elegance and charm.

Simply put, Henrietta couldn't believe Basil would give her up so easily. No argument, no demands made on her person. He turned out to be an enigma. As an esteemed member of Her Majesty's Metropolitan Police Force, he had the ear of The Queen herself.

Looking back on it now, some fifteen years later, Henrietta believed Basil had been aware of her affair with Mr. De la Croix and for some reason still married her. Though she would never know for certain.

As Henrietta reflected on the past years, her perspective shifted. She looked back on the past and rued the childish young woman she'd been. Immature, high-strung, and ripe for plucking.

She had supposed Basil might want children and assumed that reason alone had been why he married her. She felt it unnatural not to want a family. Desmond always used precautions leaving no possibility, although under the law, the child would be known as Basil's.

But Basil and Desmond were opposites. And she certainly couldn't ask him if that was why he married her.

She would remember until her dying day what her new husband did after she confessed her love for another.

He turned his cool green eyes on her and spoke in a low firm voice. "Well, then, Mrs. Reynolds-Walker, I will see to another residence for you. I had hoped you would be over your thrall with De la Croix. It appears you are not."

That's the moment Henrietta learned that Basil knew of her affair with another man.

Having said his piece, he turned on the heel of his shiny wedding shoes and left the room.

Mrs. T set her up in another bedroom until a residence became available. The days that passed until she moved into a home of her own weren't unpleasant. Basil treated her as if he would a guest. They bore the evening meal together with little or no talk. She continued to meet her lover who treated her differently as a married woman. He worshipped her, presented her with gifts of jewelry and perfumes. She knew he was pleased with their arrangement. His adoring attention and lively bedroom romps made her feel she had the best of both worlds.

Desmond insisted she share any information Mr. Walker might reveal about his position, or visitors to the house who might drop conversational tidbits about others. Did he talk about his work as a lieutenant detective? Were there papers on his desk she might read? What did he have to say at the dinner table? Had he ever mentioned his tea plantation Hilldale; and if so, did it sound as if he might put it up for sale?

Of course, Mr. and Mrs. Reynolds had been ecstatic with their new son-in-law, and frankly relieved Henrietta was no longer their responsibility. Although there had been disappointment when they learned of the separate residences, they did not attempt to interfere.

Strangely, Basil showed no hostility toward her. She even suspected his years of detective work might have shed light on her activity with Mr. De la Croix. She didn't much care what he thought as long as Desmond stayed in her life.

After several months of living under the same roof, Basil presented Henrietta with the documents giving her a home of her own. No ceremony on Basil's behalf. He'd smiled his ironic smile, handed the proof of her own home to her, and asked if there was anything else they needed to discuss before she left.

He had made it clear he would pay her bills within reason but would not tolerate excessive spending. As the years passed, she occasionally dropped by Portman Square to discuss a repair on the house, or extra money to travel, which he denied.

In the past sixteen years, from the day they married in 1855 until now, they saw each other a mere scattering of times.

Henrietta had finally earned freedom from her parents, and from the bonds of marriage. Free as a bird to do as she liked, with money of her own and Desmond's full attention, she felt alive, unencumbered, and free of guilt.

And now, years later, fifteen to be exact, Henrietta was angry and fit to be tied pacing the blues and creams of her parlor rug wondering who Desmond entertained. He hadn't sent his carriage for her for several weeks now.

She had no illusions about Desmond. He had always been a master manipulator and an expert seducer. From the start of their affair, about the same time her mother prepared for her coming-out at Queen Victoria's court, he'd already ravished her.

Henrietta noticed women flirting with him. No other man ever came close to him in looks and manner. There were occasions when his episodes of raging temper scared her, though he never touched her in a violent manner.

Acknowledging her own willingness and Desmond's tendency to be dismissive with her, she reluctantly admitted that at thirty-five she was past her prime. Through the years, he limited their private meetings at his home. Always the same, a carriage would whisk her to his home where the servants kept their distance. Several delightful hours later she would be transferred home to await his next summons. Compensation was always delivered in the form of pretty little boxes of gems the next day. She wore the jewels he gave her to remind herself he must love her, or he wouldn't show such generosity.

When they met in public they acted as acquaintances, nothing more.

Two days ago, Henrietta returned to Portman Square only to be informed by Miss Tamsin that Mr. Walker was away on business. His niece appeared agitated that Henrietta had come to see Basil. The little twit acted as if she, Mrs. Reynolds-Walker, had no business darkening their doorstep.

Henrietta would have to somehow get rid of the girl. With the fading attention from Desmond, she needed to secure herself financially beyond what Mr. Walker's allowance had been all these years. She knew his pension income from Her Majesty was a great consideration. She also remembered he owned a tea plantation somewhere in the foothills of the Himalayas.

The book she was reading slipped from her hands, *Great Expectations*. She stood and pulled the gauze drape aside glancing at Bedford Park. Several nannies pushed prams. Carriages sailed past. Hazy beams of sunshine danced in and out of the clouds. Much like herself, she thought.

The book turned out to be a story about a boy, Pip, who grows into an adult and learns that happiness and joy are far more important than wealth and class. She had always had the latter and thought Desmond would bring her the former. She had an overwhelming feeling of desperation. Nothing was going her way. A sign that happiness needed a stronger basis than being thrilled by a handsome man as her escort. Perhaps it was the aging process? Who knew jewels could appear dim when in the arms of an adored lover. Both gave her aches when she thought about them.

The maid interrupted her thoughts with a card on a silver plate. "The gentleman is waiting for an answer, ma'am."

Henrietta recognized the handwriting and her heart

leaped. She brushed the front of her dress and smiled. "Send him in."

Desmond breezed into the parlor, all smiles, handsome as ever, and reached for her hand. "You look extremely well, Henrietta. Thank you for seeing me at such short notice. Eh."

"Would you care for anything? Tea, a libation?" The maid waited at the door.

"A finger of cognac would suit."

She waved the maid out. "I'll see to it," and poured two glasses meeting him on the far side of the parlor as he gazed at the garden that was wilting with the cold nights. She sat in a needlepoint side chair. "Come sit. You seem restless."

He took the chair's companion, as she inquired. "To what do I owe this unusual visit?"

Something weighed heavily on his mind, and she suddenly thought he would finally declare himself. Her heart thumped and a smile crept across her face. He did love her after all.

She smiled at him. He always had a plan. Her heart thrilled at the possibilities of their future together.

Setting the empty glass on the side table, he crossed his long legs, his black patent leather shoes polished to a gleam. "We need to talk."

Always thrilled to glance upon his handsome demeanor, black wavy hair, thin black mustache—he still had the power to take her breath. He settled his large hands on his knees.

His manner had changed, different somehow, and she couldn't put a finger on it. She cooed, "We are talking. I'm happy to have you here in my home. Have our plans for tomorrow evening changed?" Her eyes flirted at him, as her lips pursed in a knowing smile.

His handsome Latina face and impeccable dark three-piece suit, *de riguer* in today's fashion stirred excitement in her.

She noticed an onyx ring on his right-hand glinting in the light.

Her euphoria evaporated, and she suddenly felt as if the sky would fall. "Is that something new on your right hand?"

He paused before answering. "Yes. A gift from a friend."

A creeping fear slid up her back. Was this the moment she'd been dreading?

About to ask if he'd like another libation, because she surely did, his side glance met hers. His deep blue eyes that used to sparkle with desire just before he would begin undoing the buttons on her dress were cagey, adversarial. His chin firmed.

His deep voice slithered with sureness. "You know me so well, Hen, have you an idea why I am here? I think you do." A perfectly formed black brow rose, and without waiting for her answer, he added. "It is past our time to be together. The memories we've made will turn to rot if we wait any longer to say *au revoir*."

Henrietta set her empty glass on the table. "Who is she? Do I know her?"

"Ah, my sweet. She is young and unknown to you. Just out in society." He spread his hand out glancing at the onyx on his pinky again. "Certainly, never a rival for what we shared. She's young and most willing. She reminds me of you when we first met. Curious and eager to experience what life offers."

Her heart shattered over his words.

Very little could she remember when later she tried to make sense of what he'd announced.

She walked him to the door where he lifted her chin with a finger. "Under the circumstances, I will not send my carriage for you tomorrow."

"Not a last time before we say goodbye?"

"I think not." His thin mustache lifted slightly as if he found her request amusing.

"I'll see myself out, *Cheri*." He scooped up his hat and cane and left the parlor.

Her insides crumbled. Her assuredness began to drip, her vulnerability washing her in humiliation. She had wanted freedom all those years ago and traded it for a life with this man. She'd always been a slave to him in every way.

Revenge crept in replacing her vulnerability. A savage desire for retribution clutched her heart.

Henrietta wasn't going to allow him to turn his back on the years of manipulating her, not without reprisal.

An eye for an eye.

Though she'd outgrown her blind fascination for him, he would soon regret discarding her to his dying day. All the nights waiting for him, the years she spent shackled to a man her parents chose.

And the deep dark secret she carried in her heart.

An intense emotional rage sent the glass she clutched sailing across the room crashing into a framed, full-length, golden gilt-carved mirror, leaving her image an appalling jagged rendition of someone who had been sliced into a hundred pieces.

The next morning at breakfast Henrietta was not surprised to read in the society column that Mr. Desmond De la Croix was to marry a young heiress, Miss Allison Horwrath. She glanced out the bay windows of her morning parlor. His engagement had been his motive to step over her threshold for the second time in all the years they were together.

She neatly folded the paper, setting it beside her plate, and smirked.

He played her for a fool.

His mistake.

Chapter Six

T amsin left her bedroom and walked the length of the
upstairs hall to the back of her uncle's home. A large
window draped in green velvet with embossed brass
holders overlooked the yard. From her vantage point she
could see the closed doors of the cellar and fallen leaves that
scattered the yard. She intended to say a quiet prayer for her
uncle before her day began.

Instead, she gasped as her knees buckled and she
clutched the drape as she stared at the cellar door opened
wide.

She was frozen in place as she gawked at the scene below.
She'd been found out.

Seconds passed. Panic built, and her inclination was to
run from what she'd done.

In horror, she watched Evie step out of the dark interior
and climb up the few steps, a basket of vegetables on her arm.

She set the basket on the lawn and closed and latched the door.

Weak with shock, Tamsin almost crumbled to the floor.

She unclutched the drape, hands shaking, and crept back to her room closing the door and laid on her bed until her heart calmed.

Obviously, Evie hadn't noticed the blanket at the back of the storeroom, or she wouldn't have calmly toted the basket up the stairs; she would have darted like a mouse was after her.

Tamsin felt jittery as if she'd run a mile or more and couldn't quite catch her breath.

A knock on her bedroom door was followed by Evie poking her head in. "There's a woman askin' for ye, Miss. Says her name's Mrs. Brownstein and ye've been recommended to her by a Mrs. Lennox."

Tamsin rolled off the bed, slightly embarrassed to be caught at what most probably appeared to be leisure. "I'll be right down." She was grateful to see Evie acting normally. It calmed her to know the maid obviously hadn't noticed anything amiss in the cellar. Her spate of anxiety began to ease.

Mrs. Brownstein waited on a small bench near the front door. "Good day. I'm Miss Morgan. Let's go into the library where we can talk privately."

Her first thought of the woman was that she was quite tall with stern features, rosy-cheeked, and the looks of an argument ready to burst out of her mouth.

They sat opposite each other with the desk between them as Mrs. Brownstein affirmed, "Mrs. Lennox recommended you. Her endorsement carries weight in my estimation."

Tamsin quickly tried to place the woman. Mrs. Lennox must have been a client of her uncle's. "That was kind of her."

She moved a small stack of paperwork out of the way and said, "Tell me why you need the services of the Walker Detective Agency." *That* slid off her tongue smoothly.

The woman took a folded piece of paper from her reticule and handed it to Tamsin. "This will tell you quicker than my explanation."

Yer man is alive, bound and gagged. He'll stay alive five days no more'n that. if'n ye don't come up with documents on city's plans for the new underground we'll kill em and dump em in the river. Ye needs ta put yer written answer in a locker at King's Cross Station. Put the key in an envelope and leave it with the station master. We'll kill em—we will.

She looked at the stern-faced woman across from her. This was by far above anything she would consider solving and hadn't an inkling how to even go about trying to do so.

Mrs. Brownstein's eyes narrowed. "Your first question is going to be, why me? Why would I bring this threatening situation to a small agency such as yours?"

About to agree, she listened as the woman rushed on, "I am greatly concerned about taking this to the Metro."

Tamsin asked, "Do you know what is behind all of it?"

"I'm fairly certain that I do. In 1864 Parliament presented more than two hundred ways to build an underground railway. As you are aware, the first part of the railway was completed in 1868. Parliament was anxious to extend the railway. They chose two parties out of a dozen in the running to build the second part: John Frayley, and the other is my husband.

"Several days ago, my husband who owns Rails for England, won the contract for the new section. The other company, Railway United, owned by John Frayley did not."

Mrs. Brownstein's hands clenched. "The threats began the evening the award was announced. I am certain it's Frayley's company that seized my husband, holding him for ransom. They are demanding the documents and plans for the construction of the second section. There is only one set of engineering plans, and my husband has them hidden. I searched his office and our home. I cannot find them. I'm frantic to comply with this demand."

Tamsin set her pen down, folding her hands on the desk-top. "This is a small agency, Mrs. Brownstein. I sympathize with your horrendous situation. But I am not sure we have the capabilities—."

The woman reached across the desk and grabbed Tamsin's hands. "Do not say it. I beg of you. It is his life about which we are talking. *HIS* life." She dug in her reticule and pulled out a fistful of banknotes, slapping them on the desk. "Here. Use this to begin. I will double it—triple it."

Tamsin tried to hold her composure at the sight of the vast amount of banknotes spilled out over the desk. This would be security for all of them and solve the detective resources she would need. Or would it? Maybe she could hire assistance.

Harrison came to mind.

Mrs. Brownstein struggled with her composure. "Both Frayley and my husband were friendly. Since the oversight committee of the Metropolitan Railway Company chose Mr. Brownstein's plans for the extension, things began to get well...ugly. Threats, dead chickens on our lawn, a man across the street at night observing our whereabouts."

"Why haven't you involved Metro in this?"

"At first, Mr. Brownstein thought it would all calm down. He and Mr. Frayley have been...well, were friends as I said. My husband found the quarrel silly. Childish."

Tamsin wrote feverishly and glanced at the uneasy woman. "When did he decide it had gone beyond silly and childish?"

"This morning when I received this letter and went to my

husband's bed chamber and discovered he hadn't slept there last night."

Tamsin felt a niggling regret she couldn't ease this woman. She would be completely out of her comfort area to take on this case. Especially considering the deadly circumstances of it.

What would Uncle Basil do in this situation? She already knew he would take on the case, find the documents, and put the perpetrator behind bars. That's what he would do.

Her mental quibbling grew into remorse, and she decided to speak to Harrison first before refusing this desperate woman.

"Where is your husband's place of business?"

"It's at the corner of Holborn and Southampton Row, in the Scott Development Building, on the second floor."

"Have you looked for the documents?"

"I went to his library first but found nothing. The same with his office. I went there before I came here and searched everywhere I could think, through dozens of plans. I could not find the documents these wicked people are demanding."

She stood up, forcing Mrs. Brownstein to stand as well. "If you will allow me to speak to one of my colleagues about this matter, I assure you I will get in touch before evening at the latest."

The woman dug in her reticule and pulled out a key. "You will need this. You already have his address. And please keep my confidence. I don't know what I would do without my dear husband." Mrs. Brownstein teared up and swiped at her eyes with a gloved fingertip. "I will wait faithfully to hear from you."

Tamsin took a deep breath. She'd barely regained her composure from the fright of seeing the cellar doors wide open when Mrs. Brownstein arrived. What a day this was turning out to be.

She walked the woman to the front door, then returned to her desk and sent a missive to Harrison asking if he would please stop by at his earliest convenience. Underlining 'earliest' she hoped would get his attention. She needed to be quick considering they only had five days.

Grateful for the chance to earn a great deal of money, deep down she understood the pain Mrs. Brownstein must be experiencing. Probably much like what she herself was going through with Uncle Basil dead. Though ashamed to think of the money as a motivator, she knew she would need it when the time came for them to move.

This pretense clawed at her heart, and she knew she couldn't keep it up much longer. Every minute she ached for the loss of a man who had raised her. When she was younger, she dreamt of marrying a man just like him. That dream hadn't quelled. It became a child's dream with a happy ending. And she was no longer a child, and no longer believed in fairy tales.

Friday, noon
23 September 1870

Harrison Spencer rang the bell at #2 Berkeley Street, Portman Square. Mrs. T invited him into the library while she went in search of Tamsin.

He stood at the window overlooking the street as carriages rolled past. Located in a residential area, Berkeley Street led into the bustle of London's environs. He turned when he heard Tamsin's footsteps.

She came into the room in a rush, closed the panel doors behind her, and leaned against them.

He knew her well enough to realize she was stirring the mischief pot once again. Something brewed in that head of hers and if he was correct, she would be asking his advice.

"What is it this time? Some child abandoned, or another grandmother ill at ease?"

She stepped away from the door folding her hands, chin up, eyes narrowed. Whatever it could be, it appeared worse than he might have guessed.

"I've a proposition for you. One that will pay good money. Would you like to hear about it?" She stepped two feet closer to where he stood at the window.

He should walk out the door. He really should, yet there was something provocative about her question. Blast it. "Why do you persist in annoying me with trivial pursuits?"

Her face lit with a smile. "Our last outing, the one and only time I've asked anything of you, you took over, solved the situation with shrewd insight and went merrily on your way. It occurred to me you could help with another situation that has come to my desk."

He turned his back on the window chuckling. "*Your* desk, is it? How do you think your uncle is going to take it when he returns and finds you sleuthing about London in the middle of the night dressed as a man...oh, and don't let me forget to mention carrying a loaded gun. He'll most likely have *my* head over that."

She waved off his annoying reference. "He needn't know." She turned toward the bookshelves, her hand inches from the place where she hid the two glasses of liquor the night before last when he'd died. She breathed in heavily and slid her gaze to Harrison.

He winced at the grieved look on her face. "Alright then, tell me what's on your mind. The least I can do is listen to your idiocy." He sank into a chair across the desk from where she stood, his long legs folded as he reposed thoughtfully, hands clasped on his stomach, thumbs twirling in irritation.

She shook the notion of two people sitting on opposite sides of the desk that flashed in her mind as if it were almost midnight last Tuesday. She tried ridiculously hard to keep a pleasant look on her face, noting to herself that he happened to be a man with a man's contemptuous regard for a woman's lack of intelligence. Something about having a smaller brain or some-such *idiocy.*

"A Mrs. Brownstein visited this morning. Her husband—"

"Is a man of wealth and great ingenuity who may be the recipient of a contract to build a second railway system." His gaze locked on her. "Do not tell me he is involved in something about which his spouse has a concern."

"He is being held for ransom." She passed him the misspelled and near-illiterate threat. "Mrs. Brownstein received this early this morning. His bed hadn't been slept in."

As he read, his right brow arched, and his lips pursed.

Finished reading, his interest fell to her. "Well, well, it seems old Brownstein has gotten himself in a mess. To say nothing about the temperature of the Thames."

Frustration sharpened her voice. "Is this a comedy to you?"

He pushed himself up straighter in the chair. "It looks like you have gotten yourself a bona fide case. What do you plan to do about it? And by the way, Tamsin, you realize this is Scotland Yard work. The men perpetrating this are cutthroats, the most aggressive kind of murderers. They will get what they want with a killing or two before they're finished."

"That is what I mentioned to Mrs. Brownstein. She is desperate to keep it out of the papers. She thinks it best for her husband's safety. She may also be thinking of his reputation."

She watched him run a hand through his mass of buttery-brown hair and stood, a sour frown on his face. She knew he was disturbed about this possible case. "I must advise you against taking this on. It's dangerous. It needs the mind of a man to handle the coordination of finding where Brownstein is being held. Also, bear in mind people like this could also capture Mrs. Brownstein."

Irritated at his mention of gender, she defended her situation. "She happens to feel the more public fuss will surely make it more difficult for these horrid individuals. They are already going to kill him on the fifth day. And here we stand arguing."

"Well then, perhaps I should leave you to it." He smacked his top hat on and stepped toward the door.

In a screech, she almost hollered, "You cannot leave me."

He glanced over his shoulder. "I certainly can."

"No. I need your help. This is way over my head." Her brow knitted in a dainty little frown.

With his hand on the doorknob, he turned to her. "That's a start, something we both agree on."

Her hands fisted. She'd like to slap his smirk, as if this was her fault. It was on her mind to tell him the whole truth about Uncle Basil when he stepped back into the center of the office.

"The least I can do is listen to what your plans are."

Smothering her indignation, she took a deep breath. He really knew how to rile her.

"First of all, I know you're on break from Oxford right now so I hoped you might have some time to assist me in finding the documents and freeing Mr. Brownstein."

"Have you considered once the villains have the plans, they will still murder him so he cannot identify them?"

She pulled out the pile of Fifty Pound banknotes she'd shoved in the top right-hand drawer after Mrs. Brownstein left. "Does this change your mind? Mrs. Brownstein is prepared to match it twice over if we find the documents and return her husband."

He glanced at the banknotes carelessly shoved in the drawer, then at her self-assured, smug demeanor. "I rue the day Basil brought you to his home. If something happens to you, he'll have my neck. You are the best thing that has ever happened to him. And I will be a sitting duck for his wrath."

She quickly drew in a breath as if on the verge of crying with relief. "Shouldn't we be thinking of Mr. Brownstein who is at the mercy of these hoodlums and about to be tossed in the Thames?"

―――――

Unlocking the door to Mr. Brownstein's office, Harrison stood aside for Tamsin to enter. She immediately reacted to the stench of stale smoke by holding a kerchief against her nose.

A ransacked office laid out in front of them. Not one stick of furniture stood on its legs, file drawers gaped, papers strewn everywhere.

Tamsin asserted, "This must have just happened because Mrs. Brownstein said she stopped by early this morning. She didn't mention plundering. It does not look as if they found what they were looking for."

He quietly stepped about the office scanning the shambles. With his cane, he pushed aside fallen papers. Wall hangings flung about, the images of their shapes like ghosts lingering on the walls. The leather on the seat and back of the desk chair was slashed and horsehair dangled from the gut.

She watched as he carefully assessed every corner and each of the drawers in the cabinets and the desk. Even the spittoon laid on its side, a puddle of dark brown tobacco juice staining the beautiful hand-woven red-medallion rug.

"I agree. It appears they didn't find the documents. If they had, there would be a portion of the office not in disarray. Or perhaps they simply gave up. Which might suggest Mr. Brownstein's home is next."

Agitated, he swished the tip of his cane into a pile of papers sending them adrift. "Miss Morgan, I do not like trespassing on another's property. And you must realize you are not capable of taking on a situation that involves the possibility of death, and the villains threatening such."

Addressing her as 'Miss Morgan' meant he was overly disturbed—with her.

She upended the slashed chair and sat on the edge of it, not wanting to get horsehair on her clothing, and groused at him. "I thought you a gentleman, It appears I have been deceived."

"No. No." His eyebrows knitted as he drew in a breath. "No game playing and name calling here. Remember I know you and when you get something into your head, you are like a raging bull." He squinted with pursed lips and banged his cane against the floor.

Grateful for the carpet, she practically jumped out of the chair sending it on its wheels backward smashing into the mahogany wall paneling.

"How dare you compare me—"

He came at her with an astonishing look on his face and she immediately sidestepped him, afraid he meant to strangle her. She quickly moved to the other side of the room putting the desk between them. Then, swung about to defend herself.

Totally ignoring her, he shoved the chair she vacated aside and touched a part of the wall where the chair had hit.

Chapter Seven

The panel swung wide when the chair hit it revealing a large safe, at least three feet high and two feet wide.

"Look what we found. I think these are the documents that will save Mr. Brownstein's life. What do you think?"

She gaped. First, that his attitude toward her shifted, and second, that this case might solve itself.

"Speechless, are you? A good day for me when I have learned how to keep you quiet." He slid open the desk drawers one by one, glancing inside each.

She cast him a weary gaze. "What are you looking for now?"

"The combination to the safe. I'm assuming he has written it somewhere handy, yet out of sight."

They combed all the drawers, even the underside of his chair, then turned their attention back to the filing cabinets one drawer at a time.

"Is this what we are looking for?" Crouched on the floor digging into the lowest file drawer, she found a scrap of paper with a set of numbers. She'd taken out a stack of files that revealed the snippet, tucked under the wooden rib of the drawer, a clever hiding place.

He bent over her shoulder.

"Well, well, what have we here?" His hand brushed her cheek as he swept down and picked out the scrap, then went to the open panel where the safe had been hidden. He set about trying the combination. At the sound of a click, he turned the handle and the heavy wooden door opened, revealing the metal sheeting that would make it fireproof. Impressed, he rifled through some of the papers, setting them on the floor for her to peruse while he pulled out another batch and glanced through those.

"I imagine you have an idea what it is we are looking for?" She felt extremely out of her element, grateful he'd agreed to come along.

"Information on the inner circle, or drawings, I'm not sure. Even a contract with the Metropolitan Railway Company. Remind me of Brownstein's company's name?"

"Rails for England."

"Look for mention of that as well."

For the next ten, fifteen minutes, they shuffled paper. Other than traffic on the street outside, and an occasional whistle for a buggy, it was quiet.

Tamsin's back had begun to twitch, and she stood stacking papers on the desk and continued reading each piece of paper. "I do not seem to be having any luck."

His gruff voice itched with impatience. "They have got to be here. Where else would he keep them if not in the safe?"

She closed her eyes and tried to imagine Mr. Brownstein's moments before the hooligans captured him. "Do you think he might have been suspicious of being followed and stashed them in some unlikely place?"

"He would have to be clairvoyant. And if anything,

Brownstein is the opposite of psychic. Over time, I noticed he's a bit of a bore."

"Just a thought." She continued to read each page and turned it over to read another.

A minute later, there came a creak in the floor from the hallway. He put a finger to his lips as he met her doubtful eyes.

The doorknob turned and much to their relief, Mrs. Brownstein presented herself.

"Oh, thank goodness it's you." Tamsin breathed out a puff of anxiety.

"What has happened in here? Oh my." Her hand went to her chest, and she fell back against the wall.

Harrison at once reached for her and guided her to the desk chair. "Sit a moment and I will explain."

He had gone in search of a glass of water for her, and by the time he returned empty-handed, Tamsin had filled her in on the present circumstance.

Tamsin had been fanning Mrs. Brownstein with a file and quit when Harrison arrived. The woman turned her teary gaze on him. "Is there any hope for my husband?"

He glanced at his watch, just past three o'clock in the afternoon. "Do not despair, madam. We have made great strides in the last several hours."

"You have not found what the hoodlums want, how can you say that?" Though a woman of fortitude, her veneer had begun to crumble, justly so considering the threat of dumping her dear husband's body in the Thames.

Harrison glanced at the stack of unread material still in the safe and asked. "Was it Mr. Brownstein's practice to keep his important documents in his safe?"

A moment of fluster clouded her eyes. Tamsin patted her arm. "Take your time."

"I am not sure. I think both places. He has a safe in our home, too."

Harrison's brow perked up. "I am most happy to know that because we have not found anything regarding a contract with the railways." He threw a glance at the open safe, then added, "We'll finish up here and come directly to your home, if that is convenient for you."

"Would you mind if I stay here, and we go together? I am in a bit of a fright over being in my home without protection."

Tamsin challenged, "You do have servants?"

"Oh, my yes. Wonderful staff, been with us all the years of our marriage, and all of an older age. But several are hard of hearing, and do not exactly offer the security I believe I might need."

Harrison and Tamsin exchanged a knowing look.

He offered, "I can have a man or two stay at your home. They will act as hired help. Unintrusive and yet trained to guard you, your home, and staff."

Her lips pinched and she looked at her gloved hands. "I am afraid if the hooligans find out, my dear husband might pay the price. I couldn't live with myself knowing I caused..." Her voice trailed off leaving the obvious unsaid.

Tamsin shuffled the papers into a neat stack. "We will finish shortly and be on our way then."

Harrison said, "We should not tidy the office in case Metro gets involved. They will need to see what has happened here. And I'm not in a hurry for them to discover we are on a case."

Agreeing with him, she freed the pile she organized and watched as they drifted to the carpet.

Within a half hour, the panel on the safe closed, and the chair turned on its side, the trio left the office pretty much as they had found it. Harrison hailed a transport and within a half-hour they walked into the Georgian style home of the Brownstein's on Arlington Street overlooking Green Park.

Harrison and Tamsin were immediately directed to the location of the safe in the library. A long narrow table with lamps and fresh flowers stood in front of a mahogany wall, paneled much like the office. The ladies took off the lamps and flowers and Harrison moved the table aside. Mrs. Brownstein touched a corner of the panels, and it popped open, exactly as had the obscure wall in the office.

"Here is the combination." Mrs. Brownstein held it out to him.

Harrison took it and got to work.

A knock on the library door sent Mrs. Brownstein into a pirouette, a palm to her mouth. In a dither and obviously gathering her wits, she opened the door a few inches. "I am engaged, Hutchins. What is it you need?"

"Nothing, ma'am. Just wanted to know if you needed anything."

"I'll ring if I do." The door firmly shut, she turned toward her two conspirators.

"This is beyond anything I would have thought at my age. Brownstein must be in a fit by now. Those people deserve a noose for what they have cost us in fright alone." Mrs. Brownstein paced as he pulled the handle of the safe down and the heavy door swung wide.

Browsing through the papers, he glanced at both women. "Nothing in here."

Mrs. Brownstein sat on the divan, her hands covering her cheeks.

Tamsin slowly walked the perimeter of the room and glanced into a cupboard and some drawers.

Harrison mentioned, "He wouldn't have been careless with the diagrams."

"I agree. But what about keeping something in plain sight

that others might not even glance at." As Tamsin said this, she continued to walk the perimeter of the room, glancing at the artwork on the walls.

She stopped at one particular oil of a farmer cultivating his land. "Harrison, would you be so kind as to take this painting off the wall."

Mrs. Brownstein glanced at her. "That's a painting of my father-in-law that my husband rendered when we were first married. He cherishes it though he also knows it isn't very well done. More sentimental than anything."

Harrison mentioned it was deceptively heavy when he lifted the frame off the wall.

Mrs. Brownstein gasped. "I see papers."

He set the oil on the divan and glanced at what were documents. "What made you think of this?" He turned to Tamsin.

"I noticed it wasn't aligned with the wall the way the other pictures are. It stuck out a bit more."

The women watched him slowly peel the papers off the back of the painting. She chirped, "Yes, I recall him laboring over these. My husband is immensely proud of his rendering of these drawings."

He glanced up at her. "This is what the nabbers want. You need to consider they might not release him even if we give them over."

"But...but that is their bargain." Shock manifested in her furrowed brow, wide sad eyes, and slumped shoulders. Tamsin thought she aged right before her. She wanted to embrace the woman and tell her all would be well. However, the uncertainty of the dire situation kept her from doing so. Dealing with thieves, and at this level of pecuniary advantage, could be anyone's game.

A pall hung over the threesome as they stood in the library. What could they say? What comfort could they offer her? Tamsin eyed Harrison. She could almost read his mind. He appeared uncertain about the outcome if his tight-lipped features meant anything. He closed the door on the safe and replaced the panel.

With help from Tamsin, they pushed the table against the wall, and Mrs. Brownstein replaced the lamps.

Next, she stacked the sheets of paper together and put them in a brown file. "Will you assist me in giving them to Frayley?"

Tamsin picked up her gloves and reticule from the table where she had left them when entering the room. Mrs. Brownstein glanced at her, eyes tearing up again. She appeared to have no desire to be left with only the servants.

In the moment, she pictured her uncle in his chair already dead and she hadn't had the acceptance of mind or heart to realize it. Like a dunce she initially thought he fell asleep or drank too much. She'd even thought he might have had a stroke.

Her heart ached for Mrs. Brownstein whose husband could already be dead. The thugs who seized him had neither sense of decency nor honor.

Harrison took the frightened woman's hands. "We will find him. I promise you. We still have three days before their five-day dictum is up. For the time being, hide the file and leave everything else as is. If you receive any notes, let Miss Morgan know immediately."

She seemed to shrivel as a breath of air left her. "Thank you for your assurance. I already have a marvelous place to hide these. And I will await your instructions on how to proceed."

Tamsin asked, "Should we call your maid before we leave?"

"Oh, no. No." and vigorously shook her head. "They

think he's away on business. Otherwise, they would fall to pieces. I worry about their health, you see."

As they retreated from Mr. Brownstein's library, Hutchins walked them to the front door. Tamsin had the distinct impression he knew far more than his employer gave him credit for.

Hutchins held the door as they made to step over the threshold and whispered to her. "We take care of our mistress, miss. With your involvement in this situation, you needn't also worry about Mrs. Brownstein."

Once on the boulevard, Harrison suggested they walk even though the overcast sky promised rain. The breeze carried an almost spring-like freshness. Surprising as fall was just around the corner.

He glanced down at Tamsin and declared, "I know this is your case. Just the same, a decision is of the utmost. And I want to know what you are thinking."

She couldn't share her thoughts. They were about the muddle of what she'd done with her dear uncle's remains. Her decisions were appalling. Angry at herself, and yes, completely stupefied as to how to save Mr. Brownstein's life *and* hold onto his documents.

Honestly, if she came down to it, money and security were unconditionally her motivation to take the case. Keeping a roof over her household was also paramount.

She was angry and disappointed in herself.

In answer to his question, she tried to hide her agitation. "Somehow, we need to find where Mr. Brownstein is being kept and rescue him. It's vital to do it without sacrificing the documents."

She peeked out from under the brim of her hat. His chin

jutted a bit. She knew it to be a thoughtful gesture, one he'd typically used all the years she'd known him.

"How do you plan to do that?" His cane tapped the cement as though making a valid point.

"It makes sense that John Frayley is involved. He lost a huge contract with the appointment of Mr. Brownstein. I do not expect he's the actual nabber. Maybe if we were to follow him, he'd lead us to where they are keeping our victim."

His face in profile, she noted a quirk on his lips. She felt relieved at the possibility she figured this out to his satisfaction. She almost felt as if it were Uncle Basil smiling down on her. They walked up Davies Street and crossed Oxford before he spoke again.

"I know you want to solve this on your own, but I have an unspoken obligation to your uncle, more so now that he is away. These men are ruthless, Tamsin. Their devious ambition is to force Brownstein into stepping down. They will kill him if he does not. It's as simple as that. They may kill him anyway."

They had almost reached Berkeley Street when he spoke again. "Will you allow me to take matters into my hands and try to solve this?"

"Can you assure me Mr. Brownstein will not die?"

A long minute passed. "Can *you* assure *me* he will?"

She stopped walking and looked up at him. "I'm such a failure."

Reaching for her hand, he suggested, "This is not about failure, Tamsin. Your heart is pure, and you always have the care of others on your mind. It's just that..." As if his thoughts were written on a white puffy cloud, he looked skyward.

She snapped. "What? That I'm incapable of handling those brutes? Because I agree with you."

He drew her gloved hand to his chest. "Then I have your nod to go ahead and plan an attack on Frayley and his men?"

"Only if you allow me to be a part of it." She withdrew her hand from his clasp.

His eyes reflected exasperation as he shrugged. She thought of the look Uncle Basil would get when she challenged him and chuckled.

"I hope you are simply injecting humor into the moment, because it's out of the question." The look on his face soured. He really didn't want her involved.

Churlishly she relented. "You win. I won't fight you."

A weary sigh escaped him. When he walked her up to the front door on Berkeley Street, he left her with a needling doubt she was as good as her word. Did she just agree to stay true to her promise and not interfere with his strategy to free Mr. Brownstein? The woman had the ability to drive him to distraction. Basil couldn't get home quick enough to suit. India was *not* a skip and hop across a pond.

Basil hadn't been gone for three days. Harrison walked back to the carriage as his eyes rolled up to the heavens in consternation. Tamsin could drive him bonkers.

Three days and Tamsin needed his assistant twice already. He would begin to think Basil's absence would turn into a burden of long and uneasy months. His time away could run longer than expected. Harrison pondered what could have gone so wrong his presence was required as soon as possible. He couldn't help wondering what horrendous circumstance might have arisen.

Chapter Eight

It had been a long dreary day about the streets of London, trying to put the pieces of injustice together. Upon entering the front door, Tamsin heard Mrs. T's distinctive step descending the stairs.

"I see by the look on your face that you need some hot tea?"

"A clairvoyant. Well then Mrs. T, I'll be in the library."

"You need a sit-down in the parlor and relax. You look a bit weary."

Tamsin glanced at her, having taken the pin out of her hat and hung it on the peg. "That does sound grand. Thank you."

Five minutes later, Evie carried in a tray, steam curling out of the spout of a small teapot, the scent of a lemon scone causing her to realize how long it had been since breakfast. "Thank you, Evie."

She curtsied and quietly closed the parlor door behind her.

Tamsin put her feet up on a rose patterned ottoman and laid her head back against the doily on the chair's headrest. She closed her eyes and quenched tears that were wont to fall. Despite all that had happened today, her heart knew the time had come to decide what to do about Uncle Basil's remains.

She held the cup near her face and let the steam soothe her as she took in the fragrance of earthy rich black tea. She sipped and put the cup aside as the comforting warmth slid down her throat.

Dearest Uncle, I miss you so much. I've made such a muddle leaving you in the underground room. I couldn't let you go. But I know I must. My faith failed me in the minutes I came to realize you were truly gone. I thought I could keep you close.

You'll be in my heart always. I'll do right by you, what I should have done Tuesday night.

"Miss, miss." A voice far away came to her. "Miss." Tamsin blinked open her eyes. Evie leaned in close. "You've slept away your teatime. It's time for dinner."

She pushed herself up in the chair and set her feet on the carpet. "Dinner?"

"Yes, miss. It's past six. And your tea's gone cold."

"Blame the chair, it's far too comfy."

Evie smirked. "Better than blaming you. Mrs. T will have a say so when I tell her."

"Then why would you? Let it be our secret. You eat the scone. I can wait for dinner."

Evie gave a small bob, then carried the tray out putting the treat in her apron pocket as she did so.

Tamsin fell back against the cushion. She must have needed a nap. Taking a deep breath, she pushed out of the chair and made her way upstairs.

By the time she washed and changed from her day dress, it neared seven o'clock. She quickly ate baked cod, shelled peas, and bread pudding. Feeling quite refreshed she then tackled the day's post. At midnight she planned to check on her uncle.

. . .

**Friday, 11:30 p.m.
23 September**

A heavy fog rolled across the lawn and the poles that secured the fencing weren't distinguishable, as if the fencing floated. Tamsin dropped the heavy fabric of the drape and glanced at her uncle's favorite room. A fire crackled keeping the damp from the library. She rubbed her upper arms and waited for midnight. The Westminster clock chimed a quarter-hour past nine o'clock.

His leather chair squeaked as she sat down and rifled through the top drawer, the contents of which she'd seen many times.

Off in the distance, Sally and Evie were finishing in the kitchen. Mrs. T had already said goodnight and gone to her room in the attic. Tamsin glanced at the bookshelf and the title *Crime and Punishment* by Dostoevsky made her face crunch. *War and Peace* by Tolstoy hit her as if it was a catalogue of her own behavior. When she noticed *Little Women,* she drew it off the shelf.

Curling up in the easy chair close to the fire, a blanket wrapped around her skirt, she began reading about the beloved March sisters, a book she practically knew by heart. The hour of midnight would approach faster. Her blessed uncle had purchased it and had it sent to her from America a year ago.

As time passed, the Westminster clock chimed midnight rousing Tamsin who sprang up from the chair, spilling the book of sisters on the floor.

Unraveling the shawl, she pulled it over her shoulders,

collected her thoughts, and went to the back of the house. She lit a candle and stepped out the kitchen door. The night air was damp and chilly, leaves had begun falling with the cold snap the last couple of days.

The cellar door opened quietly, thank God, and she slipped through the opening and down the stairs out of the wind. Holding up the candle she stepped a few feet beyond the crates. The glow seeped into the black night as she moved around the crates piled to hide her uncle.

The candle flickered over the plank and two crates where she'd laid him.

Nothing.

Even the blanket was gone.

As if he'd gotten up and vacated the cellar.

Absolutely stunned, she scanned the area as if he'd moved himself elsewhere and swung about holding the candle high, expecting to discover him until she realized what she was doing.

Astonished at her inanity she could have barked a laugh.

Mother of God. If she could be certain of anything in this world, it would be that he did not get up and walk out of this horrid musky underground vault.

Her heart hammered as she swung the candle high again creating shadows of the crates and boxes.

She breathed in the icy damp air. Her nose twitched with the sharp smell of parsnips as she paced three yards to the wall and back to the stairs. Back and forth.

Someone took him. Obviously, but who? Henrietta? She didn't want him in the first place, why would she want his corpse?

So, who?

Who knew where he lay?

Her heart hammered. Who could have known what she'd done? She glanced at the small circle of illumination the little candle's glow provided, her scrambled thoughts making her dizzy.

Knowing she needed to alert the authorities regarding her decision to reveal what she'd done, she must rethink. Her insides roiled, and she inhaled.

If she alerted Scotland Yard, they would know what she'd done with him.

The increase in the howl of the wind wasn't calming, and she reached the stairs to leave when the door clicked shut, blowing out her candle. Stunned for a moment, she climbed the steps and pushed the door. It didn't budge. It must have caught the latch.

Drat.

Reaching for the belt on her robe to tie it, she realized it must have slipped out of the loops. She sat on the step with her elbows on her knees cradling her face in her hands. No one would even think to look for her out here. At least not until time to prepare for the day's meal if, and that was a mighty *if*, there was need for vegetables and fruits. Evie had just been down here yesterday. Well, Tamsin certainly wouldn't starve.

Though she had no sense of time, it seemed like hours passed. She slept lightly for a time because a small crack in the top of the door jamb allowed a flicker of grayish dawn. She comforted herself knowing it would get lighter.

An egregious thought popped into her head. Our Lord and Savior awoke on the third day and rolled the stone aside. She banished the thought and scoffed at her ability to easily blaspheme. She was losing her mind.

Blast it.

Hope strengthened with the distant sound of carriages coming and going on the cobbled street as the day began. She padded about, feeling her way toward a basket of apples, and taking one in hand, she returned to the steps and bit into her breakfast as the slit of light began to brighten with the morning.

Evie would have already gone into her chamber and known she hadn't slept in her bed. She could picture her scurrying down the staircase calling out for Mrs. T. Or else, she might have taken Sally aside and asked for directions seeing that Miss Morgan hadn't been in her bed last night.

Tamsin smiled at the possibility they might think she'd been out dancing all night or gotten into some trouble or other. The influence of living in the home of a powerful detective usually bore suspicion of wrongdoing before thinking otherwise.

She rose and got herself another apple returning to the steps. Crisp juicy fruit from the tree outback tasted wonderful. She finished the second apple and set the core beside the first on the step. How long would it take the women in the house to think to check the earth cellar?

Just as she pondered the thought, she heard Charlie's baritone and Mrs. T's sharper tone, and beat her fists against the door, yelling as loud as she could.

"Give us a moment with the latch. Thank the Lord Almighty you aren't dead."

Tamsin heard his fumbling with the latch and a second later, she stumbled up the steps standing on the top step of the cellar squinting into the bright light then into his elderly arms.

A moment later Mrs. T cupped Tamsin's face with her palms and looked into her eyes. "You don't look any worse for the mishap."

"I'm sorry for worrying you. It wasn't all that uncomfortable."

As if on cue the kitchen door opened, and a chorus of feminine voices cascaded onto the back lawn. Sally, Evie, and even Cook Ames.

Evie squealed and hopped from foot to foot. "You spent the night in there?"

Sally shook her head and sighed in relief. "Look at you, all ready for bedtime."

Before she could say anything, Charlie entered the cellar and glancing about scooped up the apple cores. "Is this your dinner or your breakfast?"

With all the confusion and questions, rather than answer, she implored, "Whatever made you look for me out here?"

Mrs. T grabbed her from Charlie. "The thought of losing you was frightful. I take it you've been in the cellar all night." She didn't wait for an answer and held up the matching sash of Tamsin's robe. "I saw this on the lawn minutes ago when I stood at the window. It appeared like an arrow pointing to the way. And, then I saw Charlie begin fussing with the latch." She turned to him her cap slanted oddly on her gray head of hair. "You're a fine man, Charlie. We owe you a debt of gratitude."

Tamsin held the cotton belt in her sticky apple fingers. "I wondered where it had got to."

Mrs. T put her hands upon Tamsin's shoulders, her whole face beginning to brighten with fading panic, "Tell me why you would come out here? Was it late last night or early this morn?"

Tamsin tied the sash around her waist averting her gaze as she supplied a false answer. "I had a sudden urge to eat an apple and couldn't find any in the kitchen."

Evie asked, "Weren't you scared out here all alone with the bite-chews and goblins? I couldn't 'av done it."

Tamsin smiled at the young maid. "Oh yes you could. Especially when you do not have a choice in the matter."

Charlie offered up an excellent idea. "I'll put a bell in the cellar, ye can ring it ta yer heart's content if there be another such calamity."

As Tamsin rolled her eyes at the idea of a second mishap, Cook Ames said, "You'll be fortified once you've eaten, miss. I'll get back ta the bacon seeing as how you are fine and all," and patted Tamsin on the shoulder as she bustled toward the back door.

Mrs. T ordered the maids to return to their chores. "Nothing changes. We all have work that doesn't do itself. You've got the carpets to finish and remember not to disturb the carpet in the library."

Charlie took advantage of the distraction and whispered to Tamsin. "Mr. Spencer would have had me head. He ordered me ta keep watch over all ye women, especially ye, what with the Master gone and all."

Chilled from the late September night and dressed in her nightwear, anxiety crawled up her skin. She dearly wanted to return to the house. "How presumptuous of him. I certainly do not need anyone watching over me."

Charlie's bushy brows nearly reached his hairline. "And the proof of that is in this early morning's business, ye'd likely admit ta?"

She had the decency to blush and gave him the slightest nod then followed the others as they returned to the house. If only he knew why she happened to be in the cellar to begin with, though he might not endure the shock.

Dressed in a green skirt with a plain front, full pleats running down the back, and a matching jacket bodice with a bit of lace at the neck and cuffs, Tamsin glanced at herself in the full-length mirror. Taking a moment to see her reflection, she felt that every day pushed her further away from her beloved uncle. How would she survive without him? What was the future going to look like without him?

She hadn't slept well, not just because Uncle Basil's remains had been nabbed; but how was she supposed to investigate his disappearance?

She hadn't a clue as to what to do.

Obviously, someone knew he had been in the cellar these past two and a half days. Hardly anyone went there other than Evie, and *she* certainly hadn't seen him or the whole of England would have known about it.

Poring over the last two days, she thought of Henrietta Reynolds-Walker who arrived the morning of his death. Though she clearly had wanted to talk to him and seemed put out when told he had gone away for several months or more.

Then Harrison arrived right after Mrs. Reynolds-Walker. Tamsin could never suspect him of wrongdoing. He lived by the letter of the law and Uncle Basil had always been his noble, lionhearted victor. Mrs. Thomson had also arrived that afternoon, but clearly her legitimate reason turned out to be her grandson.

More convinced than ever that her uncle died by someone's hand, she didn't know where to begin to uncover clues. The fact that his remains had been stolen suggested someone had eyes on her ever since that night when she ran outside and looked up and down the street. The killer could easily have watched as she dragged her uncle across the back lawn. Her intuition prevailed at times like this, she relied on it.

Goose bumps spread over her arms at thought of someone scrutinizing her. Whose eyes had they been?

Convinced more than ever now that her uncle died by poisoning, she decided to take the two glasses to the Metro Police. She realized the liquid in the cut-glass carafe was also compromised. Anyone could pour a jot and be dead. She shot up from the chair where she'd taken refuge and took hold of the bottle and carafe. Where to hide them?

After a quick moment perusing the room, she pulled out a potted palm in the corner behind the desk and slid both containers behind, then returned the potted palm.

Getting a grip on her wild suspicions, she contemplated writing names of suspects. Not one person came to mind. Everyone loved Uncle Basil. He made a very good friend for anyone in need. He was a pillar of kindness in the community.

Who could possibly be a likely suspect? More so, why would someone want to kill him? She found it hard to think he had an enemy. Although his life's work involved the underbelly of London and motives were perpetual.

Most of his friends were retired Scotland Yard men who gathered once a month at the Silver Cross. He even encouraged Harrison to attend after he finished at Cambridge. Tamsin recalled how proud her uncle had been when he took his protégée to a meeting of his Scotland Yard pals.

She remembered the first time Uncle Basil had taken her to a lecture involving Harrison's class at Cambridge. Afterward Uncle Basil treated them to dinner at Simpson's Tavern. They'd walked through a labyrinth of cobbled streets and quaint window fronts, then stepped inside the dark paneled walls. Tables stretched end to end inviting conversation.

A week or two later, her uncle invited Harrison to dinner along with a friend of his, Jack Whicher, a well-known detective, who regarded her uncle as a long-time friend. It was that evening the friendship between she and Harrison had begun in earnest.

The fond memory brought a smile.

Wool gathering, pencil still in hand, and a blank sheet of paper in front of her, her thoughts dwelled on the past. Not one name of a possible suspect had come to mind.

Her heart thumped with pain at the loss of her dear uncle, and the confusion she felt.

Shuddering to think of Harrison's reaction when she confessed what she'd done, she knew his sense of honor would force him to divulge her actions to the authorities.

She'd created a mess, knowing she would most probably end up mulling all her wrongdoings from behind the thick, moldy walls of Newgate.

Evie interrupted her misgivings with the announcement of Mr. Harrison Spenser.

"I don't intend to stay long. It's been a trying day, but I've good news about Mr. Brownstein and wanted to deliver it myself."

Tamsin asked Evie to bring tea and scones, then closed the glass doors to the parlor as they sat opposite each other. "I take it, he's alive and returned to Mrs. Brownstein."

He nodded. "Even better, Frayley is imprisoned. He will have a trial, but frankly, I'll be surprised if he doesn't hang for this. Brownstein wasn't the only victim who suffered from Frayley's greed. I was able to sneak into the office of Railway United the same night we had agreed I would take over the investigation."

She coughed on a sip of tea. "You found proof of his threat against Mr. Brownstein?"

He grinned. "You won't believe this, but whoever wrote that threat of being nabbed for ramson, had written several and threw the discards in the can in the office."

"No." She laughed. "How did you find where they had taken him?"

"Apparently, Frayley had also threatened Mr. Ginsburg, head of Municipal Rails. Mr. Ginsburg went to Scotland Yard with his complaint without realizing how much damage that man had already caused. And at the same time, I went to the Commissioner.

"Mrs. Brownstein had gotten another letter from Frayley and was on her way to see you when I encountered her. From that moment on, the Commissioner ordered a detail and in no time figured out where they might have Brownstein hidden. It all worked like a charm."

She could see he was pleased with his efforts.

"Brownstein is back home. Ginsburg is satisfied that Frayley is locked up. And I received a pat on the back."

"What about all that money?" she asked.

"I'll leave that up to you." He stood and picked up his hat, giving her a hard glare. "Can we be done with this pastime of yours?"

A look of displeasure crossed her features. "I simply thought it a way to keep busy. These problems came to my doorstep. I wasn't out looking for adventure."

"They were looking for Basil. A man who made his living doing just this. You are not fit for this business. It can be ruthless, as you've discovered."

Harrison left the house slamming his hat on his head. He wanted to make an impression on her that police business should not be a woman's endeavor.

Chapter Nine

Harrison took some time this morning to look at two buildings with enough space to make a roomy gym for today's youth. Lads who had no place to go and needed something to lure them off the ragged streets of inner London.

Joshua Zillig was his inspiration. After seeing him that rainy night and the thug who tried to lure him to steal from his grandmother, Harrison was convinced a gym might have the power to redirect their instincts and bring them off the streets and into a worthwhile endeavor.

Having found a property he could afford, he hurried on his way to chambers and an appointment with Barrister Malcolm Fergus. Harrison's jaunty stride reflected how he felt about the world, his world, the one he created with initiative and an inheritance from his dear paternal grandmother. If it wasn't for her generosity, he would not have the funds to create a gym for youth.

Seven years of higher learning would have left him a pauper without her bestowal. His father offered to pay for his education. Yet there was something to be said for independence. As it happened, his grandmother had given him monies from his grandfather's bequest years earlier. At the time, Harrison had banked the bestowal where it would gain interest. It gave him a sense of independence and he liked the fact that his schooling had never been a burden to his family.

In his sixth year of becoming a barrister, four years at Cambridge, and now his second, and last year of pupillage, the time had come. One might say he had the stamina of a racehorse heading toward the flag in the barrel.

A year ago, he'd been introduced to Barrister Malcolm Fergus at a luncheon. Barrister McMaster had mentioned to him that Fergus would be a smart choice for his pupillage. He remembered the interview as if it were yesterday. He'd practically swooned with nerves, his hand jittery as they shook in greeting.

Fergus, a Scot from Edinburgh, had taken notice of the younger man's tension—obviously not very well hidden. He pushed back from his chair and jumped up, hands on his hips and decried, "Am I ta waste me time on a wordless candidate for Her Majesty's service? Ye'll need ta get hold of yer nerves, man. Yer embarking on a life of dealing with thieves and cutthroats, the underbelly of our beloved London. Criminal law is not for the skittish."

Harrison recalled letting go of his breath in a loud whoosh.

Time had passed and here he sat in the second year with half a dozen months of apprenticeship left, better known as the second-six of study. Since their meeting, he made it a point to attend every one of Fergus' eloquent lectures. Over time he considered the possibility of sitting on the Court of Queen's Bench and practicing criminal law next to the esteemed man.

With the brisk winds from the north, he bent into the fray trying to keep his top hat in place. His briefcase bulged with the required testimonies and an autobiographical documentary account for every year of his life from birth to the present. He had also written an application for Inns of Court admission. He was to hand in each set of documents that would start the wheels turning toward his eventual degree.

The day would have ended on a high note if he could have talked with Basil. His encouragement through the years, and his knowledge of law made him the perfect listener for Harrison's nervous excitement.

Of all the times for Basil to be called elsewhere, Harrison lamented that it was sorely inconvenient, though unavoidable. He knew steamships were allowed passage through the Red Sea, shortening what used to be a year's travel to two months or less depending on the weather. Add to that Basil's settling in, it might be several months before they heard from him.

Coming up on the Court of Justice, he stopped short in front of the large, carved wooden doors and indulged in a moment of reflection before entering the most distinguished law society in the world where generations of lawyers toiled to make England a better land. A bit overwhelming, nonetheless a dream in the making for him.

This distinguished building housed the chamber where he would be working as an apprentice to Malcolm Fergus, shadowing him in court and digging into files of cases not yet solved. This would be his pursuit for the next six months, the last leg of his coming to the bar. He followed the marbled corridor on the second floor to the end of a series of doors with names etched on brass plates until he came to the chamber that read Barrister Fergus. He reached for the brass knob.

A gentleman younger than he was sat at a desk pushing his spectacles up his nose making his brown eyes the size of shillings. "What can I do for you?"

"I've an appointment. The name is Harrison Spencer."

"Huntley, sir. And the barrister is awaiting your arrival." He pointed to a door on his left, "Right through there, sir."

Hat in hand, and his briefcase in the other, he stepped through the door and was immediately greeted by the lanky Fergus as he unfolded from his chair.

"Ready ta do this, are ye?" The Scot motioned to an empty table and chairs in the corner. "Let's sit thee here."

Harrison laid his documents on the table and made sure to breathe regularly. He watched as Fergus shuffled through the pile choosing several testimonies. His thick brows, a bit of gray seeping into the black hairs, rose and settled several times as he read. "Hmm...ye've some complimentary reviews Spencer. If the rest are alike, ye'll have made quite a statement for yerself."

"Thank you, sir."

Fergus reached for the folder marked *court registry* and opened it. "Yer intention ta file for admission ta practice mentions criminal law. So, ye've made yer decision have ye then?" His deep green eyes scanned the younger man's features.

Harrison pressed his elbows into the arms of the chair and sat up straighter. "It seemed easy. A retired mentor, Barrister Basil Walker had been Her Majesty's Lieutenant Detective. He captured my interest when talking of past cases. Made civil law sound, well boring."

Fergus' craggy features softened into a smile. "It's a verra simple description, but I've often thought of it as choosing ta work with people or paper."

Harrison nodded in agreement, relieved the barrister didn't think less of him.

"Ye have a mentor in Walker have ye then. A fine man ta call friend."

"Yes, he's currently attending his plantation, Hilldale."

The Barrister grunted. "Well, that explains why he hasn't answered me last message."

"His leaving came up quickly according to his niece."

"Ah. Well, I'm sorry to hear that. He's always well received in our corridors." With Basil gone for the next six months or more enjoying the merits of his plantation, Harrison intended to mention in his letter to Basil that Fergus wanted to get in touch with him.

Harrison eased up on the arms of the chair not realizing how stiff he held himself.

The barrister rose and tapped the pile of documents with his fingertips. "I'll put these in yer file. Ye've items yet ta take care of. Paying for yer writ against the AG's office, and yer Inns of Court request for admission are next on the list. I've kept up with yer work here in our chamber and find all ta be in order. Ye don't lag about like some who seem to feel as though we're running a nursery. It bodes well for ye, Spencer."

Stunned to hear the master's inner thoughts, Harrison's edginess eased. "Thank you, sir. It means a lot coming from you."

"Ye've entered the third and final stage of joining the Bar. Ye've done well with the nonpracticing six, now ye've ta face the comprehensive practicing six. After that, ye'll be in yer winged collars and gown listening to a cantankerous judge percolate senility as he tells ye about the solemn duties ye'll pay homage ta for the rest of yer life."

At the end of the interview, Harrison fairly skipped down the marble steps of the Court of Justice. He rued Basil's absence and would have shared this meeting with him. It was never so clear as now, that Tamsin missed him, too. Her scintillating presence dulled about the same time Basil left for India. She'd not been the same since. Now that the meeting with Barrister Fergus ended, he should give her the attention she obviously needed during Basil's absence.

Saturday, mid-morning
24 September

As Tamsin neared Mrs. Reynolds-Walker's Bedford Street home, her pulse increased. She could feel it in her chest. She had put this off for three days. With the horror of her uncle's remains disappearing, she could not rest until she sought every possibility. Her dreams last night filled with eerie figures draped over barrels and crates that overflowed with apples. Shaking her head of nonsense, she realized she had arrived at her destination.

The butler opened the door to the rap of the brass knocker. "Mrs. Reynolds-Walker, please." She handed him her card.

Though they'd never set eyes on one another, he obviously knew her when he scanned her card. Shoulders squared and chin lifted, he indicated she step inside the foyer, then led her to a small parlor just off the entrance.

The room appeared intimate and filled with exquisite gold filigree embellishing the cornices. Complementary patterned paper of ivy and roses adorned the walls. Over-stuffed furniture also in rose and cream patterned silk with a sofa and four chairs cozied up to a glass topped table. Shelves flanked the marbled fireplace with China figurines and other decorative items. The hearth was set though not lit. Knowing she wasn't expected, it didn't surprise her the room held a late September chill.

The swish of silk marked the sound of Mrs. Reynolds-Walker's appearance.

"Of all people, you are most surprising." Tall as she seemed, she towered over Tamsin. "What brings you to my door?"

Waving her hand for Tamsin to sit, she took a facing chair and made herself comfortable. Tamsin endured her welcome with poise knowing they did not have even a remote relationship, though they certainly knew each other.

"I guess I'm missing my uncle and found myself walking past. I know it's impulsive."

"As a small child you were impetuous. One would think you had matured." The smirk on her face did nothing for her long features. Tamsin noted her beautiful golden hair fashioned in a large chignon starting higher on her head and hanging lower onto her neck.

Obviously, she hadn't set out on the right foot with the woman. "Apparently I'm still learning."

Mrs. Reynolds-Walker straightened out a wrinkle in her dress. "I imagine it will take him time to get a letter to you."

Tamsin nodded and considered just exactly how much time it would take to receive a missive from Heaven.

"Would you care for tea?"

Drawn from her utterly obtuse thought, she nodded. "I would welcome a cup, thank you."

Mrs. Reynolds-Walker pulled on a bell rope and returned to her chair. "I know this isn't a social call. Tell me why you are here."

Trying not to blush, Tamsin plunged in. "I never learned why you and Uncle Basil separated the very day you married. Would it be too much to ask why? It's always awkward to ask my uncle anything personal."

Mrs. Reynolds-Walker's eyelids nearly closed, though not in a painful way, more like remembering an old injustice. Her hands nestled in her lap, suddenly gripped the arms of her chair. "I recall you being impertinent. Shall I say he and I simply didn't suit?"

Determined to get to the real reason why she was here, she pushed on, "Wouldn't you have known that before you married?"

A knock at the door and a maid entered. "Yes, ma'am?"

Mrs. Reynolds-Walker's gaze fixed on Tamsin for a long second. "We'll have tea."

The maid curtsied and silently closed the door. From the sound of her voice, Tamsin thought she might have asked for rat poison. Her skin crawled at the thought.

Mrs. Reynolds-Walker's chin lifted in...umbrage? Tamsin's knowledge of the woman being scarce, maybe she miscalculated an unannounced visit.

The elder woman admitted. "The instant Basil and I met I knew we wouldn't suit. My father refused to back out of the contract. He wanted the union for whatever reason I never understood. He wasn't to be crossed, a rather forceful man. We abided by his way or not a'tall. My mother's suffering went on for years."

She looked off, across the room as if recalling a memory from the past, then said, "He transferred his bullish demands to me when I reached a certain age."

Skeptical, Tamsin asked, "Surely my uncle had a say?"

"He acted as a gentleman would. I wonder, too, if he perhaps wanted a son."

"My uncle wouldn't have expected a loveless marriage."

Mrs. Reynolds-Walker stood and shook the wrinkles out of her skirt. "I don't believe he thought it would be loveless. I wasn't privy to my father and Basil's conversation. Remember, I was young and legally had no standing as far as my parents were concerned. All I remember thinking about Basil Walker is that he acted like a man of the world, quiet, handsome in his own way, and very much a gentleman though he didn't care a pin for me. I began to hope I could continue my pursuits if we married."

Tamsin slanted her gaze. "You aren't sure, or he told you he didn't care?" Mrs. Reynolds-Walker's excuse for the marriage ending before it began didn't seem logical to her. Uncle Basil was kind and approachable, easy to talk to. He possessed a knack for understanding someone's discomfort, even before the problem became obvious. As though he had a second sense and could read minds.

"Why not ask your uncle when he returns?" Her smile curved on one side as her eyes narrowed.

Taken aback, Tamsin swallowed hard. She had the oddest feeling Mrs. Reynolds-Walker knew something important. An insufferable woman, to be sure. Relief came when the maid entered carrying the tea tray.

"Anything else, ma'am?"

"This will do, Ella. You may go." She puttered with the cups and asked, "Sugar, milk?"

"Milk, please. No sugar." At least she didn't request poison.

Stirring the contents, Tamsin's thoughts drifted. She reminded herself why she came here and mentioned, "Uncle Basil keeps his private life to himself. I thought you might share the reason for living apart all this time. It's tempting to think you've been involved with someone else."

"And if I have, why would I tell you?"

Aha. She as much as admitted it. "You were in love with someone else and still married my uncle."

The steam rose from the cup, as Mrs. Reynolds-Walker barely took a sip. "How old are you?"

"Soon to be twenty-two."

"You are no longer a child. I could tell you the truth, but I've no desire to ruin an innocent's dreams of love and family and a future." Glancing over the rim of her cup she added, "Assuming you are still an innocent."

Tamsin held back a gasp knowing she deserved the jibe. After all her inquiries dealt with extremely pointed details regarding their marriage.

"I may be young in your eyes, yet I've done my share of investigating, following in my uncle's steps. Though I've not probed a murder until..." She quickly dabbed at her mouth with the napkin. What in heaven's name did she almost blurt?

"...recently?"

Over the rim of her cup, Mrs. Reynolds-Walker's eyes lit up. "Something I might have read in the *Morning Post?*"

"I wouldn't call it murder when it mentioned only the threat of one, far less interesting." Tamsin had read the same item. She picked up her teacup and let the warmth seep into her fingertips. "I am interested in why you are withholding your true feelings regarding the marriage to my uncle."

A derisive smile spread across Mrs. Reynolds-Walker's thin, sharp features. "I have been deeply in love with another man since I was sixteen." She swished a crumb that had fallen on her lap.

Tamsin almost gasped but caught herself in time. "Did my uncle know?"

"I told him the truth on the night of our wedding. His immediate response...I could have laughed...was to have the housekeeper put me up in another bedroom. And that ended any thought of the two of us. He purchased this home for me, and I've been here ever since."

"And this unnamed man is still in your life?" Tamsin sipped her cooling tea, acting as though her answer wouldn't matter, though Henrietta's indifference to her uncle wounded her sensibilities.

"Well, now, little missy. I'm sure you've read far too many

penny novels not to understand that sometimes love just takes over. I've told you what you came here to find out and this is the end of it."

Little missy, indeed. Did this woman think of her as a child? "Indulge me with one more question. Why did you come to the house on the morning after my uncle departed?"

Mrs. Reynolds-Walker's attention drifted to the ceiling with its ornamental handcrafted Louis XV style. A moment or two passed before she answered. "You're prying. However, if you are intent upon knowing, I intended to ask for a larger purse. Times are changing, as I'm sure you're aware. It costs to maintain a household."

Confounded by the woman's desire for Uncle Basil to give her a lift in income when her whole life had been wrapped around an affair with another man, gagged her. Tamsin wondered if her actions were considered bigamy, or... well, she really couldn't think what it would come to being married to one man and loving another. The devastation to her beloved uncle foremost in her thoughts, she shivered with displeasure.

"I'm glad my uncle is gone. I'm in charge now, and as I see it, you haven't any rights to his property. At least until he returns." Drat, she should know better than to attempt to intimidate this woman without careful consideration.

Mrs. Reynolds-Walker's chin rose—and she puddled her hands in her lap. "You have no jurisdiction over what the agreement is between Basil and I. However, do take note, it's ironclad. And you are nothing more than a poor little mouse in need of a home. He might decide to rid you of his roof when he returns."

Tamsin stood gathering up her gloves. "There is something to be said about being honest. Where I in your shoes, I'd be ashamed to ask for money when it's another man I loved."

Mrs. Reynolds-Walker's chin lifted a teensy bit more and

Tamsin caught the hatred swimming in her pale eyes. She also sensed the rigid anger holding the woman together. Tamsin hoped her own tone did not reveal her inner turmoil.

"When my uncle returns from India, perhaps you should make a point to hear his side of the details." She bit her tongue. *Why in God's name did she mention that? If Henrietta is the murderer, she knows full well I know he's dead. Drat.*

Taking a few steps toward the closed door, she turned just as Mrs. Reynolds-Walker sipped her tea. "Have you ever considered the life you might have lived with my uncle? He was a wonderful man, generous and kind."

"Was?" Mrs. Reynolds-Walker's features grew wary, and the cup rattled as she placed it on the saucer. "What exactly have you come here to tell me?"

"Clearly a figure of speech. You are already aware he is currently enroute to India. And I doubt he'll try to reinvent your marriage when he returns." She stepped out of the room and almost fell into the butler who stood at the door, obviously eavesdropping on their conversation.

She couldn't escape the house fast enough. Tamsin turned down Bedford toward home encountering a two-carriage accident and a large group of pedestrians who gathered on the sides as Bobbies helped several passengers disembark from one of the damaged vehicles. The other carriage rolled on its side, the horse screeching in pain. She saw a man minus his top hat, banging his cane against the cracked window as he lay sideways across the cushions.

She stepped away behind the group of bystanders and unexpectedly caught Mrs. Reynolds-Walker hurrying down the steps of her home taking absolutely no heed of the accident as her stride quickly took her in the opposite direction.

Curious, Tamsin pushed her way out of the crowd and slowly followed the woman, keeping to a distance. She turned up Bailey. Large elms flanked the street and Tamsin intermittently stepped behind them to remain unseen should Mrs. Reynolds-Walker glance over her shoulder.

The woman kept to the right on Tottenham and Tamsin stayed well behind as Mrs. Reynolds-Walker stepped up to a dark-bricked façade and knocked. She couldn't see who let her in other than a man of sizable proportion, not exactly dressed as a butler. Distance prevented her accuracy.

Once she disappeared into the residence, Tamsin took note of the address, #33 Tottenham, and headed for home.

Chapter Ten

Harrison settled back into the carriage as the driver headed for the East End's densely populated abomination where the spread of addiction and depression hung in the air like a dark pall. Fergus had thought it particularly needful as part of Harrison's awareness of what made London tick, that he should familiarize himself with the area.

He intended to better understand slumming itself. And to gather information regarding opium sales used by the inhabitants. He'd read a paper written by Lord Bellman on the rapid industrialization of London and how wide the split between West London and East London actually was.

It seemed to Harrison that the rapid changes taking place in London had more to do with England's troubles than anything else, almost like a division of two-nations.

He had gotten into a debate with several of his colleagues about the do-gooders and philanthropists who made frequent visits to the East End slums to see how the poor lived. It was depressing to know Londoner's walked the muddy streets gawking at women stretched out on their cornerstone, barely gowned, and men stinking of ale who couldn't stand against a wall without slithering into the muck and filth.

Fergus mentioned High Street, Bethnal Green, and the worst of it, Old Nichol. Harrison was bound by duty to the barrister to familiarize himself with the East End. His studies for the last five years had been taken up with his youthful self when he might have ridden through the East End with some of his bolder classmates.

Authors of the day were writing about the unrestricted use of drugs growing among the working classes. Dark London was described in such egregious detail that religious groups were beginning to campaign about the unrestricted opium trafficking.

Ching Chan, with her elderly grandmother and two young sisters, lived on the top floor in a home with six other families ten blocks from her place of work in the East End on Shoreditch. She worked ten-hour days that began just before noon and ended when the boss showed up sometime around eleven at night.

Her grandmother kept watch over her two young sisters while Ching Chan worked.

Ching Chan swept up the pieces of a broken vial and dumped them in the garbage. The shelving in her small market space wasn't the most stable. The man for whom she worked held no interest in the sturdiness of her cubby. Profit and sales were his regard.

Ho, known as the boss, ran six other cubicles like this one for another man, who was the actual owner of the cubbies. She'd never seen him.

Ching Chan would have preferred a different life for herself. She dedicated her responsibility to her little sisters and old woman. This job, as miserable as it proved, allowed her to bring food home every night when she closed up.

It was exactly eleven in the morning, and Ho unlocked the door of her cubicle. In that instant, a bedraggled woman with a youngster on her hip barged past her into the cubicle.

"What you need?" Ching Chan already knew what she wanted and why. Laudanum was known as the baby's quieter, or mother's friend. It consisted of opium, water, and treacle.

The potion caused deaths and severe illnesses of babies and children. Yet, apothecaries recommended it for colic, diarrhea, vomiting, hiccups, pleurisy, rheumatism, catarrhs, and cough.

"A bottle of laudanum."

Ching Chan's eyes narrowed on the baby in her arms. "What her trouble?"

The woman looked as if she might swoon from lack of sleep or the effects of eating opium. "Won't sleep. What's a person ta do? I'm needin' me sleep."

"Baby get used to laudanum need stronger."

The woman's heavy-lidded eyes swept the shelves behind Ching Chan. She looked exhausted, as if she could fade away.

"It made from poppy. Opium. Use make soap and lotion. For baby, mix with milk. She sleep, you rest."

"I want laudanum." Her small fist pounded the rickety counter.

"Today same price as laudanum." Ching Chan hid the pang of guilt that fluttered in her chest. When she hired on, Ho told her exactly what to say. She must always sell opium over laudanum if possible.

The woman dug into her pocket and pulled out coins, in return she received a small, folded packet of white powder.

"A pinch in milk." Ching Chan always added this, hoping to restore a bit of her own decency.

The worn-out mother shifted the child on her hip and scooped up the packet scurrying out of the shop and into the darkening alley like the rats that sniffed about.

Night hovered over the East End of London and Ching Chan knew the time of day had come that provided the best opportunity for sales. People were in despair and when the sky turns into darkness they rotate toward weakness.

Ho had taught her these things. He also warned if someone didn't get what they needed from laudanum, offer them opium. In no time, they would pay any price for the opium. If the mother ate opium, she would eventually sell her child for a packet.

Ching Chan lost her family to opium. She knew exactly the power of the lotus plant. It is why she kept from it.

In the east end there were many shops such as this one all run by Chinese who worked for the same owner. She had never met that person. It was Ho, a medium sized man, with a full beard and glasses who came around every evening to collect the day's earnings and lock up the stall.

Ching Chan worked late every night until eleven o'clock when she would leave with her groceries to feed her siblings and grandmother.

Opium was unregulated and easily accessible. Most everyone thought it a medical remedy suitable for self-medicating. Ching Chan's little stall was one of many places available to the public, the poor, and the addicted, particularly here in the East End. She couldn't claim to be an apothecary and had quickly become aware that even they make heinous mistakes when mixing opium.

She felt it her duty to make clear opium must be ingested in small amounts. Her musing was suddenly interrupted by a white-skinned woman with a bright blue hat who entered and smiled at Ching Chan. "My husband sent me to get his order. Four ounces of opium and a vial of laudanum, and I will also have a bar of your soap."

She knew the woman and her yellow-skinned husband. As she began wrapping the articles, she mused over the number of white women marrying Chinese. She knew their numbers were increasing what with the number of children born of their union. Ching Chan read the papers. She also knew Londoners from the West End were scandalized at the many Anglo females marrying Chinese.

Before her parents died, she had been sent to school to learn to read and write. She obviously had merit, but the obligation to her grandmother and little sisters hung heavy on her heart and she could do nothing except what she knew, sell opium.

"Here is parcel. A small vial of skin cream you try. It is new product."

The woman, Mrs. Wang, wore lipstick in a bright red color. When she smiled, her brown rotting teeth dominated her facial features.

Ching Chan returned the smile out of deference. In her heart she pitied Mrs. Wang and her baby.

The boss man wouldn't be pleased with her if he knew her subtle warnings to the mothers who practically wept with lack of sleep.

Ching Chan had long ago promised herself that if she had a child, she would never give it opium or laudanum. She'd seen the little bodies of her neighbors' children, their death like appearance, unresponsive, and no appetites even when food was available. They became malnourished and some died of starvation.

Her only means of working was this dreadful job. The man she worked for often demanded that she do better, push more product on unsuspecting mothers.

Ching Chan thought she saw him once when she first began working for Ho. He had slicked black hair and a thin mustache and was dressed in the fashion of a wealthy man, very much out of character for the neighborhood where opium was sold, and where mothers begged for it, even selling their bodies for it.

All she could do was what she was doing. Selling a product that she herself would never try.

Chapter Eleven

Monday, early afternoon,
24 September 1870

The maid settled Mr. Spenser in the parlor and went in search of Miss Tamsin. Who glided into the room moments later gowned in an afternoon dress of green striped silk complemented by her luxurious dark hair. Without realizing it, she gave off a look of fragility and femininity. Stunned by the vision, he simply nodded.

She sank into a chair and waved at him to do the same. "Cat got your tongue?"

"You look...different." He couldn't take his eyes off her.

"Really, Harrison. You're making me self-conscious. Shall I change my dress?"

"No." A bit harsh, he instantly wished he could take back the tone. He'd meant to compliment her and awkwardly had done the opposite.

"Good, because I'm in no mood to do so. It's been a tiring

day and all I want to do is sit here. And of course, talk with you. So, tell me, what is new with your Scottish tutor?"

He took a chair opposite and commented, "He isn't my tutor, Tasmin. And should he hear you say so, his caustic wit might melt your delicate ears. However, your asking prompts me to mention that I am so accustomed to visiting Basil on the days I've met with the barrister, I couldn't stay away from your door. The habit is ingrained in me."

"I'll be a poor substitute, but we can give it a try." She cast him an impish smile.

Mrs. T bustled into the room placing a tray of scones and tea on the table. "I heard your voice, Mr. Harrison, and thought you might need a bite or two. What with all your studies and important legal work."

Tamsin's gaze followed Mrs. T as Harrison seemed to preen while reaching for a chocolate scone. He appeared to actually puff up.

Turning to leave, the housekeeper glanced at Tamsin. "Is that a new dress? It's quite becoming."

She squirmed, feeling like a specimen in a petri dish.

He snorted as Mrs. T left the parlor, and quickly mentioned, "I came right from chambers to inform you that Brownstein's three captors will be going to trial. It's possible they could receive twenty years or more. It's becoming more of a civil case because it's involving the subway and the city."

Relieved at the change of subject, she declared, "I never did thank you enough for helping me. Poor Mrs. Brownstein, she feared going to the authorities thinking that gang would murder her husband if she did."

"Her instincts were spot on. If she hadn't first met up with you, I'm afraid to think of what the outcome might have been. I'm glad I could help."

"Don't be modest. It just goes to show that your studies

are leading you on the right path to success." She surprised him with a smile, thinking she'd been dour.

Finished with the scone chased by tea, he proclaimed, "You amaze me. The thought of taking on cutthroats and treacherous thieves never occurred to you. Reuniting the Brownstein's became your determination. Considering the vast amount of money involved, and the thugs calling the shots, I'm lucky to be sitting in the same room with you."

Her cheeks flushed. "I do appreciate your stepping in and taking over. I admit to being out of my league. I really do not know what I could have been thinking."

She ran a palm over her skirt as the room quieted with sudden lack of conversation. Her desire had been to make money, thus keeping the household from insolvency. In the end, turning the Brownstein kidnapping over to him seemed the right thing to do.

She'd made a huge mess of everything and the dearest man in the world lost to her forever. Sadness weighed her down and she turned her face aside hoping Harrison wouldn't notice. She missed him terribly and her heart ached and there was nothing to be done about it except endure.

The world outside the parlor intruded with the clop of hooves and banded carriage wheels on the cobbles of Portman Square. A whistle blew in the distance.

The bell rang followed by the patter of steps in the front hall. The opening of the front door came next. "A post for Miss Morgan."

Tamsin glanced at her visitor. "I never get posts."

He winked at her. "Always time for a first."

The maid slipped into the parlor and handed it to her, then retreated, closing the door.

"Will you excuse me a moment?" She held up the missive.

He nodded and left her to it as he sauntered over to the

stuffed bookshelves and ran a forefinger along the titles when he heard a slight gasp and turned to her.

He really didn't want to intrude yet felt trapped in the room.

She spouted, "Of all the nerve," and. "How dare she," and followed that by ripping the post in half.

He'd never seen her quite so agitated. "Anything I can do?"

The icy look she gave him might have been an adamant *no*.

Instead she threw the torn note at him. Then as an afterthought, she jumped off the settee and scooped up the pieces settling on the floor taking them back in hand.

He blazed, "Tamsin, what has gotten into you? What's in that note that has you so riled?"

She paced the edge of the thick Persian rug, her wrist at her forehead. "I'm such a fool, worse than an idiot. Oh, Harrison, if I tell you, you will just march out of here and never set eyes on me again."

The fist holding the torn note shook with vigor. "She's threatened me, and I have not an ounce of what to think."

Turning to her, he cupped her shoulders, looking her in the eye. "Calm down and tell me how I can help."

In her vexation, she tried to shake his hands off her shoulders, but he kept a firm grasp. "Sit and drink some tea, get ahold of yourself."

Her cerulean eyes locked on his and she calmed a bit. He pled, "Please sit down and let me help you?" He could feel her forbearance as her shoulders slumped.

She did as he asked and faced him still gripping the torn note and looked at her hands as if they would give her direction. Her chest fell and rose with agitation.

She barely whispered, "This may take a bit as there is something I have kept from you. A horrendous situation and I cannot truly explain why I did what I did. All I know is my heart is breaking."

They sat on the divan together. A low breath escaped him. "Nothing can be that bad."

She looked him in the eye and nodded with assurance. "Yes, there can be. And I saw it. And made a decision that has turned out to be wretchedly horrid."

Mrs. T knocked on the parlor door and entered. "Excuse me for interrupting. Sally needs two days off, Thursday and Friday. Her mother is ill, and I wanted to make sure her absence will not cause a problem."

Tamsin glanced at the door and Mrs. T. The interruption flustered her thinking, and she took a moment. "I can manage without her. Did you ask if there is anything we can do? Maybe send along something for their dinner?"

"For the time being, she seems to have taken the news calmly. I'll question her further."

After the housekeeper closed the door, he turned with a raised brow. "You have me on pins and needles."

Glancing at him, her hand still clutching the torn missive, she tried, "I don't know where to begin. It's heartbreaking. You'll be devastated."

"Obviously, this letter," he pointed at her lap, "has something to do with what you are going to say. Who it is from?"

"Mrs. Reynolds-Walker." She opened her hand and dropped the bits on the table in front of them.

Her heart clutched. "But, the worst, most horrible part is about Uncle Basil." Her hands clasped and her knuckles swiped at her lips. A tear formed in the corner of her eye.

Harrison was beginning to fear the unforeseeable. Basil in an accident? Something gone wrong in India? Basil not returning earlier than anticipated?

In her anxious state, she twisted her fingers, and he handed her a handkerchief to mangle.

"He's...he's dead."

"Who?" His glance was one of surprise.

"Uncle Basil."

Something about the emotion in her voice gave him pause. He focused on her, trying to grasp the meaning of her words. His throat tightened.

Basil?

Dead?

He slumped back against the settee, wordless.

His mind fixed on her statement.

"How do you know this?"

Tamsin put her hand on his, her face crumbling with emotion. "It is awful being without him. It's terrifying."

He swiped his cheeks with the back of his hand. "How long..."

A sob rolled out of her and a gush of tears. "He never went to India."

"What?" His hands fisted.

"I found him in his library at...about midnight three nights ago..."

His voice low with disbelief, he asked, "The same morning I came by? Are you telling me I was in this house with him dead?" His face paled. "You said he had gone to India. Bombay."

She nodded and handed him the now damp handkerchief. "I lied."

She watched him as he gazed about the room and came to settle on her as if she was an anchor. "How did he..."

"I'm sure it was arsenic."

He embraced Tamsin holding her tight as they both dealt with the emotional devastation. She had not realized how much of a burden it had been to keep his death to herself. It was like a mountain of grief and secrets.

He held her in his arms, his chin nuzzling the top of her head.

As she quieted, he asked, "Where are his remains?"

She extricated herself from him and gave him a weary glance, then looked away. "I dragged him to the underground vault."

His eyebrow rose as he waited. His finger under her chin, he drew her sad, red gaze back to him. "You mean he's in the root cellar?"

At her nod, he said, "Explain everything to me about that night."

Haltingly she told him about the argument that woke her, finding his body and the two glasses of liquid. The front door wide open, and the unlatched gate that made it certain someone had been with him. She also admitted her great fear of losing her home and that the household staff would certainly lose their employment. They would all be out on the street.

She admitted hiding him until she could figure out a solution. All the while she tried to discern who would have murdered him and kept coming back to Mrs. Reynolds-Walker. She clearly felt he died by poisoning because of the two glasses.

"When you walked me home from Mrs. Brownstein's and asked if you could take the reins on that investigation, believe me when I say how relieved I was. Uncle Basil's death is haunting me, and I knew I had done the wrong thing and I wanted to go to the cellar last night after everyone had gone to their beds. I wanted to apologize to him and do the right thing. I can't believe how selfish it was of me to think I could somehow keep him for a bit." She gulped on a sob of remorse.

He placed a hand on her arm. "It's a heart wrenching situation no matter how you look at it. I could have helped you. I am sorry you felt the need to keep this from me. You did not have to go through this alone."

She slowly lifted her gaze to him trembling a bit at the mouth. She feared telling him the rest.

Harrison stated the obvious. "There has been a murder and by law I cannot keep this from the authorities. I cannot think of a reason anyone would want him dead. If you are right about the poison, without question it had to have been deliberate."

"I think it best I notify the Yard for you. Things might be a bit dicey with him dying three days ago. But I think we can explain this in a way it will make some sense."

Her side glance was meant to warn him.

He spouted, "What, in the name of God, Tamsin? Is there more you have yet to tell me?"

"You needn't blaspheme."

"Tamsin, I am already jeopardizing my future. Get on with what I have *yet* to learn."

Her head shook as if deciding for herself what to do.

"How long are you going to drag this out? I loved the man, too, you know. He was..."

She could see he tried to keep his emotions in check, hating the mess she had made of her beloved uncle's murder.

In a meek voice, she began, "As I had been doing, last night I waited till the house grew dark, and crept out to check on him."

She paused.

He eyed her wearily.

"His remains are gone."

Harrison sucked in a breath.

"Someone knows what I've done. The murderer must have watched me drag him to the cellar."

"You could have been a victim. Had that occurred to you?" He shoved a hand through his thick hair. His voice rumbled with anger. "I am at a loss to understand how you could live with Basil's death...and now his disappearance... how could you not go to the authorities? Or, at the least, come to me?"

She cupped her mouth with a hand as a muffle of words tumbled out. "I'm sorry. I wasn't thinking right. I had no plan...just pain and emptiness. And our future, this house."

He took her hands in his. "Well now you have me, and somehow we'll get through this."

Obviously confused and restless, he stalked to the window as though he could find a solution out on the grounds. His shoulders sagged and her heart ached for his loss, their loss.

As unfair as springing this on him proved to be, she felt a sense of relief sharing the massive burden. "I inadvertently locked myself in the cellar last night and was rescued this morning when the staff began looking for me. My sash had come off my robe and Mrs. T saw it on the lawn."

"Do they know about Basil?"

"Not a word. They think he's on his way to India. You are the only person I can trust to know the truth. And, of course, there is the murderer."

With the gray sky filled with clouds of a watery sort behind him, Harrison turned his back on the bay window and flashed her the semblance of a wry smile. "The three of us are going to get rather cozy before this is over."

She swiped at her cheeks. "I should have taken you into confidence at the first."

A moment passed as he tried to understand all she'd said. "I think I know why you did not. You loved him more than anyone, and he was taken from you. You reacted out of a keen sense to not let go."

Her attention went to her hands crossed in her lap. He returned to the settee and slipped his palm over her hands gently squeezing them.

"Tell me what is so damning in the letter Mrs. Reynolds-Walker sent?"

"If you can fit the pieces together, read it."

"Just tell me." Frustration etched in his voice.

"She wrote that I am never to darken her doorway again. That I obviously had an odious reason for going to her home and upsetting her with questions about the past. That I am a rash, interfering, and difficult person, and it's no wonder my uncle keeps his distance.

"She also threatened me with calling the Metro if I came anywhere near her. She intends to tell them I am unstable."

He pinched the upper part of his nose and said, "I would like to know what caused you to seek her out?"

"Because I think she murdered him."

"That's a very serious allegation. She would have been within her rights to defend herself if they had physically fought."

"Uncle Basil...hitting a woman? Hardly." She shivered in disgust.

"Stupid of me to mention, sorry."

"I am not so foolish that I accused her. Really, do not think me so ignorant. I wanted to get a feeling, a sense of her. In all the years she's been in our family, I have never really conversed with her. When she came by her only interest was her small purse and having enough to live on."

"I agree you were watched the night he died." His deep voice carried a warning. "And she possibly thought as his wife, she legally inherited, so that could be construed as motive. Except she doesn't know he's dead. You didn't tell her, did you?"

Shrugging her shoulders, she quite saucily mentioned, "If she murdered him, she would know."

"That's defamation, Tamsin."

"I have always found it difficult to be around her."

"That's beside the point."

"What am I to do?"

"For the moment, nothing." His voice guarded and filled with warning, he added, "Promise me, Tamsin."

Her lips pursed and she somberly nodded. "I do have something else to tell."

"I don't think I can take any more at the moment."

Ignoring his complaint, she said, "When I left Mrs. Reynolds-Walker's home an accident happened on the next corner, and I stopped for a moment with the crowd that gathered. I happened to notice her leaving her home. She hadn't mentioned another appointment. Finding that curious, I followed her to #33 Tottenham off Bailey, a dark brick three-story."

Harrison pulled a small black book from his breast pocket and wrote down the address.

Then he asked, "I would like to see this hiding place. Could we meet out back at eleven? Or is that too late for you?"

He wanted to see her uncle's remains and the spot where she kept him behind the vegetables.

She sighed. "Eleven would be good."

Chapter Twelve

Saturday, near midnight
24 September 1870

T hick black clouds scuttled in front of the orange moon leaving very little light. The night threatened an onset of pelting rain pounding the roof, and perhaps a safe, snuggly feeling as one bedded down.

Harrison stood next to an old elm creaking in the wind and waited for Tamsin as she slipped out the back door. Wrapped in a black shawl and stealth of movements, she would have been invisible but for the lone candle she carried. Harrison unlatched the door, and they proceeded down the squeaky wooden steps, closing the trap behind them.

"Do not touch the floor, stay on the step and point to exactly where you hid him."

"I wrapped him in a blanket and after rearranging several crates, made a bier behind the vegetable bins over there." She pointed to the far corner of the cellar.

Harrison took the candle from her, lifting it high. "Essentially you hid him from view should your maid need vegetables or fruits."

"Yes. It was Evie's job to gather Cook's needs. She hated being down here, much too scary and dark for her. I would say her trips might add up to once a week or less."

"I'm assuming she wouldn't linger for any considerable amount of time."

"She's skittish as a cat."

He stepped carefully to the rear of the musky cellar holding the candle high. "This must be the spot?" He could see drag marks across the dirt floor, and her footprints as she came and went over the past three days, and the fresh steps from being locked in last night.

"Yes." She rubbed her arms remembering what she'd done.

"You mentioned a blanket."

"It's gone."

"Hmm." He bent down, holding the candle close to the earth floor.

"What?"

"I am looking for footprints other than yours. It looks as if someone has brushed them out." Having said that, he noticed the print of a large boot.

"Does Charlie ever come down here?"

"There would not be a reason for him to do so. Why?"

He stepped away from the shoeprint and lowered the candle for her to see.

"The size makes me think it definitely belongs to a man."

He held the candle low and very carefully stepped where the floor hadn't been scuffed, waving the candle about. He discovered another print different from the first. Part of the left heel was missing. He stood up, stretched his back, and voiced, "There were two men in here. Recently, I'd say."

"How do you know that?" On the step, she became

almost of a height to him. His eyes glistened from the reflection of the glowing candle.

"Two sets of prints. One print left a clear impression in the dirt, a left foot with part of the heel missing. They carried Basil out. Two men wouldn't have had need to drag him."

He stood close to her, allowing the glow of the little candle to spread over them. "What kind of wicked person would poison him and hide his body?"

He cupped her elbow, "Let me help you out of here."

Back on the lawn with the door latched, Harrison mused, "We will have to find the body, otherwise we can't prove his murder."

He handed her a scrap of cloth. "Does this look like the blanket in which he was wrapped?"

Her heart wrenched as he laid it in her palm. The cloud cover continued to mask any glow from the moon, and he'd blown out the candle. "When we get inside, I'll look at it."

She turned to him as they stood at the bottom of the stairs leading to the kitchen door. "I can testify to the fact he is dead. Doesn't that count for something?"

"It should." He patted the collar of her jacket back in place. "This time of night might not do for us to be seen together. I'll come by Monday and we can hash this out." He stood on the lawn as she walked up the steps, opened the door and stepped inside.

Staying to the shadows, he quietly walked away.

In her room, Tamsin pulled the patch of material out of her pocket and knew instantly it was the same that covered her uncle. Her throat tightened.

Will you ever forgive me?

She tucked the piece of fabric covered in faded yellow primroses in her top drawer for safe keeping.

Monday, 9:00 a.m.
26 September

Tamsin left for the apothecary taking with her the two glasses of liquid tucked into a basket.

When she entered the establishment, Mr. Fowkes was busy rearranging containers on the shelf behind the counter. He turned and with a big smile said, "The to-be famous murder mystery writer. How are we today, Miss Morgan?"

"Fine, thank you, sir." Setting her basket on the counter, she asked, "I hope you will help me with a twist in my plot."

He swiped his palm on a towel and leaned against the counter.

"This might seem an odd request. You see, I've two glasses of liquid and wonder if you can tell me if arsenic is in either of them."

His bushy brows rose at the same time his mouth gaped as he noted the glasses she'd taken out of the basket and put on his counter. "And why would I want to do that?"

"Because I need to know if there is arsenic in either of them." Her eyes widened as she locked her gaze on him. His voice didn't sound particularly interested in her request.

"You're the mystery writer, how's it you don't already know?" He backed away from the counter and crossed his arms, squinting at her, and obviously suspicious of her motives.

She shrugged. "A good question, sir. I do know. Please understand that I'm following in the steps of my character in asking you to do this."

"If you took water out of a well anywhere in London, there'd be a trace of arsenic. It's in everything in London's grand system of bringing fresh water to us all." His sarcasm was tersely cogent.

"I will pay you to do this, sir." She worried he might refuse.

Squinting at her, he took a long minute to decide. "You are a determined young lady, miss. I'm not acquainted with authors, are they all like you?"

Taken unaware by his interest, she said, "I don't really know."

"I'd say writing must be an art of sorts." He tapped the counter with his fingertips. "I'll test it for you, but I don't want money. I'd rather you mentioned me along with Mr. Marsh in your opening remarks."

Relaxing a bit, she inquired, "Who might Mr. Marsh be?"

"The gentleman who developed the test to discover the amount of arsenic in London's drinking water. He used sulfide and hydrochloric acid. I'll do the same."

"I'm most grateful to the gentleman, and to you, Mr. Fowkes. Thank you for naming the chemicals. That will come in handy when I write the scene." She tugged on her gloves and added, "Shall I wait, or come back later?"

"I'm not busy right now and this won't take long. If you've shopping to do, or you can wait?"

She eyed a chair facing Upper George Street. "I will while away the time window watching."

"You do that." He scooped up both glasses and walked through the curtains that divided his public room and the rear of the building where his private office must be.

Traffic on Upper George Street was clogged with slow carriages taking up most of the width of the cobbled lane. Maids scurried with baskets on their way to the marketplace just around the corner and down two blocks. A few vendors tucked up against the buildings, did their best to advertise their product in spite of the late afternoon traffic.

Across the street from where she sat, a bald man brushed paste on a poster and slapped it against the wall. She read *Harry's Barber Shop Open* and thought what an unsuitable name for the barber. She couldn't help but snigger at his pink pate, not one hair to be seen.

Next door to the barbershop there appeared to be a steady line of pedestrians stepping over the threshold of *The People's Voice* written on the lintel. The sign inclined her to think of a dissatisfied group wanting reform of some kind.

Three little tykes, hand in hand on their way somewhere without supervision, made her curious why their mother would not be with them. At least they knew enough to stay on the walkway rather than the street where the bustling carriages splashed puddles of filthy water from the downpour last night. They stopped at a bread-maker's window pressing their noses up against the glass until a woman wrapped in a smudged apron came out the door and handed each a biscuit. The baker's kindness warmed Tamsin's heart.

Something clanged to the floor in the back room distracting her.

Mr. Fowkes called out. "Nothing broken. I'm almost finished."

She settled back in the chair and mused about Harrison's promise to investigate the address on Tottenham, where she had seen Mrs. Reynolds-Walker enter.

Mr. Fowkes came through from the backroom carrying both glasses. "As you already know, both glasses have a high degree of arsenic."

She left the chair and stood at the counter. Not until this moment, did she realize she had held out hope his death would have been natural. Her heart twisted in agony that he had been the victim of cruelty. Both glasses were poisoned. She'd have to think about that.

Mr. Fowkes set the empty glasses down. "I've disposed of

the poison, so you needn't worry it might get into the wrong hands."

She held back a gasp. Bother.

He'd also cleaned the glasses. She had intended to use the smudges on them in the slight chance they could duplicate a fingerprint. Uncle Basil had talked to her about the innovation that can prove guilt or innocence. She had read that Sir William Herschel used fingerprinting for identification and Uncle Basil told her it would revolutionize the future of crime. Though, at the time, Scotland Yard didn't use the procedure.

"Something amiss? You look struck." He packed the two glasses in her basket.

"Nothing, sir. Other than I'm most grateful for your help."

He smiled at her in such a way, she felt he was patronizing her. "I've written this down on my letterhead exactly as it tested. You keep this for your novel so it can be exact. I'll keep one for me own records to remind me of you and your story. And if you need any other assistance, I'll be glad to help." He winked at her. "As long as you're using arsenic as a means to kill, you might want to know that when lesser amounts are given in the weeks or months leading up to death, a final larger dose will kill immediately."

"Why would a killer not want to just give a larger dose and be done with it?"

"It's clear you're a novice. Your readers will expect you to be well versed on this subject, I'd imagine. Giving a large dose all at once would be agony for the victim before it completed the task. Given in smaller amounts leading up to the larger dose would bring on a quiet death without fuss, in most cases."

His bushy brows rose, as his watery eyes settled on her.

"You wouldn't be playing games with me now would ye, missy?"

For a moment, her heart jumped. She bit her lip. According to Mr. Fowkes, it was a certainty her uncle was being poisoned for a week or two before his final drink. "Why would you say such a thing? I want to be accurate, 'tis all. A writer's authenticity is important. Just ask Mr. Dickens."

His skeptical brows stayed put, yet he smiled. "I'm not in the same social circles as Mr. Dickens. And I look forward to reading your exactness."

Out on the lane, Tamsin's heart calmed. He was a nice man. She hated lying to him. However, she saw no other way to get the answers without raising all kinds of questions. For a quick moment, she felt he'd been on the brink of questioning her more deeply, thus her quick exit.

Uncle Basil's habit was to pour a drink from the cruet every night while he went over his day and made notes.

So, who put the poison in the cruet?

It was certain someone had been with him in his last minutes. Mrs. Reynolds-Walker came to mind, of course. Tamsin thought she should take the glass bottle to Mr. Fowkes, but then she dreaded he would figure out it wasn't a novel she wrote. And then he would most likely report her to Scotland Yard.

While she was out, Harrison arrived and made himself comfortable in the parlor until her return. She quickly deposited the basket in a corner of the library.

He followed her. "What have you there?" He peered over her shoulder. "Seems like you want it hidden."

She put a finger to her lips just as Mrs. T walked into the room.

"A post came for you." The housekeeper said. "I laid it on the desk. Will it be both of you for lunch?"

Harrison glanced at Tamsin with expectation, and she nodded to Mrs. T.

The housekeeper smiled at him. "Your work must have slackened somewhat. It's good to see you a bit more now especially with the master gone."

When the housekeeper left the library, Tamsin closed the door. "Are you just now coming from chambers?"

He nodded, as he leaned back against the wall of books. "Apparently, a large gang of drug runners has been under surveillance for quite some time and recently the detectives assigned to the covert operation had a breakthrough."

"Why does the Yard even care? Drugs aren't under any restrictions for purchase or otherwise."

"It has been apparent for quite some time there are drugs being undercut and that is causing a rise in crime."

"Parliament should do something about regulating medicines. Perhaps make them less accessible. Maybe then we wouldn't have so many people dying. I saw pictures of opium houses in *The Daily* that should warn and deter folks. I thought Her Majesty's men handled problems such as this."

"They do. I'm not well known, I have a low profile, Fergus has asked that I get involved. It's as if Basil put the idea in his head." He glanced heavenward and added, "Like he's playing chess with me and I'm the pawn."

Tamsin laughed. It felt so foreign. She laughed again. "Goodness, that felt good. You are thinking of Uncle Basil in one of his roles—finding the underlying cause of things gone awry."

Harrison, hands in pockets, rolled on the balls of his shoes. "He always treated me special, right from the first as a lad when we met." An unmistakable sadness in his voice almost brought tears to his eyes and he blinked.

She noted his struggle and wished she could say something appropriate. However, words could never salve their loss. A moment of quiet came over them as they exchanged glances, recalling a gentleman they both loved.

She inquired, "Did you get a chance to go by the house on Tottenham?"

"I checked out the address in the office. It's a séance parlor, run by a Madam Patwell."

"Really?" She wondered if Mrs. Reynolds-Walker tried to connect with the *other world*. Could she be the one who poisoned Uncle Basil, then tried to connect with him? But why, after years of denying him any relationship at all? It must be the money. She reminded herself that Mrs. Reynolds-Walker was not above suspicion.

The woman was more than capable of sneaking into the house and poisoning his cruet. Even though it was years ago, she had lived in the house long enough to know where things were. Perhaps even clever enough to have kept a house key?

However odd it may seem deep inside, Tamsin had convinced herself of the woman's guilt. Though she didn't know how to go about proving her allegation.

"Fergus gets a monthly sheet on nefarious activity and the house on Tottenham is listed as one—it has been on the list for years according to my source."

Evie knocked on the door and poked her head in the library. "Luncheon is served."

They seated themselves at the table laid with cold-cuts of ham and a ragout of the savory spice of sweet-herbs with chunks of lamb boiled in wine. Warm buttermilk biscuits dripping in soft butter were Harrison's undoing. He admitted, "I'm ravenous."

"I am, too." She unfolded her napkin and placed it on her lap.

"Mrs. Labady isn't much of a cook. Though I'd never

broach the subject with her. She's very sensitive about the matter."

"I'm surprised your landlady does not employ a cook. Seems she would do so with as many boarders as there are. Did you once mention there were six of you?"

Dishing two spoonsful of the ragout into a bowl he handed it to her, then prepared one for himself. "Yes, keeps her in the kitchen mostly."

"Not a job I'd enjoy by any stretch of the imagination."

He chuckled as he reached for a biscuit. "You must have been on the run this morning. You were just taking your wrap off when I arrived. What were you up to?"

She whispered, "I do not want the maids to hear. I took the two glasses of brandy, or whatever it was the night Uncle Basil...well, you know...I took them to Mr. Fowkes and he analyzed them." With a chunk of lamb at the end of her fork, she pointed it at him giving substance to her words. "They were both laced with you know what." She rolled her eyes then popped the morsel into her mouth and began chewing the delicious lamb.

He swallowed the delightfully infused meat. "I guess that puts an end to the why he...well, you know," and bit into the warm biscuit.

She chewed the lamb and a small sound of contentment whimpered out of her. Swallowing, she added, "Mr. Fowkes wrote out his findings on a piece of letterhead and gave it to me. I mentioned to you that he thinks I'm writing a mystery novel. I am not sure why he would put his judgement on letterhead and give it to me. He made a copy for his files, too."

Harrison's face sobered as he said, "He's decided you are up to something. The answer on his official paper is proof of what he thinks should you need to show it to your...hmm, editor?"

Tamsin asked, "Why is the house on Tottenham being watched?"

"I suspect it has something to do with a previous death."

"A death?" That caught her attention.

"It was proven the woman died of natural causes. Yet they keep an eye on the place from time to time."

"Do you think it would be clever if I attended a séance at Madam Patwell's?"

He felt a drip of butter on his lip and patted the napkin against it. "I think it could be dangerous for you. What if Mrs. Reynolds-Walker is there? Surely you cannot disguise yourself to the point she will not recognize you."

"What if I dressed to look like an elderly widow with a cane, gowned in black with a thick veil over my gray hair?"

He chuckled at the thought. "I see your mind is already set. My better judgement warns against it. We both know you will do what you please." He sat back in his chair and pulled out his watch.

"Have you an appointment?" Her dark brows rose with the question.

"Not for a while. You make me fidgety 'tis all." He didn't smile when he added the last.

She shrugged and sipped water thinking of him as very much like Uncle Basil. "You are a clever man to know you have lost the game. Is there anything more to the drug war you are investigating?"

"It's not a drug war. But it involves opium shipped in at outrageously low prices. The mastermind is unknown, and well hidden. It would be easier to infiltrate the greenhorns at the bottom of the pyramid."

"I don't understand. What is the point of any business selling their product at a low price?"

Harrison tucked his watch back in his pocket. "That's the

kicker. We can't figure it out. No crime has been committed. I've been tasked with finding an answer for the barrister."

Evie entered the dining room and took the dishes away asking if they would like tea. Harrison mentioned he must leave in a few minutes.

Tamsin waited until the maid left the room before she asked, "How do you go about finding something when you don't know what you are looking for, exactly?"

"Smugglers bring in tea from India as a cover for drugs that will be undersold. The drug king is unknown. The men working beneath him have been under investigation for an exceptionally long time. Whoever he is, he's very clever."

"Would Uncle Basil approve of your involvement? He was always your champion."

Harrison shrugged. "He might be concerned that I am not finished with my last six. I took on this investigation when Fergus asked. He needed an unknown on the fringes, and that is fundamentally all I am."

Tamsin patted her lips with the napkin and inquired, "What if Madam Patwell is involved in the drug pricing war?"

"That's a stretch of the imagination if ever there was one. The woman is an elder and reading palms or tea leaves or whatever for at least two decades."

"Wouldn't it be shocking if she were the mysterious leader of the opium problem?"

His gaze caught the grin on her face. "If only Basil could keep you in hand. Sometimes you scare the very *divil* out of me."

His response received a hearty laugh from Tamsin as she said, "Do not think unkindly of me. I am doing my best to earn our keep around here."

He blinked. "Why would you think you need to earn your keep?"

She drummed her fingertips on the napkin and drew her hand away keeping her voice low. "He lived on his pension, and I am concerned that once it is known he is gone to his eternal reward, the pension will disappear."

He couldn't respond as he had bitten into the last buttermilk biscuit, soft butter dripping from his fingertips. Her look of woeful sincerity urged him to chew the scrumptious tidbit before answering.

Wiping his fingertips, he said, "Your uncle was wealthy, Tamsin. Beyond his pension he inherited a great deal from his father. And his plantation brings in double the income it takes to run this household."

Her head tipped as she squinted, as if she had not understood a word he said.

He added, "I thought you took care of all his bookkeeping. Surely you knew his worth?"

"Household accounts are my task. I have no idea of Hilldale's profitability, nor about his inheritance."

"For one, the plantation is so successful, he had received a request to purchase the plantation with cash, mind you. No small amount that would have been."

He watched her breathe, her right-hand shaking. He had shocked her, and she was speechless with what seemed like relief that they would not be put out on the lawn.

"He was heavily endowed, Tamsin. And you are his only heir."

"How would you know this?" Her head drew up at that, her eyes red with emotion. She quickly patted the napkin over her face.

"I was one of his witnesses in the drawing of his will. I just assumed you knew all about it." He hadn't agreed with her actions the night she found Basil dead. Yet it made sense to him now that she would prolong notifying all the people who needed to know he was gone. Harrison sensed her insecurities with his own loss. She was in charge of the house-hold, and announcing his demise was more than she could deal with right now.

He wanted to come around the table and hold her. He also did not want to arouse any suspicions with the staff and stayed put. "Tamsin, I would comfort you, but I do not want to make a scene."

Not quite understanding what he meant, she mumbled *right* and dabbed at her face. "Sorry."

She dipped the end of her napkin into her water goblet and dabbed at her eyes. "I had no idea. He is, was...incredibly kind." A sob escaped. She pressed a palm to her chest and drew a slow breath. "I did not..." her face scrunched as if she would wail aloud. "I want *him* back not an inheritance."

He leaned toward her, putting his elbows on the table, hoping to calm her. "He loved you and most likely intended sharing all this with you at some point."

Covering her ears, she sucked in a deep breath.

The air in the dining room stifled. The normalcy of the undercurrent of talk from the kitchen drifted to them. This conversation seemed surreal, yet necessary. He would have preferred it to occur in private, not in this fishbowl.

Tamsin tried to hum a cheerful tune and her voice broke. She kept on until she gained control over her emotions.

He felt helpless when raising his glass. "To you, Tamsin."

They sipped their tea and the flush on her face began to subside. They must not allow the staff to become aware. Not yet, in any case.

As she sat opposite him, he recognized her struggle to stay calm. A series of emotions flitted across her features, disbelief and confusion being uppermost. Her eyes darkened almost cobalt blue. Sadness twitched the sides of her lips as she fought to control herself. She fiddled with a spoon, an edgy, nervous thing she did when sitting at the table and confronted with a problem.

It surprised him to discover how much he knew about her.

Chapter Thirteen

Tuesday, morning
27 September 1870

T he next morning before leaving Mrs. Labady's boarding house, Harrison received a message from Cambridge friend Mickey Garrity, in the hopes they would meet for lunch at two o'clock at the Silver Cross.

Traffic was bottlenecked over a loose wheel on a carriage. Vehicles jammed and people yelled. The offending driver acted as if he'd drunk way too much wine, and the sad-looking excuse of a horse neighed its plight.

A blustery wind shook red and gold leaves from their limbs, transporting them in the air like miniature kites. Harrison paid the driver and left him stuck in traffic with all manner of vehicles as he barreled down the street thinking of his busy day ahead.

Arriving at chambers, he wasn't surprised to see a stack of legal decisions waiting for him to peruse and file. The ones he questioned, he set aside for the barrister's attention. It was just one more learning tool for a soon-to-be lawyer. It also spoke of Fergus' faith in him.

The next several hours passed in rapid succession and Harrison glanced at his watch, realizing his lunch with Garrity gave him just enough time to stop by Royal London Hospital and perceive what he could about corpses.

Hailing a ride, he ruminated over the cryptic details of what had happened to Basil. Whoever took the corpse most likely planned to sell it to a medical school, because that's where the profit would be. The thought terrified him. Basil deserved much better than winding up as a specimen on a slab where a swarm of eager, would-be doctors dismembered him piece by piece.

The idea sickened him.

The buggy rolled to a stop and Harrison jumped down, paid the fare, and made his way to the main entrance, asking for directions to the mortuary.

Little more than ten minutes later he found himself at a door, the upper panel made of milky glass and imprinted with the word Mortuary. He readied himself to face what he might discover as a nurse swathed in black bombazine head gear with a white band across her forehead, and greeted him.

"May I help you, sir?"

"I am looking for my father's corpse. I understand it was removed from our home and brought here. Or so my elderly grandmother told me."

"Would he have had identification on him?"

"I doubt it. He had been preparing for bed."

"When would he have been brought in?" She rifled through a stack of paper. He envisioned many corpses on the other side of the wall, lined up on carts and awaiting their fate. Was Basil among them? It gave him the shivers to think of him on a cart under a sheet with a tag on his toe.

She now had the stack of papers in hand, he could see dates written in a bold hand at the top of several of the pages.

He noted 24 Sept. stamped on two of the pages as she had laid them face up on the counter in front of her. He was suddenly unsure he wanted to go through with finding Basil's corpse.

"I can identify him. Sixty years old, grayish auburn hair, just under six feet, a stocky sort."

"I'm sorry sir, but without real identification I can't do anything."

He leaned over the counter. "I just described him to you; it doesn't get any more real than that. Green eyes, too, by the by."

"Sir, I'm quite sorry." Her voice etched with ice.

A man, who had been working at a counter with his back to them, turned to look at Harrison.

The gentleman said, "You heard the nurse." His voice was tinged with hostility.

"Yes, I did. And I am rather frantic about how to go about finding my father considering the unusual circumstance of his death."

The man, dressed in a well-cut, three-piece suit of dark gray superfine appeared to be someone of importance. He put his pen down and stepped behind the nurse. "What exactly made his death unusual?"

Harrison had strategized his story. "My elderly grandmother was the only one home and her hearing and sight are hindered. She arranged for someone to take him to the hospital, however she cannot tell me who that might have been. I arrived home and knew only what she said. So, I came here first."

"My name's Upton, and you are..."

"Harrison. Harrison Spencer."

"Well, Mr. Spencer, I'll take you in back and you can see

for yourself if we have him." He glanced at the attendant. "It's alright, Maebell. I'll take responsibility for this."

She gave him the papers she had gathered. "These are the information sheets on the bodies recently brought in, sir." The narrow-eyed look she gave Harrison made him think of a lizard about to strike.

Upton marched down the marbled hall to a door at the end where he held it open so Harrison could enter. The chill of the cavernous room struck him. The walls were lined with cupboards and several tables of bodies were covered in linen. The reality of the situation hit hard. One of these could be his mentor.

Upton moved toward the nearest table. "Are you ready?"

He nodded and Upton pulled back the sheet exposing the head of the dead person, who happened to be a male and thankfully not Basil. His battered face churned Harrison's stomach.

They moved on to the next table, and then the next, each time causing Harrison's heart to beat heavily in his chest. And each time, someone else was beneath the sheet.

Upton glanced through the papers the assistant had given him, then asked, "When did he arrive?"

"Two days ago." Harrison inhaled through his mouth and wondered how someone could work in this environment for long periods of time.

"Then you've seen the bodies that are current. You might try St. Mary's and possibly other mortuaries. I don't mean to sound vulgar. Dead houses are quite popular when a body is found and there is no identification."

Harrison clutched his hat and nodded, thinking of the worst possible scenario; that Basil was already used as a specimen. "Thank you, Mr. Upton. I appreciate the time you have given me."

Upton clapped him on the back when they returned to

the long white hallway and made their way toward the front. "It's a nasty business, this. I do hope you find your sire."

Harrison hailed a ride as he stepped into the fresh air. A part of him was relieved to not have discovered Basil's remains.

He was now on his way to the bank ready to purchase the perfect gym for his hoodlums to-be. He hadn't revealed to anyone his little project. Afraid of a negative reaction, he wanted to establish the gym and outfit it, and staff it before inviting anyone to see it. Although, he did want to bring Tamsin, Joshua Zillig, and the lad's grandmother, Mrs. Adele Thomson, around before the grand opening. He just wasn't ready yet.

Tuesday, afternoon
27 September 1870

Harrison, confined by his promise to Tamsin, did not reveal anything about Basil's death. And at this point, they had nothing to go on other than the two glasses of liquid doused with arsenic, and no motive that he knew.

Maybe Mickey Garrity would have an idea.

Garrity had dropped out of Cambridge to become a detective. He abandoned two years of prelaw and began working for Davis & Fenway, a small detective agency somewhere in Southwark. Harrison and Mickey had been sparring partners for two years on the boxing team.

When Harrison reached the age of twenty-two and graduated from university, he entertained the idea of detective work before deciding to change his educational goal and become a barrister. That's when he met Mickey who dreamt of being a sleuthhound. They were about the same stature, tall, with large shoulders, though Harrison was a bit leaner.

Stepping into the darkened wainscoted hall of the Silver Cross Pub, it took a moment for Harrison's vision to adjust. His friend had tucked himself into a corner on the far left. The place smelled of cigars and stale ale. The front of the ancient tavern faced west, and all the windows twinkled with multi-colors of stained-glass filtering the late afternoon sunshine.

Shaking hands Mickey blurted, "You're a sight for sore eyes, old chum. Take a seat and let's order some bangers. I'm half starved."

Once the server took their choices, Harrison got down to business. "I have a problem that I cannot go into detail about, you'll just have to trust me. Someone has stolen a body that I am tasked to find. And fast. Got any ideas?"

His friend's face brightened like a lantern at midnight. Then his substantial shoulders shook with merriment. "You always were good for a laugh."

"This isn't a joke. I would like to give you specifics, however, I am keeping this under my hat for the time."

"Well, then, what is it you need?"

"The body had been hidden and the next night it was gone. There is the possibility I might know who took it."

"Who might that be?"

"The wife."

Mickey shook his head as if ridding himself of confusion. "I'm lost. You think the wife stole her husband's body? Wouldn't it be hers to bury?"

"They never lived together. I'm afraid the body will be sold to a hospital or worse."

Harrison glanced at his friend whose interest appeared to shift between hilarity and concern. "I know this sounds preposterous."

The savory mouth-watering scent of bangers and hash arrived along with two mugs of frothing ale.

Nothing could come between the detective and his bangers. The conversation came to a halt as they dove into the meal.

After two healthy chomps on the sausage dripping with rich onion gravy and followed by a long swig of the cool ale, he agreed, "You're right, you'll want to find the body quick. The wife could be a revengeful bawd and want him cut to pieces or dumped in the Thames."

The distasteful image caught Harrison just as he nearly put a forkful of the delicious meat in his mouth. He laid the utensil, meat still intact, on his plate and said, "Exactly what we... I am thinking."

"Who's this *we?*"

"The one who found the body to begin with."

"Ah. I thought it was you. You're sheltering someone. The plot thickens." He swigged at his ale and swiped the froth from his upper lip. "Are you certain the one who found the body isn't the killer?"

He shook his head. "Not...no. Couldn't happen."

"What'll you do next?"

Harrison patted his breast pocket. "I created a list of dead houses and mortuaries in London. And if no luck, I'll get over to Guy's or St. George, or one of the other infirmaries. No one would transport the body far. They would want to get rid of it and get paid."

"You always have your finger on the problem. I'll give you that." Said with a heavy amount of sarcasm as he eyed Harrison then wolfed down on the last bit of banger, chewed, and swallowed. "What's with the secrecy? Why are you involved?"

"My problem is finding the body before it's destroyed, or worse recognized." The moment the words were out of his mouth, his breath caught. He could tell his friend smelled a fish.

"Ah, I'd know him then? Amongst our sort, is he?"

Harrison turned his attention to the gravy and onions congealing on his plate. Bringing up the subject with a nose hound like Mickey was brainless on his part.

Mickey ventured a guess, "One of our Silver Cross men?"

Damn. Harrison lacked the stamina to look him in the eye. "Hardly. This one is old. Really old."

After a long minute of silence, the detective pushed his empty plate aside and set his elbows on the table. "Tell me it's not one of our men."

Bloody damnation. He was as cunning as a fox.

Harrison forked the last bite on his plate and ignored the question. Though how he would swallow the food could be a challenge. For the moment, he wouldn't answer.

"Hell, and the devil. What have you got yourself into?"

Harrison's irritation at his own stupidity swelled. His mouthful needed to be chewed but it tasted like sawdust.

Silence hung between them.

Mickey emptied his mug and banged it on the tabletop. "The jig's up, lad. You might as well spill the beans. If it's one of our men, you sure as hell are in a mess. You might be diggin' your own grave."

Having finally swallowed his mouthful, he scorned Mickey. "As usual, you've misinterpreted my initial question."

Mickey pulled out his watch. "I've got another half hour set aside."

Harrison smiled. "You'd do better to spend it on yourself than here with me. I'm up to my ears in reading old documents and filing affidavits for Fergus."

They reached for their fresh mugs as the waiter set them down.

Harrison changed the subject. "What can you tell me about the opium pricing?"

Leaning in, Mickey spoke in a low voice. "It's the blazes. We feel like we're close, but never a name."

"The Woman's Society is in an uproar about the use of the drug for young children. Hard to believe mothers would give it to them. So far, there have been eight known deaths. No telling how many go undiscovered."

Mickey asked, "Do you remember Evans, a tall lanky chap, quiet like a mouse, worked in the file room at the home office?"

"Does not ring a bell." He pulled on his mug.

"Evans thinks, given time, he can remember the name from an old case dating back a few years. He said he'd look up the file."

Harrison glanced at his watch.

Garrity asked, "Give me a minute more, old chum. It does me good to talk this out." He set his mug down. "Have you ever thought of coming on board with my group?"

In the middle of quenching his thirst, Harrison almost spurted his drink. "*Your group?* And who might that be? Those ruffians under Fenway? He gives them far too much sway with his investigations."

Garrity's eyes narrowed as he stared at Harrison. "I don't run the place I just try to follow orders. It's a bug up the chief's ass. His ruination will be criticism over the way his men mishandle his orders. That's how he rolls and the rest of us take hold and hang on."

"Chaotic then? You plod on in good faith the job gets done? Why don't you talk to his superior, maybe there'll be something in it for you."

Garrity took a pull on his ale ignoring his friend's suggestion.

Harrison was tired of the conversation going in circles

and drew the napkin from his vest and folded it on the table. Besides, he had a pile of paperwork waiting for him in chambers. One of Fergus's latest organizational ideas. "I'll make a few subtle inquires when I get back to chambers. You never know what might come up that would appeal to you."

He nodded. "I'm good where I am, just lettin' off some steam, old chap. You take care with your situation."

Harrison cast him a side glance. "No worries here, just a ton of work."

Garrity reached into his pocket and tossed coins on the table. "We should do this again."

Harrison paid his share of the tab and grabbed his hat and briefcase. He wasn't interested but said, "We'll do this again when we can. Good luck with Evans."

Garrity waved as he headed for the door.

Big Ben chimed a quarter past four, barely heard above the din of carriages, riffraff, and hawking.

Chapter Fourteen

"Come in," Tamsin welcomed to a knock on her bedroom door.

The housekeeper entered and gasped, eyes wide with shock as Tamsin's image appeared in the reflection of the mirror.

"Who died?" Mrs. T clasped a hand to her cheek. "Do not spare me, just say it outright."

"It isn't what you think." She reached Mrs. T and pulled her to the cushioned chair by the fireplace.

"Not what I think, you say? Look at you, in mourning from top to bottom."

"I'm masquerading."

Doubt appeared on her ashen face. "You have accepted an invitation to a ball? My everlasting dream has come true, then. But black is not your color. Especially if you are intending to meet someone. Anyone."

Tamsin stood from the crouched position as she had assisted the housekeeper into the chair. The grandmotherly woman was always trying to push her into frivolity with people her age. "Anyone? I'm not desperate, Mrs. T. In fact, I am far too busy to even think of *anyone*, let alone *someone*."

"It is unbecoming of you to use that tone with me, young lady."

"I apologize. I'm impersonating an elderly widow. Though I do need a walking stick." She eyed the still unsettled woman. "Would you happen to have just such an ambulatory tool?"

Mrs. T's hand fell from her cheek, as did the beginnings of hope on her face. "What is this about? I'm responsible for you with your uncle so far away. It appears I might not be up to the challenge."

There again the loss of her dear uncle, that only she and Harrison knew about. And, well, one other unknown, the assassin.

"You need not fret. I'm working on a case that involves going to a séance. But I cannot go as myself." Tamsin's sassy retort forced Mrs. T to hold back a smirk.

Though her eyes scraped Tamsin from head to toe. "You will have to go a mite to convince me you are an elderly lady, my dear."

"I plan to hobble and lean on a cane if one can be found, and I intend wearing gloves and keep my face well hidden."

"We can take care of the walking stick. Charlie used one not long ago when he twisted his ankle. It's your clear unlined face and lovely dark hair that will not suit. Although, I do believe I can help. First, however, I must know if you will be in a safe environment. I rather think these kinds of people are charlatans."

Ignoring her remark, Tamsin asked, "Can you make me look really old?"

"You need not say it like it is something to achieve. I am living proof of what is to come. Be grateful you have decades yet."

"I cannot begin to think of you as old. Especially the kind

of old I hope to look like when I walk into Madam Patwell's parlor."

Mrs. T patted her side braids and glanced into the mirror. "You will be surprised to know as I've never admitted this to anyone, least of all your dear uncle. I used to be on the stage, small though it was, and many years ago before I married Mr. Thistlewaite. I could not dispose of that trunk full of costumes because it symbolized my youthful and carefree days. *And* my independence."

Tamsin pulled back the black tulle from her face. It seems Mrs. T hadn't been an elder all her life. "Do tell."

"I hope worms haven't gotten into it after all this time, but I have an old-lady's wig that might just work. We can do the rest with makeup."

Enthralled, Tamsin followed Mrs. T to her private domain in the attic. The trunk was draped with a lovely apple-red and olive colored shawl. Tamsin had not been in Mrs. T's attic room in quite some time. It had the appearance of a cozy and warm room smelling pleasantly of lavender.

After opening the trunk, Mrs. T drew out a few folded items, setting them on the bed. A hat box appeared, and she drew out a grayish wig done up in the regency style, soft braids meant to fall over the ears and a bun in the back. Tamsin thought it would do perfectly.

Mrs. T watched as Tamsin adjusted the wig on her head. "When is this séance?"

"Four o'clock."

"Oh my, well. We are in the nick of time then. I do not suppose you want to tell me what this is all about?"

Drawing the wig off her head, Tamsin turned from the mirror. "It's a lark. I have always wondered how they contrive to hear the dead speak. I thought it would be interesting."

"You keep your wits about you. I wish your uncle were

here. I would like to know what he thinks. Sometimes you get wild notions, lassie. I suppose this is one of them."

Beleaguered by guilt for keeping this dear woman in the dark about Uncle Basil, Tamsin was distraught. She could barely look Mrs. T in the eye. Her voice cracked as she said, "Thank you for the loan. And I will tell you all when I return."

Mrs. T's face lit with mischief. "Ask this spiritualist if there is a handsome young man in your future."

Tamsin's eyes narrowed. "I can hardly do that as an elder."

"Tell her you're asking for your lovely granddaughter." Her eyes twinkled with delight as she patted Tamsin's cheek.

Tamsin made her way toward Madam Patwell's, thinking over the information she'd already shared with the spiritualist. In her mind she went over what she had written to the oracle about a cousin who passed recently. Testing the waters to see how she handled spiritual insight, Tamsin hoped she would expose her fraud. What possible trickery could she use to exploit a death? Talking to the dead simply could not happen.

Intrigued to watch Madam Patwell use her methods, Tamsin abided by her philosophy of nothing ventured, nothing gained.

She lifted the brass knocker and let it fall against the plate. A tall man, the butler according to his vestments, opened the door. His brow was scrunched as if he disdained the welcoming of anyone. "How may I be of service, madam?"

She lowered her voice, hoping to sound elderly. "Madam

Patwell invited me to visit at four. The name is Mrs. Deerfield."

"You are expected." He reached over and closed the door behind her. He wasn't much younger than the woman she portrayed, which made it easy to amble behind him. When they approached the second door on the right, he stepped aside and allowed her to enter.

"Madam Patwell will be with you shortly." His bushy brows narrowed beneath his bald head, a cobweb of dark blue veins spidering down the sides. She shivered with thoughts of phantoms gliding around her in the dark room. Reminding herself this wasn't real took the edge off.

Alone now, she surveyed the room. Heavy drapes drawn against the gray skies that threatened rain, a lamp on the buffet sent a weak yellow stream into the corners where six chairs were tucked up against a table. A sturdy dresser with drawers stood against the wall. Two urns filled with peacock feathers at each end, a pastoral landscape adorned the wall between.

An unremarkable space, she wondered if this is where the séance would take place. Adjusting her veil, she cupped her hands atop Charlie's cane and stood waiting as her heart fluttered in her chest.

"Welcome to my parlor, Mrs. Deerfield."

Tamsin jerked to the left and in the last moment remembered to lower her voice. "You startled me."

A small-boned woman, in an unadorned dark gray dress, her light blond hair flowed like a veil down to her waist. Her hands held together as if in prayer, she silently approached Tamsin, her pale eyes giving the impression she could see through her.

Tamsin shivered. It was as if the ethereal woman came out of the woodwork. How she accomplished that, Tamsin couldn't decipher. Obviously, she'd been watching her in secret. Creepy. Luckily, she hadn't tried to adjust her wig or some such telling movement that might give away her disguise.

This might be the first of many traps the psychic sets for her unaware victims.

"You are to refer to me as Madam Patwell."

She pulled out a chair indicating Tamsin should sit. The table was covered in a dark red cloth with gold-like fringe at least six inches in length. A candle flickered in the center.

"Have you ever talked to your loved ones?" She sat across from Tamsin and spread her hands wide on the sturdy red linen.

Tamsin felt her question odd because who can talk to the dead? "This is my first visit to a medium."

"Who is it you wish to make contact with?" Her soft voice drifted in the room.

"A cousin. I mentioned him in the note."

"You did, indeed. Our policy is to get to know each other and the next time we meet will be our first attempt to contact him. I need his name and when he passed."

Quickly assembling her thoughts, Tamsin hadn't been prepared to answer pertinent questions. "He passed in 1868 September."

"And his name?"

"Colin Redman." She'd chosen Uncle Basil's birthday and felt comfortable giving the woman a fictitious name.

"I'm surprised you've waited two years to seek an audience with your departed one."

Tamsin fiddled with her gloves, not looking at the woman. "I needed this time to accept his death."

"Were you close? Were your memories fond ones?"

"He made quite an impression on me. He was a caring man loved by many. Unfortunately, he died in an accident. I need to inquire about land he owned, I don't know what his plans were." She dabbed her eyes with a lacy handkerchief. "We were the last remaining family. Now it is only me."

She hoped she'd satisfied Madam Patwell's curiosity with a few details, along with the tears, false though they be.

The oracle sat rigidly in her chair. Her stiff manner and soft voice, as if she might wake the dead, gave a sense of emotionless control. "In a day or two I'll gather several seekers, such as yourself. It's quite tiring for me. I need to space the gatherings. There are so many who want to communicate with their loved ones. I'm sure you understand my predicament." She picked at her skirt with a forefinger and thumb then readjusted her shawl to fall over her head and shoulders as if she might pray. Tamsin also noted she kept her chin tucked which gave her an odd angle in which to make eye contact. Eccentric to be sure.

"I do want to ask if your dearly departed Colin Redman was near you in age?"

Tamsin asked, "Why is his age relevant?"

Madam Patwell took a long moment to answer. "In the spirit world, the more one had in common with the deceased, the more likely we will be able to call on him."

That made sense, and Tamsin said, "Yes, we were. He is the last remaining in his family, and I in mine. Our mothers were sisters."

Madam Patwell stood indicating their visit had come to an end. "I am thankful I can offer my services for a reunion with your cousin. There is nothing we can do here on earth when we are the last of the living except hope for a loving and productive meeting in my parlor."

Tamsin realized a soothsayer's flourishing could only come from gathering as much information as possible in order to build a characterization. It wouldn't surprise her to know the woman believed in mystiques. Yet it did startle her that a bright woman, such as she appeared, would believe she could speak to the dead. Tamsin eagerly awaited the séance.

She would be looking for all the tricks.

The butler entered the parlor as if on cue and Madam Patwell drifted or floated—for that is what she appeared to do —to the dresser taking up a book. "Today is Monday. Would Wednesday at two o'clock be convenient for you?"

Tamsin stood up and reached for her reticule. "That would be fine. Wednesday at two then."

On the walk home, she leaned on the cane and practiced walking slow, which turned out not to be difficult as tight as Mrs. T had bound her stays. September would soon come to an end. The weather reminded her of the winter not long off.

Uncle Basil had brought so much energy to their home. She had taken their life for granted. He loved the crackle of the burning fireplace logs and merry conversation spilling from the kitchen. Surprisingly, the routine of the household stayed almost the same with him gone. Probably because the staff knew it would return to normal the minute he walked in the front door.

She was saddened to think what it would be like when the rest of the household knew the truth.

Today was bread day and Sally would be elbow deep in flour kneading the yeasty dough. Uncle Basil always loved coming home on Monday's, ready with a quip to tease Mrs. T. The staff missed his warm and inviting presence.

If ever she were to catch his murderer, she pitied the person. Since the discovery of poison in his drink, revenge flooded her thoughts. Henrietta Reynolds-Walker's image came to mind, and she gripped the head of the cane with a fierce vengeance.

It remained to be seen if the unscrupulous woman would take her troubles to the mind-reader. Tamsin knew she must be growing short of funds, evidence being her visit on the morning Uncle Basil died. Followed by her own visit to Mrs. Reynolds-Walker's home where the woman mentioned her purse again.

Before turning up Orchard Street and home, she glanced back to see if she had been followed. The only other person heading in the same direction was a lad with a stick engrossed in supporting his blue hoop to stay upright. Breathing easy, she turned the corner and climbed the steps to her front door.

Chapter Fifteen

Tuesday, 3:00 a.m.
27 September 1870

M rs. T made her way in the dark with the stub of a
candle lighting her way and knocked on Tamsin's
bedroom door. She stepped up to Tamsin's bed
just as the young lady's eyes opened and her groggy voice
croaked, "Did I sleep in?"

The housekeeper reached for Tamsin's robe. "No, dear.
I'm waking you because someone's been in Mr. Walker's
library and made a mess of it."

"What time is it?" Tamsin tossed off the covers and
swung her legs over the side of the bed slipping to the floor.

"Just three. It looks like thievery to me. Though I cannot
imagine what there would be of value. The master would
have most probably taken all his important papers with him."
Suddenly she covered her mouth with her hand.

"What?" Tamsin grabbed the robe out of Mrs. T's hand.

"I have not looked to see if the safe has been opened. I'm almost afraid to."

Slipping her arms into her robe, Tamsin flew down the stairs. Mrs. T kept to a slower pace lest she fall.

A horrendous mess greeted her. Books tossed carelessly around the floor; drawers open with contents emptied. The decanter and glasses crushed on the floor as if someone stomped them with a boot. Whoever did this must have made quite a racket and she wondered why it hadn't aroused her.

Thinking back to the interrupted sleep the night she found Uncle Basil dead at his desk, made her heart pound. She fell back against the wall and gasped for air. Overwhelming sadness clutched her heart. Havoc has rained over this home and its occupants once more. What is it they want?

Mrs. T caught up to her and put her arms around the slight body, hugging her. "There, there. Take a minute or two. It's a shock and with your dear uncle so far away."

Shrugging out of her arms, Tamsin swiped her cheeks. "Sorry, it is appalling to know ruffians would enter our home and do this." She wanted to scream or...God forbid, punch a wall, something to release the anger rising in her blood.

She immediately inspected the front door, and it didn't have a scratch on it. Either Mrs. T forgot to lock the door, or the perpetrator used a key.

In that moment, she knew it had to be Mrs. Henrietta Reynolds-Walker.

Surveying the ransacking, they wondered what the thieves were after. What would Uncle Basil have that was obviously important? She thought she knew everything about him.

Pressing a corner of the mahogany panel, it released and revealed Uncle Basil's safe. She closed the panel and glanced over the wreckage throughout the office.

Because the decanter and glasses were crushed, she

wondered if the thieves who took his body returned to the scene of his death. She'd hidden the glasses and decanter behind a large plant in the corner of the bookcase, but they'd been found and crushed. Could the killer be trying to get rid of incriminating poison in the glasses?

The web created by his death grew stronger yet still no logic.

"What do you think?" Mrs. T wondered.

Tamsin asked, "What woke you?"

"I cannot say as I know. I heard a distant sound and thought I should see if all was well."

Tamsin put her arm around Mrs. T's shoulders. "The villains could have hurt you, or worse. It's frightful to even think of you investigating by yourself."

"I took the back stairs and had my slippers on. They never heard me coming."

Tamsin almost screeched. "You faced them?"

"Not so they saw me. They had totes already filled with papers and were making their way to the door."

"How many?"

"Two. Youngish, I would guess by the way they dressed."

Tamsin hugged her. "I am so grateful you were not accosted."

The quarter-hour chimed and out of habit they simultaneously glanced upward. A quarter after three. "Will you be able to return to your bed and sleep?" murmured Tamsin.

"If we apply ourselves, we can make short shrift of it and finish our night's sleep. The last thing we want is for Sally and Evie to think someone was in the house as we slept."

"How true, Evie would be gone in a moment if she knew strange men traipsed through the house. Thank you for offering to help sort out all this. But this is my responsibility. I know his filing system and where everything belongs. Hopefully, I will be able to discover what might be missing. You go on up. This won't take long."

Mrs. T patted Tamsin's cheek. "Such a sweet lass you are. Did I ever mention to you how much the Master changed when you came to live with us?"

"I might have been too young to understand a great many things about that time. Though I know he loved me and did his best to care for his sister's child, it must have been confusing for him, dropped into his unsuspecting lap as I was."

"You opened his life and let in sunshine, my dear. You were a blessing." She lifted her robe and turned toward the back stairs.

Wide awake now, Tamsin couldn't think of sleep. She stepped up to the desk, leaned in, and spread her palms atop.

What is it they want from you, Uncle? What were you working on that has caused such a turmoil, and most probably caused your death?

The clock struck the fifth hour and Tamsin's eyelids kept closing. She decided to finish organizing later. Stacking papers and shuffling notes into order, his desk no longer looked as though it had been ransacked.

She made note of the fact Uncle Basil's pension files were missing except for three pages that had drifted under his desk. Most of the housekeeping bills were intact. His correspondence with the Home Office had been rifled, and she couldn't tell if anything was missing. Even though he'd retired, there were occasions where he'd assisted because of prior knowledge. However, she hadn't had access to that file and of course, it seemed impossible to know if documentation had been taken.

At the back of the drawer there was a piece of wood behind which two files remained hidden. One was labelled

Blackbeard, and the other Mr. Ramsey. He had deliberately hidden them, and they appeared untouched.

It looked like information about drugs. She wondered why her uncle would involve himself in opium. Then she wondered if the drugs weren't the target. Perhaps it was Blackbeard or Mr. Ramsey himself.

Exhausted, Tamsin closed the doors to the office and returned to her bed as wisps of dawn's early light softened the horizon

Tuesday, mid-morning
27 September 1870

Barrister Fergus entered chambers as if he were a gust of wind and barked at Harrison to follow him, as if he were his master's dog.

As he entered the barrister's private office his superior barked, "Shut the door," and hung his hat and cape on the coat tree.

"Well, Mr. Spencer, we've gotten our orders. How does it feel ta be working on this case?" Fergus didn't wait for an answer, and added, "I'm to handle the criminal investigation as temporary Deputy Assistant Commissioner. We'll be undercover working for the Home Office."

Fergus slapped a file on his desktop. "The Home Office approved ye and Mickey Garrity, who's been kept out of the limelight for most of his career. He's a detective with a long string of successes. They've put a lot of faith in both of ye."

Harrison wondered about the references the barrister made over the last few weeks, and asked, "You've been elevated to Deputy Assistant Commissioner?"

The barrister glanced up from his search in the drawer and looked at his pupil. "It's a special assignment handed ta me several weeks ago. We are ta investigate the use of opioids and make a recommendation. I've not said anything yet to either Mickey or ye. But the special committee wants ta make a recommendation to The Queen's committee. First, they need information we are ta gather."

Harrison's eyes lit up as if a lightbulb came on. "Mickey and I are to assist you then?"

"Right."

Harrison's brain began to spin with excitement.

Fergus blinked. "What? Ye think it's grunt work and yer above it?"

"Completely the opposite, sir. I am honored to have been chosen."

Fergus rifled through another drawer finally finding what he was looking for and pulled out a diagram spreading it on his desk. "We've been informed there's to be a large shipment coming in at night on the first of October at C Dock. They'll unload the cargo at the west side of the docks." He pointed to the map and tapped on C Dock.

"In the meantime, acquaint yerself with this file, and I'll see that Mickey reads it too. Ask any questions ye might have."

Harrison nodded and picked up the stack of papers. He viewed working undercover with Mickey as tolerable. He deliberately hadn't mentioned he knew the chap because Mickey revealed to him in strictest confidence about the possibility of an opium war on England's shores. Harrison had been a bit taken aback at Mickey's revelation at the time. Casual conversation about classified government information could get him sacked, or worse in irons, if he shared any of it. He'd always known Mickey tended to brag about some of his conquests.

The name of the person or persons who undercut the cost of the drugs was still unknown. Mickey and Harrison were to attempt to identify the head operative and stay out of sight lest they be discovered. Their orders were explained as more of a fact-finding expedition.

Harrison understood in the last briefing that another five children recently died, that they knew of, from opium. If this effort saved lives, it would be well worth the trouble. In the meantime, he would read over the file Fergus gave him and be prepared for a midnight surveillance on the first of October at London's C Dock.

Harrison waved down a transport to Lombard Street where a former church had been turned into a makeshift mortuary. He'd recently gotten word of a murder victim's unclaimed body.

It took one second for him to know the putrefying body in no way resembled Basil.

He hired a ride to St. James Westminster where there was a former factory transformed into a mortuary. The caretaker walked him through the tomb-like structure, each corpse tagged with pertinent information when available. The noxious effluvia caused Harrison to breathe through his mouth as he stalked the boards upon which bodies were laid out two and three to a stretcher.

Harrison lifted a shroud for the umpteenth time, when a deep scratchy voice said, "Ye ain't a cowardly fella, are ye? I aint' had a one of 'em comin' after me in the dark."

The hair on his nape curled. He thought the place was empty and dropped the cloth over the cadaver's face, as he spun around. A cleaning lady sprouting a toothless smile cackled at him. "Did'na mean ta scare the wits out o' ye. Jest couldn't pass the chance ta tease. Gets mighty lonely in here."

Feeling foolish, he said, "I'm searching for a friend. It looks as though he's not here." There were four rows of planks and at least six bodies in a row. Basil was not among the cadavers. He nodded to her as her cackle followed him out the door.

He left the stench of rotting flesh and hired a driver to take him to a railway arch adapted to hold corpses under the watchful eye of mortuary staff. He found two men eager to assist in reuniting him with Basil. It ended with him being dissatisfied. Basil's remains were not among those stuffed and piled against the brick walls.

After the third railway arch walk about, Harrison abandoned this avenue of seeking out Basil and took a deep breath of fresher air, almost ready to call it quits.

One last stop for the day, St. Mary's Hospital. He knew bodies were accepted at Cambridge's medical facility where they were used for teaching. A rumor had spread that someone had been smart enough to set up a system whereby the clerk at St. Mary's used a wooden box and filled it with sand for burial leaving the family with the firm conviction their loved one had been buried in the church yard.

When in fact, the body had been turned over to the medical school for dissection and learning purposes. Harrison's source had also mentioned it could be four months before the cadaver would be dissected and dismembered.

He wondered how much the clerk at St. Mary's got paid, and if the Reverend had any knowledge of the money-making scheme going on right under his nose.

Arriving at Cambridge Medical facility, he was directed to the anatomy department.

The name plate read *Front Desk, Anatomy Department.* The young man at the helm looked over the rim of his horned spectacles and asked, "What may I do for you, sir?" His bulbous nose appeared to stop his glasses from falling off his face.

Harrison flashed his second-year law school card and said, "I am looking for the remains of a man that was stolen from his house before he could be buried." He tapped the card on the desk, attempting to dazzle the young man. Who, it appeared, didn't care a whit about Harrison's legal background. He looked to be about twenty, making Harrison his superior by seven years.

His smirk irritated Harrison. He'd like to bash that fat beak and break his glasses. So much for acting like an adult, to say nothing of the long day searching stinking morgues for a dead man he admired and loved.

"You have a predicament, sir. We are a teaching school. Our cadavers have been signed over and allotted to our medical school. They aren't property to return, sir." Heavy on the *sir* as if he spoke to a numbskull.

"What if I threaten to tell *The Times* your medical school should be investigated?"

Big Nose stood up, huffing as if he'd just been challenged to break the law. When in fact, he was already a part of doing just that.

"I have not got all afternoon. Either you let me in to look for this missing cadaver, or I go to the offices of *The Times*. Which is it?" He made a big deal of digging his watch out of its vest pocket and looking at the time.

The young man removed his glasses and with thumb and forefinger pinched his nose. He glanced at Harrison. "I can't leave this desk, sir. Though I can let you into the room. Everyone's gone home for the day, and no one will be the wiser. As of this morning, there are thirty-nine cadavers. Most are in drawers, the rest on tables."

Harrison pointed to the door on the left. "This one?"

The young man nodded and returned his glasses to his conk.

The room felt cool, yet not enough to cover the foul stench that seeped in and around the cavernous space. Bleak light filtered through windows high on the walls. He inadvertently bumped a table leg as he moved to the next cadaver. If he didn't find Basil soon, it might happen that he'd already been taken to the medical school's lab. God forbid.

Before he opened the big box drawer where several corpses were neatly hidden out of sight, he first went table to table looking at the faces. Most corpses were marked with information about the disease or accident that killed them.

He hadn't completely dealt with the loss of the man he admired. Uncovering each face and discovering it wasn't Basil had begun taking its toll. He couldn't imagine how Tamsin would handle this.

And the thought struck him, how would Tamsin handle the possibility of him being cremated? There would be nothing left to bury.

It took him another hour to finish up. As he opened each drawer and pulled back the sheet, he expected to see Basil's dark red hair. To no avail.

He wanted to get smashed and forget the faces that had taken up residence in his brain.

Harrison hadn't gone two blocks when a man, dressed in work clothes, grime on his hands and face, approached him. "I hear yer lookin' for a body?"

He stopped and slowly turned to the bloke. "What did you say?"

"I got somethin' ye might want." He stuffed his hands into side pockets and spread his legs wide, looking Harrison up and down. "Yer lookin' for that lawyer what died after bein' poisoned? Lived up on Portman Square."

Shocked, he turned around and stepped toward the fellow. In a threatening voice, he growled, "How would you know what I want?" The underbelly of London seemed to have information unknown to others.

"Cause someone told me it'd be worth a pocketful ta ye. Ta know what 'tis I know." His dark brows rose with defiance.

Blast it. Harrison felt like a loose cannon, and then this ironmonger smelling like a pickled herring approaches him, and he's itching to rid himself of the mounting frustration. "What have you that warrants my interest?"

"Like I said, I know what yer missin'. And I know where 'tis."

"What'll it cost me?"

"Three shillings."

Stunned all Harrison could think was that amount could darn near pay his rent for six months. "Where's the proof of what you boast?" He stepped closer to the fellow to determine if he looked like an honest bloke. The beggar shrugged his shoulders and turned away.

Harrison hailed him. "What's your story?"

He turned to look at Harrison. "I'm tryin' ta put vittles in me little ones' bellies. I got laid off and findin' work ain't easy. When a friend told me of yer friend, well..." he shrugged his shoulders.

"You were going to stiff me and run like hell—you haven't a clue who I am or what I'm looking for." Harrison clenched his fists.

"Thought ye'd say that. Set your orbs on this afore ye decide I don't know nothing." He handed Harrison a piece of the blanket that Harrison recognized as matching what he found in the earth cellar and gave it to Tamsin. It sent shivers down his arms.

His jaw dropped. After a moment's thought, he bargained, "I don't have that kind of money on me. Meet me at St. James Park at the top step of the Duke of York monument—tomorrow night at seven."

"Me name's Bennett." And off he scurried with an obvious limp. Harrison wondered if he'd been wounded in the war.

Chapter Sixteen

Wednesday, early afternoon
28 September 1870

Harrison was making headway with the rebuilding of a structure to be called the *Basil W. Walker Gym for Youth*, and very excited to reveal his endeavor to Tamsin and Fergus, among others, but the building still had a way to go. He'd kept it a secret, but it was getting close to the time when the name will be etched into the marble overhang above the front doors.

It was less than a mile from Joshua's grandmother's home, making it convenient for the youth in the Argyle Street area that just happened to be one block from Metro Police Station. To Harrison, it was appropriate, if not ironic. Better the youth of today get to know the Men in Blue, who would no doubt drop in on occasion. Perhaps it might bring some of the bitter youth to recognize there are other decent and meaningful paths to their future.

Mrs. T fussed over Tamsin's wig, setting it properly on her head, tucking in the stray hairs of her natural dark auburn. "As an elder, I should send Sally with you. It doesn't seem fit for you to traipse around without a maid, being old and all."

"I had not thought of that." She took up Mrs. T's hand and squeezed. "You are so dear to help with this."

A blush appeared on the housekeeper's cheeks as she comforted. "Precisely why I've brought it up." Shaking out the black bombazine, she waited for Tamsin to gather up her underskirt and step into the circle of the dress.

"After I finish with your buttons, I'll send Sally up."

An hour later, following a discussion of expectations for Sally, Tamsin walked like a frail elder as they made their way up Tottenham.

Tamsin prepared Sally by mentioning the possibility of Mrs. Reynolds-Walker's arrival. She asked her to be especially observant. If the woman appeared to recognize Sally, she should turn away and not address her. As expected, Sally, a rather modern young woman, looked forward to the game, as she thought of it. Tamsin also prepared Sally to be circumspect if questioned by the butler. He was wary, all eyes and ears.

Sally whispered, "Will I see ghosts?"

Tamsin couldn't help but laugh. "Ghosts or spirits are figments of one's imagination. You can be sure of that. This is a ruse to take money from those less suspecting."

"Are you sure? I looked forward to seeing what one might look like."

"If there was such a thing as ghosts, I am not sure I would be here." She slanted a wily glance at her maid before leaving her in the outer parlor and entering the séance room.

Madam Patwell was already seated at the head of her

table when the butler admitted four people who had gathered in the entryway. As they sat at the circular table, they were introduced by Madam Patwell. Beginning on her left, Madam Patwell introduced Mr. Atwell, Mrs. Billingsly, Tamsin as Mrs. Deerfield, and Miss Hargrave.

Wrapped in a glittery gossamer head covering, her long blonde hair falling about her shoulders, Madam Patwell added, "We were to have a fifth. It appears she's been detained." Her eyes shifted to the butler who nodded in agreement before backing out of the parlor and closing the door.

Candlelight barely spread across the table laid in dark red linen. In a feathery soft voice Madam Patwell explained, "We have two new seekers with us, Mrs. Deerfield hoping to contact her departed cousin, Colin Redman, and Mrs. Billingsly desperate to make contact with her ten-year-old daughter who died in a fire."

Mrs. Billingsly's cheeks whitened, tears spilling over. She was obviously quite emotional. Tamsin couldn't think of anything more sorrowful than losing a child to a fire.

Patwell placed her hands on the table palms up and proceeded, "This is an ancient and mysterious ceremony meant to be honored. Today is a living embodiment of the sacred occasion to grow closer to our loved ones who have passed on."

She closed her eyes as the room dimmed. Tamsin heard low breathing, and a creak of bones when Mr. Atwell shifted in his chair; otherwise, nothing for several long minutes.

She had no reasoning for what happened next as the participants bowed their heads. Everyone held hands. Mrs. Billingsly squeezed Tamsin's hand as if she were startled or afraid. With her veil shielding her somewhat, Tamsin eyed everyone at the table. She noted expectations, and nervousness, but nothing extreme.

A misty, smokey atmosphere seeped into the room, the light from the candles flickered, the cat squealed and jumped from the dresser onto the floor, its long tale vertical and back hunched. Mrs. Billingsly gasped and clutched Tamsin's hand.

Amused at the theatrics, Tamsin noted that Mrs. Reynolds-Walker was not a participant. It would have been entertaining to see how she would react during the séance.

Keeping her head bowed, Tamsin peeked at the other participants when suddenly Madam Patwell began to moan and sway in her chair. Words mumbled forth from the seer and the black cat reappeared on her lap, then it stepped to the table and padded around the circle sniffing clasped hands.

Tamsin had never seen such a show and was grateful for the veil. She didn't wish to appear frivolous.

Of a sudden, Madam Patwell stood, her eyes shut, mumbles getting louder, her arms outstretched as she pleaded to something or someone. Tamsin noticed the others were now staring at her. Mrs. Billingsly grasped Tamsin's hand tightly causing Tamsin to fear her fingers might be permanently bent. The misty air thickened, and candles continued to flicker. When Madam Patwell swooned and fell back into her chair, the cat screeched and jumped off the table.

The medium's large grey eyes opened wide, lusterless in the low light. She pointed dramatically at each of them stopping at Tamsin.

"You," she shrilled.

Tamsin felt a twinge of fear, and Mrs. Billingsly tried to let go of her. But Tamsin, a bit unhinged, clamped their hands together.

Breathing as if her last, the seer scratched out, "Your twin wants to contact you. He warns that danger lurks in your sphere."

A cold shiver encased her. How in the world would this charlatan know she had a twin? A brother who died at their birth. Furthermore, her disguise as an elder removed her from being Tamsin.

It went beyond her belief that this woman could possibly be a true psychic.

Tamsin didn't buy into the scam.

She mentally scolded herself. Patwell had obviously done some research. Which could be deemed a miracle because the woman didn't even know her. Tamsin's heartbeat increased.

Unless she'd been followed home the other day.

All heads turned to her accusingly, as if she'd done something horrid.

"You," repeated the highly agitated woman, the seer's voice sounding as if it floated through a tunnel.

Mrs. Billingsly snatched her hand away as if Tamsin had the plague, and the seat partner on the other side immediately followed suit.

She'd been singled out, and retaliated, "I was an only child, Madam. You have been misinformed."

At this moment, the butler announced the arrival of Mrs. Reynolds-Walker, who quickly seated herself and apologized. She scanned the small group, and her gaze came to rest on Tamsin who wondered if Mrs. Reynolds-Walker had been alerted to her presence and not as Mrs. Deerfield, rather as Thomasina Morgan.

As Mrs. Deerfield, Tamsin mustered indignance and stood banging her cane on the floor, demanding, "Your spirits have been misinformed. It's not likely I'll return if you continue with falsehoods. I came here to speak to my cousin, Colin. Not to be vilified with a lie."

Murmurs skittered about the table as if mice had been let loose and Mr. Atwell scooted his chair backward. "I for one, will not condone this." He stood in an aggravated huff.

Madam Patwell sounded out of breath, as she oohed and

coughed. Her power had run out. She urged Mr. Atwell and Mrs. Deerfield to take their chairs. "Perhaps I can explain what might have happened."

With some reservation, he did as she demanded, though he did not draw his chair closer to the table. Tamsin listened to her explanation and followed the example of Mr. Atwell.

Out of the corner of her eye, she caught Mrs. Reynolds-Walker ogling her. She hoped it was because of her outburst, and not that she recognized her. The Madam indicated she wanted everyone to resume holding hands, which they promptly did. Mr. Atwell and Mrs. Billingsly gave Tamsin nods of acceptance as they took her hands again. Those nods caused Tamsin to think Patwell might have a history of giving false information.

Or not.

At this point, with the surprising turn of events and the seer's outburst, things were becoming rather interesting.

"As I mentioned," the seer explained, "We have two new visitors, Mrs. Reynolds-Walker being one of them. When I go into a trance, I summon and then interpret the messages that come to me. It could be any one of you, I never know who the spirit might choose. All I can suggest is the spirit misinterpreted who the receiver of the message should be."

Mr. Atwell inquired, "Does that mean one of us in this room has a twin?"

"Someone in this room does. Absolutely." Her grey cloudy eyes slowly scanned the group, resting again on Tamsin.

After an intense moment, Madam's shoulders sagged, and she declared, "I am sorry, the spirits have been frightened off. They've left the room. I feel nothing." She patted her brow with a handkerchief. "There will not be a fee today. And we can reconvene tomorrow at two if any of you wish to return. Please accept my sincere apologies." She sounded contrite when adding, "I have no control over what comes out of me during a trance. I am simply a vessel for the spirits."

Tamsin noted affirmation from the others meek as lambs and all in agreement.

One by one everyone stood and left the parlor.

As they gathered in the foyer, Mrs. Billingsly turned to Mrs. Reynolds-Walker. "Did you notice in *The Daily* that Mr. De la Croix escorted Miss Allison Horwrath to the October Ball? She's a stunner. He's a lucky man though she'll cost him plenty if he proposes. She shops at Madam Fornier's and Francois Boutique."

Tamsin had her back to the women and yet wanted to see the look on Henrietta's face. She dared not turn around lest she give herself away.

Later, as she and Sally made their way back to Portman Square, she noted a lad playing with a blue hoop several doors down from Madam Patwell's residence. It struck her that two days earlier she'd been followed by a boy with a blue hoop. Yet that didn't explain how the seer would know about a twin.

Unless Madam Patwell ordered the boy to follow her. That might mean Madam Patwell could have been aware that Mrs. Deerfield was linked to Uncle Basil and knew about Tamsin's background.

There could have been a time years ago that Uncle Basil might have mentioned her stillborn brother to his estranged wife, though she doubted it. Her own mother, from Tamsin's earliest days, never referred to her twin. Shrugging off the memory, Tamsin knew from her own experience, young children have little recall.

It had been quite by accident she discovered she was a double birth. She also learned her name, Thomasina, is the feminine form of the given name Thomas, which means *twin* making her think she'd been named for the dead infant and her parents meant she lived for both.

As they made their way back to Portman Square, Tamsin asked Sally, "Was there anything odd about the last woman who stepped into the foyer? Did she say anything to the butler?"

"He took her cape and umbrella, then asked if a young woman in her early twenties arrived. The butler said 'no'."

When Mrs. Reynolds-Walker first arrived in the séance room, she glared at Tamsin. And Tamsin worried she might have been discovered. Upon consideration, she decided the woman disregarded her as a reason for speculation. As bold as Mrs. Reynolds-Walker was, she would have confronted Tamsin if she knew what she had to say was true.

Her disguise as Mrs. Deerfield might just have worked.

Harrison checked his watch. At five after seven, there was still no sign of Bennett. He walked to the side of the Duke of York Monument and leaned against the marble wall.

The blustery day served up dark clouds clustering in the west. From where he stood on the top step, which served as the base of the column, he numbered very few people scattered about. None looked as if they were on a mission.

As a youngster, his family would visit London on occasion. Always a thrill, he and his brother would climb the spiral stairs inside the column of the Duke's Monument. They would count the 168 steps taking them to the platform that overlooked the city of London where a bronze statue of the Duke in his Garter Robes was magnificently displayed.

As he reminisced, he noticed a man in the distance walking slow, head up as if he surveyed his surroundings. Could it be Bennett, and if so, it looked as if he brought

friends with him. Two or three from the looks of it. He sauntered, shoulders back, a tam covering his reddish hair.

Harrison drew out his fob, at nearly five after the hour.
He glanced about the park realizing the crowd had dwindled
knowing it to be early evening when most were at home.

Bennett's friends stayed behind as he limped up the
stairs, for their meeting at the base of the column. "Good day
ta ye. Have ye got the money?"

"Not so fast my friend. How am I to know you even have
the corpse I am looking for?"

"I showed ye the piece of blanket he's wrapped in. What
more proof does ye need then?" He crossed his arms in front
of his chest, muscles bulging.

Harrison looked beyond the man to his friends who now
stood at the base of the stairs. Bennett crossing his arms must
be a sign.

"Them lads will show ye where he's at when we're done
here."

"Before I hand anything over to you, tell me where the
corpse is." He stepped close to Bennett. "I am not the fool
you take me for." He pulled open his jacket showing the man
his firearm.

Bennett unfolded his arms and not surprisingly his
friends, who stood at the base of the steps, moved back. At
the same moment several men of Harrison's acquaintance
came out from behind the colorful elms dotting the autumn
landscape and closed in toward Bennet's group.

Plain to see from where they stood on the stairs, he had
anticipated the need for precaution.

He blurted, "Now that we understand each other, you
tell me where I can find the body."

Bennett's face scrunched with confusion. "I...I don't
know."

Harrison grabbed him by the scruff of his jacket and

shook him. "How did you get that patch of blanket?" Several inches taller than Bennett and fit as a fiddle, Harrison was a force to be reckoned with. He didn't necessarily take delight in the fear swimming in Bennett's eyes, although his patience clearly at an end trying to find Basil's remains.

"A...a woman who works in one of the dead houses. She knew him. She'd seen him helpin' out a mate a long time afore this. She said he'd be worth a lot ta his kin."

Harrison's fists clenched. He itched to pound his anger out on something. "Which mortuary?"

"Battersea. Ne'er a stone's throw of the marketplace."

He released Bennett's jacket pushing him back on his heels. He almost tripped to the ground. He wished he'd not roughened a man with a bad leg—and children to feed.

He waved his arm for his men to disperse, which suddenly released Bennett's friends to scurry—which they did. He glanced back at Bennett who had a befuddled look on his face, as if he wasn't sure what had just happened.

"Take this for your trouble." He dropped a crown in Bennett's palm as he thought of those empty-bellied children.

Chapter Seventeen

Harrison had stopped by Tamsin's home on Portman Square last night after his encounter with Bennett to explain the lead on Basil's possible whereabouts. It sounded quite likely he could be at the mortuary in Battersea. Though he didn't understand how the remains had gotten so far from London.

Tamsin blurted, "That is possibly twelve miles from here. At the very least it would take half a day to get there. How ever did he end up in Battersea?"

"If it is him, we'll need to transport the body back to London. It would be foolish to use the railway. I will see to a carriage." Without sharing his concern, he felt it was more about the condition of Basil's remains at this point.

Thursday 7:45, a.m.
29 September 1870

As prearranged, and nearly eight in the morning, Harrison drew up in front of #2 Berkley Street in a rented buggy. A heavy fog circled the walkways and road.

Tamsin had been waiting for him and carried a basket as she hurried down the path before he barely had a chance to alight.

He took the basket from her and assisted her into the vehicle.

"I thought we could use some scones and lemon water."

"Thoughtful as usual."

"You can thank Mrs. T. I'm jittery enough over what lies ahead and have thought of nothing else besides finding his remains."

She glanced at a bulky package on the seat in the back. 'What is that?"

"St. Mary's was most obliging when I asked if I could purchase a grave cloth. They gave it to me."

A thoughtful nod and no words.

He snapped the reins and off they went.

Heading south over Victoria Bridge, the morning sunrise rose on the back of their vehicle filtering through the trees and mist.

"Remind me how you discovered the possibility of Uncle Basil's remains in Battersea?"

He related last evening's altercation. "Someone in Battersea who works at the mortuary knew Basil and identified him to Bennett. The woman proclaimed the corpse to be him."

"I would think he could hardly be recognizable." A flock of sheep drew her attention to the rolling hills.

"I agree. Another reason to prepare that it might not be him."

Tamsin sat quietly for a while, deep in thought. After crossing Victoria Bridge, they turned west.

"The scrap of blanket Bennett gave you makes me think it could be him."

He pressed her gloved hand. "I am optimistic."

"I can see that." She chuckled and glanced at his profile as he kept his eye on the road.

"How did the meeting with Madam Patwell go? Did Mrs. Reynolds-Walker show up?"

"She arrived late and gave me a rather dark stare. I worried she recognized me; or she could have simply been curious about a stranger."

She glanced at his profile as he snapped the reins. "Speaking of which, I am eager to entertain you with Madam Patwell's tricks. She has a black cat that arches and hisses on cue. It jumps on the table and walks along each person's clasped hands. I feared being found out when her theatrics began. She has paraphernalia that creates fog in the room, and her voice becomes very manly and deep as she pointed to each of us. She shouted out *You*, at me declaring to the group I was a twin."

"Do say. Rather clever of her." He gave the reins another snap and the horses picked up their gait.

"Her pronouncement shocked me. Then I remembered my disguise and immediately stood, smacking my cane on the floor declaring I was not a twin."

"I wish I had been sheeted like a ghost and jumped out at that moment." His eyes twinkled with glee.

"You mean like the brother I never knew? That would have certainly amused everyone. The butler quickly showed up and the lights were turned brighter, and Madam Patwell told everyone to calm down, saying she would not charge for the séance. And to return tomorrow, because all the spirits had disappeared—left the room."

"Maybe you should go on stage? Your drama would intrigue the audience."

She cast him a derisive glance. "Not on your life."

They had driven past a small village, chimney smoke swirling into the gray skies, sheep grazing over the hills, creating a lovely pastoral autumn scene. Elms, beech, and cedar swayed against the background of dark blue water off in the distance. Despite their reason for the journey, it was delightful and gave her peace of mind as thoughts rummaged about in her head.

"Do you think Mrs. Reynolds-Walker ever loved my uncle? Did she kill him because he put her up in another home?"

"They lived apart for many years between his putting her up in a home of her own and his death. I guess anything's possible. What would be her motive for killing him?"

"Her inheritance."

"Basil kept her decently cared for."

"Yes. Even so, with him dead, look at what she inherits."

He sighed and sat straighter on the padded bench. "Your uncle saw to her finances separate from his business and household. He wasn't a man to hold a grudge and I never heard him speak a word of ill about her. Most men would have reacted in a derisive manner, using money as a weapon. Though not Basil. I never understood the situation between them. They did not divorce, and he certainly had the right. No one would have blamed him."

"I confess to wanting to push her out the door the morning he died, showing up as she did. I cannot quite convince myself that she is not involved. I mean, it may have been longer than two years since her last visit, yet there she came knocking on the morning of."

"Don't waste your thoughts on her. She is not worth the effort. Self-centered and rather immature I would guess. She did your uncle a favor by leaving him. She could never have been accepted in his league."

She suddenly recalled her visit with the woman. "Did I tell you I visited her several days after he died?"

"I'm curious why you would do that?" He glanced at her

profile as she looked down the road ahead. Rolling hills were dotted with bleating sheep. The sky a moody gray suggested rain.

"I'm not certain. Something to do with her standing in his library, and he was in a bundle in the root cellar, and I hated her in that moment. She was so alive..."

She swiped at her eyes and took a deep breath. "...I had a sense she wanted to see how we all handled his death."

He patted her gloved hands. "Take care, Tamsin. This is not an easy time for you by any means. And keeping quiet about his demise puts a lot of pressure on you."

"Excuse me. I don't want to make this an odd day."

He chuckled. "Everything is odd right now. But we'll get through the tough times."

She shrugged ignoring his sentiment. "Do you remember the note she sent to me never to darken her door again? In case you have forgotten, I am rash, interfering, and difficult."

"Well on that score I would have to occasionally agree with her."

She cast him an ugly pout. "Honestly, I'm trying to figure out who had motive, and you think it is fine for her to threaten me with calling Metro if I come anywhere near her. She intends to tell them I am unstable."

"Remind me why you sought her out?"

"Because I think she murdered him."

"If I were Mrs. Reynolds-Walker—"

"You aren't," she snapped. "And she does not know I think I murdered him. So why would she disparage me?"

A smile crept upon his features as he recapped, "Because you are rash, interfering and difficult?"

"Would you like a scone?"

"That would be satisfying."

"Just a moment while I sprinkle lots of hot chili pepper on it."

"My favorite. Thoughtful of you to bring it along." He held out his right hand and she placed it on his palm and immediately bit into it. Three bites later he murmured, "Hmm. Tasty. And thank you for not sprinkling it with chili powder."

"Well, I really wanted to, but I didn't bring any."

He chuckled. Hmm. "Delicious."

"Would you like lemon water?"

"I would rather another scone first. Mrs. Labady hadn't finished her breakfast preparations when I took my leave." He snapped the reins again.

The carriage headed directly into dark clouds forming in the west. "We might be in for a bit of rain. I am glad the closed carriage was available." He glanced over at her. "It would be a shame to get your pretty frock all wet."

Ignoring him again she said, "She told me she is deeply in love with someone."

"Are we still talking about Mrs. Reynolds-Walker?"

Turning to him with a scowl on her face she vented. "Are you purposefully trying to be difficult? Yes. We never finished talking about her."

"Do we have a name for this man?" The clouds were darkening.

"I asked; however, she avoided my question. She's been in love with him since she was young."

"I wonder if Basil knew. Perhaps that is why he put her up in another living arrangement." He added, "With his life's work as Lieutenant Detective to Her Majesty, it would seem he had access to any information he asked for."

"He never mentioned anything negative about Mrs. Reynolds-Walker to me. The poor man, he deserved much better than he got."

"I think he lived exactly as he desired. He could have married anyone he preferred. You know, some men have not the notion to marry. I've thought with his power to investigate whomever he chose he could have already figured out what she was after and married her anyway." He glanced over at her. She looked thoughtful. "Marriage is not for everyone you know. And you were his beloved niece who filled his home with excitement, love, and a future."

She looked at him. He had never spoken to her like this before. "Do you believe he realized her deception?"

"At his level in The Queen's service, it seems unlikely he would not have investigated her when her father approached him about a possible marriage."

After a few minutes of thought, she asked, "What would he have found out about her that would turn him off about saying yes to the proposal?"

"My guess is she loved another, and her parents were pushing an arrangement with Basil. He might have been aware of her infatuation with another man."

"I am grateful for your honesty. And I will think about what you've said before I take it to heart."

"Be grateful for the roof over our heads. It is about to pour, tuck your cloak about you."

They arrived in Battersea having missed the worst of the squall.

The mortuary appeared as pictured by Bennett, a stone's throw from the market adjoining the graveyard on Brick Lane and somewhat inconvenient for anyone who had business with the overseer. It was hard to believe the ancient structure of the stone watchhouse accommodated so many cadavers. A wood shingled top kept the weather from rotting the dead quicker than normal, or at least until holes could be dug.

Harrison knocked on the wooden slab of the old door. A

slight man, wrapped in a filthy apron, wiped his hands after he opened the door. "What can I do for ye?" His gaze slid to Tamsin and a smile came to his lined face.

"We are looking for the remains of Basil Walker. Miss Morgan is his only remaining family member, his niece to be precise. We have been informed that someone who works here recognized his corpse. The woman who did so had known him in London."

"Ye can call me Jack if'n ye please. The only other person working here is Rosy. She lived in London for many years afore coming back home here. She's off tendin' ta her daughter havin' a bairn. Can't say when she'll be back. She's most likely ta be the one yer askin' after."

Tamsin drew the piece of blanket out of her pocket and tenderly held it in her hand. "The person who knows Rosy gave us this." She showed him the scrap.

Tamsin thought of Uncle Basil wrapped in this blanket when his body was snatched.

Jack scratched the top of his head. "Miss, iff'n I let ye inside ye'll most likely keel over from the stench. I don't recall what any of 'em was wearin'. They were most likely stripped of what they wore. They's jest take the clothes and sell 'em. Too many blokes are brought here from London, twice a week 'tis."

"Why here?"

"No place else. They's dyin' faster than land's available."

Harrison closed his eyes for a moment. He'd certainly seen the truth of that with all the dead houses, mortuaries, and hospitals he'd visited in the past week.

"Yer welcome ta look see." His squinty eyes glanced from one to the other.

He raised a brow at Tamsin. "Well?"

"I am not leaving until I am content that he is not in this watchhouse."

Jack scratched his left ear. "Go on then. I'll take me break. Give ye some room."

Repelled, not only with Jack scratching his body parts but also the thought of Uncle Basil packed in with dozens of other deceased people churned her stomach.

He stepped in front of her, taking her hand. Having visited numerous dead houses, he had been prepared and knew she was not.

A wall of bodies stacked one upon another faced them as they entered the gloomy room. Tamsin held her wrist to her nose. He handed her a handkerchief.

"How do we go about this? How did you..."

He put his hand on her shoulder and said, "Breathe through your mouth and look for features that are uniquely his. I would suggest his auburn hair. I would say his shirt or pants or shoes. Though you can see most of any good clothing has been taken off the bodies."

"I will focus on the hair, and trimmed beard. His mutton chops and around his mouth and chin, all the same auburn." She wheezed. "Dear Mother of God."

He clutched her shoulder. "What?" And leaned into her face. He could see her eyes smarting.

"This seems impossible."

He softly urged, "Think of auburn hair and a neatly trimmed beard."

He stayed behind her as she made her way through the narrow aisle of bodies. In most cases ten or so stacked one upon another. This had to be one of England's greatest atrocities.

Tamsin gripped his hand as it squeezed her shoulder, as if he were a lifeline of sorts. An intrepid young woman, eager to do right by her beloved uncle, the mainstay of her life. It nearly broke his heart to witness this search. Worse, perhaps, than what he did all last week, because now he knew of the fruitless endeavor; last week he hadn't thought so.

Every time he walked through the door of a building for the dead, he'd felt on the verge of discovery.

"Look. Look. Up there on the top. There he is. I see him." She pointed upward and he immediately noticed the corpse she meant.

It did look like him, though the body wasn't nearly tall enough. "Take in the length. He's not the height of Basil."

She slumped into him, and he gently shook her and persuaded, "Let's get on with this."

The building was certainly substantial. The lantern Jack gave him provided the right amount of light to see faces. Eyes open, eyes closed, one case where the head hadn't stayed attached. He grew more concerned about Tamsin than finding Basil.

Edging their way through the mass, bodies stacked to the right, they breathed through their mouths. They'd been looking for perhaps ten minutes or so when he thought he spotted Basil's remains. Without saying anything and as they made their way along the aisle, he realized the corpse wasn't a match. At that same moment, Tamsin stopped edging her way having spotted the same body. He waited and let her decide for herself before moving on without remark.

Turning another body-ridden corner, he voiced, "What do you think?"

"I need to see this through," she said with finality and a broken-hearted whisper.

They inched their way as he held the lantern high, so its light spread. Tamsin stopped and Harrison held to her shoulder as she glanced at a body remarkably comparable to Basil. The corpse had a red blotch of skin on his lower arm and hand, so not Basil.

"I am so sorry. This must be the hardest thing you have ever endured."

She drew in a breath and stepped forward as one might think a soldier would do. It was unbelievable how many souls died in the last month or so. How many families were broken with loss, how many children left to make their way on the streets. With every step, Tamsin was heartbroken. If she didn't find him here, what was she going to do?

They were making another turn that would ultimately bring them to the front of the square of the old watchhouse where they began. The stone building's contents were the most horrid and disgraceful compilation of humanity she'd ever seen. God bless the dead and those who tried to find loved ones.

She slowed taking infinite care to look at each face, some with gaping mouths perhaps grieving the last moments of their lives or the horror that killed them.

The outside light filtered through the open door of the dungeon-like stone watch building.

Jack waited for them and reached for the lantern Harrison gripped. "Well, sir, I'm takin' it ye dinna find who ye were lookin' for."

Tamsin turned away from them and walked a few paces down the street.

He handed Jack some coins and thanked him. "No, we did not. We appreciate being allowed to look, however. Thank you."

On the ride back to London, Tamsin kept to herself. Harrison guessed she was hurting and allowed that she needed time to come to grips with the situation. Breathing in fresh air cleaned by the dousing rain earlier was cathartic. It would take some time before she took a breath without the memory of what she'd just experienced.

Two and a half hours later, Harrison walked her to the

door when they arrived at #2 Berkeley Street. "I've been meaning to ask if you would be interested in lunch with some of my family tomorrow?"

"You never talk of your family. I had no idea they lived in London."

"It's my mother and several of my siblings. She's in town for a convention and usually brings them along with her."

Tamsin's brow knitted. "A convention?"

"Maybe more like a meeting. She's an archeologist. Her group meets several times a year in London, and she would not miss it unless she is on a dig in Egypt. Say you will come. I'll pick you up at one."

"You are full of surprises. I would be delighted."

Chapter Eighteen

The solid wood door at #47 Brook Street opened almost immediately after Harrison dropped the knocker against the brass plate.

He moved aside, allowing Tamsin to enter and introduced her to his mother's butler, Mad, whose name Tamsin soon learned had been shortened by Harrison's youngest sister when she tried to say Madinger as a toddler. Mad stuck, and Missy, a toddler at the time, giggled every time she repeated the moniker.

Three young ladies swarmed to the entrance hugging, kissing, and exclaiming their excitement at seeing their eldest sibling.

Entranced, Tamsin grinned as three sets of eyes stared at her.

The delightful trio were taking note of her, their eyes

bright with curiosity. Harrison offered, "I would like you to meet a co-worker and friend of mine, Miss Tamsin Morgan."

Beginning with the youngest he announced, "My sisters. Melissa known as Missy, Priscilla, known as Prissy, and Cecilia known as Sissy." Each curtsied as their name was mentioned.

Coquettish giggles abounded as Tamsin wondered how often he brought home guests. She decided never or at least not often enough.

The housekeeper descended the staircase wearing an apron, pockets bulging with odds and ends. She appeared to be very friendly and immediately bussed Harrison on the cheek and then turned to her; causing Tamsin to realize this woman was Harrison's mother.

He introduced her as Mrs. Crawford-Spencer to Tamsin.

"My dear, I am so pleased to meet you." She smelled of spice, a mix of nutmeg and cinnamon, and her smile reached her lovely hazel eyes—Harrison's eyes.

Tamsin gave a slight curtsy. "It is a pleasure to meet you, ma'am. Thank you for the invitation to lunch."

"You must call me Martha. Ma'am is reserved for when I'm older and grayer."

The sisters tittered at their mother's declaration. Sissy whom Tamsin thought to be the eldest, mayhap seventeen or eighteen said, "Our mother is that way. You will see, she's quite modern." The words were said with a measure of pride.

Tinged with amusement, Harrison interjected, "Let's move in out of the draft if you don't mind. I for one want to stand in front of a fire for a minute or two." Harrison had already handed over his overcoat, cane, and hat to Mad and left the women in the foyer as he made a beeline for some warmth by the hearth.

Sissy, Prissy, and Missy gathered around their guest as

their mother said, "You will have to excuse their exuberance. I have had them closeted with their books until now."

Tamsin couldn't recall when she'd been in the company of such unexpected effervescence—three lively and lovely young ladies. She turned to the eldest of the three, Sissy. "What did you learn this morning?"

Quite straight forward, Sissy stated, "I hope to follow in my mother's footsteps and become an archeologist. I wrote a small essay on Alexander Henry Rhind, an archeologist of whom my mother thinks a great deal."

Her golden-haired sister, Prissy, cajoled. "She thinks it will get her some time off from her necessary reading. You know, flattering our mother."

Harrison caught the drift of their conversation as they entered the parlor and glanced at Missy. "Have you outgrown your tricks; do they still work?"

"Mother has...has...gotten a lo...lot more serious with...us...late...lately."

Martha glanced at her son. "At least you and your brother were dedicated."

Prissy blurted, "She refuses to allow me to read what I prefer. She keeps me grounded in the Middle Ages."

Harrison faked a gasp, "She doesn't allow you those penny dreadfuls, does she?"

His mother laughed, but Tamsin noted at least two frowns making her think they would like nothing better.

Missy, the youngest, turned her hazel eyes upward to their guest. "Th...th...they trie to fo...fo...fool mama."

Tamsin patted Missy's hand. "I would wager no one fools your mother."

"Yo...yo...you're right." Her beautiful eyes danced with delight.

They had all entered the warmth of the parlor, and the daughters urged Tamsin to the center of a large divan so they could sit together. Tamsin said, "I know very little about archeology, just what I have seen and read when visiting the Museum. You must enjoy the subject quite a lot."

Sissy said, "Not if you have grown up with it. Our father is an archeologist, also. The air we breathe is filled with the study of the ancients. And always Egyptian. Sometimes I think I swallow thousand-years-old Sahara dust."

Missy quickly added, "I...I...do not mind *arcklogy*. I saw pictures in my reading book...ye...ye...yesterday of Cairo. Tha...that is where I want to...to...go."

Tamsin noticed another word mispronounced. She wondered if the girl was simply excited. She considered that Missy being the youngest and trying to get a word in before one of her sisters grasped the moment, might be the cause of her stutter.

Martha had been chatting with her son and mentioned to Tamsin, "I take the younger children on my ventures and school them myself."

"What fortunate lives you lead."

Martha beamed at her daughters. "We thank the good Lord as we count our blessings."

Mad entered the parlor and announced luncheon.

Harrison turned away from the fire and offered his arm to Tamsin.

Missy slipped her hand into her mother's, and they all headed down the hall to the dining room.

Martha said, "I hope you are in the mood for seafood, Tamsin. Cook prepared a fish pudding for us followed by one of the girls' favorites, gingerbread with pineapple."

She felt quite special to share this afternoon with such a delightful family. Dining with them made it even better. "I have not had fish pudding in a great while. And gingerbread is a preference of mine."

Sissy and Prissy quickly sat on each side of Tamsin.

Missy directly across, leaving their mother at the head, and Harrison next to his youngest sister. A quick prayer was said, and then it seemed everyone talked at once then laughed at the confusion they created.

Their mother averred, "We must allow our guest to enjoy her meal."

Beginning with Tamsin, a maid carried the dish of fish pudding around the table allowing each person to spoon their portion. The rest of the accouterments followed, spice for the pudding, slices of brown wheat bread, and cut up celery, tomatoes, and cucumbers.

Tamsin noted Harrison appeared quite content to be in their presence. He teased Priscilla, "You do not look the same without your spectacles perched on your cute little nose."

A blush appeared on her cheeks as she glanced at her mother then her brother. Tamsin thought her to be fourteen or fifteen and suspected she left them off because of company. "I guess I forgot. I was in a hurry after lessons."

Tamsin chimed in. "When I wear mine, I forget I have them on. When I do take them off and set them aside, I forget where they are, and it is always when I need them most. I think sometimes I should have a pair in each room waiting for me."

Harrison scooped up a spoonful of pudding and glanced at her. "I don't think I've seen you with spectacles."

"Probably because I've put them somewhere." She grinned at Prissy. "It can be rather bothersome."

Prissy smiled at Tamsin with something akin to adoration and nodded her pretty head of lovely golden hair in agreement.

Martha asked, "Did you know your uncle and my husband belong to the same club, The Silver Cross? Has Mr. Walker ever spoken of it?"

Surprised at the connection, Tamsin didn't quite know what

to say. He had talked of this or that over the years. However, she could not recall him going into any depth about their meetings. With Harrison in and out of his library over the years, it seemed as though she would have heard a reference or two.

Prissy mentioned, "Our father is interested in anything to be puzzled over."

Martha glanced at her eldest daughter. "She's right. He is a professor of archeology. But his underlying passion is solving mysteries."

"I do not recall my uncle mentioning Mr. Spencer. I do know your son is one of his favorites." She felt horrid misguiding Martha, pretending Uncle Basil lived. Patting her lips with the napkin, she glanced at Harrison to discover him staring at her.

He winked, easing her anxiety.

Sissy giggled. Tamsin did not dare look at the youngster knowing she'd misinterpreted his wink.

Tamsin asked of Martha, "Harrison tells me you travel with your daughters to Egypt searching for artifacts. You lead a truly exciting life."

Sissy spoke up. "We're learning the history of the world. Finding the past and understanding how the future unfolds. How history encourages us to grow."

"Well said." Martha smiled at her eldest daughter.

Harrison mentioned, "My mother would rather be in Egypt than England. She has brought the girls to London in preparation for just such a journey. My brother Edward would be with her now, except he is at Eton and would not miss his exams even for a dig in the ancient pyramids."

"I had no idea you had such an energetic and intriguing family." All eyes were upon her as she tried to imagine such a household and what it would mean to be involved in their passions.

Harrison said, "Tamsin has been raised by her uncle. Her parents passed when she was quite young. So, you can envision the impact on her of meeting all of you at once." He scanned his sisters as they struggled not to gape. Thankfully good manners had been instilled at an early age.

The youngest, Missy, asked, "I would think your ho...ho... home is quieter than ours."

Tamsin could have laughed at the thought. All the preposterous occurrences since Uncle Basil's death ten days ago were no match for the silence in her heart now that he was gone.

"I would have given anything to have had a sister, and there are six of you. You are fortunate young ladies."

A smile brightened Missy's sweet little face. "Mostly I ... am."

Her sisters chuckled.

A maid cleared their plates and upon reentering the dining room, the sharp, pungent scent of ginger drifted in with her. At home when Cook peeled and grated the ginger root, its strong aromatic scent reminded her of the season of pumpkins, and red and gold leaves drifting in the air.

Martha asked, "Harrison tells me you run a detective agency. It must be an amazing occupation. I suspect your uncle must have planted that seed?"

"None other. Since I've finished with school, I felt out of sorts and Uncle Basil asked if I would be interested in working in his office, keeping ledgers up to date, filing, that sort of thing. It was quite by chance that I began investigating for him."

Prissy asked, "Do you carry a gun?"

"Prissy?" Puzzled her mother.

"I'm curious. I might want to be a lady detective someday."

Mrs. Spencer's eyes widened just a fraction. "You have a long way to go before you get to that age, sweeting."

Tamsin did not want to answer in a manner that would upset her mother. She chose her words carefully. "I have once, and actually had no need of it in that particular circumstance."

Her gaze slid to Harrison. She had given him Uncle Basil's Webley Bull Dog to hold, fully loaded, which he had quite taken exception to.

"What kind of cases are you interested in? Murders? Or theft?"

"Whatever seems to cross my desk. For instance, recently I had need to dress as an elderly woman and attend a séance. The woman used a black cat to mesmerize her audience. It turned out to be quite funny. The cat screeched, hunched its back, and scampered off the table leaving four people in shock."

"You weren't, were you?" inquired Prissy.

Tamsin smiled at her. "No, I was more interested in the reactions of the others. Besides, I do not believe in séances."

The maid came into the dining room and whispered to Martha, who asked, "Would anyone want more gingerbread and pineapple?"

A chorus of yesses resounded.

"Mother, what is a séance?" Prissy was the inquisitive daughter.

Martha glanced at Tamsin. "Would you like to answer her?"

"Well," Tamsin glanced at the degrees of interest on their faces. "A séance is the gathering of several people who think they can speak to family members who have passed away. Some people believe this can really happen. Most intelligent people know that it is not possible."

Missy spoke up instantly. "Wh...wh...why not?"

"Because when people die, they can no longer talk. Right?"

"So, why are there people who think they can?"

"They are duped by the person who falsely claims to have a special knowledge. Charlatans make a living off vulnerable, grieving folks."

Sissy, enraptured by the topic, glanced at her mother. "Would that student of father's who claimed the paper he turned in was his, be a charlatan?"

Martha swept her palm over Sissy's arm as she leaned in. "The same. Rogues come in all sizes and colors my dear. That's why it is always best to know the person you entrust."

As the afternoon began to fade Harrison inquired of his mother, "How long will you be away this time?"

"I expect we will return early in the new year. February most likely. Edward will have his term break, and the girls will be missing their friends. Most importantly, there is your second six. You will be done and receive your robe and wig."

"As usual, you have us all figured out, Mama. How you weave your magic is beyond comprehension."

Martha dug in the pocket of her apron and drew out a small figurine. Tamsin held a giggle when she realized it was meant to represent Harrison as a Barrister in his robe and wig.

"See what your eldest brother will look like when we return." She handed the figure to Missy and watched it travel from hand to hand ending up in Harrison's.

"I believe you have exaggerated this portly figure, mama."

His sisters giggled, the youngest blushing pink.

Tamsin joined in the fun. "You will have to be circumspect when dining on bangers and mash as you head into the legal world."

On the walk back to Portman Square, Tamsin mused, "You certainly have an original family. I am happy to have spent time with them. Thank you for including me."

"I knew you would enjoy my sisters. It's one of the reasons I wanted you to accompany me today."

"And the other reason?" Her lips twisted in a smirk.

"No other." He shrugged.

"What are you hiding from me?"

"Nothing specific. It's just that...well, our trip to Battersea was unpleasant, and I thought we could both enjoy the company of my sisters, each unique in their way, and my mother. A woman of great strength and conviction."

As they walked north on Orchard Street, Tamsin agreed. "Our visit did shake off the remains of yesterday. Thank you for your thoughtfulness. Tell me why you do not talk about your delightful family."

He almost laughed. "When do we ever have a moment for reflection? A crisis of something or other is always boiling."

Reaching George Street, they turned east on Berkley Square. A light wind had kicked up. She realized how true were his words. "You never mentioned your father's interest in detective work. Am I correct in thinking that is when you became interested?"

"My father likes the chase if you will. Like my sisters said, *the puzzle*. But Basil was my influence. His attention to detail." He glanced at her, the afternoon sun making her eyelashes glisten. He was grateful she appeared to have enjoyed the time with his family.

"Your uncle's precision in thinking through issues bordered on perfection. Indeed, if he were investigating his murder, it would be solved by now."

"I have told you repeatedly Mrs. Reynolds-Walker killed him. I just haven't been able to prove it yet.'"

Shaking his head as if considering her dogged determination, he opened the gate to her residence.

As she entered, Tamsin said, "Your mother lives like a queen."

"My father enjoys making her happy."

"Yet, you keep your family at arm's length."

He scrunched his brow. "I might. It's called preservation. They tend to smother me."

Before she turned to the steps, he suggested, "Let's sleep on the problem of Basil's whereabouts for the night and tomorrow bring all our reasoning and possible suspects into focus. I have an hour or so in the late morning if that would suit."

"Yes. I've been thinking."

Again, he shook his head. "When aren't you?"

"I'll let Cook know you will be here for a late breakfast. Thank you again for a delightful afternoon."

Harrison almost revealed his secret about the *Basil W. Walker Gym for Youth* to Tamsin. What held him back was that it wasn't finished, and he wanted it to be a special occasion. The walls were plastered, the floor was ready to be laid, and he was genuinely thrilled to be able to honor his mentor in this way.

Chapter Nineteen

T amsin rang and Sally appeared. "If Mrs. T can spare a few minutes, would you ask her to join us?"

"Yes, miss."

Tamsin went to the far wall of the parlor and leaned against it, looking out at the leaves scuttering across the lawn. The gray skies looked ominous as the dark clouds moved slowly across the firmament. Her emotions were scattered from all that had happened. And now she would be destroying Mrs. T's peace of mind. If she could be considered family, she would have been a loving aunt to Uncle Basil.

Tamsin had been able to keep herself together these eleven days. However, revealing the truth of his absence to Mrs. T put the stamp of reality to his death. Her heart pounded as she turned from the window.

Harrison greeted the housekeeper, and she took the chair he offered.

Remorse skittered over Tamsin as she looked at the housekeeper, mob cap atop her soft white hair, glasses edged toward the tip of her nose. Her black bombazine with white apron and white cuffs that never seemed to show dirt. A pleasant and lovely-minded woman who had kept their home running smoothly all these years. As much a part of the household as Uncle Basil was.

Mrs. T's voice had a slight tease as she glanced at Harrison. "I see you didn't finish the scones, Mr. Spencer. Were they not to your liking?"

"Quite the opposite. Your scones are my favorite, ma'am. But it's been brought to my attention that I should watch my girth."

Mrs. T smiled as her gaze fell to Tamsin. And Tamsin saw her expression change. It must have been apparent from the look on Tamsin's face that something had shifted in their lives.

Tamsin gave her a moment before saying, "I have something to tell you that is going to come as a dreadful shock. Perhaps it might also enlighten you regarding some oddities of late in our household."

Mrs. T cupped her hands. She sat in the chair offered, her shoulders rigid, her chin raised as if she were ready to do battle.

Tamsin's remorse churned. "The night my uncle supposedly went off to India, eleven days ago..."

Mrs. T nodded.

"...he didn't go to India as I led you to believe. He...he was murdered that night at his desk."

For a long moment the room fell to silence until Mrs. T asked, "Not Mr. Basil?"

Tamsin nodded. Words were hard to come by. It was like that night all over again.

Bewilderment creased Mrs. T's face. Her hands gripped

the arms of the chair. "Murdered?"

"He never planned to go to his plantation. It was a ruse on my part because when I found him dead at his desk, I didn't know what to do."

A few seconds became a very long minute as Tamsin saw the puzzlement in her eyes. She did not blink as she stared at Tamsin, putting the pieces together.

Tamsin guessed she was trying to sort things out, trying to cope with what she just learned. Harrison continued to stand behind Mrs. T not knowing if she would swoon.

Suddenly, Mrs. T bent her head downward, a shaky hand to her chest. "I knew something had happened. I couldn't figure out what. Though I knew it had to be horrid. Your behavior of late has been strange and distant."

"It breaks my heart to have to tell you this. I should have told you sooner. You, of anyone, should have been taken into confidence. It rattled me horridly and I was quite afraid. I didn't ask for Harrison's help for several days."

Mrs. T guessed, "You hid his remains in the cellar."

She whispered, "Yes."

"May I inquire if he...his remains are still there?"

Tamsin glanced at Harrison as he finally took his seat. His never-ending capabilities provided strength as he revealed to Mrs. T, "Someone has taken the body, and we are in a state of uncertainty as to who and why someone would do so."

Mrs. T appeared to regain control, her face losing its ashen cast. "The morning when we found you in the cellar, is that when his remains had been taken?"

"Yes. I went out for three nights in a row to check on him —well, on his remains He was gone on the third night when I unintentionally locked myself in the cellar."

Mrs. T said, "It must have been that same night I went to the kitchen to get a glass of water. Just past eleven I heard noises, scuffling, on the back lawn. I thought Charlie had gotten up to something. Though it seemed a bit late for him. He is a creature of habit and usually tucked in by nine.

"I opened the back door to make certain it wasn't him and noted a shadowy motion, as if an animal slunk behind the elm. I couldn't be certain and the scuffling I thought I heard had stopped. I shut the door, locked it, and went back to bed."

A wisp of relief overcame Tamsin. The suffering and anxiety tormenting her seemed to ease. This lovely elder who helped raise her and to whom she owed a world of debt.

Harrison's gaze shifted to Tamsin. "Thank the almighty you were not about yet. Knowing you, in all probability you would have charged into the yard and met the perps face to face."

Ignoring his little jab at her predictability she asked, "You think there was more than one?"

"Your uncle was a stocky and well-built man. It would take at least two men to carry him. Think how he worked out, boxing, dueling. He was fit as could be."

"I moved him," she rejoined.

"You dragged him on a blanket. There's a difference. And, if you told the truth, I'm fairly certain it took all you could muster to do so."

Mrs. T swiped at tears sliding down her cheeks. Anguish for the housekeeper burned Tamsin's soul. The woman had cared for her uncle for as many years as she had lived in this house.

She knelt in front of Mrs. T taking up her hands. "We've shaken you horridly, Mrs. T. Is there anything you want to ask?"

She cupped Tamsin's cheek. "I knew something happened. The recent mayhem in Mr. Walker's office seemed to confirm that." She turned to Harrison. "I'm assuming you feel we are safe?"

"Nothing has come about since thieves ransacked his office and Tamsin doesn't seem to think anything is missing. Without discovering the body, we are at an impasse. I have combed every dead house, mortuary, and hospital that allowed me entry, with no sign of him."

"How...how did he die?" She slipped her hand from beneath Tamsin's and swiped at the side of her cheek where a tear dribbled.

Tamsin got to her feet and took the chair next to the housekeeper.

"He was poisoned. Arsenic. At least evidence seems to prove so."

Mrs. T swiped at another tear, obviously attempting to keep her emotions in check. Harrison added, "He showed no signs of suffering. It appeared to be almost instant according to Tamsin."

Mrs. T's pale blue eyes widened. "You were with him when this took place?"

"I would say I arrived in the library within minutes, perhaps seconds." She avoided looking at Harrison, the memory of that midnight churning in her heart knowing the killer stood in front of him and watched him die. She wondered if she'd ever be able to rid herself of that image.

He continued, "We are attempting to solve the murder on our own, which is why we have delayed alerting the Home Office."

Mrs. T's eyebrow quirked as she asked Tamsin, "Is that why you attended a séance?"

"Little good that did, except to discover Mrs. Reynolds-Walker is a patron of Madam Patwell's parlor."

Stoic in times of trouble, the housekeeper kept control. Knowing full-well the cost of doing so, Tamsin ached for her. "I'm so sorry to have this horrid news to tell. However, I couldn't keep this from you any longer. I know how much you cared for him. He viewed you as one of our family and was grateful for your presence in our lives."

Mrs. T said, "I did think it strange he left without a good-bye." She dabbed at the persistent tears in the corner of her eye. "It wasn't like him to do so. He never left without instructions."

Tamsin asked, "You need to keep this to yourself for now. I don't think Cook or Evie would do well knowing, and I am beyond doubt Sally would be the worst for it should she know."

A silence hung over the room. Mrs. T sighed and swiped at another tear. Her voice unsteady. "What about Charlie? Is he to be told?"

"You are the only one we have taken into confidence." Tamsin glanced at Harrison for an answer. He gave her a slight nod and she continued. "Would you mind telling him? And insure he does not reveal my uncle's death to anyone?"

Harrison said, "I've already spoken to him about due vigilance. He's prepared knowing Basil is away."

Mrs. T stood with her palms on the table steadying her. Overcome, she breathed a sigh of profound sadness. "Such a wonderful man. In some ways, he was almost like the son I wished I had. Such a shame there is hatred to a degree that would end his life. I hope the two of you catch the criminals who did this."

Tamsin stood and hugged the elder. "Be assured your position is secure, and when you inform Charlie, make him aware as well. Always the caretaker, my uncle made provisions long before this for all the household should anything unfortunate occur."

Mrs. T's lips pursed as if afraid her emotions would show. "He was an exceptional gentleman,"

Tamsin quickly asked, "You need time to absorb all this. Let me get you a cup of tea. You have had a terrible shock."

"No. No. I'll be alright. You've set my mind at ease about India." She paused a moment, her lips pinched. "I might tell the maids I have a headache and sit awhile in Cook's chair and have her give me a bracing cup. I'll get on well enough. I am relieved you shared this. It must have been hard to do so." She glanced a moment at Harrison. "Thank you for your support of our Miss Tamsin." She quietly slipped out of the dining room, closing the door behind her.

Tamsin and Harrison exchanged glances. Bit by bit Uncle Basil's murder was coming to light.

Saturday, 1:00 p.m.
1 October 1870

Harrison cleared his throat drumming fingertips on the tablecloth. "This is an inappropriate time to bring up a dinner request. My mother has invited us to join her at a small gathering to raise money for the families of the 481 lives lost when the HMS Sylvan capsized off Finisterre. It's to be held at Lord and Lady Hempstead's home."

Tamsin looked up, still feeling the tightness in her throat. "Your mother certainly travels in high society."

"Are you interested?"

"I'm mourning, Harrison. My heart grieves."

His chin bowed to his chest. "I know, believe me I know. But no one else does and until then I think you should continue as natural as possible until this is all figured out."

He took her hand in his. "I'll be there with you the whole time. And you might just come across some information that helps us."

He added, "The Hempstead's are old family friends from

Cambridge days. And my mother wouldn't ask, except Father decided to come to town, and I would like him to meet you."

"How can I refuse to meet your father. Certainly. When is it?"

"Day after tomorrow. And to sweeten the pot, Tennyson will be reading one of his poems."

She shifted a sly eye to him.

> *"And by the moon the reaper weary,*
> *Piling sheaves in uplands airy,*
> *Listening, whispers, 'Tis the fairy*
> *Lady of Shalott."*

He chortled. "I take it that is a yes, assuming Tennyson reads your favorite?"

Chapter Twenty

Saturday, 10:00 p.m.
1 October 1870

S hafts of pale autumn moon saved the night from being as dark as the inside of a coal mine. The cold Thames angrily slapped against the docks spitting salty foam into the air.

During the day the streets teemed with maritime life, boisterous sailors on leave with one aim, to drink themselves into oblivion then stumble back to their ship and snore the night away.

At night blackened chimney's regurgitated thick curls of smoke darkening what light a faint moon might lend. Fog curled around the slippery wooden walkways. Shops were closed for business at this late hour. Goods a captain requires were displayed in the windows; sextants, time pieces of great accuracy, and compasses mounted in front of the helmsman were stilled without the roll of a ship.

On this night of mischief, the brackish Thames, lined

with innumerable piers, warehouses, jetties, and the occasional dolphins, was quiet. The moon hung in the west clouds constantly shifting cutting what little light it provided.

Away from the East India and St. Katherine's docks, only the slap of waves against the bulwark cut into the silence. Swirls of murkiness along this stretch helped to keep Harrison's and Mickey's cloak-and-dagger watch for the unloading and transfer of opium out of sight. They weren't in danger of gun fighting or throat slitting. Their instructions were to stay out of sight and take note of the action at C Dock.

An easterly wind roiled the sharply pervasive stench of dead fish. It crossed Harrison's mind that he could never live on the water. The thought of a nice sail on a bright wind-swept day would be grand, however maritime life held little interest for him.

Mickey whispered, "Did you bring any ales?"

Harrison glanced at him. "If I had my druthers, we'd be at the Silver Cross. But duty calls?"

The detective grunted as they tucked into an uncomfortable niche on the dock hunched behind a string of barges. Their orders were to stay hidden and figure out the shipman in charge. The chatter of lightermen sifted through the air unaware their movements were being observed from one dock over.

The ship presently unloading took four hefty men to lift a crate. As the night wore on, twenty crates were transferred from the boat to drays. As each wagon loaded with ten crates, the dray took off. They had been instructed to establish a supervisor in control of operations. So far, they hadn't taken note of anyone fitting that role. The fourth wagon was in the process of loading.

Time passed slowly. Gunmen stood on the barges watching the removal of crates. Harrison guessed it wasn't baled hay they were transferring, more like opium, a drug a significant portion of the population seemed to crave. Though legally sold in the markets, some producers undercut the competition. In the last few years, opium wars on English turf had begun to escalate.

Fergus had an uncommon role in this operation. The Head of Home Security had asked him if he knew of a wily chap able to insert himself along the docks. He suspected a load of opium would be delivered, and if so, he'd report to the barrister with his findings.

Home Security needed a relatively unknown person to keep this out of the public eye. Fergus trusted Harrison to look for the head of the operation who had cleverly eluded the Bobbies in previous opium drops.

The Daily enraged readership to the point of exasperation for the Home Office over the wide use of opium and the death rate due to overdose.

Thus, Mickey and Harrison found themselves hiding on the docks and spying. Looking for someone who could be in charge. Someone important. Someone who would no doubt end up in the gaol once their findings held merit.

The wind increased with the tidal waves slapping against the docks. After an hour of watching the ritual of unloading and reloading, Harrison whispered to Mickey, "I want to get closer to the road, and see what is going on up there. I don't see anyone at this end who might be our man."

"And leave me with this crappy detail? I'm trying not to fall asleep."

Harrison pushed at his shoulder. "Talk any louder and you might get the wrong end of a gun in your mouth."

Mickey sulked and mumbled a word Harrison hadn't heard in a long time. That was saying something considering his bully-boy language.

Harrison crept along the dock away from the unloading. The lightermen were on top guiding a crate as they conveyed it to the men who loaded the dray. Friendly insults were traded back and forth.

He moved swiftly along the pier, ducking behind the storage bins at each docking point. The near moonless night provided just enough light to keep him from falling in the water.

Sneaking along the furthest side of the dock stacked with bins of stored cargo, he reached the area where the Thames slapped against land. He ducked behind a storage crate, with barely enough footing to crouch and stay dry. He stepped carefully, lest his boots become sodden. He might end up swimming.

Nearly a dozen armed men surrounded the wagons. His eye caught a flicker of light up on the road, he guessed from a lucifer used to light a pipe or cheroot? Could it be the very person they had been ordered to look for? Whomever, the person was tucked in a carriage with the top up. A barely definable outline of a man's hat suggested to Harrison it could be their man.

A light sparked again, as he crept along the gravel path and stepped onto dirt and withering weeds crunching beneath his boots. He stopped to see if he'd aroused the man in the carriage. Nothing.

Hiding behind a stand of prickly bushes tall enough to cover him, he had a direct look at the cab and the person smoking, though it was difficult to discern facial characteristics. Listening for movement from the vehicle, he took a breath of ease knowing he'd not been seen.

Suddenly the cab door opened, and the occupant jumped down. He took three strides from the carriage directly toward Harrison who held his breath.

Unbuttoning his flap, the chap relieved himself.

From where Harrison hunched, he could have seized his leg. The stench of urine was strong. Harrison used the moment to etch the fellow's features in memory. Macassar oil groomed his hair. His mustache was trimmed to the thickness of a pencil-point. Harrison dared not look in his eyes. It spooked him how uncanny it would be if they caught each other's gaze.

The cut of his clothing spoke of wealth. His shoes, though he stood in damp foliage and muck, were highly polished black leather. At that moment a cloud rolled in front of the moon and cut off further inspection.

Harrison barely breathed. It felt like forever before the bloke finished, buttoned himself, and returned to the carriage. As he began to crouch his way out of the low brush, he heard a rifle shot seeming to come from the C Dock.

The sudden flash of light was accompanied by gunshots *dut, dut, dut*, not unlike a soft version of lightning bugs hitting oil lamps. He ducked and drew his gun. The carriage, two or three yards from where he crouched, took off at a moment's snap of the reins, speeding toward the west. Harrison now had a direct line as far as the first dock, beyond that a thick haze shrouded the scene.

Utter chaos. Men yelling, "load the wagons." The surrounding space filled with specks of light as gunfire tore through the air, screams rent the night, bodies splashed into the briny Thames.

Wagon drivers snapped the reins, and the last wagon took off, men scrambling to catch a ride.

The stench of fish and salt was overcome by a sulphury metal compound.

"Help me," came a cry from his left.

Harrison slipped through the mist. "Say something so I can find you."

"Here..."

Harrison knelt. "Where are you hurt?"

"...neck...leg."

The moon completely darkened he could barely make out how the man laid. He felt the warm spurt of blood near the carotid and grabbed his handkerchief, stuffing it into the wound, then grabbed the man's good hand. "Press hard, while I look at your leg."

Finding the leg wound, instantly he realized the knee was torn to shreds. He ripped the pant leg off with his pocketknife, making a tourniquet.

"...tell...me...wife..." whispered from dying lips.

Harrison felt for a pulse though he knew the fella had passed. Life taken in an instant; the dead man's wife would be shattered. Shaking the thought away, he stood and glanced about for his partner. The mist was so thick he couldn't see where his next step would land.

His instinct told him, the person in the carriage must be involved; perhaps the head of the operation, the man Fergus was eager to catch.

The earth stood still except for the gentle slap of waves against the docks and an occasional groan. Peace came instantly on the heels of the murderous assault and sent a creepy sensation upon him; that, and the stench of sulfur.

Spooked, he slowly backed off the dock and made his way to the far side of the wooden anchorage without prompting any fire, almost tripping over several dead bodies as he made his way to the level ground.

Where the deuce was Mickey?

Chapter Twenty-One

Saturday, 11:30 p.m.
1 October 1870

T he thick mist and near moonless night hampered his search for Mickey. The stench of sulfur prompted him to be quick, plus the possibility of a gunman intending to kill anyone foolish enough to linger.

Harrison longed for a hot bath and a large glass of brandy. However, they had prearranged to meet with Fergus in the lobby of Lincoln Inn after the business at the docks. He regretted the day he felt obligated to assist the barrister in this covert plan to discover who was operating the surge in opium. He assumed this wasn't about just one man, it was more about the operation of what the man hoped to accomplish.

Reaching the Inn, his footsteps echoed in the large, marbled entrance. Glancing about, he didn't find the barrister among a small group carrying on an enlivened conversation on the far right of the sixty-foot domed structure. Their talking muffled across the nearly vacant expanse.

A deep voice from somewhere behind him, groused, "My joints are sore."

Harrison spun about. "Where the hell did you disappear to?" Mickey looked like a drowned rat. Harrison noticed he seemed to favor his right arm. He also noticed the group on the other side of the hall gaping at them. No wonder, dripping wet and smelly from the briny water.

"I fell in the river."

Harrison looked him over and decided he may have had an accident. Still, something itched in the back of Harrison's mind, the possibility Mickey was covering up his whereabouts. The old Mickey, the one from their academy years, had Harrison thinking this Mickey ran off to report to someone else. Someone who was covertly fattening his wallet.

As if he had read Harrison's mind, he said, "It's not likely either of us will get extra pay, so what's your yank?"

Displeased, Harrison glanced at the large wet hulk. "Why'd you skip out?"

Ignoring the question, Mickey snarled, "Did you find the carriage?" It was obvious he had a different agenda regarding tonight's troubles. Harrison decided to let it go for now. "Turned out to be a red herring. I tried to get back to you. The crossfire kept me down."

Mickey grunted and turned away. Harrison was wary of his behavior. He knew something irritated him. What? Before he could come to any decision, Fergus came through the hallowed doors of the Lincoln Inn.

"Okay lads, let's go up to me chamber where we can discuss the evening in private."

They trailed after the barrister walking up the marble stairs, their shuffling footsteps echoing as if a small army invaded.

Seated, and with two fingers of fortified wine for each of

them, Fergus asked, "Rough night?" He looked directly at Mickey who gulped his drink and fixed his gaze on the empty glass clutched in his beefy hand.

Finally, Mickey answered, "It was a mess. Once the shooting began, I couldn't make out who was who." He jerked his head toward Harrison making it appear as if Harrison had left him in the lurch. "He scampered off, says he wanted to check out the carriage up on the road."

Fergus ignored the complaint and glanced at Harrison. "Did ye come across anything useful?"

"By the time I reached the carriage a bloke was getting out of it to relieve himself. I was less than a couple of yards from him and couldn't move without giving myself away. The shooting started and he jumped in the carriage and was off. I'd say five minutes tops before the gunfire ended and I tried to get back to Mickey."

Fergus finished his drink and laid the glass on his desk then looked at the duo. "So, nothing came of tonight. No facial recognition, no names mentioned. Nothing."

Mickey offered, "The first hour or so, we were privy to banter back and forth as they unloaded the crates." He shrugged his shoulders and looked at Harrison, then added, "Nothing of any import was revealed in the crosstalk."

Harrison nodded in agreement.

Sunday, 8:00 a.m.
2 October 1870

Early the next morning, Harrison made his way back to Chambers. There had to be fifty or more individuals coming and going, a much different sight from last night's late hours.

Harrison found the barrister in his office. The door ajar, he lightly rapped his knuckles against the frame.

"Come in. I'm surprised to see ye this early after the late night."

Harrison eyed a large stack of books on the end of the barrister's desk, obviously just delivered from Lincoln Inn's library. "I didn't report everything to you from last night, sir."

The barrister swung his chair around, and with a dubious scrunch of his bushy brows, waited for Harrison to get on with it.

"This is going to sound like a tattle. It's about Garrity. He couldn't have known I saw a carriage last night. Unless he knew there would be one at the scene?"

Fergus' hard glance alerted Harrison to the barrister's own possible unease about the Davis & Fenway detective. "What are ye inferring?"

"I'm not sure. I've known Mickey since our school days and he's quite capable of playing ends against a middle. When I made my way back to our secure place he was not there. And when I asked him, he said he fell in the river."

Scrunching his bushy brows, the barrister looked skeptical. "Ye don't believe him?"

"I do not. Which is why I withheld information until now when it's just the two of us."

Fergus nodded to him to continue.

"Last night, I hid in the bushes before the man stepped outside the carriage. The clouds separated, giving me a few moments to take note of him. He relieved himself almost in front of me. You once said the man you looked for had slicked and gelled dark hair, a thin mustache, tall, dressed very well, and polished black patents. And a black onyx ring on his right hand."

"That's some description." His eyes narrowed, "What, no eye color?"

Harrison ignored his sardonic humor. "I was very close and had barely seconds of observation. I could hear him breathe."

"I hope he didn't get his water on ye," he smirked.

Harrison's brow knitted. "I'd have had a hard time not reacting."

"Well, yer discovery may turn out ta be the missing dimension. Good work, young man."

As he left the barrister's chambers, Harrison suspected Fergus had an idea who the perpetrator could be. Harrison also wondered what role Mickey played in all this. A chill came over him as he contemplated his colleague might be working for the wrong people.

Sunday, 7:00 p.m.
2 October 1870

As the north star began to twinkle upon the streets of London, the carriage driver pulled up in front of Portman Square where Harrison stepped out, giving the address of their next destination to the driver.

Breathing deeply in the chilly night air, the leaves scrunched under his shoes as he opened the gate and strode up the walk.

He looked forward to the leisurely evening ahead, and the opportunity to mingle with his parents' friends. It was an opportunity to raise funds for the families of the Bridgestone disaster, yet it also promised to be entertaining. He needed a diverting evening.

Tamsin appeared eager by the looks of her. She'd done up her thick chestnut hair with flirty curls dangling on her cheeks. A dark blue cape with the cowl falling onto her shoulders gave her an air of elegance. She wore white satin gloves. He'd never seen her dressed like this and had always thought of her as an older child. He wondered when the child disappeared, and this lovely woman materialized.

"You've done something to your hair."

"If that is a compliment, thank you, kind sir." She glanced at him with a smirk of interest. "You look devilishly handsome."

Settled in the carriage across from her he said, "Being out with you amongst my parents' society promises to be entertaining."

"In what way?"

"I phrased that oddly." His long legs stretched out across the floor of the carriage. "We are either at your dining room table, or...I don't know, looking for your uncle's remains...trying to solve the murder and never in a situation like we will be. I'm very much looking forward to an evening of simple pleasures with you."

Tamsin drew the cape over her olive-colored gown and rested her gloved hands in her lap. Instead of responding to him, she probed another avenue. "It sounds as if you've had a hard day?"

As evening darkened and streetlamps lit, he saw snippets of light drift across the clear skin of her face and considered how beautiful a woman she had become and wondered why he just now noticed the change.

"Yes. And I hope you enjoy the evening as well. Just stick with me until you're comfortable."

She snorted. "What, you think I am incompetent in society?"

He chuckled. "Not a'tall. More than anything I hope you enjoy yourself tonight. As I've never known you to shy from any situation, I believe you will."

Her long-sleeved glove draped, and she tugged it back in place. She had borrowed them from Mrs. T and discovered they were a size too large for her. She could not justify the expense of purchasing new ones.

"You needn't worry. I have it on good authority Lord Tennyson is reading and that will certainly be the highlight even if all else fails."

He laughed outright.

She pondered, "You must have had a very busy time of it to forget the reason I agreed to accompany you. Tell me, what exactly is the purpose tonight, other than the famed poet reading?"

"Lord Hempstead's mother happened to be one of the passengers who perished in July when the Bridgewater caught fire and sank, taking with it the crew and 481 passengers."

She smoothed out her cape and glanced at him. "I read about it in the paper. Ghastly. The poor Hempstead's. It is a wonder they are making merry, is it not?"

"Have you ever noticed how people are willing to assist in time of trouble? I think it's a form of that. Donating money to charity to assist those who are in dire need, all in the name of 481 people who are deceased. Think of it as a consolation of sorts. On occasion, my mother and Lady Hempstead have raised funds for other disasters."

"You are most fortunate to still have both parents and your brother and sisters."

The sun was beginning to set. A streak of orange and red lit the sky as he focused his gaze on her and considered what she must be thinking.

Instead, he said, "Did I mention that my parents are hosting Lord and Lady Hempstead tonight. I look forward to introducing my father to you."

She ignored his comment and offered, "I shouldn't have

said that." She clasped her gloved hands together. "I hope I didn't sound like an unfortunate sole. Life gives us only what we can handle. Uncle Basil always said that." She eyed him with a look of mischief. "I'm very much looking forward to meeting your father tonight. And your mother again, of course."

He looked deep into her eyes as the shadowy lantern on the outside of the carriage swayed. "You have been through your own misfortune. Your statement came from a sensibility, a deep understanding."

"You are a kind man, Harrison. I appreciate your friendship."

He turned his attention on the street as the carriage passed a small group of men holding up placards. They caught a glimpse of strikers yelling as the driver swerved onto Edgware Road away from the crowd and headed west.

Minutes later she asked, "Tell me, is your father as interested in archeology as your mother?"

"He's the Department Head at Oxford. That's how they met, so I was told."

"In Egypt? Or here?"

"The first time at university. And later again, in Egypt."

She pushed back a dangling ringlet. "Do you mind telling me a little about the disaster? I read the account in *The Daily*, however there was no mention of where the ship burned."

"It was the Fifth of July. The Bridgewater had left Cork sailing east beyond Land's End when it somehow caught fire. There were no survivors, those that made it to lifeboats ended up capsizing from the weight. As I heard, it was terrifying to say the least. A crowd gathered on shore watching the boat go up in flames and listening to screams for help.

"By the time other boats arrived, bodies were floating. It was a grievous sight, wives, children, whole families amongst the flotsam they had taken with them. It is approximately where the English Channel meets with the Celtic Sea. I understand boats set out from Land's End but were forced back to shore when a nasty squall churned the waves ten, twelve feet high."

"Oh Harrison, how awful. Those poor families. No one survived?"

A moment or two slid away before he spoke. "Over the next few days, bodies, and fragments of lives lost washed up on shore along the coastline. All the detritus that was retrieved was transported to Lord Hempstead's warehouse, and the bodies that were found were sent to morgues.

"The Bridgewater had been expected within seven days or so of their departure from Cork to London's Docks. Lord Hempstead eventually received a listing of the names of those who were onboard."

She laid her gloved hand on his and squeezed. "I am honored to participate tonight, and most happy to contribute."

"That was not the intention when my mother invited you."

"Nonetheless, I wish to do my part to ease the burden of families who lost loved ones."

She paused a moment before mentioning, "I read an article in *The Daily* this morning about a gun fight thought to be opium importers on the docks. Would you happen to know anything about that?"

His gaze slid to her, wondering if somehow she knew his involvement in last evening's gun fight. He didn't respond.

"I take solace in the fact you do not have to be involved in such horrific doings. Opium wars, from what I have read, always leave dead people behind."

Shrugging, he turned his attention to the window and the passing scene.

Chapter Twenty-Two

A line of carriages inched toward the front of Hempstead's lavish home, where blue and gold uniformed footmen assisted with disembarking.

When their hansom cab reached the approach, a footman opened the door and set the step down. Harrison vacated the cab and took Tamsin's gloved hand into his as she stepped down. The faint sound of music from the open doors filtered to the street.

Horses nickered and snorted; guests shuffled forward on the paved drive converging toward the mansion, where more footmen took wraps. Further into the foyer footmen offered trays of crystal goblets bubbling with champagne. The foyer was lit with what must have been a hundred candles.

As Harrison escorted Tamsin inside the magnificent home, they found themselves surrounded by fluted ionic columns that circled the foyer. She was not surprised by the number of people gathered to aid the surviving families. The elegant evening was a first for Tamsin and she had Mrs. Spencer to thank for including her.

Harrison guided her with a light hand at her back toward a tall, handsome man whom Tamsin considered must be

Professor Spencer. Father and son were the same height and stature. Though Harrison's hair was much lighter, their resemblance was striking.

Harrison shook hands with his father. "Allow me to introduce you to Miss Tamsin Morgan. Basil Walker's niece."

The Professor cupped her hand as his golden eyes sparkled. "I recall you as a lovely young lass not more than five or six. It's a pleasure to meet you again, Miss Morgan. I hope your uncle is in fine fettle. It's been a while since I've journeyed to London." He leaned closer to her. "I understand he is out of town, otherwise we could have caught up. Please give him my regards."

"Yes, sir. I certainly will." She did not recall meeting him, but after all, she'd been young enough not to have had the encounter mean much. She suddenly felt awkward with mention of her uncle and profoundly hoped he would not go on about him. She did hate being evasive, or downright lying when it came to that.

Harrison must have guessed what she was fussing about because he immediately changed the subject. "We are particularly impressed with Lady Hempstead's and Mother's involvement in raising funds for charity on behalf of the families of the disaster. Where has she got to anyway?"

He glanced over the sea of guests milling about in the central section of the main hall. Feathers, ribbons, and combs decorated upswept hairdos of women gathered in circles to catch up on gossip. Their husbands and escorts, goblets of various libations in hand, exchanged the latest blather creating quite a hubbub. Nowhere could he lay eyes upon his mother.

Tamsin knew who he sought. "Your mother is helping Edith. I would suppose both women are overwhelmed with how many are in attendance." Mr. Spencer once again glanced over the heads of the bursting throng. "I wonder if it is the draw for Tennyson's reading or the noble cause to help others?" His bright eyes glanced at them as if waiting for an answer.

"I'm quite thrilled to be able to hear the poet recite." Tamsin added, "and, of course the opportunity to make a donation for the suffering families."

She noticed that Professor Spencer's smile was quite like his son's when Harrison interrupted her chain of thought by asking, "May I get you a drink, Father?"

"Ah, thank you. I have it from good authority, Thomas Maybell is here. I want to grasp the opportunity to ask him about his latest tour of Ethiopia." He glanced at them. Tamsin noted his intention already decided when he asked, "You don't mind, do you?"

She held back a giggle at his obvious desire to find his friend. She didn't know him well enough to tease.

Harrison gave his father a leg and waved his arm toward the swarming crowd. "Have at it, sir."

His sire cuffed him on the shoulder. "Ever the jester. Then I'll be off." He winked at Tamsin and turned on his heel and was immediately swallowed up in the throng.

As Tamsin and Harrison were stuffed in the corner of the great hall, he mentioned, "We might not see him the rest of the evening. Let's make our way to the punch bowl. Perhaps we'll find Mother as we move about."

"Your father is a charmer." Her gaze swept his face. "You are graver than he."

"So, I've been told."

Harrison led with Tamsin staying close though his height assured her she would not lose him. She noticed the intricate crown moldings carved with the Greek key only because of their place high on the wall and imagined how lovely the rooms would look if fewer people stood about.

The crowd eased as she followed Harrison toward the

great hall and turned into another parlor. The ceiling was handsomely decorated with details of cherubs circling a large, elegant chandelier in the center. Pictures hung from golden ropes dangling from brass rods a yard or so lower than the ceilings. The mass of invitees kept her from seeing the actual oils.

The strains of violins, flutes, harpsicord, and cello swirled throughout as they eventually came upon a serving table set against the wall. A huge bowl of white sparkling wine was offered up in crystal goblets by a footman dressed in the Hempstead blue livery.

Guests edged down the laden table selecting succulent morsels of shrimp chilled on ice, slices of ham, little sausages wrapped with bacon, pineapple chunks and tiny nuggets of beef in a dark sauce.

"Well, at least we have elbow room." Harrison passed a plate to her and took one for himself.

"Mr. Spencer."

Harrison glanced up to see Barrister Fergus. "Ah. For a moment I thought someone was asking after my father."

"He and I met in passing a few minutes ago." The barrister's gaze shifted to Tamsin.

"Allow me to introduce Miss Tamsin Morgan. She is Basil Walker's niece." Harrison glanced at her. "The barrister is the reason I changed my focus from common law to criminal."

Taking a breath for a moment, she surprisingly noticed how alike her uncle was to this man. Auburn hair, mutton chops. Though her uncle was a bit shorter, and his eyes were green, not blue.

Aware of the esteem Harrison held for this gentleman, she was pleased to finally meet him. "It is an honor, sir."

He smiled and nodded though appeared to be preoccupied. "'Tis a pleasure ta meet ye, Miss Morgan. Your Uncle is a favorite of mine." He glanced above her head for a moment. "Will ye excuse me, miss." His gaze shifted to Harrison. "I've a need to speak with Harrison a moment."

Tamsin nodded in affirmation and tried not to stare. His mutton chops and ruddy skin she thought of as a symbol of strength and authority. The few prominent men she'd taken note of lately embraced the trend. But it was his similarity to her uncle that took her breath away.

The barrister was explaining to Harrison, "I just saw a chap resembling the description ye gave me this morn. If ye will excuse us, Miss Morgan." His glance shifted to her, "I need Harrison ta follow me and see if 'tis the same man I've been looking for. Would ye mind terribly if I take him off?"

She attempted to show concern and narrowed her vision. "Is this work related?"

"We've been caught, Harrison." Fergus chuckled. "Nothing ta worry about, miss. Just a wee look to satisfy me suspicious mind."

"Then you must assure yourself, sir."

Harrison seemed eager to follow the barrister and Tamsin urged, "Don't worry about me. I'll follow and keep tight, so we do not separate." He quickly spun around and tagged after the barrister who, Tamsin concluded, must be working around the clock.

Though she had no recourse other than follow the men, the scent of shrimp and little canapes teased her appetite. She kept pace behind them. The barrister turned to the right and continued down a hall that appeared less occupied. They entered a ballroom, and Tamsin set eyes on Mrs. Reynolds-Walker almost immediately and stepped back into the hall. She had no desire to meet that woman and planted herself in a corner to wait for Harrison.

Curiosity being what it implies, she peeked around the corner to catch a glimpse of her uncle's wife who chatted up a small group. Tamsin recognized one of the women from the visit she made to Madam Patwell's séance parlor.

Glancing into the ballroom again, she noticed the women were still talking, and she had a creepy feeling her disguise at the séance that day hadn't worked. Mrs. Reynolds-Walker must have guessed at her disguise and informed Madam Patwell of her twin. There could be no other explanation for that disastrous revelation.

What did that mean, given Uncle Basil's murder? What is the connection? She could not rule out the ransacking of her uncle's library. A deliberate search for information, no doubt. Oddly enough, however, the Blackbeard file, tucked in the back of a drawer behind a wooden square concealing it properly, had gone unnoticed. It had been in the same position as when she had left it before the robbery.

Tamsin glanced around the corner again noting Harrison standing with the barrister and an elder woman. Harrison was concentrating on something beyond Tamsin's sight line. She stepped into the room quickly, sliding behind a wooden pedestal adorned with a large fern, thinking her gown the same shade of green, she hoped she would go unnoticed. The intensity of his focus bothered her. He looked for something, or someone, and she craned her neck to peek to the far right.

A tall, handsome gentleman with slick black hair, as if he'd oiled it, and a thin mustache, was engaged in conversation with a lovely blonde woman gowned in a Princess dress, made fashionable by the Princess of Wales, so Tamsin had read in *The Daily*.

She smirked, thinking the train a subtle suggestion the wearer was socially above the rank of *walking class*. Tamsin imagined the lovely blonde's satin ensemble dragging the floors and streets. She assumed they were of an age. The oily-haired man appeared much older, she would guess him in his late forties or early fifties.

"Would you care for some refreshment, miss?"

Spooked at the sound of a deep voice, she could barely move, tucked as she was behind the fern.

"What?" And immediately raised her head almost knocking the plant off its platform.

Reaching for the base of the plant as it wobbled, she lost her balance. Thankfully, the footman grabbed hold of her arm.

"Steady, miss. I've got you."

Perfectly stable, tray full of drinks in one hand, and her in his other, he nodded. "Well, done, miss. Step back from the pedestal and all will be as it should."

Mortified, she did as he asked and gained her balance as she backed out from the space between the plant and the wall.

Thankfully, no one seemed to notice the fracas.

He dipped the tray and asked, "Would you care for a drink?" Gentleman enough not to enquire about her wily concealment, his bright eyes laughed at her though his mouth maintained a rigid thin line.

"Thank you. I believe this will steady my nerves after the fright you gave me." Her fingers circled a long-stemmed goblet filled with a bubbly substance, lifted it to her nose to sniff and drank it down in one gulp.

Exactly what she needed, She replaced the empty goblet, took another one and walked off in the opposite direction of the waiter, Mrs. Reynolds-Walker, and the dark-haired man.

Affairs of this kind were not her specialty. She could never claim even a fraction of the *haut ton's* state of elegance and hadn't a notion of what to do next. So, she wandered about the halls among beautiful ladies in gorgeous colorful gowns, noting whose trains swept the floors *ala* Princess of Wales fashion. The air filled with conversations in different languages, French, German, and another she didn't recognize.

Half-way through her second bubbly she felt stifled and flushed. A cursory glance at the far end of the ballroom showed a wall of patio doors shut against the shivery autumn evening.

She followed the sound of music entering a large room where dancers frolicked to the Viennese Waltz. She watched for some minutes as the graceful couples swept and swirled about the ballroom.

"Miss Tamsin. A pleasure to see you."

She spun about recognizing Mrs. Spencer's voice. "As am I to see you. You must be gratified by the attendance."

"We are thankful for the kindness of others to share what they have with those less fortunate." She glanced about. "Why don't I see my son? He should be out there twirling you about."

Tamsin almost giggled. "He might be afraid I would step on his shoes. He is fussy about such things."

Mrs. Spencer's brows scrunched. "He is up to something, isn't he? Tell me the truth, I won't flinch. You know I'm not that kind of mother."

"Perhaps you should hear it from him." A waiter came by and took her empty goblet, offering another which she declined.

"Why isn't he here escorting you? I'll find him and remind him of his duty to you."

"Oh, no. Don't." She quickly scanned the room not seeing a head of curly, sandy colored hair. Tamsin would not be so bold as to tattle on him to his mother. She might not be aware of his involvement in the underbelly of London. Yet, Tamsin thought his mother brilliant, and she *had* raised him. Still, she would not spill the truth about anything he seemed disinclined to tell her himself.

"He excused himself and should be back any moment now."

"Oh. Well, I—"

"Martha, I've been looking everywhere for you. We have more donations than we could have imagined. If you will spare me a few minutes..." She glanced at Tamsin then back at her friend. "I've interrupted your conversation, haven't I?"

"That's fine. Arabella, this is Miss Tamsin Morgan, a friend of Harrison's and the niece of Basil Walker. You would recall him as the Chief of Investigations for Her Majesty, retired now, of course.

"Tamsin, this is my good friend. Arabella Newmann. She is overseeing the donations for the unfortunate families. Are you sure you are fine until Harrison returns?"

"Absolutely," Tamsin replied, smiling at the pair.

"Well. If you will excuse us, duty calls."

"Certainly, and I will tell Harrison you were looking for him."

Her voice trailed off. "We will be in the blue parlor."

She watched as they squeezed into the thickness of guests toward their destination and took refuge in a corner soaking in the display of wealth and the upper classes. As a child, Uncle Basil took her to a Schiller and Mendelssohn Festival. The exceptional harmony began her love of music. She was remembering the festivities, the music, and the gowns the ladies wore as she glanced about the lush rooms, and the opulent decorations.

"Allow me to introduce myself, Mr. Daniel Stow. Would you care to dance, miss?" He made a small bow.

She looked up at a smartly dressed, dark haired man, about Harrison's age. Flustered, she tried not to bark, "No. I would not."

"You are intent on the movements. I noticed your foot tapping."

As awkward as she felt, she hoped he would not pester her. "Perhaps I enjoy the rhythm of the music."

He gazed down at her, his lids closing a teensy bit as if narrowing his sight—almost as if he inspected her through a telescope. "I believe you would rather be out there on the floor."

He appeared to flirt with her. She hadn't the experience of knowing for sure. And where had Harrison gone? Mayhap dancing and enjoying himself for all she knew. He would be in his element here. Most of the people he'd known all his life.

Mr. Stow's attention turned to the musicians; they were about to begin again.

She glanced into his twinkling eyes.

"I am a family friend of our hosts, Mr. and Mrs. Spencer, and of course, the Hampstead's. And I would be pleased to have this dance with you."

"I am afraid you will find me a neophyte." Heat crept up her neck at the admission.

"No worries. This is a slow tempo. Just follow my lead. May I ask your name?"

Someone, Mrs. Spencer perhaps, should initiate an introduction between them. But she had never considered herself a prude, and he had asked her to dance, so she blurted, "Miss Morgan."

He held out his arm and off she went led by a stranger who wanted to dance.

With her.

He turned her about in step to the music calming her fright she would step on his shoes. They parted and came back together in tempo. To her surprise, she had not stumbled and followed him nicely. She concluded Mr. Stow must be an instructor.

"You, Miss Morgan, are a natural. You haven't missed a step."

She felt a dreaded blush. "Thank you." Being shorter than he, she focused on the second button from the top of his vest as he swept her about.

When the music ended, he escorted her off the floor. "Would you care for punch?"

More blushing. "No thank you. I've got to return to my...people."

Stupid. Her artlessness embarrassed her.

He bowed and stepped back. "Thank you for the dance. Perhaps we will meet again and enjoy another turn about the floor."

His twinkling eyes and obvious delight brought a moment of sheer panic. She turned, barely hearing his last words, and headed to the room where she last saw Harrison.

Who was nowhere in sight.

How could she be so alone in a room stuffed with humanity? Feeling awkward in her fancy ruffled dress the color of dill pickles, with her hair piled high, she slowly made her way around the perimeter of the dance floor attempting to throw off the awkward feeling.

Did she feel brainless, and childish? Insecure? Embarrassed?

Yes, to all because she is most definitely uncomfortable.

Pickles, indeed.

Chapter Twenty-Three

"There you are."

She slowly turned to face Harrison.

"Where have you been? I've searched everywhere for you."

He'd left her to fend for herself, most likely off tending to Barrister Fergus' bidding.

Accusingly he grumbled, "Dancing with Daniel Stow? That will get you nowhere in the relationship quarter. He's a rake. Ask anyone." His eyes narrowed in contention. He certainly had a way of dashing a rather fond moment into shards. She felt like pinching his nose, that should wipe the nasty smirk off his face.

All the years she'd known him, he had hardly shown displeasure toward her. Well, strictly speaking, that wasn't entirely true. He had been horridly unsettled when she took on the case of Mrs. Adele Thomson's grandson, Joshua Zillig. She sighed at the fuss *that* caused. Although, the outcome had been worth his distress which put a smile on her face at the thought.

She also recalled he'd been beside himself when she handed him Uncle Basil's Webley Bull Dog revolver. A loaded revolver if she admitted to the truth. The memory caused a giggle at the horrified look on his face.

Perking up she saucily mentioned, "You abandoned me. I thought..."

"Thought what? You could come here and pick up with anyone, ignoring the fact the invitation came from my mother?"

His ghastly remark chased away her giggle. She glared at his knitted brow and pursed lips. She felt like engaging in verbal battle with him. He had no provocation for that remark. Clamping her lips shut should a rebuke fly out unexpectedly, she said not a word, and stalked toward the buffet table leaving him to stew in his own vexation.

What did he take her for, a fool? Besides, he had left her to fend for herself amid this extravaganza.

Ugh.

She noted footmen encouraging folks to the ballroom where chairs had been set up for Tennyson's reading. He certainly earned the title, *darling of poetry*; she'd read that in *The Daily*.

Giving up the idea of the buffet table, she intended to get as close as possible to the dais where Tennyson would be reading and headed in that direction along with a great number of other guests. Enthralled, and feeling childlike at the promise of listening to her favorite poet, she walked up to the front row and took the second to the last single seat. Within moments Mrs. Reynolds-Walker sat next to her.

Oops. Awkward.

She quickly turned to the person on her left, a young woman digging in her reticule and drawing out a lacy handkerchief to pat her forehead. With a quiver in her voice the woman confessed. "I get nervous at large events. Nonetheless, I could not miss out on Lord Tennyson's reading."

Her furtive glance at Tamsin sealed her declaration.

Tamsin mentioned, "I understand how you feel. I could not pass up the opportunity either. I'm Tamsin Mogan."

"Pleased to meet you, miss. Cathy Bligh."

She felt Mrs. Reynolds-Walker's eyes burning into her neck. With intent she kept up the conversation with Miss Bligh, inquiring, "Have you heard him read before?"

"Not at an event like this. I don't travel in his society. I'm here because my great aunt perished in the Bridgewater fire." She dabbed her eye with her frilly handkerchief. "Sorry. I do miss her. She would love to be here with me. I am partly doing this for her because she enjoyed a friendship with Lord Tennyson. He often asked her opinion of his poetry."

Tamsin could hardly express her surprise. To think that she was sitting next to the niece of a friend of Lord Tennyson's.

Miss Bligh said, "He was a regular at our little cottage. A gentleman through and through, nevertheless quite reticent. Though he enjoys reading his poems to a willing audience."

A moment passed and she added. "We were friendly as he lived next door to my grandmother and often sent me snippets of something he had worked on and would ask my opinion."

No longer able to contain her surprise, Tamsin practically gushed. "What an honor you must feel."

Cathy Bligh's attention went to her hands wringing the handkerchief. "Not really. I cannot find fault with anything he creates, so I am uncertain I did him any favors."

The young women quieted as Mrs. Spencer and Mrs. Hempstead walked to the front of the room, attempting to quiet the crowd. Tamsin smiled at her new friend, endeavoring to ease her anxiety, what with Mrs. Reynolds-Walker sitting within inches of her right elbow.

Mrs. Hempstead began the introduction. "Lord Tennyson has generously agreed to read to us this evening donating his time in an effort to increase the proceeds to be distributed amongst the families suffering the loss of loved ones."

She then turned to Mrs. Spencer, who added, "We are honored that the esteemed Lord Tennyson's schedule brings him to London. He graces us with a reading of several of his latest, and an early favorite, *The Lady of Shalott.* Delightful verses dedicated to the memories of our dearly beloved family members who perished in the boating fire on the fifth of July."

Lord Tennyson, a man in his early sixties, tall, and hand-some had requested a comfortable chair on the platform from which he intended reading. It created an appropriate back-drop for the sensitive nature of the gathering. As if each person listening had an exclusive reason to be in the chamber with him.

A hush fell over the room as his Lincolnshire burr spilled out over the crowd. He announced his first reading, *Far-Far Away.*

After much appreciation for his first reading, he announced another favorite, *The Charge of the Light Brigade.*

Finished with the poem about self-sacrifice and heroism, he paused a moment sipping from a glass of water before saying, "My next reading is *Lady of Shalott,*" which earned more than a few hand claps.

Finished with the epic poem, he announced, "I have one last poem written for this occasion and dedicated to all those lost to us on the fifth of July. *An Ode to Hearts Lost.*

The room quieted once again and his burr began with a poem about loved ones who wander in a garden smelling the scent of the flowers, walking arm in arm with new-made friends as they travel the journey Our Lord has created for all of us.

It was a good half hour or more before his Lincolnshire

voice lingered over the last few words of goodbye for all 481 loved ones, together with the captain and crew of 12 who are now resting in peace with the Lord.

You could hear a pin drop in the large room until someone choked on a sob. Lord Tennyson had not moved from his chair, a finger of his hand still on the page where he had read the poignant eulogy.

It suddenly came to Tamsin the meaning of this gathering for everyone in attendance. Not one of these mourners had had the privilege of saying goodbye to their loved one. This wise and wonderful gentleman had given them a tribute to cherish with his gift of poetry.

No one moved. Cathy Bligh held her lacy handkerchief to her nose. Her bright eyes swimming in unshed tears she glanced at Tamsin and whispered, "Thank you for sitting beside me."

Tamsin patted Cathy's hand hoping to soothe her as both young women stood and gathered their programs. Footmen were passing out copies of the reading, beautifully done with a lacy scrollwork of gold ink embellishing the date and the title, *An Ode to Hearts Lost*

Enthralled, Cathy wore a look of pure devotion on her pretty round face.

In the same moment, Mrs. Reynolds-Walker stood smoothing out her skirt and Tamsin was forced to recognize her presence. "Miss Tamsin. Your sympathy for the unfortunate families is enduring."

"And your empathy is gracious." The last time she'd set eyes on her uncle's wife they were at the séance. Mrs. Reynolds-Walker's pinched features caused her mouth to pucker as if she'd swallowed a lemon.

Tamsin drew on her gloves wondering what to do next. Mourners approached the dais where Lord Tennyson now stood. Cathy Bligh leaned close. "Would it seem bold of me to talk to him?"

Mrs. Reynolds-Walker inserted herself in the exchange. "I dare say, not if you lost a member of your family in the fire."

Seeing as the woman thrust herself into their conversation, Tamsin introduced them. "Miss Cathy Bligh, Mrs. Reynolds-Walker. Cathy's great aunt perished in the fire."

"Please accept my condolences." She folded her copy of the poem and stuffed it in her reticule.

Knowing the depth of Cathy's friendship with the poet, Tamsin offered, "Come Cathy. I'll stand in line with you."

Cathy showed signs of grieving, and with a quivering smile said, "You are too kind."

Stepping ahead of Mrs. Reynolds-Walker, Tamsin took Cathy's elbow, and they walked toward the dais where the great poet received gratitude and expressions of appreciation for his reading.

From a distance, Tamsin side-glanced at Mrs. Reynolds-Walker who talked to her female companion. Tamsin did not recognize the woman.

Sunday, 9:00 p.m.
2 October 1870

Harrison waved at Tamsin hoping to catch her attention. She and another young woman finished talking to Lord Tennyson and left the dais. He stepped up intending to talk to her when the barrister cut into his line of trajectory with narrowed vision honed on him. He had obviously discovered something from the exasperating scrunch on his face and needed Harrison's attention.

Harrison glanced a moment at Tamsin, and she realized he was technically working for the barrister when Fergus whispered, "I've got it on good authority who might have authored last night's gun fight." His wary gaze looked over the crowd.

Tamsin nodded to him and left in Cindy's direction.

Harrison murmured to Fergus, "You want to discuss it here?"

Fergus' brows scrunched as he leaned in. "I recall ye distinctly mentioning slicked-back oily hair, and a slim mustache. That is what ye said, right?"

"I did."

"Can ye tell me if he's here?" Fergus raised his head glancing about the large room.

Harrison tried not to show his ire. He knew she was miffed at him. Yet he felt obligated to identify the greasy-haired, thin mustached man.

"Shall I stroll about and look for him?"

"Hold on, let's think this through. Ye are certain he has no reason to recognize ye, right?" Fergus set his libation on a table.

"Right."

"Well, then, let's amble about the rooms and find the chap. And ye tell me if he's the one in the carriage last night. Don't approach him, do nothing that would allow him to get suspicious."

"Right, sir."

The barrister's eye lids lowered, a sure sign he intended to toss a sarcastic bone or two at him. "And cut the *sir*, it's a clear giveaway ye're on the clock."

The next twenty minutes or so, Harrison, drink in hand, slowly moved about the rooms and halls. He nodded and every so often stopped to have a casual word or two with acquaintances. About to enter a small room next to the ballroom, his three sisters approached. Missy said, "We have been looking for you. Mama said you arrived. We hoped you brought your delightful friend, Miss Tamsin."

He craned his neck. "She is here somewhere."

Sissy challenged her brother. "I thought you would keep her close. Otherwise, I predict you may lose her. And that does not bode well for us. We like her. More so than the redhead you brought to lunch a month ago."

His brows knitted. "You need to button up."

Sissy giggled when Prissy interfered. "The redhead was two months ago. And her name was—"

"That's enough, Prissy."

With serious business at hand, the chatter of his sisters vexed him. "Can we not discuss my private life in public?" His eyes narrowed on both girls who quickly smothered their lips with gloved hands lest he hear their titters.

Their merriment cut into his mission, irritating him. He gazed at the outer area where he immediately spotted his prey. A black-haired gentleman with a thin mustache dressed in a perfectly fitted tuxedo stood across the room. His thoughts immediately went to last night's bloodshed on the docks and hiding behind a large bush kneeling on damp rotten leaves as the man nearly pissed in his face.

As the crowd parted, he had a full view of the gentleman. Unquestionably, he matched the description of the person Fergus sought—even to his highly polished leather patents.

Cutting off the conversation with his snickering sisters, he excused himself and went in pursuit of the Scot finding him at a banquet table filling his plate.

"He is here."

Fergus, plate in one hand and a large spoon filled with potatoes in the other as he stood in the buffet table, had a look

241

of bother on his face, said, "Well, there goes a perfectly good meal."

Harrison offered a possibility. "I think he's here for the duration. He didn't look ready to leave."

Grumbling, the barrister turned away from the banquet table, handing his partially filled plate to a footman, then barked at Harrison. "Where?"

"In the archway of the ballroom. You won't have a problem identifying him. He looks exactly as you described."

Within minutes both men stood with their backs against the snap and crackle of the fireplace enjoying the scent of apple wood, and casually glancing about the room.

"On the left, the curved hallway. He is talking to a woman in blue, with a feather in her hair."

Fergus turned ever so slowly, and drank from his goblet, then turned back to Harrison. "Are you absolutely sure it's the same person?"

"I'd swear to it." Harrison's attention returned to the crackling fire.

"You've just confirmed one of the biggest opium dealers in London."

"What's his name?"

"Desmond De la Croix. And if my sources are correct, that's his fiancée. The one with a feather in her hair. Undoubtedly an American. Her father is under surveillance for illegal importing. The authorities in New York have contacted Scotland Yard and are keeping an eye on Earl Horwrath. My guess is De la Croix and Horwrath want to keep their fortunes in the family with the marriage."

A bit puzzled, Harrison asked, "I don't understand. If he's one of the kingpins, why didn't you consider him when investigating this current situation?"

Fergus glanced around the hall where they stood and lowered his voice. "It's a long story. The Commissioner asked me ta investigate the opium problem. It's why I had ye and Mickey inspect the docks. In the meantime, the Commissioner decided we were barking up the wrong tree and scratched him off the list. He thought De la Croix wouldn't involve himself in something this small."

"From the number of crates unloaded last night, I'd say it qualified as a good-sized operation."

The barrister looked long and hard at Harrison, as if he were considering something. "It appears as though De la Croix's business is growing worldwide without any obstruction. We've been aware of his connections in New York. He's got backing, no doubt about it."

Harrison's jaw dropped. "Someone is aiding him? A powerful someone?"

Fergus scratched his jaw, and Harrison suddenly remembered something Garrity asked him. "A week or so ago, Garrity wanted to know if I knew a De la Croix."

"And do ye?"

"You just told me his monicker. I've never met him."

The men dropped the conversation as Tamsin made her way toward them. The newly harvested remarks his sisters shared about liking her took up space in his head, pushing Fergus' criminal investigation out of his mind.

Stepping into their little circle, she inquired of the barrister, "I hope you've solved your mystery and are able to enjoy yourself."

"Perhaps not as much as ye. I saw ye at the reading. I suspect ye're partial to the poet." His grimace widened into a rare smile.

"Tennyson is a favorite." She turned to Harrison. "Were you able to spare a few minutes with Lord Tennyson? I understand your mother thinks the world of him."

"Doesn't everyone." His disenchanting remark caused her to grimace, and he quickly added, "Unfortunately, I was attending my sisters. They asked after you, by the way. You'll have to tell me all about Tennyson when we are in the carriage. Apparently, I am behind the times when it comes to poetry."

She tried not to laugh that his sisters knew more about the famous poet than he did. Somehow it seemed natural that he wouldn't. "That I will do. Now, if you'll excuse me," she nodded to the barrister, "I promised a friend I would accompany her to the donation table."

"Miss Morgan, spare a moment, please." Fergus gave her one of his unusual smiles.

She arched an eyebrow.

"Have you ever heard your uncle mention the name De la Croix?"

"I can't say as he did. It's not familiar a'tall."

The Scottish barrister glanced across the large room at De la Croix and his fiancée. They certainly were popular. His future bride was a lovely young thing, very gay and lively.

Almost as an afterthought, he asked, "Please keep the name De la Croix between us for now."

Nodding, she went off in the direction of the donation room where Cathy Bligh waited.

On her way, Tamsin mulled over the name De la Croix. The question toyed with her memory, but nothing sparked. And, yet for some reason the name did sound familiar. Would Uncle Basil have had dealings with the man?

She overheard Harrison asking his mother how she happened to know De la Croix, and she said through charity work. She hadn't an opinion of him other than he appeared egocentric.

Chapter Twenty-Four

O n the other side of the ballroom, Tamsin and Cindy stood in line slowly making their way toward the table where they intended to donate to the Charity Fund. Tamsin noticed Mrs. Reynolds-Walker's hand shaking and inquired, "Are you ill? What's wrong?"

The woman opened her beaded purse and shoved a wad of money at Tamsin. "Please indulge me. Place this contribution for me. I'm queasy and need to go to the refreshing room. Will you be good enough to bring me my receipt? I'll wait for you there."

Without waiting for a reply, she left giving Tamsin no time to refuse. She watched as the woman slipped through an opening the servants were using to navigate a quick passage to the kitchen.

"Is there a problem?" asked Cathy.

"I'm not sure. She isn't feeling well, and she handed me this." She showed Cathy the wad of banknotes. "She wants me to donate this in her name and mentioned she would wait in the refreshing room for her receipt."

"That looks like quite a lot of money. You must be good friends for her to ask you to do this."

"I'm mystified. And rest assured, we are certainly not friendly." She glanced at Cathy. "I haven't a clue how much she is donating. Should I count it?"

Cathy glanced at the wad of banknotes clutched in Tamsin's hand. "It looks as though they are counting each donation as it is received," easing Tamsin's mind, as she continued, "do you know if Mrs. Reynolds-Walker lost someone in the disaster?"

"No. I really don't know her well."

Nearly an hour passed, and Harrison's anxiety was increasing by the minute. At least half the several hundred in attendance had said their goodbyes, the halls were less crowded. The musicians had retired to the kitchen where they were no doubt being fed.

Prissy and Sissy approached him asking the whereabouts of Miss Morgan, and he had been forced to admit he had no idea. Though he knew she must be somewhere in the mansion. After all, they were riding together.

It neared ten thirty and had been a long day, and after last night, and his meeting with Fergus that had lasted until one in the morning, he was more than ready to surrender to a quiet evening at his lodgings.

He walked into the front parlor, then a smaller parlor, and finally the library. Tamsin couldn't be found. He had no idea other than she took another ride home. His twisted thoughts went to Daniel Stow. Had he offered and she agreed? Surely, she would have said something to him.

His mother approached, thanking him for attending and staying through the entire occasion. She inquired about Miss Morgan, and he felt a bit shy that he did not know where she had got to.

She added, "We are not leaving for another half hour. Your father and Mr. Newmann are working with The Bank of England representatives. Then we will be on our way."

More attendees left and the crowd dwindled to less than fifty. He made one more lap through the halls and rooms, even asking a maid to check the refreshment room for Tamsin Morgan; the maid affirmed the room was vacant.

He had not paid her much attention this evening. Thanks to Fergus.

It occurred to him she might have left in a snit. She wanted to talk earlier, and he mentioned there would be time enough when they were in the carriage to catch up on the evening's events. Thinking of it now, he'd sounded rude, possibly giving her reason to find another carriage home.

Retrieving his coat and hat, he decided to have the driver take the route to Portman Square. He mentioned looking for a friend of his, a young woman in a blue cape, who might have left the party early. The driver had argued about it being late and a heavy mist taking over, what woman would walk in such a mire?

Harrison did not want to explain about Miss Morgan being a modern woman and all that entailed. Most elderly men would bristle at her unseemly behavior.

Arriving at #2 Berkeley Street, he scrambled out of the cab and took the steps two at a time. Mrs. T answered the bell with a smile on her face, that slowly turned to alarm as Harrison began.

"Please tell me Miss Tamsin has arrived."

"No, sir. Wasn't she with you this evening?"

Harrison stepped inside and took off his hat. "I couldn't find her. I assumed she left before me. I hoped she would be home." His hazel eyes scanned the foyer and a long breath escaped.

Mrs. T's palm went to her lips, her eyes darkened with concern.

"It is a misunderstanding, Mrs. T. Don't think the worst. I will figure out where she is and have her returned to you."

"When did you notice her missing?"

"Oh, maybe half past nine or there about. With the commotion and all, maybe a bit later. I waited until most of the guests were gone. I know she is not at Hempstead's. And I cannot figure out who she would have left with. It seems out of sorts for her. We had plans to return here together."

Mrs. T swayed slightly, and Harrison took her by the elbow and directed her to the parlor. "Mr. Basil and now this." She choked on her words.

"Don't go there. It's a simple case of confusion. That's all." He stood over her as she caught her breath. "I will retrace my steps to Hempstead's and see if she returned there for any reason."

"Get word to me immediately."

"The next time you see me, she will be in hand. I promise."

Harrison immediately left and directed the driver to Hempstead's estate. Upon entering their home, he explained to the butler his reason for returning and wondered if Miss Morgan had shown up.

Harrison's mother and Mrs. Hempstead were walking out of the large parlor arm in arm, laughing, when they noticed him. "Did you forget something, dear?"

"Well, oddly, yes. Miss Tamsin. I cannot seem to find her. Do you recall her talking to anyone in particular?"

Mrs. Hempstead spoke up. "A Miss Bligh. They sat together during Lord Tennyson's reading. They seemed to take a liking to each other. Miss Bligh is a very shy young woman. Her grandmother was a favorite of Tennyson's. They were neighbors, perhaps you know this."

"No. I did not. Would you know how I might get in touch with Miss Bligh?"

His mother said, "Miss Morgan never gave me a reason to think her irresponsible. Are you overwrought? Your father tells me you have been working late into the night."

He turned an arrogant stare at his mother. "Me, overwrought? This is a young woman who defies weakness and cares a great deal for her friends. Which is why I am questioning her going off without a word. It's not at all like her."

Mrs. Hempstead rang for the butler and asked him to find her book of addresses. When he returned, she opened the page explaining, "Miss Bligh stays with family when she is in town. I have their address." She wrote the information down and handed the paper to him.

"Thank you. I would be remiss not to mention how gratifying of you to open your home to all the families and friends of those who died. It allowed everyone an opportunity to mourn and to hear Lord Tennyson's soothing eulogy. I was honored to be a part of it."

With that, he excused himself and spun about practically running to the door.

The ride took fifteen minutes until he knocked on the wooden door where Miss Bligh was staying. The door opened, and hat in hand, he handed his card to the woman.

She read the card and looked up at him. "You are Harrison Spencer?"

"Yes, Ma'am."

She widened the door for him to step inside. "What can I do for you, sir?" She swiped her hand on her apron looking as if she was making rounds before going to her bed.

"I understand Miss Cathy Bligh is staying with you. We were both at a memorial service today, and I am looking for a mutual friend, Miss Morgan. She sat with Miss Bligh. I would like to ask her a few questions if I may."

"It's right late, sir. I dunno. Wait here."

He immediately wondered what his next step would be if she refused to see him.

Within minutes, Miss Bligh showed him into the parlor. She took a chair, and he followed suit. "Is there a problem? Is Miss Tamsin alright?"

"I was told you sat with her at Lord Tennyson's reading. She and I rode to the memorial together and when I looked for her to leave, I couldn't find her anywhere. I checked with the housekeeper at her home, and she had not returned. It is unusual for her not to do as she says."

Miss Bligh inquired, "You must be hoping I know her whereabouts?"

"Well, as far as I know you were the last in conversation with her."

"That isn't exactly true. Mrs. Reynolds-Walker engaged her as we all stood in line to make our donation. The woman appeared quite upset and asked Miss Tamsin if she would make the donation for her and meet her in the refreshing room when she was done to give her a receipt for the donation."

A soft-spoken young woman, with cinnamon-colored hair, Miss Bligh cupped her hands. "I am not one for gossip. On the other hand, Mrs. Reynolds-Walker gave her a large number of banknotes all rolled together, and as Miss Tamsin was concerned for the woman...I mean to say, it was quite noticeable that she was overly agitated about something. Miss Tamsin's obvious concern led her to be most helpful toward the woman."

Harrison drew a breath. His thoughts scattered in several directions. "You mean to say, Miss Tamsin made the donation for Mrs. Reynolds-Walker and then went off to the refreshment room to give her the receipt?"

"Exactly. We said our goodbyes with a promise to have tea within the week. It was the last I saw of her."

He quickly turned, hat in hand. "Thank you for the information. I certainly don't mean to alarm you. I'm sure everything is fine. Tamsin most likely stayed with Mrs. Reynolds-Walker to be sure she was taken care of. I will not take up any more of your time. I know it is quite late."

They walked to the front door where he took his leave.

Jumping in the hack, he wasn't sure where to go. Mrs. Reynolds-Walker's home, or Tamsin's. He felt he might have been overreacting when explaining to Miss Bligh and suddenly felt quite silly. Tamsin knew how to take care of herself. With that thought in mind, he ordered the driver to return him to Portman Square.

Mrs. T and he were in the hall when he felt a web of angst hover over him. "I cannot stop from concerning myself. She certainly is not compelled to keep me informed about her whereabouts. She would reproach me, no doubt. When I heard it was Mrs. Reynolds-Walker to whom she last talked, well..."

"We both know her disdain for the woman. It's not difficult to think of Mrs. Reynolds-Walker's wicked frame of mind toward our girl."

Our girl.

When did he feel responsible for her? Why should he feel accountable, other than she was Basil's niece, and Basil had a profound love for the daughter of his deceased sister.

Harrison knew Tamsin to be strong, and of stern character. She did not suffer fools readily. He glanced out the window overlooking the front lawn and the gate at the end of the walk illuminated with the golden glow from the streetlight. Clarity had him recalling the night Basil died and the gate that swung open. Tamsin had told him this, and the two glasses of poison, one half empty, the other full.

Mrs. T asked, "What if Mrs. Reynolds-Walker lured Tamsin to her home?"

Becoming more agitated by the moment, he glared, "Why would you think she was lured? She could have gone on her own. Miss Bligh mentioned Mrs. Reynolds-Walker appeared ill and had to leave the premises. She had given Tamsin her donation and asked that she bring her the receipt when done. Miss Bligh saw her hand it to Miss Tamsin and thought it a rather large stack of banknotes."

Mrs. T rung her hands. "It's probably nothing. Yet, I cannot seem to relieve myself of Master Basil's murder and now--"

"Don't say it." His arm shot upward, palm facing the elder. "The only plausible thing to do is go to Mrs. Reynolds-Walker's residence."

"I agree, Mr. Harrison. I want to accompany you, except it might seem eccentric with the housekeeper trailing along behind."

A sheepish smile appeared on his face. "As if I am incompetent?"

"I would never accuse you of that."

"It is late. Not a good time to drop in on someone you don't have much regard for."

"I implore you to come straight back here. I will not be able to breathe easy until you do."

Donning his hat, he jumped in the coach and ordered the driver to #14 Bedford Square. He drew out his fob; it was far too late when he dropped a brass lionhead hard against the front-door knocker.

The butler took his card and left him standing in the foyer. Within a minute, he returned and put him in the front parlor. "Madam will be with you shortly."

Harrison stepped to the large bay window overlooking

the lawn. A shaft of the new October moon beamed through the nearly bare oak limbs looking like long gnarly fingers.

Her home appeared comfortable with all the accoutrements of a mid-century structure. His memory of when she wed Basil came back to him. Tamsin was a young child at the time. It had been obvious she would have liked a mother figure; however, that turned out to be impossible for Mrs. Reynolds-Walker. Basil never shared his feelings about the marriage, legal yet incomplete.

The pad of her steps on the marble floor alerted him to her arrival.

"Mr. Spencer, you have chosen a horrid hour to knock at my door." She entered the parlor patting a strand of hair that had escaped its mooring. She breathed heavily, as if she'd run from the opposite direction of the house.

"I'm here because I understand you gave Miss Morgan a great deal of money this evening to put toward the donation for the families of the victims?"

She let out a breath of air. "Why, yes. Are you an emissary come to thank me at this late hour?"

He flapped his hat against his leg. "I'm hoping you relate what Miss Morgan's conversation was with you?"

She waved him to sit as she took a chair. "May I offer you a drink? Whiskey, scotch?"

He continued standing. "No. It appears Miss Morgan may be missing. What I need from you is your last conversation with her."

She patted her hair again. "Oh, well, easy enough. I felt faint and asked her to make my donation for me. I know her to be trustworthy, and I needed to leave the lineup."

"What exactly did you say to her?" He stood at the end of the divan near the chair she'd taken. The tip of her shoe tapped against the carpet.

"Only that I requested she take my banknotes and make the deposit for me, then bring me the receipt."

"How long did it take her to do your bidding?"

"She never showed. I stayed for a while. More time than I thought necessary considering I did not feel well, and then I left. I needed to return home. Just now I thought you were she with my receipt."

He eyed her attempting to see tension. "Did she say anything suggesting she had somewhere else to go?"

"Not that I recall." Her fingers tapped on the end of the chair arms, as if he had interrupted something important.

"If you should hear from her, will you let me know?"

"Where would I send a note?"

"Mr. Walker's residence should suffice."

His gaze hardened on her. "It appears you have recovered from your ailment earlier this evening. How fortunate." He smiled at her and let himself out.

Once outside, Harrison walked toward the south and snuck into a dark area of bushes and trees circling at the rear of Mrs. Reynolds-Walker's residence. He stood in the dark outside the stable listening, for what he knew not.

If he were to return to the Hempstead's estate, he could inquire if Mrs. Reynolds-Walker's donation had been made, that would ensure what Tamsin's last effort was. Though he felt Miss Bligh would have made mention of that fact.

A nicker came from the stable.

He guessed there would be one horse whose duty was with a carriage and a trot on Rotten Row. There should be a groom in charge, and he knocked on the door, conveniently ajar. No answer. He stepped inside the stable a lit lantern at the far end apprising him that someone worked nearby.

"Hello."

"Anyone home?" He gained a few steps toward the lantern when the groom came into focus.

"Lookin' for somethin'?"

"Yes, a carriage that transported Mrs. Reynolds-Walker to the Memorial Service this evening."

"And who might ye be?" The lad lifted the lantern.

Harrison guessed him to be no more than fifteen at most, and of slight build. "I'm sorry to bother you. I was at the same affair and seemed to have lost my gloves as I escorted Mrs. Reynolds-Walker to her carriage."

The lad looked him over and came to a decision. "Follow me." They walked to the end of the stable. There were three stalls, two of them empty, attesting to a less prosperous time. He noted the carriage at the end of the stable.

"Ye can see, sir, 'tis small. Take the lantern and have a look."

"They are my favorites, or I wouldn't be so fussy." Harrison opened the door and held the light high, looking for anything he could find that might be Tamsin's. A handkerchief, a glove.

"No luck. I appreciate your allowing me to look."

"Right, sir. I knowed their hands was full of the miss who was poorly."

Without reacting Harrison handed him the lantern. "Yes, the dark-haired woman in the blue cape. I hope she feels better soon." He turned away, then looked back. "There was no need to fetch a doctor, was there?"

The groom, busy untangling a lengthy rope shook his head. "Nay, sir, looked more like she was sleepin'. I could tell m'lady worried over her."

"How so?"

"I had ta fetch the butler who carried her into the house. M'lady told me not to worry about the lass as she'd fallen and hurt herself. She assured me the lass would be right as rain in no time, or she would've sent me for the doctor."

Harrison left the stable and walked toward the road in

case the groom stood watch. He turned and looked at the house for a minute or two assessing the probability of entering.

They brought her here and that meant she was inside, no doubt about it. And, kept against her will, probably drugged. He winced at the ire she would spew once it wore off.

Crossing over to the other side of the street he ran past several houses where his driver waited.

He puzzled over why Mrs. Reynolds-Walker seized her. Tamsin wasn't wealthy. Well, she would certainly fall into a great deal of wealth. Mrs. Reynolds-Walker wouldn't be privy to that...

...unless she knew for certain Basil was dead. And if she knew he was dead, she would likely assume Tamsin would come between her and Basil's wealth.

Suddenly ideas took on possibilities. He let out a worried breath. Tamsin had said all along Mrs. Reynolds-Walker murdered her uncle. Could she be right?

As Harrison approached the waiting gig, he laid out a plan.

Chapter Twenty-Five

A bat flew over as Harrison leaned toward the driver, a dense fog circled the ground. "I'm in a bit of a fix and need your assistance. I'll pay extra if you agree to an odd request."

The driver, reins curled about the break-stick, cupped his hand over the piece of wood. He'd been employed through the evening and Harrison remembered him from several trips over the past months. "Whatcha got in mind?"

"I will pay triple for the use of your cab until I am done sometime late this night."

His red-rimmed eyes gleamed in the light of the lantern hanging from the cab. "Whatcha up ta, mister? I'll not be part of anythin' dangerous or thievery. I've got a family depends on me wages."

"I'll honor that, sir."

"Tell me what yer up ta? I'll not be lied ta, so beware." He tightened his fist about the break-stick.

Harrison stood near the cab and leaned closer so as not to shout. "This will sound harebrained. I swear it's God's truth. A friend of mine, a young lady, has been nabbed and held for God only knows why, maybe ransom. I've got to rescue her tonight before they decide to hide her somewhere else, or worse, which they're capable of. And you are the only person with a cab who I can ask to assist me."

"Where's she now?"

"In that home three down on the right that I just came from."

"An yer sure she's there?" His eyes narrowed as he considered Harrison's proposal. Harrison couldn't fault the man. After all the circumstance was highly unusual, and worthy of suspicion.

"As sure as I can be. The stableboy as much as told me so without knowing what he was revealing. By the by, I'm Harrison Spencer, studying for my law degree. And God's breath, I hope I don't get caught."

"Yer not sneakin' off ta git hitched, are ye now?" His face was bright with mischief. "I know all about Gretna Green, I do. Got inta a bit of a mess with a couple months back and swore I'd cut off a hand before I'd ever get caught doin' wrong again."

The cabbie's story threw him for a loop. "I'm thinking nothing of the sort, sir. I'd laugh if I weren't so worried about this young woman. She is the niece of my dear friend Basil Walker."

"He's The Queen's detective?"

"The very one."

"Why ain't he troublin' himself? Why's it ye?"

"He happens to be in India."

The driver cast a squinted glance at him as he weighed

his decision. "I'll take ye for an honest man, Mr. Spencer. Because I've driven Mr. Walker many a time. Ye can call me Samuel. So, what's first?"

Harrison took off his outer coat and hat, tossing them on the seat. "I'm going to find my way into the house and search for her. I suspect she is in an upstairs room. I believe they've got her doped, so they will not worry she would escape."

"Ye know all this?"

"I'm guessing."

"Take me knife just in case."

Harrison reached for the steel blade, sheathing it. "You are prepared for anything. Hopefully I will have no need of it." Off he went slithering around the back of #14.

The lights were off except for the front parlor. He tried the kitchen door to find it locked and strained to lift a window in a bank of windows to the left. The second one was unlatched, and he slowly lifted it and waited to see if anyone in the house heard him.

Nothing.

As his vision adjusted to the dark, the embers from a fire and a foggy beam from the moon assisted him. A convenient bench beneath the open window allowed him to crawl through and stand on the slate floor. He took off his shoes, leaving them near the door, and slowly made his way toward the front of the house where the light from the parlor aided him with a faint glow onto the foyer and steps leading to the second floor.

Peeking around the wall from where the lamp shone, Mrs. Reynolds-Walker sat at one end of a divan. Her head leaned against the upholstered back as she softly snored. He noted a nearly finished glass of amber liquid on the table in front of her.

He hoped it had been a triple scotch straight up.

A faint glow of the parlor lamp spilled out onto the foyer

aiding his ascent on the stairs. He hoped the woman lived alone as he quickly looked in each bedroom. Of the three he'd opened there were no signs of Tamsin, and he crossed the hall toward the fourth door. No Tamsin.

The next door turned out to be a small closet, linens perhaps, and his foot bumped up against a bundle on the floor. A yellow glow from the light spilled out from the parlor and through the balusters. He stood quietly for a moment sensing the sleeping household when he felt a puddle of warmth at the tips of his stocking feet.

Dropping to his knees, he groped the bundle. By God. Tamsin, gagged and bound in a lump on the floor and unconscious.

He whispered in her ear. "Tamsin, it's Harrison. Can you hear me?"

No response. What he didn't want was for her to moan, or suddenly scream.

His fingers probed for rope knots on her legs and hands untying the thick hemp as she softly moaned. He left the scarf that gagged her in case she might scream.

"It's me, Harrison. Don't make a sound, do you hear?"

"...head."

"I've got you. Don't make a sound."

He lifted her in his arms, thankful for her lithe frame.

Halfway down the stairs, the glow of the light in the parlor shifted. He hoped Mrs. Reynolds-Walker had passed out, and continued down the stairs, one step at a time. The house creaked here and there with a wind that had begun. A step from the bottom he stopped, hoping to round the corner and get to the kitchen.

The glow from the parlor appeared to have dimmed further. Could it be running low on fuel? Mrs. Reynolds-Walker hadn't awakened. Tamsin was beginning to weigh heavy in his arms and he turned into the hall toward the kitchen. It was tricky, but he bent over and nabbed his shoes without dropping her, then snuck out the door. He walked in stocking feet away from the house into the thicket of bushes and trees and out onto the road where Samuel waited.

In the carriage, he laid Tamsin on the bench and put on his shoes. She moaned when he took her in his arms.

"Seems as though it went well." Samuel snapped the reins, forcing his horse to trot.

Harrison ran a fist through his hair and smiled into the darkness glancing at Samuel's back. "Without your help, this rescue would not have been possible. I'll put her in the hands of her housekeeper. Mrs. T will take good care of her."

"Seems that's what ye've done, govn'r."

Tuesday, 10:00 a.m.
4 October 1870

Harrison woke with a start and grabbed his watch. Nearing ten o'clock, he'd nearly slept the morning away.

The memory of last night rushed at him and he jumped off the divan realizing he was in the parlor of Basil's home, and a wrinkled mess. He immediately thought of Tamsin and adjusted his vest and ascot, then went looking for Mrs. T. He didn't have far to go. She had her hand on the parlor door-knob when he reached out to open it.

"I hope you are somewhat refreshed, Mr. Harrison."

"I'll do for now. Have you been up to see her?"

"She's groggy and goes in and out of sleep."

"I've got to report to the barrister. Fergus must be in a sweat by now."

Mrs. T inquired, "Can you spare a moment for coffee and a slice of pie at least?"

"Tempting, but no. I've got to go. I suggest you bring Charlie into the house." He snapped his fingers with a thought. "Better yet, I'll stay here and send a note to Fergus. Can you spare one of your girls to run an errand?"

"Certainly."

He went to the library and wrote a quick note explaining the situation, certain the barrister would instantly react to the kidnapping of Miss Tamsin.

"Malcolm Fergus has the authority to post guards and will do so the minute he is informed of last night's doings. You will have protection within the hour."

"I'll send Sally to you. And have Cook fix a proper breakfast."

"Mrs. T?"

She turned about on her way to the kitchen. "Yes?"

"I would like to see her."

Her face softened. "Certainly. We will go up after I talk to Cook and the maid."

Sally tied the ends of her modest cap beneath her chin and pulled her cloak over her shoulders, then appeared at the library door just as Harrison finished blotting, folding, and sealing the information about last night. "You are to go to Lincoln Inn, second floor, and ask for Barrister Fergus. Hand this only to him. None other. If he should be in court, wait for him." He handed her the letter. "Thank you, Sally."

She gave a small curtsy and spun promptly on her way.

Mrs. T returned to the library and took Harrison upstairs to Tamsin's chamber. As the door swung wide, there sat Tamsin leaning against the headboard swathed in a shawl, her dark hair brushed off her shoulders and tied with a ribbon. The small grin she offered was practically hidden by the huge dark circles under her eyes.

"You sure gave me a fright last night. How are you feeling?" Harrison stepped close to the bed, not taking his eyes off her.

"Stiff and drowsy. Mrs. T tells me I owe my rescue to you?" Her sapphire eyes lacked her usual twinkle. It grieved him that such a vibrant woman came up against a ruthless scourge.

"Am I to understand Mrs. Reynolds-Walker lured you to her home, and drugged you?"

"Yes. She feinted at being unwell and asked me to escort her to her carriage. Someone grabbed me and that's the last I recall."

"Miss Bligh helped me put the pieces together."

Tamsin laid her head back against the headboard and closed her eyes. Her voice sounded weak. "Yes. We were in line. She heard the conversation."

He glanced at Mrs. T. "I will be downstairs waiting for the guards."

"Before you go," asked the housekeeper as she drew back the covers, "will you lift her to a more comfortable position down on the bed so she can rest her head on the pillow. He slid his arms under her and in the blink of an eye moved her. She was warm and he was reminded of last eve when he carried her to Samuel's carriage.

Chapter Twenty-Six

Tuesday, noon
4 October 1870

S ally burst through the front door, breath heaving in and out. "Your Barrister Fergus is on his way, sir." She tore off her cloak spluttering, "You must be a very important man, Mr. Spenser. Half-way through reading your post, he was barking at everyone to do this, do that."

"Thank you, Sally. You've done your mistress a grand assist."

He plopped in a comfortably padded chair in the parlor and rested the back of his head. Within seconds his eyes shut.

A far away voice barked, "Ye're neglectful in yer duty lad."

Harrison's eyes opened, then widened as he realized who had spoken. He jumped out of the chair brushing the sleeves on his jacket.

The smell of strong coffee honed his senses. He laid eyes on Barrister Fergus who smirked, "Sleeping on the job, aye?"

Harrison drew his fob out noting the time of a quarter past noon.

A Bobbie, dressed in his fine blue uniform, entered the parlor, and handed Fergus a sheaf of papers murmuring low. Harrison caught the name Basil Walker and saw through the gauzy curtained windows facing the street where three more of London's finest stood on the walk outside the gate. The maid brought in a tray of coffee and scones and set them on the table. She handed Harrison a cup with his required two lumps of sugar then backed out of the parlor.

Harrison noted Fergus didn't miss the familiarity when the maid served him.

"From the little I've deduced, ye've been busy since we parted company last night." Fergus sipped at a cup of brew, as his dark eyes locked on his pupil.

Harrison ran a hand through his mussed hair and reached for his cup. "Yes, sir. You could say that." In that moment, Mrs. T poked her head in the room and wiggled a finger at him to come to her.

Fergus caught the gesture and rolled his eyes.

"Is it Tamsin? What's wrong?"

"Our miss needs to talk to you."

Harrison stepped outside the room. Whatever her concern was, it weighed heavy. He mentioned, "Barrister Fergus will want to talk to her. Is she well enough to come down do you think?"

The look on the housekeeper's face seemed almost laughable as she pled, "I've done everything except lock her chamber door to keep her from running down the stairs as it is. I told her I would ask you first."

"If she's feeling up to it, please ask her to come down."

"Right, then." She left him standing in the hall.

Within minutes, the three of them, Tamsin, Harrison, and Fergus sat at the dining room table. The barrister began by addressing her. "Ye look well considering what I've learned about last eve. Ye're a strong young woman, Miss Morgan."

"Tamsin, please, sir." Her wrists were red from the rope burn, and she was still a wee bit foggy brained. Though fragility didn't stop the yen for revenge that consumed her.

Harrison suggested to her, "I know we haven't had a moment to talk about this, but..."

She laid her hand on his and nodded. "I know what you are going to say, and I agree it's time. Over time."

"Are you up to it?" Harrison needed her assurance.

"This is my third cup of tea. I think I can manage."

Fergus glanced at them with narrowed eyes full of suspicion.

She wondered if his legal background had already alerted him to confidential matters. Straightening her shoulders, she met the Scotsman's hard stare.

"I will begin at the start of all this, sir, so you will understand why I broke the law."

His bushy brows chased up his forehead. His assessing glance fixed on his pupil a moment before returning to her. He leaned back in the chair, his hand gesturing that she should begin.

"On the twentieth of September, voices woke me just before midnight. I came down to see what was afoot and found my dear uncle dead. Poisoned, I was to learn later, as he sat at his desk."

The barrister's face looked like he'd just seen a bombshell explode. He lurched forward in the chair. "Ye just said Basil is dead?"

"I am deeply sorry to tell you. Yes, he is."

The revelation seemed to hit him as if he'd been punched in the face. When he adjusted to the appalling disclosure, his voice wasn't so commanding. "Enlighten me."

Crushed by the sadness in those two words, she said, "I hardly know what to say to you. Except that I know your friendship has endured for decades. I am so sorry."

He gestured for her to continue, for the moment keeping his silence. A bit of color returned to his features.

"When I came upon the scene just before midnight on the twentieth of September, Uncle Basil was in his chair in the library. There were two glasses of brandy, or some such, one half gone, the other untouched. I had the contents tested by an apothecary and they both contained arsenic. I later learned the contents of his decanter also contained arsenic, leading me to concur that my uncle had been ingesting it for some time.

"The front door was ajar, as was the gate at the end of the walk, though no one appeared to be about."

Fergus raised his palm stopping her recitation. "Didn't he travel to India?"

She took a deep breath. "That is the story I told when asked." She paused. "You see, when I realized he was dead, I became terrified. And thinking about the staff and myself and that our home would be taken from us, and we would be out on the street."

"Surely, Miss Tamsin, you knew your uncle would have arranged—"

"Yes, yes of course. However, at that moment I wasn't thinking rationally. The loss of my dearest person—my mind went to the worst possible imagining."

She put a hand to her cheek, visions of that night clear and sharp.

"Where are his remains?"

She drew in a long slow breath folding her hands on the tabletop. Last night's drugging left her sluggish. A familiar lump in her throat tightened.

Relating the events to the barrister and witnessing his

shock upon hearing of Uncle Basil's death, was horribly traumatic. She forced down the lump in her throat.

"I decided to hide him for a bit. I needed time to think. I can't describe how desperately afraid and worried I felt. The dearest person in my world gone from me. It is hard to reconcile, especially considering who his killer might be."

"And who might ye suspect?" His voice quivered as if he was stressed. Or, mayhap baffled.

"I'll get to that part in good time. Allow me to continue, please."

Fergus' rigid jaw, and ice-cold eyes, made her believe he found her melodramatic. He certainly wasn't a man to tolerate other's foibles. "How could it be possible for ye to physically move him? I mean ta say, ye aren't a large woman by any means."

Without a doubt, the gaol would be her next home. "I wrapped him in a blanket and dragged him to the cellar."

He scraped back his chair, stood, and walked to a window facing the back yard. "Is that the cellar in question?"

"Yes, sir."

He said nothing for a few minutes, probably digesting her facts about the loss of a man as noteworthy as her uncle. When he turned back, his glare burned into Harrison. "At what point do ye enter onto the scene?"

Harrison glanced at Tamsin, "Was it the third day or the fourth?"

She whispered, "the third." Her heart hammered.

Harrison quickly said, "Tamsin took me to the cellar that night the twenty-fourth of September at midnight."

Fergus turned from the window his features dusted in a black rage. "Take me to him."

She smothered a gasp. Harrison glanced at her.

"NOW!"

"It's impossible, sir."

He headed across the room to the door.

"Sir! His remains are missing."

He whipped away from the door incredulity plastered on his wooden face. "WHAT?"

"We've looked everywhere. Mortuaries, hospitals, dead houses."

Harrison added, "We had a lead about Battersea and rode there. Unfortunately, it wasn't him."

In an eerily controlled voice, Fergus asked, "Miss Tamsin, who else knows Basil is dead?"

"Mrs. Thistlewaite, the housekeeper, and she in turn has been instructed to tell the all-around man, Charlie."

"So, whomever killed him has now taken his remains?"

"It looks that way, sir."

He glared at Tamsin as if he could turn the skies to fury. "I take it ye've been investigating his death yerself? With the help of my law student?"

Harrison's face turned ashen.

The barrister made it sound as if she'd committed the murder. The skin on her arms prickled. "Yes sir. We made some discoveries particularly after his library was ransacked several days later."

If the scorn on the barrister's face proved anything, he might be on the verge of apoplexy. He glared at Harrison. "Keeping me in the dark is a criminal offense. Of the two of you..." he growled, glaring at Harrison, "...surely one of you knew better than to conceal his death. And apparently, with Miss Tamsin's mention, the robbery of his personal files."

Harrison's face flushed. "Yes, sir. I take full responsibility."

Tamsin argued, "No, sir. I take full responsibility. Harrison did not arrive until the next morning after I had already hidden his body. And I didn't say anything to him for several days."

The barrister waved his hand as if to blow off Harrison's shame. "Ye seem ta know plenty about your uncle's business. How much damage to his files?"

"It looks like some files were taken."

At this, Fergus rubbed his forehead and groaned. Hands on his hips, he turned toward the window once again. "Don't spare the details."

"The housekeeper woke me at three in the morning. Sounds from below woke her and she took the back stairs. They didn't hear her coming. Because of their goodly size, she was sure they were men with totes filled with whatever they could take from the file drawers. The moment they noticed her they ran out the door, leaving some of my uncle's papers behind. He had a secret panel in the back of his drawers where he kept items of importance."

"I'd say hiding information behind a wooden panel was smart of Basil. He must have anticipated such a thing. Do ye comprehend that whoever wanted him dead puts ye in a very dangerous situation? Ye may be next, Miss Tamsin, has that occurred ta ye, either of ye? Aye?" Not waiting for an answer, he continued to lecture.

"Also, ye tampered with a crime scene when ye cleaned his workspace. Another score against ye."

His demeanor exuded the law and his standing as a prominent barrister, and all the other hats he wore because of his brilliance. His daunting manner sent chills through her. He may even think of them idiots, she as being the worst of course. Because she'd dragged Harrison into this dreadful situation.

Harrison's dark hazel eyes shifted to her. She'd already deduced from the look on Fergus' face that they were in serious legal jeopardy.

Fergus's voice dripped with sarcasm. "Firstly, I've had me hands tied these past weeks with Basil's sudden trip to India," his dark blue eyes sparkled with a mix of irritation and dissatisfaction.

Tamsin knew the Scot was angry, yet not well enough to know his degree of vexation.

Her activities were criminal and having dragged poor Harrison into this mess might just cost him his law degree.

Everything he did was meant to help or protect her. The ramifications of that dreadful, life-changing night weren't over yet. It appeared most likely that she'd end up in prison. What an ignoramus she was proving to be.

The barrister had been speaking and she'd been gathering wool. She gave him her full attention rather than contemplating her dismal future.

"Basil retired from Her Majestie's Service to become my lead investigator. His detective work was superior. Out of the limelight, retired, and as cunning as the devil. The code name for his current file is Ramsey."

He turned to Tamsin. "Would ye be familiar with that name?"

"Yes, sir." She had supposed it to be a cipher for someone or something her uncle investigated. "Uncle Basil always used puzzling markers."

It occurred to her his murderer might have known of her uncle's connection with Fergus. If so, he...or she... might also be aware of what her uncle and she were working on.

The barrister said, "I found where Basil used the name Ramsey as a possible code for someone he suspected. I could go back to my own files and see if Ramsey is mentioned in one of them."

"Once a thief, always a thief," chided Harrison.

"Something like that."

Fergus scanned the Blackbeard info, then the White papers. And remarked, "Both the White and Blackbeard portfolios suggest Basil was interested in a connection between two unknowns. He obviously found the link yet hadn't gotten back to me before the trip to his plantation."

She bit back her unease. Was Uncle Basil murdered because he discovered the link? She felt ill.

Harrison said, "At the fund raiser you sought the dark-haired man with the thin mustache. Who we figured out to be the same man at C Dock the night of the shooting."

"By Christ," he shouted, pounding the table with his fist, "It feels like we are on the brink of discovery."

Tamsin asked, "It's Desmond De la Croix, isn't it?"

A moment of incredulity passed when he barked, "Until I investigate further, I'll wait to disclose my thoughts."

Surprising the men, Tamsin asserted, "Mrs. Reynolds-Walker killed Uncle Basil. And she's in it together with that man De la Croix."

Fergus turned a hard eye on her.

Harrison had heard her declarations far too many times to be shocked by the outburst. Although this time she obviously added De la Croix to her list of suspects.

Fergus harrumphed. "Why do ye think yer uncle allowed her to live off his income and never seek a divorce and remarry?"

"My uncle was a saint."

"I might agree with ye, except I knew him well. And no one's that perfect." He set the pencil he was rolling between his fingers on the table and sat up straight, as if about to stand.

Tamsin said, "I happened to see Mrs. Reynolds-Walker and De la Croix at the Fund Raiser leaving the library together. He kissed her before allowing her to precede him into the reception."

The barrister sat back in his chair. "And that provides us with what?"

Harrison glanced at his hands, a smirk on his face.

A bit unsure, after Fergus' sarcastic question, she said,

"Well, it wasn't a kiss from a brother. I had the impression they were lovers. Even though Mrs. Reynolds-Walker went to great lengths to indicate they were anything but."

"What makes ye think that?"

"I visited her after Uncle Basil died and she told me she was in love and made it very clear my uncle wasn't the one she meant. After I saw her with De la Croix at the Charity Ball, I realized that's who she's been in love with all these years."

Chapter Twenty-Seven

Malcolm Fergus crossed his legs as he twisted in his chair. He picked up the pencil again and twiddled it through his fingers. After a minute, he cleared his throat and announced, "Just between the three of us, I've a mind that you might be the murderer, Miss Morgan. You have motive, you have proximity, and you stand to inherit a fortune."

Her mouth dropped open, then she snorted. "Are you daft?"

He turned to Harrison. "What say you?"

The color drained from his face. "I—I'm—sir. I couldn't disagree more. I've known both Tamsin and Basil for years, witnessed how they loved and cared for each other basically, for the last ten years. And no finer relationship have I seen than that of a father figure and a niece." He raked a hand through his hair. "It's beyond the pale that you would suggest such a thing."

Tamsin realized Fergus was dead serious. She stood and splayed her palms on the table surface. "How dare you suggest such a monstrous thing? He was my family. He was the father I'd lost." Her hand clenched and unclenched as if she might strike him—with meaningful pleasure!

She spun to face the window fists clenched at her sides. "Leave my home and never return. I never want to lay eyes on you again. SIR!"

A chuckle came from the barrister. "Well, ye've convinced me of yer innocence. I had ta know for certain."

She stormed around the table and came up so quickly he didn't see her hand raise and come down on his cheek with a mighty slap, then rubbed her stinging fingers.

He held his reaction and kneaded his mutton-haired cheek where her hand struck. "Sorry to be so blunt, miss. I was after a truthful reaction to my statement."

"Well, then I suppose this wasn't the first time you've had your face slapped?" And without waiting for an answer she spouted, "It won't likely be the last either."

Rubbing his jaw one last time, he defended his accusation. "I hope ye'll accept my apology, but I did have ta ask ye. And it's clear ye have a problem with Mrs. Reynolds-Walker. If she's the killer, seems ta me she'd put herself elsewhere and not at yer threshold."

Tamsin said, "The morning after I discovered his body she arrived on our doorstep demanding Basil's presence. That's what made me suspect she knew he was dead and wanted to see my reaction."

"What was yer reaction?"

"You are a cold-hearted beast. It hardly bears mentioning how I felt when I discovered him dead."

She was developing a headache and felt wound up tighter than a clock. Last night's peril at the hands of that wicked woman, and the barrister's declaration she murdered her uncle, didn't help.

"And ye Harrison? What are yer thoughts?"

"I'm inclined to think he was murdered because he was getting too close to the truth about something. Or someone was forcing his hand, and he wouldn't budge. I really don't think Mrs. Reynolds-Walker has motive worth killing him. Except possibly the inheritance she thought she would receive. I do have a strong sense she's involved somehow, however."

As the dining room quieted, Tamsin could hear distant talking from the kitchen, and the clip clop of carriages on the street, mingled with the tapping of the barrister's fingertips on the crinkly pages in the file.

"Basil's notes suggest someone was undercutting the cost of opium contributing to price wars, and not paying tariffs or levies. He made a list of small shops on the east end, and a note regarding their income. Which suggests he'd done some significant research."

Harrison reached for the list and looked it over. "May I borrow this? I'll stop by several of the shops and see if I can discover anything."

"Excellent idea." The barrister lifted the Blackbeard file and a piece of paper slid from it. He scooped it up off the floor and was about to add it to the file when he saw a name written across the top. De la Croix.

"This is a note Basil wrote to himself regarding the possible sale of Hilldale to one Desmond De la Croix. It's dated nineteen September 1870. He passed the paper to Tamsin. "What do ye know of this?"

"It's dated the day before my uncle died." She read the few lines and handed it back to Fergus. "I know nothing of this. He never said a word to me about selling his plantation. But I wouldn't regard that as unusual. Perhaps he was dangling it out there to get a reaction."

He pressed his elbows into the arms of the chair. "Then I find it an unusual coincidence that ye put the word out Basil was visiting his plantation."

Her cheeks pinkened. "I tried to give myself some time to figure the why or who of his death."

His deep piercing eyes dug into her.

The urge to slap him again was strong. She reeled in her impulse, uncertain if his reaction might put her in Newgate. Slapping him the first time allowed a release of pent-up frustration. What might she feel with a second one?

"My uncle owned quite a few shares in the Darjeeling District of the East India Company. His shares were bought in the early stages of the experiment in the 1850s. The feasibility of growing tea in the foothills of the Himalayas and other parts of India was being explored. By 1863, seventy-eight plantations had been set up. The experiment was a huge success according to my uncle. And still is as far as I know."

"Ye are the sole beneficiary. Ye stand to gain a fortune selling Hilldale."

She felt the heat rise on her neck and closed her eyes to shut off the suspicion swimming in his and countered, "Will it be enough money to return him to the living? Because that's the only reason I would be interested in selling the plantation."

That shut the barrister up for a long moment.

The atmosphere in the dining room chilled. She knew what he was suggesting. And why not? She was the one who found him, moved him; tampered with the glasses and carafe of poison; to say nothing of what she would inherit. The wealth involved in her uncle's death wouldn't bring him back. All she wanted was for him to walk into the dining room and tease them all for the fuss over his sudden disappearance.

Harrison cleared his throat. "Basil regarded the plantation as a future income for Tamsin should anything ever happen to him. He made mention of this to me about a year ago when he asked me to witness some legal papers he was signing."

"Harrumph." The Scot shoved the torn paper into the file from where it had fallen.

Her vexation toward the barrister and to some degree toward Mrs. Reynolds-Walker made her fidgety. She wished he would finish with his questions and leave her in peace. A nap sounded about right.

"Their marriage was never a real marriage."

"It appeared to be legal." Fergus paused a moment. "Did you ever hear her talk of Desmond De la Croix?"

"I heard her say things about a man she loved, but she never mentioned a name."

"I know you are aware of him, having seen his name in Basil's files."

She sensed his sharp awareness was due to his love of detective work. "I was suspicious that he might be Mrs. Reynolds-Walker's lover."

"Because they kissed?"

"Don't be absurd. Much more than that. She's loved him since she was very young."

"Did she tell you that?"

"I already told you; she spoke to me of someone she was very much in love with. But she never mentioned his name."

"Like most women, yer a daydreamer."

Tamsin kept her thoughts to herself. He was goading her, and she wasn't going to give him any satisfaction with another vulgar display, though her hand itched just the same. She'd never slapped another person in her life. Why was the urge so great to do just that to this man?

He spread his arm over the files and drew them close, flipping the cover and poring over the contents. Again.

Tamsin suggested, "Can we find a reason Desmond

wants a tea plantation? Could it be a cover-up for the opium shipped to England?"

Harrison suggested, "The tea import would certainly provide cover for the actual opium runs. Historically there aren't any sanctions against importing either product."

Fergus nodded thoughtfully and asked Tamsin, "I know ye were young, just the same, did ye ever reason out their marriage? A possible rationale or motive?"

"As you say, I was a child. I wouldn't have had any understanding of them as a couple, nor the why of their marriage."

Chapter Twenty-Eight

J abbing a finger on the Blackbeard file, the Scot barked, "I'm familiar with Basil's handwriting and right here in his hand is a description of a fashionably dressed, greased black hair, slim mustache, and tall..." he glanced at Tamsin, "...with no name. Unless he's Ramsey, which means he's Desmond De la Croix. Apparently, Basil has had a line on him since the fall of 1865."

Harrison asked, "If this is our lead, should we assume De la Croix somehow got wind of Basil's interest in him and had him killed?"

With a glint in his eyes he claimed, "A definite possibility."

Tamsin asked, "Does this suggest that we might have solved my uncle's murder?"

"Not so fast, lassie. We dinna have proof of the link that Basil proposes. But it does give us an avenue ta explore."

She added, "I have another question." The barrister's left brow hiked up his forehead. "As you know, Mrs. Reynolds-Walker nabbed me last night and drugged me. I think she should be taken in for questioning. I want to know what you're going to do about that?"

He rested against the back of the chair, his stern voice belying the fact he looked a bit weary. "Strategically speaking, nothing right now. She's a small fish in the game that is being played out. 'Tis not that I don't sympathize with ye being treated badly. I see ye as a member of this team and right now we still don't have all the facts. Most of what we discussed is conjecture, not fact."

Harrison looked uncomfortable regarding Fergus' declaration. Tamsin dared not fault the barrister, he was after all Harrison's superior. Harrison had to get through the next few months until he became a full-fledged lawyer. Until then, he cautiously tip-toed around his administrator. Yet, he took a deep breath before suggesting, "Should there not be a reaction to snatching up Miss Tamsin, sedating her, and shoving her in a closet?"

The barrister looked from Harrison to Tamsin. "You are to be commended, Harrison. Searching for Miss Tamsin and returning her to her home barely scathed; you have seen to her welfare."

He asked Tamsin. "You do agree?"

Well, what could she do except nod and then thank Harrison.

Feeling a bit lacking in significance, as if drugged, bound, and stuffed in a closet was trivial, she wondered if the barrister considered her expendable.

Fergus gathered the folders in front of him and shoved them into his briefcase. He stood, announcing an end to the meeting.

"At this time, I won't be bringing Mrs. Reynolds-Walker in for questioning. It might rock the boat. Ye're under watchful guard around the clock, lassie. And I believe ye respect the law enough growing up in yer uncle's home that ye are very aware ta be careful."

He'd just spoken to her as if she were a child. Irritation

inched up her nape. "You think me dispensable, but it is my dear uncle who was murdered, and I demand to be kept abreast of any new information."

Fergus didn't answer her and as Harrison stood and the men shook hands, he said, "Thank you for the guards, sir."

Fergus faced Tamsin. "Give me yer word ta stay put, lass." He towered over her, his dark-red mutton chops and harsh green eyes daring her to refuse. He wasn't asking, he was commanding.

She grudgingly nodded.

"I do feel for ye, miss. I'll not allow her abuse ta slide. Seems ta me, she might have wanted ta rattle ye thinking maybe ye were getting a bit too close for comfort."

He added, "I'm going ta me chamber. I've a need ta catch up on me reading. I don't expect ta find a connection between De la Croix and Mrs. Reynolds-Walker. But miracles do happen. I think Basil was far enough into the investigation ta have left suggestions if that were the case.

"Ye'll be safe with three Bobbies outside. It would be advisable not ta leave the protected sanctuary of yer home." His mutton chops and ruddy skin couldn't hide a small smile directed at her.

"If for some unforeseen reason ye must, take one of the men with ye. This is a command, not a request." Again, he waited for her agreement.

She met his gaze openly and thought of her dear uncle and the years of protection and comfort he'd afforded. She supposed the barrister was that same kind of man, nonetheless he irritated the heck out of her. Her nod was barely discernable.

Grim faced, he turned to Harrison. "On yer return from the East End come by chambers. This is not a request." Off he went, slamming his hat on his head as he stepped out of the dining room and trod down the hall.

The instant Tamsin heard the door close, she turned to Harrison. "That doesn't bode well for you. Is he always so irritating?" Tamsin tugged on the cuff of her sleeve.

A sound not unlike a growl came from him. "In his defense, I thought he was within his rights to expect us to follow his directive."

"You mean me, don't you?" She tugged rather strongly on the other cuff, almost making him think she would have preferred slapping him, also.

"I didn't say that. However, since you brought it up, yes, I do mean you." He cocked his head and pursed his lips.

She glared at him. "In the end, when all this gets solved, I think you will see I was right. It is Mrs. Reynolds-Walker who murdered my uncle."

The smile he gave her wasn't really a smile, it was more like a lopsided grimace that was forced into a semblance of congeniality. His long legs stretched out from the chair as if he'd been sitting too long. "I can see you're feeling better. And I need to be on my way, chiefly now that I have my evening taken up with the barrister. There are just so many hours in the day."

He rose and with his hand on the knob of the door to the dining room, turned to her. "Just a thought, why don't you stretch that brain of yours and explore a reason why Mrs. Reynolds-Walker would want to kill Basil, other than the fortune he left behind."

He took up his hat and locked eyes with her. "Swear to me you won't do anything to harm yourself and others while I'm gone."

She smothered the urge to stomp her foot, or...or yell. And forced herself not to say one word. Instead, cursing him with an evil eye felt about right, assuming there was such a thing.

With as sweet a voice as she could manage, she inquired, "I don't know what you mean by that?"

"Tamsin, if I have to tie you to a chair, I will." He went so far as to put his briefcase on the table and his hat atop it.

She put her hand over his as it rested on his briefcase. "Don't be a meddler. Why would I want a repeat of last night? I'm not stupid you know. Besides the place is crawling with Bobbies."

His scrutiny glued to her; he waited a few seconds obviously not trusting her. "So, help me God, Tamsin if you do anything to put yourself in harm's way, I'll..."

"What, lock me up? Seems *your* barrister wants to do the same."

He picked up his briefcase and hat, briefly smiling his adieu and left. The dining room suddenly fell silent, yet remnants of their meeting lingered in the room.

Harrison irritated her with his pompous Fergus posture. She fretted with anxiety over Mrs. Reynolds-Walker's nabbing and drugging of her. And, if she was totally honest, her heart grieved ever more for her uncle and his guidance.

Since she was old enough to understand about Mrs. Reynolds-Walker, she harbored a dislike of the woman.

Tamsin recalled when she was thirteen or so and overheard two adults talking about her uncle's marriage. She was visiting with a friend from school and the friend's mother and another woman were talking about Mrs. Reynolds-Walker. They suggested she married for money, and acted unmarried when it came to a certain gentleman.

Later that evening, she had questioned Uncle Basil about what she overheard, and he had answered just enough to satisfy her inquisitiveness until she was older and realized he'd been evasive about divulging truly personal aspects.

She had also asked Mrs. T about Uncle Basil's marriage. She had gotten to an age when she recognized how unnatural his marriage arrangement was. Most of the time, she forgot he was married.

Maybe it was time for her to have another conversation with Mrs. Reynolds-Walker.

The moment Harrison went off to find transportation to the East End she snuck out the kitchen door darting across the backyard and walked to Marylebone Street effectively avoiding the Bobbies.

Tuesday, Late Afternoon
4 October 1870

Harrison hailed a cab and when he articulated Brunswick Street to the driver, the man leaned his elbows on his knees, clutched the reins, and declared, "Get someone else, gov'."

His stern voice told Harrison there was no use arguing. A bit dismayed, he walked a block or so until he caught up with another driver and waved his cane saying, "Brunswick Street."

The driver announced, "It'll cost ye full price, upfront."

Harrison pulled out two shillings and indicated the driver should keep the change, then he opened the door and bounded inside. They'd been a few minutes on the road when the cab intermittently lurched and slowed.

Usually at this time of day, the rush decreased somewhat, he wondered if there was an accident ahead. Though he didn't relish his task of going into the back streets of dark London as the newspapers labeled the area, he intended to visit one or two of the small shops that dealt in opium.

His afternoon would be spent searching for a needle in a haystack as he had scant information on which to rely.

Walking the slimy lanes of Blue Gate Fields searching the opium shops was a daring endeavor.

Just four days ago, he and Mickey were at C Dock around midnight investigating the unloading of a massive delivery of opium under the guise of tea. Fergus had directed them to keep an eye out for the man whose identity they sought. Without realizing it at the time, Harrison had been within a few steps of said man.

They'd botched the discovery a week earlier when Mickey insisted they visit a den down a filthy alleyway. The place was thick with foggy air and beds littered with opium users.

Hopefully he would have a chance to get close to the drug-dealing miscreant one more time.

He knew The East India Company, a chief supplier of tea was one of many in an unregulated market selling popular items such as opium soap, pills, lozenges, enemas, and confections. Some enterprising chemists diluted the strength of opium with alcohol and sold it as a cure-all.

Local individual shops were not on the same playing field as the larger apothecaries and pharmacists. The smaller ones made their own potions and distillates. It was easy to purchase pure forms of opium bundled in one-pound blocks, regardless of the 1868 law limiting sales of the drug.

As the taxi made its way across King Street, he took in the decay and canker of filth. He didn't for one second wonder why the first cabbie refused him transport to the east end.

Pennyfields was a mixture of slimy residentials, tiny rotting retail shops, and small manufacturing. Reading statistics on the last census, he had taken note of the German, Irish, and Chinese infiltration, workers filling the need for men at the Docks.

As they turned a corner, he noted a sign, Roaring Lion, and jabbed his cane against the roof of the carriage, the driver pulled over. He noticed several women idly chatting in front of another den, The Dragon's Delight, and stepped out of the gig. A metallic stench rolled up causing him to grimace. It had been a while since he walked the downtrodden filth of dark London streets. Reform was coming, though it was mighty slow.

A sly look on the driver's face caused Harrison to believe the man figured he intended to spend a day or two in an opium crib.

Upon entering the dilapidated establishment, he noticed a few scattered customers sipping ale and keeping to themselves. A woman scrubbed the counter and kept an eye on him. The strains of an argument coming from the kitchen drifted to the front room. The hefty woman, dirty rag in hand, appeared disinterested in the goings on, and asked, "Ye be wantin' ta quench yer thirst, sir?" She brazenly looked him up and down.

"I'm looking for a shop, the proprietor being Suzy Wang. Would you know of it, or her?"

A sly smile spread up her ruddy cheeks. "Everyone knows Suzy's place. Out the door and up three blocks. If yer after a crib and pipe, ye won't be leavin' her place for a day or two. She'll set ye up good and plenty."

He nodded, and literally felt her eyes boring into his back as he left the dingy pub. She pegged him as a druggy. It appeared that the east end's locals labeled most anyone walking the streets as opium heads. Limehouse Causeway housed Ah Tack's lodgings and was another gathering spot famous for its clientele's addictions.

If Fergus hadn't taken him up on his suggestion, he'd never have walked the destitute and bleak streets. Where was it going to end? Was it ever going to end?

The skies were overcast with gloomy sediment. The squalid, low-class housing and shops formed a bulwark where the exotic Oriental underworld of Limehouse Causeway began.

A few strides down the pavement, he noticed a closed sign on a door. A woman, Chinese of a certainty, sat on the curb. She glanced up at him, her eyes pink and runny, a puddle of vomit between her sandals. She waved her hand as if shooing him away.

As he strode toward Wang's shop, the mix and muddle of desperation and addiction rent his insides.

He continued down the street encountering the horrendous stench of sewage and destitution. Groups of three or four in dark doorways eyed him as he passed. Four shops later, a door was held open with a brick and a woman of Chinese derivation was rearranging items behind a glass countertop. He entered.

"I help you, sir?" Though speaking English, the sing-song chant of her words was distinctly Chinese.

"I would like to speak to the owner. Is he in?"

"Me in charge, sir." She finished rubbing her rag across the glass and looked directly at him.

"Do you own this business?"

Her mouth and eyes opened wide. He'd shocked her. "No, sir."

"I want to talk to the owner."

"That impossible. He never come."

This approach wasn't going to work. "Can you tell me who I might talk to?"

"You want try some? I give you small packet try." Her face lit up as if she finally understood him.

His fingertips drummed on the glass as he tried to think of a way to get through to her. "Who is your next in command? Who helps you?"

She continued to smile. "Boss, he take care everything."

"Is Boss in? May I speak to him?"

Behind her, the curtain to the backroom opened and there stood a representative of the Chinese wrestling nation all wrapped into one mountain of a man. His shoulders bunched up against both sides of the opening. Harrison could almost laugh if he wasn't feeling like an ant about to be squished under the behemoth's massive feet.

"You want buy? Or talk?" His arms were the size of tree trunks.

Harrison's inclination was to turn and run like hell, but that wouldn't get the information he needed. Besides, he was not one to run from problems. He usually headed directly into them.

"I'm looking for a gentleman, whose name I don't know. He's about my height and has a black mustache and slick black hair. I would like to do business with him. I'm wondering if you can help me."

The wrestler took a step forward and gently put his huge, beefy palms, the size of dinner plates, on the glass top. If it was possible, his slanted eyes narrowed even more. "Bao say we no meet him. You no trust her?"

Okay, it was time for him to back off. He nervously plastered a smile on his face, tipped his hat, and backed out of the shop swiftly, making his way to the vehicle.

Just as Harrison was closing the door on the cab, Bao—as referred to by the wrestler—ran outside the shop waving a piece of paper at him. She shoved it in his hand before he closed the door, then sprinted back to her shop. Sitting back in the cab, he pounded the roof with his cane.

As they took off, he unfolded the paper and read three words, him la Croix.

He knew he couldn't return to the shop. It might mean Bao would pay the price, and he wasn't up to having his brains smashed in between the hulk's massive hands either.

As the carriage took off, he noted several more women

had arrived at the first shop. The closed sign remained on the door. He figured with a name in hand, he needn't visit the notorious Frying-pan Alley in Spitalfields, or Palmers-Folly, or Petticoat Lane.

The horrific living conditions in which mothers were forced to raise their children caused him grave concern. Was history going to provide the British with the scope of drug addictions and its effects on humanity?

Chemists and doctors were not the only prescribers. It was common knowledge the small shop sellers in the East End had a lucrative business selling the powder. Even grocers, general stores, and booksellers sold opium.

It was Fergus's and Harrison's suspicion that the man they sought was a regular supplier of this drug at a very low cost. Over the last several years, small shops popped up undercutting the cost to the public. It wasn't a coincidence that the deaths of children had also risen.

And now he had a name. The name, La Croix. Something to possibly boost the barrister's attitude.

Chapter Twenty-Nine

T he feel of Uncle Basil's five-cylinder Webley Bull Dog revolver gave Tamsin more than enough courage even though she'd taken the ammunition out of the chamber. She felt sure that pointing a gun at her adversary would be enough to scare Mrs. Reynolds-Walker into surrendering.

She patted the pocket of her skirt as she crossed over Bayley Street.

The killer had poisoned Uncle Basil, and Tamsin's intent was to bring that person to justice this afternoon. For the second time ever, she approached the home where Henrietta lived in a brick Georgian style home with black shutters, symmetrical windows, columns, and manicured shrubbery.

She drew back the brass knocker and let it fall against the plate. The door opened, and Tamsin saw recognition in the butler's eyes. "Mrs. Reynolds-Walker please. My card."

Without saying a word, he opened the door wider and allowed her entry. She'd shocked him by showing up after being nabbed last night. From the look on his face, he'd obviously been in on her abduction.

Stepping into the foyer, he shut the door and led her to the front parlor, not asking to take her cape. Removing her gloves, she kept them in hand as she wondered what else the butler knew.

Mrs. Reynolds-Walker had forced two pills and a glass of water on her and her world had spun into a deep black hole. Her next memory had been Harrison's voice far off in the distance.

Entering the parlor of her adversary, she recalled the gold filigree embellishing the cornices, and the patterned paper of ivy and roses adorning the walls from when she visited Mrs. Reynolds-Walker in late September.

The butler's receding steps echoed on the marbled foyer as he undoubtedly made his way to his employer. She slid her hand down her skirt, reassuring herself the Webley was at the ready.

Standing with her back to the unlit fireplace, she waited. Thoughts of her uncle mixed with the revenge she sought for his death.

Squaring her shoulders, her fingertips tapped against the woolen overdress of her skirt, again taking strength from the hidden revolver.

Mrs. Reynolds-Walker had a sharp-witted look in her eyes. She was wearing a broad felt hat with cream colored fluff of some sort waving in the air. Obviously ready to leave the house, she crossed the room motioning with her arm that Tamsin should take a chair, as she herself sat in an upholstered Queen Anne with cabriole legs.

Tamsin continued to stand in front of the unlit grate.

"You have brass showing up here." Her hostile stare bored Tamsin.

Tamsin took a deep breath. "I'm registering a complaint regarding your accommodation last night."

"You resort to jesting? I'm surprised as to why you are here."

Her fingertips brushed the Webley through the wool of her skirt. "You killed my uncle, and after your treatment of me last night, I'm quite certain your intention was to kill me, too."

"Why would I murder the man who holds my purse?" Mrs. Reynolds-Walker shifted in the chair and clutched the padded arms with her thin-fingered hands. "You on the other hand, invite one to do you harm."

Tamsin took a step toward her. "You admit to drugging me, tying me up, and shoving me in a closet!"

Her response was a slight shrug of the shoulders. As if what she did wasn't worth a response. "It appears little harm was done."

"Certainly not to you. I could press charges."

Mrs. Reynolds-Walker's answer was another shrug. Her lips curled slightly. "I doubt you will. You could hang for killing your uncle and taking advantage of his wealth."

Tamsin's shock caused her adversary to laugh outright. "Surely you realize you're in a serious predicament."

Gaining back her senses, Tamsin rebutted. "Why did you murder my uncle? He treated you with respect."

"What matter. He's dead and gone. And your lies about his travel to India will turn against you. It will take many months of investigation to figure out if he is, indeed, dead."

Tamsin's knees weakened. This woman as much as admitted she'd killed him and took his remains from the cellar.

Tamsin drew out the Webley Bull Dog revolver from her pocket and pointed it at Mrs. Reynolds-Walker.

"I'm taking you to Metro Station."

Henrietta opened her mouth to scream when exuberant rowdy laughter burst through the front door. Two men tumbled into the hallway as cold air rushed through the foyer.

The revolver in hand, Tamsin gestured with it, forcing Henrietta to move to the corner of the room as two men shuffled and laughed in the foyer.

She heard the butler mention Mrs. Reynolds-Walker was in the parlor with a guest. Tamsin took a deep breath realizing the revolver was all she had as defense and it was unloaded. Dear God help me she whispered.

She tucked her hand into the folds of her skirt clutching the Webley and cast an evil eye on Henrietta. "One word, and with pleasure I'll get even for last night."

As they fumbled their way into the parlor, the men took notice of Mrs. Reynolds-Walker and Tamsin. A tense atmosphere between the women was apparent. Though Mrs. Reynolds-Walker realized introductions were expected. "Miss Morgan, may I introduce Mr. De la Croix, and Mr. Garrity."

They nodded and each fell into a chair. It was obvious they'd been drinking. "We've intruded, have we not?"

Mrs. Reynolds-Walker glared at Tamsin.

Tamsin was not sure what her next move should be. It seemed she was in an impossible position having just been introduced to the man the barrister and Harrison had been looking for.

The butler asked, "Should I serve refreshments, madam?"

Mrs. Reynolds-Walker glanced at Tamsin who said, "Under the circumstances, I think not."

Mr. De la Croix stood and walked toward Mrs. Reynolds-

Walker. "It's been a while. You look as though you are readying to leave."

Henrietta stepped back. "You know you are not welcome here. You need to leave." Her words were bitter. "What would Miss Horwrath say if she knew you were here?"

He stumbled over a foot stool as he reached for her hand, and she backed away from him. He righted himself, laughed off his near fall and turned to his friend, Mickey. "I believe we've come at an inappropriate time."

Mickey sidled near Tamsin. She quickly glanced at Mrs. Reynolds-Walker and stepped closer to her. Fear clutched her and she fisted the revolver in her pocket. She was in way over her head and feared this was not going to end well. If only she had loaded the cylinders with ammunition.

The large younger man, Mickey Garrity, reached for her arm, and she spun about, drawing the Webley from her pocket and pointed it at him. "Move away from me, now."

Mr. De la Croix took a step toward her. "Now here, miss. You don't want to do anything stupid, do you? Put the weapon down and we'll all go about our business."

"If you take one more step, I'll shoot you."

Mrs. Reynolds-Walker finally allowed her screech to rend the air sending shivers through Tamsin's already compromised composure.

The butler, who must have taken up hearing space outside the parlor, entered in a rush. Tamsin pointed the gun at him.

What was she doing? An unloaded gun, and three men about to pounce.

The butler lunged and she reflexively pulled the trigger, which shot off a loud bang, and sent De la Croix thudding to the floor.

Mrs. Reynolds-Walker screamed, "You murdered him."

She dropped to her knees at his side brushing his oily hair off his face and patting his chest.

In Tamsin's shocked moment, the butler grabbed the revolver from her and spun her around causing her to fall into a chair as he pointed the weapon at her.

The butler then shook the woman trying to tell her De la Croix wasn't going to die, and to shut her caterwauling. Apart from the fact that he was shot in the knee, bleeding, and squealing like a stuck pig, it was apparent De la Croix would live.

Tamsin was outraged as she registered that the revolver was loaded when she was certain she had checked all the chambers. Positive that she had done so, she jumped up from the chair and as the butler bent over De la Croix, she pushed her foot into the butler's backside and sent him sprawling over the wounded man then grabbed the gun.

He lunged upward at her as she pushed the barrel of the Webley in his face.

"I wouldn't if I were you."

Backing off, the butler's hands shook as they dangled at his side. His face paled.

Tamson stood against the wall waving the gun between a sobbing Mrs. Reynolds-Walker and the butler who quickly knelt again at De la Croix's side and brushed his employer away as he tore the trouser leg free of the bleeding area.

"Don't anyone move, or I'll shoot her," warned Tamsin. Her arm steady on Mrs. Reynolds-Walker, her fear erased. She felt in control. Though how long would it take before one of them lunged at her, was anyone's guess.

Kitchen help ran into the parlor followed by two maids. They banged into each other as the cook stopped short at sight of the gun in Tamsin's hand.

"Don't shoot, miss. I mean no harm. I heard a gunshot." Her eyes were as big as saucers.

The butler grabbed the towel out of the cook's hand and began blotting up the blood around the knee as De la Croix groaned in pain at the pressure being applied to the wound.

Tamsin eyed the bleeding knee and the shredded pant leg, and the blood. The butler appeared quite efficient as he wrapped the towel around the wound saying, "it might be a flesh wound. A doctor will know more."

The suave, thin-mustached man groaned in pain as he lay prone on the floor.

Her carelessness and ignorance of gun safety caused this, and despite his wrongdoing she cringed at the pain etched on his face. She'd never in her life hurt anyone.

De la Croix was the subject of much consternation this morning when Barrister Fergus was at the house. She doubted he would be pleased she'd shot the man he'd been looking for all this time.

Mrs. Reynolds-Walker's attention had fixed firmly on De la Croix the moment he drunkenly stumbled into her parlor. More than likely, especially considering her wailing over his injury, he was the man she loved, the man for whom she left Uncle Basil. When she could talk to Harrison, she intended to ask what his thoughts were on the subject.

De la Croix, the butler, cook, two maids, Mrs. Reynolds-Walker, Mr. Garrity, and herself created a small crowd in the parlor.

Mr. Garrity grinned at her. Not a good sign. It meant he felt he could best her. The name Mickey Garrity was familiar; however, she couldn't remember why. Had it been Harrison who mentioned him? They'd been in school together, she seemed to recall.

She glanced over the faces in the parlor and kept the gun in plain sight of everyone, her finger on the trigger.

She motioned for one of the maids to come to her and whispered to the girl, as she surveyed the crowd. "I need you to go to #2 Berkeley Street and bring back the Bobbies. Tell them about the shooting and what you see here, and that Miss Morgan is here."

Waving the Webley at each person, she whispered to the maid, "Can you do this?" At her nod, Tamsin said, "Go now. Run."

The girl dashed out of the parlor.

Tamsin glanced at the faces looking at her, and commanded, "All of you sit on the floor."

Mrs. Reynolds-Walker started to sit in a chair and Tamsin snarled, "You sit in that corner on the floor." The woman jerked a cushion off the divan and threw it in the corner where she collapsed.

The rest complied with her command, though she knew it was the Webley that kept order in the room. Certainly not her. She had to admit, the weighty little gun gave her a sense of power. She wished she knew if there were more cartridges in the chamber. If she overlooked one, there could be more. Nonetheless, the situation was tenuous, and she dared not show any sign of weakness.

Garrity crouched on the floor next to De la Croix. They spoke in hushed tones and Tamsin pointed the gun at Garrity. "You move to that corner." She indicated a corner further away from De la Croix.

The cook and maid cried out as the Webley passed over them when she commanded Garrity.

A moment of calm from the group allowed Tamsin to look at De la Croix. He appeared to be the kind of man to whom women would flock. Frivolous women who were not interested in integrity or honesty. Women like Henrietta.

Mrs. Reynolds-Walker's face was covered in red blotches. Her hands clutched, and her breath was uneven. Tamsin hadn't any remorse over the woman's plight. She was Uncle Basil's killer, and it ate at her heart to think of it.

The men weren't going to be docile for long. They could easily overtake her. She hoped the maid was swift. There were six people sitting on the floor in varying degrees of vexation and all she had was a revolver between herself and them: an unloaded revolver, most likely.

Several Bobbies paced up and down and around Basil Walker's home waiting for their next order. Another Bobbie was on the front stoop of #2 Berkeley Street, when a maid rushed forward and alerted them that Miss Morgan wasn't in the house. She was holding a revolver over people in a house at #14 Bedford Square and had shot one in the knee.

The maid was almost trampled as the officers sped in different directions. One sped to Lincoln Inn to alert the barrister; another to the hospital to send an ambulance to #14 Bedford Square; and the remaining two Bobbies put the maid in the police vehicle with her directing them to Mrs. Reynolds-Walker's home.

Harrison happened to be in chambers with Fergus when a Bobbie arrived alerting them to a wild woman brandishing a revolver at #14 Bedford Square. Harrison was able to give the driver directions to Mrs. Reynolds-Walker's home.

By the time they arrived at #14, the officer had relayed all the information he'd been given to the barrister who unholstered his gun.

Harrison went ahead of Fergus into the house, exploding into the parlor where it was reported Miss Tamsin had shot Mr. De la Croix. Brandishing his weapon, he came up short, noticing Tamsin holding her Webley steady, and in complete control.

He scanned the parlor, his gaze coming full stop at

Mickey Garrity who sat in a corner, his legs stretched out before him.

That's when Harrison took note of Garrity's boot—part of the left heel was missing.

His discovery suggested that Mickey may have worked for Mrs. Reynolds-Walker, or Desmond De la Croix, or possibly both.

The ambulance arrived, and two men carried a stretcher inside the home.

One of the men gawked at De la Croix, "Me stars, but if it ain't Harvey Ramsey. Seems ye met with some mischief. Haven't seen ya in a very long stretch, old pal."

In misery, Desmond De la Croix closed his eyes and moaned as they lifted him on the stretcher. He managed to hiss, "Shut your hole."

The barrister stepped into the home in that moment and halted the two hospital men dressed in white jackets and lifting a wounded man on the stretcher. The tall, burly hospital medic informed him Harvey Ramsey was shot in the knee. Fergus surveyed him, his thin mustache and slick black hair. He couldn't help but smile at the paradox in which De la Croix had unwittingly found himself.

The helpful medic offered, "He's an old mate, sir."

Fergus ordered a guard to accompany the stretcher and stay with the prisoner—he was under arrest as of this moment.

Having weeded out some of the confusion, Fergus then glanced at the scene before him. Two men on the floor in opposites corners. A woman in another corner, sitting on a cushion, a ridiculous hat shifted at an awkward angle on her head. Three kitchen maids, and Miss Tamsin standing against the opposite wall clutching a revolver.

Harrison noticed relief on Tamsin's face when he entered

the parlor and went to her, requesting she hand over the revolver.

His request surprised her. After all, she'd been in charge for an hour or more and doing quite well she thought. Common sense, and a grimace from the barrister however, urged her to do as Harrison requested.

Fergus excused the kitchen maids, ordering them not to leave the premises and not to discuss what went on in the parlor until he could talk to them later.

Tamsin moved away from the wall where she had taken up her authority and stepped toward the barrister, whose full attention was on the officer as he recited what he knew about the situation currently at hand. The officer was crediting her, Tamsin, with swift action, and complete control of the situation.

Harrison had stepped into the hallway. She could hear his voice questioning the butler.

It was then Fergus turned his steely-eyed glare on her. "Well, it appears ye do not follow direction verra well. I recall telling ye to stay in yer home until further notice."

"About that, sir." He carried the weight of authority to the point she almost felt as if she should curtsy.

He cut her off with his palm slicing the air between them and winked at her. "'Tis shocking ye haven't killed someone. I'll take yer affidavit later, Miss Tamsin." And with that said, he walked over to Mickey Garrity, who had gotten off the floor and was dusting off his pants.

The barrister questioned Garrity. "What possible reason would bring ye ta this home?"

"I was with a friend who had business here. He said it would take a minute. He was retrieving something. As you can see, we inadvertently got involved in an unpleasant altercation."

The Scot's bushy brows rose, "Was yer friend the fellow on the stretcher?"

Garrity hesitated only a moment. "Yes, sir."

"Desmond De la Croix, also known as Harvey Ramsey?"

Mickey suddenly appeared reluctant to admit to friendship with De la Croix, who he realized was toxic.

"Well, it seems ye keep unsavory company. What do ye say ta that?"

"I've been in an undercover operation, sir. Nothing I can speak of right now." Mickey shrugged his beefy shoulders.

Fergus eyed him speculatively. "Seeing as how I'm in charge of this particular murder investigation it's a wonder I don't have yer name on me list." He eyed Garrity, obviously dissatisfied with what he saw.

A Bobbie came up to Fergus at that moment and whispered. The barrister nodded and said, "Garrity ye are under arrest and will be escorted to the station and locked up until further notice." He then turned to the Bobbie, "Frisk him and lock him in the wagon for now."

Garrity rounded on the barrister, "I've done nothing. You have no right..."

Grabbing him by the neck collar, Fergus said, "I've every right. Don't make matters worse for yerself. I'm the one with the power ta make yer life miserable. Tread careful, Garrity. Threatening me will bode ill for ye."

Harrison returned to the parlor and quietly mentioned to Fergus about the left heel imprint in the root cellar, and the left heel on Garrity's boot.

Malcolm Fergus smiled. A unique occurrence. "Well, this might wrap up sooner than expected. Take two of our men and do yer best to dig up the footprint in Basil's cellar. It'll be evidence in court should we need it."

Harrison considered Garrity's participation in Basil's murder and anger knotted his chest. What possible reason would justify killing a man like Basil? He knew Garrity was a wild card, but Basil was a gentleman in The Queen's personal guard.

Garrity appeared brainless. A noose might be in his future. Basil Walker was nearly thought of as a saint in most quarters. He intended to pay close attention to Garrity from this moment on.

Tamsin watched as the barrister nearly cleaned out the parlor. Mrs. Reynolds-Walker was rubbing her arms, her back to the room as she looked out the large bay window facing the street. Tamsin wondered what was going on in her thoughts right now. Her lover all these years on his way to the hospital and then the lockup. She wondered if Mrs. Reynolds-Walker had ever known his real name, Harvey Ramsey.

A tiny bit of regret engulfed Tamsin as she glanced at the pitiful woman. Did she realize her lover of many years was on his way to lockup?

This might be her opportunity to find out why she murdered Uncle Basil.

She walked across the room to the large bay and in a challenging voice asked, "Why did you murder my uncle?"

Mrs. Reynolds-Walker was at least four or five inches taller than Tamsin and looked down at her. The pupils of her blue eyes, dark as crows. Tamsin's heart wrenched as she scrutinized this self-involved, vain woman whose arrogance was bred into her from an early age. A woman who could take the life of a man and not think twice.

"I want to know why you poisoned him."

Henrietta smirked at Tamsin. "You little fool. It's time you grew up."

At that moment, Fergus returned to the parlor and barked an order for Mrs. Reynolds-Walker to get in the wagon; he was holding her under lock and key.

The last Tamsin saw of her, she was handcuffed and

soldiered out the door to the waiting wagon for her inglorious ride to Metro Station. The autumn-colored leaves on her broad felt hat sagged from the day's trials and several strands of her golden hair had fallen from their pins. From the look on Henrietta's face, Tamsin suddenly realized the woman had been prepared to leave with Mr. De la Croix and Mickey Garrity when all heck broke loose.

Tamsin glanced furtively about the hall. Bobbies stood throughout the doorway and outer lawn of the mansion. Others walked near the gate as Fergus and Harrison scoured the wagons before leaving for Newgate. They gave one last pass through the front hall, and parlor. All were dispersed.

All except Tamsin, and she reentered the parlor, sat in a chair by the unlit fireplace, and sighed in relief. Through it all the reason for her uncle's death was yet to be known. She felt as if she could cry the rest of the day away.

Hearing the fuss on the street, carriages and paddy wagons grinding their wheels on the drive, and conversations between the rough voices of officers, Tamsin felt a twinge of ease and took a deep breath. Barrister Fergus was in complete control.

She sank deep into a chair and laid her head back unsure what was to be expected of her. The house grew quiet, and she'd closed her eyes a moment when a large hand cupped her shoulder.

"It's been a long day for you. I'm not surprised to catch you napping."

At the sound of Harrison's voice, she sprang off the chair. "I... well, it was quiet."

"Let me take you home." He reached for her hand and together they darted through the foyer and outside to his waiting carriage.

Fergus was talking to two Bobbies and waved his arm at

Tamsin and Harrison. "I'd like a word with ye before ye leave, miss."

He walked toward them. "Yer a force to reckon with, I'll give ye that. Ye know the danger of standing against a small mob, now, don't ye?"

She was shocked; was he complimenting her? "I didn't plan any of it, if truth be known, what happened in the parlor just fell into place. And between the three of us, I hadn't a notion the gun was loaded."

His bushy brows narrowed on her. "Ye could've been killed."

"I'm aware of the chance I took, sir. My intention was to scare Mrs. Reynolds-Walker into confessing to the murder of my uncle."

"And did she?" He seemed mildly interested in her answer.

"I never had a chance to question her. It turned into complete chaos, particularly when I accidentally shot De la Croix."

"Do ye have a motive in mind?" His bushy brows came together in a squint.

"I did think at one point she killed him because she wanted to marry De la Croix. But his engagement to Miss Horwrath took care of that possibility. Then there was Uncle Basil's wealth that she would inherit." She stopped guessing and shrugged.

The wind whipped up a pile of dried leaves sending them into a swirl. With hat in hand, he said, "Yer revolver served ye well."

"It was my uncle's. I felt as if he was with me."

With a slight smile, he said, "Perhaps justice has been served at Basil's hand; after all it was his gun."

He turned to Harrison, "If Miss Tamsin is up for it, bring her around to the station in about an hour. I'll be questioning

Mrs. Reynolds-Walker." He turned to her. "Ye might be of service ta the investigation."

She was nonplussed and again felt obliged to drop a curtsy; which she didn't because it would be ridiculous. "I'd like nothing better than to listen to her excuses and lies."

He slapped Harrison on the back and said, "Say four o'clock at the main station, then? I'll let her stew for an hour or so. She's more likely ta offer up information the longer she sits on a dirty wooden chair, in a stinking dank room."

"Yes, sir. We will be there."

Tamsin and Harrison walked toward the waiting buggy. The ambulance had already left with De la Croix. Fergus had sent two Bobbies back into the house to question the assistants in the kitchen. Mickey Garrity was on his way to jail and somehow the world seemed to shift on its axis as red and gold leaves sailed across the clear blue sky on this blustery autumn afternoon.

Before the day was gone, Tamsin would know her uncle's killer, and the why of his murder. A pragmatic woman, the information wouldn't set her heart at ease. Nevertheless, knowing would give her some relief.

Chapter Thirty

Wednesday, 5:00 p.m.
5 October 1870

Fergus sent three Bobbies to the only known address for De la Croix. They had to force open the locked entrance. As Fergus had supposed, the enforcement officers found a stack of papers with Basil's signature or name on them. The same papers stolen from his home nine days earlier.

A quick review suggested Ramsey was looking for information about the tea plantation in India that Basil owned. The original sale with title deed, and surveys of Hilldale, were among those stolen. When they found the purloined papers, they were in the process of forgery to appear as though Basil had sold the property to Ramsey.

Harrison opened the heavy pebbled-glass door to the Metro Police Service at Whitehouse Place allowing Tamsin to step in ahead of him. A front desk officer greeted them. Harrison was asking for Barrister Fergus when the man himself strode through a narrow dark corridor into the front of the station.

"On the mark, I see." He smiled at Tamsin. "Miss."

They followed him down the long hallway from where he had emerged and into a room with one small window with iron bars. For the interrogation, a table and three chairs centered on the slated floor with two more chairs placed against the wall.

A stale damp odor in the room intensified the unpleasant atmosphere.

Tamsin had wondered what an interview room could consist of, now she knew. It was bleak, stinky, and depressing. Courteously, Fergus asked if she wanted to sit at the table or against the wall. She chose the wall.

Harrison claimed a chair at the table alongside the barrister. An officer opened the door and led an annoyed and handcuffed Mrs. Reynolds-Walker into the dank room. He indicated she sit in the chair across from the barrister and Harrison. Henrietta had removed her large hat and had taken pains with her hair since they last saw her.

Smudges darkened the skin beneath her eyes. She looked tired and uncomfortable though the officer had just removed her handcuffs. Those weary eyes scanned the entire room from the iron grates covering the window to the closed door, and back to her three interrogators.

Fergus began, "Ye know Miss Tamsin Morgan, Mr. Harrison Spencer, and meself so let's get on with this, shall we?"

Having yet to say one word, she nodded slightly.

"I've brought ye here hoping ta get some insight into what happened at yer home earlier today."

A bit of life appeared in her eyes. "I was expecting a late lunch with friends. The day couldn't have gone more awry."

"How long have ye known Mr. Ramsey?"

She drew her hands from the table and cupped them in her lap. "I've known him as Desmond De la Croix, never as Mr. Ramsey. It was shocking to know he went by a false name. I met him at my debut cotillion when I was sixteen."

The barrister wrote on a pad then looked over at her. "Just to be clear, his legal name is Harvey Ramsey. De la Croix is fraudulent. Now, Mrs. Reynolds-Walker, I would like to know how well might ye know Mickey Garrity?"

"Only through his friendship with Desmond." Her eyelashes fluttered. "Oh, my, I mean Mr. Ramsey. They've been companions for—I'd have to say years. You must know he works for Davis & Fenway. I believe he might be a detective."

"On another subject, would ye tell me about yer marriage to Basil Walker."

Her gaze shifted to Tamsin, who was staring at her. "There isn't anything to say. It all happened years ago. My parents forced the marriage. They thought Basil was an advantageous catch, and that I couldn't do better than to marry him. He possessed a sterling reputation and was a member of gentlemen clubs." A slight smile lifted the side of her mouth. She added, "My father put great influence on a man who belonged to clubs."

She turned thoughtful for a moment. "My parents wanted the marriage and there was no denying them. What more can I say? I was young and under their demands."

"Ye've made it clear why the marriage took place. I want ta know what it was like being married."

Her gaze shifted to Tamsin once more. He could only speculate what that was about.

"I was in love with someone else. As I was forced into

marriage, I couldn't see myself carrying on the duties of a wife. I didn't feel like a wife to Mr. Walker. So, on our wedding night, I told him as much."

"How did he react ta what ye told him?"

"He appeared to understand. He had his housekeeper put me up in another room. And eventually he found a home for me to call my own. Everyone was happy. My parents, Mr. Walker, and especially myself."

He made notes on the pad, and appeared quite thoughtful as he took a minute or two before responding. "Why would a man as wealthy, nice-looking, and certainly as intelligent as Basil put up with such an arrangement?"

A haughty lift of her chin might have said it all, but she snapped, "I would not know. And as I was pleased with the outcome, I didn't waste my time on speculation." She sputtered as if suddenly heated with disgust, "It isn't as though he didn't have a life of his own. He was well known and respected. And certainly, hadn't needed a wife to complete him."

"So, ye took it upon yerself ta marry him, escape your parent's domination, and once married, decide ta free yerself of yer new husband. Have I got it correct?"

She huffed at his insensitive understanding. "I can't expect you to grasp the tension I felt at being practically sold off by my parents."

He tried not to show his aversion. This woman revealed tendencies toward manipulation, control, and a general lack of empathy or concern for others. He found it hard to understand why Basil would marry her. What was his motivation?

"Ye kept up appearances socially?"

"No. I had no desire to be seen with him in public."

He noted that remark on his pad, stretched out his legs, sighed, and looked at the suspect before him. Young as she was years earlier, she must have been heavily in the thrall of

Ramsey. She laid her cards on the table; and it appeared she deliberately married Basil, then revealed her feelings for someone else.

Fergus suspected there was more to the story.

Still guessing, Fergus wondered if Ramsey wanted the tea plantation enough to use Mrs. Reynolds-Walker as a willing go-between in a possible purchase?

Or, perhaps Basil had planned to sign over his plantation as a gift to her. But she felt trapped and refused him. She might have thought Basil wanted to be a real husband to her.

He took a deep breath. His musing was pure conjecture. One other thought was Mrs. Reynolds-Walker was truly in love with Ramsey.

"Did ye already have a lover?"

For the first time, she seemed to come to life. Her eyes blazed with reaction. However, she didn't answer his question.

"I'll take that as a yes. I'm guessing it's Harvey Ramsey. Am I right?"

If glares could kill, Fergus would be dead. He chuckled. "I'd let ye go for now. But I dinna believe for a moment ye wouldn't run and hide."

Her eyes were mere slits of anger as the guard snapped the handcuffs on her wrists. After she was taken from the interrogation room, he turned to Tamsin and Harrison, asking, "Where there any surprises in what Mrs. Reynolds-Walker had to say?"

Tamsin said, "Clearly, my uncle meant nothing to her. After he died, I made a visit to her home. She mentioned being in love with another man since she was a young debutant. I had the feeling they were still together all through the years."

"Perhaps Ramsey will be more forthcoming. I'm curious how much real influence he has on her."

Harrison said, "Wouldn't it be a surprise to discover Mrs. Reynolds-Walker is behind the murder?"

A smirk lit Tamsin's face. She knew she didn't need to remind them of her firm declaration.

Wednesday, 7:00 p.m.
5 October 1870

With Mrs. Reynolds-Walker incarcerated, Fergus arrived at the City Orthopedic Hospital to spend time with Ramsey. Tamsin tagged along to hear what the man had to say in his defense.

Harrison had work waiting for him on his desk in chambers. He needed to catch up on the sworn declarations of facts compiled thus far and begged off, certain he'd hear about the interview at the proper time.

As expected, Ramsey was in bed. Fergus had no fear that this man would be going anywhere soon; not with the damage done to his knee. Tamsin had seen to that.

A nurse was in attendance and mentioned the patient needed his rest. Fergus assured her, "He'll be getting plenty of rest, don't you worry about that. I just need a couple of minutes of his time. 'Tis all."

The nurse appeared agitated. "I've had detectives go after the wounded before. See that he's not riled."

The Scot paid her scant attention as he walked around the bed and stood looking down at Harvey Ramsey. His leg was in a contraption that lifted a few inches off the bed. "What've ye ta say for yerself?"

Ramsey pointed a finger at Tamsin. "She shot me in the

knee without provocation of any sort. I want her behind bars."

"We'll see ta her incarceration in due course. Right now, I've questions of me own. Is it true ye wanted to purchase Mr. Walker's tea plantation?"

It was a minute or two before Ramsey spoke. "At one time, I did. But he wanted more than I was willing to pay."

"When was this?"

"I was interested as far back as maybe twelve years. I've brought the purchase up several times since then. But he wouldn't budge on his price."

Tamsin spoke up. "Sir, I recall my uncle mentioning a conversation he had with someone, whom I have come to believe was this man. He told me the man was tired of waiting for a decision about Hilldale and just might do something illegal and he meant to keep an eye on him."

"What were Basil's reasons for not selling?"

"He felt the prospective buyer had motives that were illegal. He wondered if Hilldale was a cover-up in the transport of opium. Something to do with undercutting the price."

Fergus looked at the helpless Ramsey cuffed and in a sling. 'Twas his own behavior put him in a predicament. "I'm thinking ye knew why he wouldn't sell ta ye. And ye had him killed because of it."

Ramsey shut his eyes. "I'm not up to this. That gun wielding..."

"Now, now, Ramsey. She was working under the auspices of the crime department. She was doing her duty."

"Some obligation ye gave her. She's a—"

Tamsin turned away from the bed and looked out the window. The barrister had called her action a duty and it thrilled her to pieces, like cool water cascading over a firewall.

He stepped in front of Ramsey cutting his view of

Tamsin and inquired, "Where were ye the night of Tuesday the 20th of September, about midnight?"

He moaned. "I'm a cripple. My leg may never be of use to me again, and you want to know where I was in September? How the hell do I know?"

Fergus leaned over the bed and grabbed Ramsey's shirt in his fist. "By God, ye'd better have an alibi, or ye might just hang for the murder of Basil Walker. Yer choice, Ramsey."

With that, he turned, clutching Tamsin by the elbow and walked them both out.

His intention was to scare the be-Jesús out of Ramsey who had been a scammer for years, though he knew the man wouldn't scare easily. Using the date of Basil's death should bring a response that would involve Mickey. They'd both say they were together, which would be provident because Harrison had Mickey's boot print from the cellar.

Out on the street, Fergus smashed his hat on his head and turned a sour look on Tamsin. "Well, that dinna give us much. A waste of time ye'd say?"

"It was interesting to watch you probe Mrs. Reynolds-Walker and Ramsey. I'll be interested to hear what Mickey Garrity has to say. I would not have thought of the three of them in a conspiracy against my uncle. Your questioning brought out a connection between them."

She glanced up at the tall barrister and noted his attention fixed on her, giving her a thrill of sorts. As if he respected her conclusion.

"If ye'd been a man, I think the law would have taken an interest, aye?"

"Quite possibly." She smiled inwardly at his thought, as if her uncle had spoken.

It was late, and the streetlights were on. Fergus hailed a ride for Tamsin and then he returned to Metro.

Garrity waited in the interrogation room, in handcuffs and stocking feet. He scowled at the barrister.

Sullen and quiet, Garrity sat in a chair across from his jailer. His facial flushing had subsided a bit from earlier in the afternoon because he'd been without his drink for several hours now.

Fergus wondered how tight he and Ramsey were. Harrison had mentioned earlier on in the investigation that Garrity wasn't on the up and up. Harrison had an unusually keen sense of people, Fergus admired that.

"How do ye like yer accommodation?" The Scot shifted his briefcase to the floor beside his chair after he drew out a paper covered with written notes.

Garrity cocked his head. "You owe me an apology, and an explanation as to why I'm here. And I want my boots back."

"Let's begin with what ye and Ramsey were doing that ye were tanked up earlier. How long have ye known each other?"

"A year or more." His handcuffs rattled against the tabletop when he moved his forearms. The treatment he received greatly agitated him.

"What's the basis for yer relationship? Business, friendship?"

"A bit of both. I was helping him purchase some property."

"Where might that be?"

"Here and there. He fancies himself an entrepreneur. You know the type, someone who thinks of himself as a speculator."

Fergus' voice mingled with a touch of humor. "Ramsey put on airs. His fancy name a façade to draw unsuspecting wealthy individuals to his offerings." He waited for a reaction, and when Mickey didn't respond, he added, "Ye know the type, a manipulator. He uses others to accomplish his own desires."

Garrity still didn't react to the crack against his buddy.

"I'm surprised that ye have so much time ye can help a friend buy land, and tip a few with him, all the time working for Davis & Fenway. Do ye get special hours? Maybe I'm sitting on the wrong side of the table."

Garrity's face turned sour. He grunted and slapped his palms on the table. "You're running out of time, Fergus. You can't hold me without cause. I'll be out of here in an hour or so." He shoved his chair back from the table, his cuffed hands laying in his lap.

"We've got evidence against ye. Ye'll be our guest for a while, maybe for life."

A moment of silence filled the air. He could see the Irishman calculating the odds against him. "'Tis a matter of yer left boot missing part of the heel. An exact replica of what's on the dirt floor where Basil's body was taken."

The reddish hue on Garrity's face turned ashen.

Fergus waved to the guard who had been standing outside the room. "Ye can tell this cretin, he needs someone ta bring him shoes, because we won't be giving his back."

Then he stood, grabbing up his briefcase and left the room without another word to Garrity. Let him stew and wonder about the heel on his boot and how it would affect his future.

Chapter Thirty-One

Thursday, 9:00 a.m.
6 October 1870

S cotland Yard Commissioner Thomas Merryweather had appointed Barrister Fergus as temporary Deputy Assistant Commissioner, the third highest rank ever given for criminal investigations on a temporary basis.

Basil Walker had been working with Fergus on what was thought to be a rather small criminal inquiry until his fateful murder on the 20th of September.

The investigation was undercover. There were only three people who knew, Commissioner Merryweather, Barrister Fergus, and Basil, who had retired from Her Majesty's Service, and was now dead.

On this particular blustery day, Fergus entered the Commissioner's office, removed his hat, and approached the desk. Merryweather closed a ledger he'd been working on and gave his attention to the barrister.

"It's good to see you, scowl and all." He turned to a

cabinet behind his desk and removed a bottle of whiskey pouring two-fingers for each of them and handing one glass to Fergus. "Can't be all that bad, can it?"

Fergus wasn't one to drink early in the day. He knew Merryweather imbibed whenever the chance occurred and wasn't about to say no to his superior. "Thank you, sir. Ta yer health." And sipped the contents. When the Commissioner sat, Fergus took a chair.

"Are you getting close to a solution?"

"I'd say, with three possibilities. Me money is on Ramsey. Though Mrs. Reynolds-Walker is a strong likelihood."

"And the third?" Merryweather settled in his leather armchair.

"Mickey Garrity, a detective for a small firm, Davis & Fenway. From what we've gathered, he's been involved in some dirty work for them. The other two however are quite suspicious."

"Have you got them under lock and key?"

"Yes, sir. All three have been photographed, and pertinent information documented, age, height, so on and so forth." He smiled at his superior. "Exactly according to the Habitual Criminals Act, sir."

"Will I see a conviction sooner rather than later?" Merryweather sipped at his brandy, his dark eyes eager for the possibility. He was impatient to get this case over with and get on with a proper farewell to a man who was respected by many citizens and friends, and most of all, Her Majesty.

"I need some time, sir. One of the suspects is in the hospital with a crushed knee. A casualty of arresting him. I should have this figured out within a day or two at the least."

"You never fail, Fergus. It's a shame you chose the bar. I could have done greater things with you on my staff." Finishing the last of his whiskey, he set the empty glass on his desk.

Basil had been a loyal friend of long duration. Brilliant and principled, he was assassinated in the prime of his life. Fergus wasn't resolved over his friend's demise and hoped seeing justice done would bring closure of some sort.

What he said to the Commissioner didn't reveal the dull pain that festered. "I enjoy occasionally playing detective. Gets me out of the office and into the action. It was always exciting working with Basil."

"Yes, yes, a terrible loss. I can imagine how the rest of London will react once the announcement is made. He was greatly admired."

Fergus set his glass down and glanced over the many accolades framed on the Commissioner's mahogany walls. The shelving held tomes filled with Merryweather's interests. A huge desk was the focal point of the room. An eye catching red-and-blue, oriental rug with a center medallion of cream and gray livened the dark wooden floor.

He thought of his own chamber, stacks of papers, books opened to important points all scattered about, all needed in the process of problem solving. If he were to file them away, they would be out of sight and thus forgotten. He wasn't normally a judgmental sort when it came to his or other offices but decided to suggest to Harrison that a bit of sprucing up would be in order.

Merryweather asked, "You aren't thinking of stepping away from your undercover roll?"

"Not a'tall. Keeps me blood pumping."

Merryweather got up from his chair and came halfway around his desk. "Basil's death is hard to accept. How has his niece taken to all this?"

Fergus' gray bushy brows lifted. He was surprised Merryweather thought of her. "She's adapted considering we've not revealed his death yet. I think once the press gets wind of his passing, she might crumble. I hope not, of course. Miss

Morgan is a strong young woman to have carried this burden these past weeks. We think of the weaker sex as fragile of heart and mind. He'd be proud of her. She's made of sturdier stuff."

The Commissioner noted, "Because she was raised by Basil, not some flighty-minded female. I've always considered men to be the strong backbone of a family. Sheltering the weaker sex and so on."

"Right. Then you should know Miss Tamsin is very much involved in this case by her own insistence."

Merryweather's jowls sagged when his mouth was closed, giving the appearance of an ornery mastiff. He was no doubt contemplating Miss Tamsin's role in Basil's murder.

Fergus wondered what the Commissioner's wife and daughters would have to say if they became aware of his characterization of women. He appreciated that the gentleman had six daughters to marry off, especially considering he'd never had a son that would have helped to balance the sex in his family. Fergus pitied the husbands that were yet to be chosen.

"And you know nothing about Basil's remains?" the Commissioner asked.

"Naught a hint, sir. Be assured my office is involved. Harrison Spencer, near to taking the bar, has put in hours and hours of investigating Basil's death.

"We'll get our pound of flesh." The Commissioner had the demeanor of an elder from a bygone era.

Fergus sincerely liked the gentleman.

Thursday, 11:00 a.m.
6 October 1870

Fergus, Tamsin, and Harrison agreed to meet this morning at Metro where Garrity spent the night in lock up.

It was blustery with the occasional heavy rain splatters. Tamsin avoided the miserable weather arriving by hackney just as Harrison climbed out of another vehicle. They took the steps together into Metro meeting the front deskman who informed them Barrister Fergus was in cell number six on the second floor.

They turned the corner and walked down a long corridor of cells filled with prisoners. As the law men strode the filthy hall, the inmates yelled threats, as others begged for clemency. The inmates were disturbing and crude, as the corridor filled with their trash talk echoing off the damp, mildewed brick walls.

Harrison tried to shield Tamsin as they hurried along, and a guard threatened the criminals if they didn't shut up. It was useless and he encouraged them to walk fast and ignore their surroundings. Within minutes they arrived at the interrogation room.

The three settled in just as Garrity was delivered in handcuffs. The barrister noted that someone had provided him with boots. The guard pushed the prisoner into a chair.

A belligerent grimace on Garrity's face. He used his shoulder to nudge the guard who brought him in. The guard shoved him in the chair, the prisoner kept his head down finding the tabletop to be interesting enough.

Fergus wasted not a moment. "We'll get right down to business. What if I told ye Basil Walker is dead?"

Garrity ignored the question.

Fergus slammed both his palms on the table nearly hitting Garrity's cuffed hands. "Answer me."

"What the blazes do I care? I didn't know him."

"That's odd. Your boot print was in his cellar."

"You'll have to prove that." he growled.

Fergus chuckled. "And that we have. Yer boot print from the cellar with the broken heel. There won't be any dispute during yer trial."

"Trial for what?"

"His death. Have ye forgotten the reason ye were in the cellar ta begin with? I suspect ye intended ta dispose of his remains, but yer partner had already done so without letting ye know. When ye showed up, ye left yer boot print. It's as good as yer signature."

Garrity kept his silence and continued to eye the tabletop.

"How long have ye worked for Ramsey?"

Garrity shrugged.

Fergus pounded his large fist on the table. "Answer me."

"On and off—several years."

"What did ye do for him?" He spread his arms on the table, cupping his hands.

"This and that."

Again, Fergus pounded his clenched fists on the table causing Garrity to nearly jump out of the chair.

"He wanted me to find out things for him. Rifle Walker's desk, keep an eye on who went to the cellar at night, stuff like that."

"Seems ta me such duties are beneath yer worth to a man like Ramsey. He must not have paid well?"

This time Garrity's gray eyes locked on Fergus. His voice resounded bitterly as he ignored the reference to Ramsey. "I waited till dark. The same woman went down into the cellar each night."

Fergus leaned against a post and questioned, "Tell me about the third night."

"I wasn't there the third night."

"That's a damn lie and ye know it. Were you the one to carry Basil's body out? Ye and who else?"

There was a very long pause before Garrity said anything. Fergus knew if he talked he would implicate himself. "I wasn't there the third night."

"Have ye any notion of who that might of been?"

He shook his head.

"I'm figuring that's the night ye left yer boot imprint when ye stole his remains?" He used the pencil in hand to point at the boots on Mickey's feet. "Because I see ye wearing a pair fit for fancier affairs now."

Garrity slanted a derisive glance at the barrister.

Fergus lowered his head, his chin resting on his chest. He could sense Garrity's resistance. He was going to be a tough nut to crack.

"I'm guessing the one who showed up was his niece." Garrity fiddled with his hands that were locked together with the handcuffs. "The last night, I don't know if it was a man or a woman. The person was tall, dressed in pants and their head covered."

Several minutes of silence passed when Fergus asked, "Whose idea was it ta murder Basil? I'd guess it wasn't yer's."

"How would I know. I never met the man."

"Ah, ye've met him both alive and dead. I have it on good authority that ye got in a fight at yer place of employment, David & Fenway, that ye knocked out a few teeth of a co-worker when he ratted on ye about a case ye were working. Basil was brought in as a witness ta other beatings ye'd meted out. Seems ye were fairly quick with yer fists over the years. And ye didn't have a fondness for Basil Walker because he had yer number."

Garrity glared at the barrister and professed it a blatant lie. Fergus wondered what, or who, he was protecting. "Ye'll save yerself a lot of jail time if ye confess who murdered him." He drew his fists off the table thinking the game Garrity played was rather tiring.

"Seems ta me yer willing to take the responsibility for Basil's murder. I'd say the person yer protecting will owe ye big, as yer probably going ta hang for it."

Garrity scanned the faces of the other two in the room who hadn't spoken a word. Harrison was a man with many scruples as he knew well enough from their years at Cambridge. The woman he knew because she kept him at gunpoint earlier and Ramsey had told him she was Basil's niece.

The Scot watched him assess Miss Tamsin. She looked as though she'd already made up her mind. She had guts though, brandishing a gun at them, taking charge of the group that had gathered in Mrs. Reynolds-Walker's parlor.

Fergus asked, "What is yer relationship with Ramsey?"

"He paid me to keep watch on certain properties he was interested in purchasing. My post with Davis & Fenway kept me busy, I wasn't always available."

Fergus scraped his chair back and stood, as did Harrison and Tamsin. Garrity glanced at Harrison a long moment, then looked away. "When will I be out of here?"

Fergus smiled. "If I were a betting man, I'd say ye've got a roof over yer head for many a year ta come. I'm not satisfied yer not the killer. But as it stands right now, yer crime is aiding and abetting in a murder."

Garrity was escorted to his cell.

Tamsin and Harrison were expected to join Fergus in his carriage as they made their way to City Orthopedic where Harvey Ramsey remained handcuffed to a hospital bed.

The trio's purposeful strides echoed on the marble of the second-floor hospital corridor. It was eerily silent otherwise, and a relief from the damp moldy halls of Newgate.

They stopped at the desk to inquire about Ramsey's room number, then continued down the hallway almost to the end, where a high-collared Officer in Blue stood outside the door.

"How's the patient?" asked the barrister.

"Cross I'd say sir. Wanting to be let go."

"Is he awake?" They glanced into the room. Ramsey's head was turned toward the window. If he heard their voices, he didn't show it.

"I don't rightly know, sir. I've been sitting in this chair for the better part of the morning. The doctor has been in, no one else until you arrived."

"Take some time for yourself if you like. We'll be here perhaps an hour."

"Thank you, indeed, sir." He couldn't get away fast enough.

Fergus strode into the patient's room and walked around the bed to find him asleep, or acting as if he was. He jiggled the bed with his hip.

Ramsey's eyes opened. He grunted and closed them. With his left hand handcuffed to the bed, he couldn't move overly much.

"Come, come, Ramsey. You've got visitors."

His eyes slit open, and he groaned.

"I've some questions that need answering. Ye've had a day ta think about yer circumstance, so let's get on with it."

He tossed his hat on the windowsill and drew up a chair to the side of the bed. "Ye know Harrison Spencer and Tamsin Morgan, I'm sure. They're here to aid me in getting the facts straight."

Tamsin stood at the end of the bed. "Basil was my uncle. I happen to know you were interested in his plantation in India. Did you make an offer to purchase that land?"

He swept his right hand over his face, covering his eyes and groaned.

"You needn't hide Mr. Ramsey. All we want to know is what you were looking for when you snuck into my home and went through my uncle's files."

When he didn't answer, Fergus jarred the metal bed frame with his hip again, eliciting a groan from the wounded man, who said, "I was interested in any offers he may have gotten for that property in India. He was avoiding me."

Tamsin moved from the end of the bed to stand nearer him, looking down at his face. All the years she'd suspected Mrs. Reynolds-Walker's duplicity, this was her chance to know if it was Desmond De la Croix she loved.

"Mrs. Reynolds-Walker told me she loved a man who was not my uncle. Was that man you?"

When he didn't answer, Harrison stepped forward. He placed his hand gently on the surgical wrappings on Ramsey's knee. "It might be wise for you to answer the lady. She's entitled to know the truth after all these years." He gently smoothed his hand over the bandages.

Ramsey breathed in a shaggy breath of fear. He looked from Harrison to Tamsin and back again. "You might say I gave the woman the impression I loved her. She was like a gnat pestering me, wouldn't let go. So, what's a man to do but use what's near at hand."

Harrison stepped back from the bed as Fergus turned from the window. His Scottish accent full of discontent, he asked. "Are ye saying she did yer bidding?"

"It's not like I took advantage. She was more than willing to do anything I asked." Fergus' impulse was to belt him in the face and get rid of that smug attitude.

Dazed for a moment at Ramsey's crudeness, and though Tamsin had suspected Mrs. Reynolds-Walker of nefarious behavior, she had never gone so far as to think of her as an actual thief. "You mean she snuck into my home and went through my uncle's files?"

"She thought it a lark."

Fergus barked, "What do ye know of Garrity?"

"He'll do anything for money."

The Scot chuckled. There's a large segment of society who would do the same. "How long has he worked for ye?"

"Three, maybe four years."

"Whose idea was it to murder Basil?"

"Oh, now don't jump to that conclusion. You'll need proof and you don't have it because I didn't kill him."

"My team found many files that had been stolen from Basil's library. He had planned to sell Hilldale Tea Plantation to ye." He waited for a reaction from Ramsey.

When the man didn't respond, Fergus said, "The contract we have in our possession is drawn up by ye and is clearly a forgery."

"You can see I'm not in the best of health. I'd like to be left alone."

"Knowing the law as I do, I'd say yer wish to be alone will happen soon enough. When there's a murder, a rope around the neck usually evens out the injustice."

He didn't give Ramsey a chance ta react when he added, "Garrity was yer grunt, getting his hands dirty for ye. Whose idea was it ta kill Basil so that ye could take over ownership of Hilldale?"

Ramsey plopped his arm over his eyes and let out a breath of anxiety. "Not mine."

"But you know whose it was, right?" Harrison stepped away from the bed as Fergus took his place.

"I could guess, but I won't talk until I've been promised a release."

The barrister chuckled. "One trick for another, aye. Ye can rot in hell before I give ye a pass. As I see it, I've got enough on ye ta be sent up for the next ten or twenty years. Of course, if I find out ye killed Basil Walker, it'll be the rope for sure."

He stepped back from the bed as Ramsey dropped his arm away from his face. There was raw fear in the whites of his eyes. Hopefully, he'd given the prisoner something ta think about.

Harrison motioned to Tamsin that they should step outside the room. In the hall they moved to the window at the end of the corridor overlooking the streets of London and the traffic stuffing the roads. A bend in the Thames was visible from their perch. Big Ben bonged the three-quarter hour sending the time across the river and over the streets of London.

In her heart, Tamsin knew Mrs. Reynolds-Walker killed her uncle. It didn't make sense that the barrister was stuck on getting a confession from Ramsey. Would tomorrow bring a confession, or a denial from the strong-minded widow?

Chapter Thirty-Two

As the trio left Metro, Fergus suggested dinner. Tamsin declined saying she was a little done in. In truth, she was exhausted.

Harrison tried to warn her about what exposure to violence can do to oneself. Death, especially when unexpected, is shocking and surreal all of itself. Compound that with the murder of a loved one, and it becomes hard to cope with the loss and move forward. It's not uncommon for family members to find recovery long-lasting and life-altering.

The day had been exhausting and tomorrow wouldn't be any less stressful. He suspected Tamsin anticipated a difficult interrogation with her nemesis.

At this point, all Tamsin wanted was to know what happened to her uncle and his remains.

Fergus left Ramsey's room Harrison and Tamsin waiting for him near the stairwell. It was late afternoon, and the trio were fatigued from the grueling day.

Grateful to be out of the wind as they sat in Fergus' carriage, they agreed to take the evening off and meet up tomorrow morning.

Harrison walked Tamsin to her door. "Let's hope this will be the last cross-examination. It's getting to be too much for you."

She snapped at him. "I need you to stop hovering over me like a big brother." Her eyes narrowed with justification. "Though I do appreciate your caring I'm not a porcelain doll on the verge of cracking." She squeezed his hand then let go. "Enjoy your evening and I'll see you in the morning."

Having left Tamsin at her doorstep, Harrison climbed into the carriage. A big brother? If she were to think of him at all, brother certainly wasn't the acclaim he had in mind.

Fergus chuckled. "Big brother? I had you pegged for something a little more enduring. Ye might have to polish yer approach."

Harrison's mortification robbed him of words. He looked out the window at the crush of people and carriages, basically ignoring his mentor.

"Don't be sore. "Tis been a long time, but I could polish up some niceties ye could use."

Was the barrister giving him a bit of a rub? He'd not seen this side of him, ever. Harrison threw the Scott a scathing glance only to discover the man was enjoying himself immensely.

Harrison had no desire to continue the line of conversation and changed the subject. "She needs a quiet evening in the sanctuary of her home."

"Right. Losing Basil is finally catching up with her. We will all be glad ta get this over and done."

The carriage maneuvered south toward Westminster but the heavy mix of vehicles on Oxford Street was caught in the crush of five o'clock traffic. The blustery wind earlier had turned into a deluge gushing down the cobbled streets like a river, increasing the mashup.

Fergus suggested, "I believe our Miss Tamsin has begun the mourning process. The signs are there. She's quieter and withdrawn. Now that we are narrowing our list of suspects, perhaps she's beginning to realize what the future holds without him."

Traffic thinned a bit and the carriage rumbled over a rough patch of road, as Harrison spoke up, "Do you recall when you were informed of Basil's death, what a cold-blooded shock it was?"

"I'll never forget. Why do ye ask?" He had pulled out his pipe and was holding it between his teeth, without lighting it.

"In retrospect it feels like a year or more. And to think it's just been a smattering of weeks. I agree with you about Tamsin. Perhaps it's another step in the grieving process?"

"When has she taken the time these past weeks to mourn? She's been under considerable strain."

They withdrew and became silent, each recalling when they learned of Basil's death and the shock of losing him. It was why they now struggled to find the responsible person and make him or her pay for his murder.

Harrison wondered, "We should initiate a conversation with her about a memorial service? It could be held in a chapel, or perhaps something more intimate at the house? What do you think?"

Fergus rubbed his palms together hoping to get some warmth. "I think you are a true friend. And I will be glad to assist with whatever she chooses. When you bring it up, let her know to include me in the plans." His large hands in gloves, he slid them to his knees. His voice was low and mournful, "I'll never have a friend like him again."

They rode in silence for a few minutes, when Fergus

declared, "I'm fairly certain we'll wrap this up tomorrow after our interview with Mrs. Reynolds-Walker."

Harrison pulled his gaze from the window where he'd fogged it with his warm breath. "You're sure she's the killer?"

"We know he died in his chair. And we know it was poison that killed him. Which means Garrity, or Ramsey, or Mrs. Reynolds-Walker would have been in the room with him. I need a little more information before I decide, but either way, if it's not her, it's more than likely Ramsey. Garrity is a smalltime hood. As much as I dislike his ethics, I don't see him as a killer.

"Yesterday I would have added Garrity to the list. But I'm thinking Ramsey used him more for his dirty work. The discovery of Garrity's boot print might mean he was more likely there to dispose of the corpse."

Harrison bit his lower lip in frustration. "It's hard to accept that a man as well liked and respected as Basil died in such a pitiful way."

"We'll come up with a splendid way to honor him. But first things first. Let's nail the bastard. It's The Queen I'm concerned about. She won't take his demise lightly. I rather think whoever killed him will wither their life away in the gaol, or dangle from a rope."

"Right, sir."

Harrison's boarding house came into view and Fergus rapped his cane against the ceiling. "Thanks for the lift. See you in the morning."

Friday, 8:00 a.m.
7 October 1870

Harrison's landlady, Mrs. Labady, accommodated her six residents at eight o'clock sharp with breakfast in the dining room. There was very little chitchat among the boarders. She preferred her roomers to dine and get on about their day, though she never inferred they do so in words. She was a bit cleverer than that.

It was the empty tray she carried in from the kitchen and began picking up used dishes, that led them to realize their leisure was over. By the time they finished a bowl of porridge sprinkled with cinnamon, two slices of bacon each, and buttered toast slathered with her specialty of strawberry-blueberry jam, she deemed it time her boarders left for their respective employments.

Briefcase in hand, Harrison headed for Whitehouse Place and thought of Tamsin. Last evening, she appeared exhausted and downcast by the time the carriage had pulled up in front of her home. Usually she was full of energy, and questions, and ready to form opinions.

Through the process of interviews, he'd noticed how quiet she'd become. Today might prove to be more than she anticipated, and he wondered what he could do to support her. It was obvious her emotional turmoil since Basil's murder was at a peak.

Fergus and Tamsin were already seated when Harrison arrived.

She greeted him with a weak smile. "You walked all the way from Mrs. Labady's? Isn't that quite a lengthy trek?"

"I needed the exercise."

Tamsin glanced about the dark cell and held a handkerchief to her nose to ward off the damp, musky scent. The only window, high up on the wall, was locked. Yet up to the present time, this building, old as the hills continued to serve justice.

She had read somewhere it was originally built in the twelfth century and rebuilt and added onto many times. It was remarkable that in this modern world of 1870, it continued to be used as a prison.

Fergus mumbled as he dug into his briefcase, "Let's see if Mrs. Reynolds-Walker will be agreeable today. Perhaps she's had enough of her cell."

Tamsin wondered, "We must be in the oldest section."

"That we are." He chuckled. "Do ye think it would inspire ye ta tell all and get on with yer life if this was going to be yer home?"

She was about to respond when the door opened, and a warden seated Mrs. Reynolds-Walker and cuffed her left hand to the chair.

"Will this be all, sir?" the sentry asked the barrister.

Fergus glanced at everyone and nodded. "I believe so."

Friday, 10:00 a.m.
7 October 1870

As the door to #6 closed, Fergus looked directly at the ruffled and worn-out inmate. "I hope yer not too inconvenienced by yer accommodation."

"What matter to you," she snarled. "I'm grateful rats haven't eaten my shoes."

His stern gaze swept over her. A woman of leisure, and a nice annual purse from Basil. He wondered if she had put it all together these past few days. She certainly had the time.

He'd asked at the desk and the only person to visit was her butler, who had given her a basket of food that she more than likely was forced to share with other inmates or suffer dire consequences.

Fergus pictured this pampered woman sharing space with all manner of humankind. It must be a fright for her. But he simply couldn't muscle up regrets on her behalf.

The battered hat was gone, and she'd twisted her hair into a semblance of neatness. For obvious reasons, the jailer had taken her hair pins. Her jewelry had also been taken from her and given to the butler.

Fergus placed a paper on the table and pushed it across to her. There were several questions written down that he wanted answered.

Why did ye poison Basil?

Where have ye put his remains?

Who helped ye move his body?

Why do ye think Mr. Walker continued to give you an allowance and purchased a home for ye when it's clear ye had no respect for the man?

He watched as she read the questions. He fantasized her as a mythical monster rearing up its ugly head, teeth gnashing, with no consideration for anyone but herself.

Leaning back in his chair, he calmly asked, "Why did ye poison Basil?"

Without thinking, she tried to cross her arms, forgetting her left hand was cuffed to the chair. Anger sparked in her eyes.

Again, he asked, "Why did ye poison Basil?"

"What makes you think it was me?"

"Because ye needed ta get yer hands on the deed ta Hill-dale. So, ye poisoned his drink and stood in front of him as he drank it, all the while he was unsuspecting of yer motive. Ye poured two glasses but didn't touch the one for yerself.

"Once he was dead, ye planned to search his office, but someone was coming down the stairs so ye fled out the front door."

"Why would I want the deed to a plantation in India?"

"Because someone forced ye ta get it from Basil's library."

Humiliation darkened Henrietta's eyes before she glanced down at her lap.

"Where are Basil's remains?" asked Fergus.

She took a deep breath and glared at him. "Even if I knew I wouldn't tell you."

"Ye being such a proper lady, was it Garrity who moved the body from the cellar? I think the pair of ye stayed near the house and spied on Miss Tamsin as she dragged her uncle's body to the cellar. Ye saw her grief and felt no remorse for what ye'd done. Murdered a good man. A man who never faulted in his care of ye."

Sucking in a breath, she spat out her irritation. "Your imagination runs wild. Perhaps you should become a prognosticator." She struggled to keep a shred of dignity.

Grappling with his own impatience obviously itching to shake the hell out of the self-absorbed, deceitful women, the Scot took a deep breath not able to shake the knowledge his friend was dead because of her.

He needed to find her frailty, when suddenly an idea struck him.

"From The Queen on down, there is testimony to Basil's generosity, kindness, and willingness to help others. He was one of The Queen's favorites. Her Majesty was verra sorry when he retired. I can't imagine her wrath when she's told he's been murdered and by whom. Makes one wonder what lengths she'll go to for retribution."

The prisoner paled at his mention of Her Majesty.

"I have it on good authority Basil boosted yer parents' income when they were in need. I believe that took place several weeks before ye married him. They wanted to see ye settled with a highly respected gentleman and know that ye would always be taken care of.

"It's understood ye had a lover throughout the time Basil courted ye and after yer marriage. Did Basil know about yer affair?"

She stared at him, her mouth slightly agape, and jerked on the handcuff mumbling something.

He felt he was on the right track and continued. "Out of curiosity, I'd like ta know if ye ever revealed the name of yer lover and how ye managed to keep two men interested."

Other than the breathing of the four people in the cell, a great silence hung in the air and a vile eye raked his face. If looks could kill, he'd be a dead man right now.

Down the hall, an iron gate screeched as it slammed shut. A man's deep voice with an east-end accent shouted a string of obscenities, and the sound of a truncheon banged against the iron gate.

After which, silence was restored.

Mrs. Reynolds-Walker lowered her head. Perhaps she was considering her dire situation.

Tamsin spoke up. "I want to know why you led my uncle on, why you pretended to be interested in him. Was it money? Prestige? What was the lure that made you accept his offer of marriage in the first place?"

The woman's head snapped upward as she again tugged on the arm that was cuffed to the chair. She was clearly upset and in a muddle indicating a tantrum was possible.

In her growing rage, she started to say something and stopped. Then opened her mouth again, then shut it. Her eyes wild with frustration or anger or perhaps both. Gritting her teeth, she looked like she was going to spit.

Fergus felt she was ready to explode. He glanced at Tamsin and winked at her, receiving a doubtful glance in exchange.

Again, a loud scream from one of the cells rang down the corridor of metal and stone, followed by footsteps running toward the sound and muffled hubbub, then a truncheon banging against the bars.

"I have a question for you, Mrs. Reynolds-Walker."

The woman glared at Tamsin as if she had no right to ask anything.

"I'm simply curious, was it you who told Madam Patwell I was a twin?"

Mrs. Reynolds-Walker laughed crudely but said nothing.

Tamsin had her answer. The woman was enjoying the upper hand by not revealing she was the one. It just proved Mrs. Reynolds-Walker already surmised her luck had run out.

Of a sudden, the woman mourned, "The love of my life has cast me off." Her face contorted, looking almost like a shriveled, rotten orange.

Fergus hid a smile and Harrison blew out a thin breath. Tamsin's eyes widened and her mouth looked like the letter 'o'.

"You know nothing about what I've been through. My whole life crushing down when the man I loved thrust me off." She screeched and pounded her hand on the table. "HE was the reason I married Basil. He forced me into that marriage, telling me lies about how our love would never change, it could only get stronger.

"I've loved him since the moment I first met him. I was a young girl ready to make my debut. He'd come to the house to meet with my father about business. And that late afternoon we were alone for a few minutes during which he asked if I would meet him in the park in an hour.

"It was magic being with him, well...our times together were..."

She blushed a deep red realizing what she almost revealed. Her voice softened. "The most handsome man in the world chose me. How I wanted to tell the other debutantes about him. He could have his pick of any of them, and it was me he chose."

She paused a moment in reflection. "As you can imagine, my debut was no longer the most important event of my life. I basked in Desmond's love."

"Ye are talking of Harvey Ramsey. He's nothing more than a common thief," said Fergus.

"I never knew him as Ramsey. He was my Desmond."

Tamsin turned to Harrison and the barrister. Both looked dumbfounded.

She could hardly ask without showing pity for Mrs. Reynolds-Walker's stupidity. "You've been with him since you were a very young girl." She was leaning against the farthest wall and wondered how Ramsey and Henrietta stayed together all these years.

Mrs. Reynolds-Walker's overwrought voice was painful to hear. "I gave my all to this man and he announced he's to marry another." Her sorrowful eyes shifted to Tamsin.

"It's pitiful you're such a lousy shot. If I'd gotten my hands on that gun, I would have made him worthless to any woman."

"You might have saved us all a lot of trouble," said Fergus.

Her eyes narrowed on him as if she wasn't quite sure he was agreeing with her. "I gave him my youth, and what did I get in return?" Her wild eyes scanned the room, settling again on Tamsin.

She patted her chest as if she needed to breathe and continued with her dramatic monologue. "My suffering has been bittersweet. One day he loves me, the next he loves that bawd, the next he insists I stay married to Basil, then he no longer cares.

"I shocked Basil the evening of our wedding when I confessed to my love of another. He scoffed saying ridiculous things like the wedding tired me, and I was experiencing megrims."

She shifted in the chair, tugging on the handcuff and glared at the three of them obviously finished with her story.

Fergus coughed into his fist. "Basil had no idea you loved Desmond De la Croix?"

A fleeting look of yearning crossed her harassed features. Her voice softened. "I hadn't a clue what Basil thought, nor did I care. The housekeeper put me in a room as far from Basil as she could manage as if I'd sneak into his room." She laughed at the ridiculous thought.

Tamsin had been standing and plopped into a wooden chair unable to speak. She suffered for the uncle she loved so much.

She swiped at a tear running down her cheek. "It was the best of both worlds, wasn't it. A lover on the one hand, and a wealthy husband on the other." Her laugh was shrill, as if she was well aware the joke was on herself.

Breaking out of her stunned state, Tamsin challenged, "Except that your vow of marriage to Basil was a lie. You had no intention of being a wife to him. Yet, he was decent enough to put you up in a home of your own and give you an allowance."

The woman seemed to drift into memory for a minute, a look of satisfaction on her pinched face.

Tamsin challenged, "What was the real reason you came to the house the morning after my uncle died?"

"We were married, weren't we? I have every right to check on my allowance." She sat up straight in the wooden chair and needled Tamsin with a glare. "Nothing will change that."

Harrison asked, "You mean to say you considered Basil as your husband even though you turned your back on him the evening of your wedding?"

With eyebrows raised, she challenged, "Am I not Basil's legal widow? Everything he owns is now mine."

Fergus grunted, "I see yer game, and I'll see ye hang for it."

Tamsin stalked around the table and leaned into Mrs. Reynolds-Walker. "Why would my uncle put up with your duplicity for fifteen years?"

"Who knows? I certainly didn't understand him. Nor did I care."

Tamsin laid her palms on the table next to the woman. "You killed a decent and wonderful man. Why? Help me understand why you would take his life."

Mrs. Reynolds-Walker abruptly meant to stand forgetting for the moment that her hand was cuffed to the chair. The chair tipped putting pressure on her wrist and she glared down at Tamsin. "You haven't any proof of that. Why wouldn't I care for the person who paid my bills."

Harrison righted her chair and she sat.

Fergus scraped back his chair and strode to the cell door knocking on it. A deputy stuck his head in the room, and he said, "Ready the prisoner to be taken out. She'll be under my supervision and returned within two hours."

"Yes sir."

Mrs. Reynolds-Walker turned on the Scottish barrister. "Where do you think you are taking me?"

"You'll see."

"I'm not moving until I know where you are taking me." Her lips pinched and her eyelids narrowed.

He laughed. "Ye no longer have any rights until proven

otherwise. I say ye are leavin' with us, and so ye shall." He yanked the chair out from the table, then jerked her upward waiting for the guard to unlock the cuff.

A Bobbie hurried from #6 to arrange for a carriage. The guard unlocked the handcuff from the chair. Tamsin and Harrison gathered up their articles and the barrister led the way downstairs.

Everyone was seated in the police carriage, Mrs. Reynolds-Walkers's hands were again cuffed, and two Bobbies stood on the running board outside the carriage as the driver snapped the reins.

Tamsin sat across from the barrister. She knew he wouldn't want to be questioned in front of the prisoner and remained silent. Likewise, she couldn't converse with Harrison, though the route they were taking was in the general direction of the hospital. She thought Fergus must be returning to the hospital and Ramsey.

What did that man have up his sleeve?

Chapter Thirty-Three

Friday, 1:00 p.m.
7 October 1870

Arriving at the hospital, Fergus ordered two Bobbies to escort Mrs. Reynolds-Walker down the hallway and wait for his signal before bringing her into Ramsey's room.

After the guards moved away, he whispered instructions for Tamsin and Harrison to stand near the door, outside the curtain where it had been pulled around the bed to give the patient privacy. Then he entered Ramsey's room.

"How's the knee?" he asked, with a somber expression.

Ramsey sputtered, "Come to gloat over my brush with death?"

"I'm here ta listen while ye describe exactly what happened between ye and Mrs. Reynolds-Walker and Basil."

"If I talk, I walk." Stretched out on the white sheets of his bed, his leg in a sling, one arm tucked beneath his head, and the other cuffed to the bed, his dark eyes slanted toward the barrister waiting for his reaction.

The Scot's tolerance was waning. "This isn't a negotiation. Ye either give me the information I want, or it's a cell for ye. Yer choice."

Ramsey waited a minute or two before his dramatic monologue. "Henrietta was always a pain in my ass."

"Watch yer language. There are women at hand."

He glanced at the closed curtain. "Miss Morgan? She's a good looker."

Fergus barked, "None of yer fancy talk, Ramsey. Lay it on the line, or ye'll be in a wagon on the way ta yer next home."

"Just having a bit of fun. I'm bored tucked in here day after day. Your guard dog, Jocko, watches my every move. I'm not going anywhere with my knee the way it is."

Even though Tamsin and Harrison stood behind the curtain listening to Ramsey, Fergus could picture Tamsin's cheeks turning pink. She was pretty. Ramsey had paid her a compliment, crude though it was.

"Basil, me, and Henrietta. That's what you want to hear about?"

Seemingly bored, the barrister cast a weary glance at him.

"I first met Basil when introduced by another gentleman at White's one evening. When I discovered he owned a tea plantation, I had a chance to see if he might be interested in selling, if the price were right. A few years back I wanted more control over my import business and figured having my own plantation would be the ticket."

"I think ye mean yer contraband," added Fergus.

"Now, now. If you want me to continue, you'd better play nice."

The Scot's eyes narrowed, but he kept his mouth shut.

"A few years later, I heard of Basil's possible sale of Hilldale and encouraged Mrs. Reynolds-Walker to cozy up to her estranged husband. Which, she said she tried to do, but he hadn't any interest in her, or in selling his plantation. She could have been lying. She's a good liar."

"Sounds to me as if she was tired of yer using her."

He chuckled. "There isn't a woman alive I can't wrap around my finger. And Henrietta was always eager. She'd do anything to please me. Always has, always will, I suspect." He adjusted the sheet over his upper body as if a chill took him.

Fergus had enough. "Ye're verra sure of yerself. She was a married woman ye realize."

Ramsey laughed aloud. "Let's just say the lady loved someone else and Basil didn't make the cut, husband or not."

Ramsey droned on, "I made it clear to Henrietta what I wanted from her. She promised me she would convince Basil to sell the plantation. He was always cordial toward her, and she felt she could bring him around."

For a moment or two, it grew quiet until someone in another room bellowed for a nurse, followed by the sound of pattering at a quick pace down the hall.

At the same moment another nurse came in and opened the curtain asking Ramsey if he needed anything. In so doing, she revealed Harrison and Tamsin standing behind the curtain and scanned the three visitors quickly. "Are you family?"

"No, ma'am. I am Barrister Fergus here to take testimony of a death in which yer patient may or may not be involved. And these two are my assistants."

Fergus was dusting the charm off Ramsey. Since Ramsey's hospitalization, it was obvious the nurses paid him extra care. The barrister figured the women thought him quite agreeable, in spite of the fact he was cufflinked to the bed.

The nurse's eyes widened. "Then I won't interfere, sir." She smiled at Ramsey as she adjusted the curtain around his bed before leaving.

Fergis barked, "Get on with it, Ramsey."

The patient cocked his head toward Fergus. "You think I'll admit to Walker's death, but that isn't going to happen. I didn't murder him.

"Henrietta took matters into her own hands. She was plenty worried about money, and knew he had a bundle that she expected to inherit. Doesn't that say it all? We'll see about Hilldale now, won't we Mr. Big Man. Somehow, I envision lady luck will choose me as the victor."

"Ye mean a busted knee is triumph over defeat?" The Scot fisted his hand with an overwhelming urge to push in his face. He countered the urge, of course, though it was strong. He could only imagine what Tamsin and Harrison were thinking.

Scuffling in the hallway distracted all of them for a moment.

Ramsey changed his position on the bed drawing his free arm from behind his head. "I'm not the one who killed The Queen's man. And I'm satisfied staying here for the next few days until I can put weight on this leg."

Fergus held on to his self-respect, though it was difficult. For a fleeting moment, he considered Ramsey's other knee but squelched the idea. With his leg in a sling and one hand cuffed to the bed, the irritating prisoner was basically locked in place.

In a calm, indifferent voice, he asked, "With so much confidence in yer future, I take it ye know who killed Basil?"

Ramsey shrugged. "Isn't it obvious? Henrietta. She slipped arsenic in his drink. She'd been in his house several weeks earlier and mixed it in the carafe. She's a sly one. He'd been drinking small amounts all this time. That last night, she slipped a large amount into his glass and stood across his desk as he took sips during their conversation.

"She delighted in explaining to me how satisfying it was to watch him die. If it hadn't been for his niece coming to check on him, she'd have stayed longer."

"What would you guess was Mrs. Reynolds-Walker's motive?"

"His wealth, clearly. She's in line to inherit quite a bundle. She's excited about her future as a very wealthy woman."

"How is it you were privy to her plans to kill Basil?"

Something, possibly a tray, clanged on the tile floor in the hallway, they all heard glass shattering. A woman's scream, loud enough to shake the dead, curled in the air.

Fergus yanked back the curtain from around the bed and with stunned appreciation of the moment, watched as Ramsey realized Mrs. Reynolds-Walker heard every word he'd said.

The woman sprang onto the bed charging Ramsey bringing her hands cuffed in iron down on his knee. Ramsey screamed at the top of his lungs and tried to reach her with his good arm. She scraped his face with her fingers, shouting piercing obscenities that more than likely could be heard throughout the hospital.

Tamsin froze with shock. Harrison, who'd been leaning against the wall in a corner of the room, couldn't reach the bed. One of the guards lunged at Mrs. Reynolds-Walker but not before she pounded Ramsey's face and knee quite dreadfully.

The assault on the patient was so sudden, he couldn't defend himself. His leg was wrapped in a sling and tied to an apparatus hanging from the ceiling, and his left hand cuffed to the bed, made it easy for her to yank the sling that held his leg. She bit his arm like a dog going after a bone and again banged the cuffs on his already bleeding and severely injured knee.

Fergus had been talking to one of the guards when the assault originated. He charged into the room and reached across the bed to grab her hands, but she'd snatched a fork off Ramsey's tray and stabbed his hand with it. She skewered Ramsey's arm, all the while with an ear-splitting screech ricocheting off the walls and down the corridor, alerting all within hearing of the horrendous attack.

A guard elbowed his way into the chaos attempting to clutch the woman's shoulders. She swung her arms around, slashing her handcuffs and fork at his face.

The barrister lurched around the bed and grabbed the woman, dragging her off the patient. She bellowed obscenities at the bedridden Ramsey, foul words of deceit, and lies, yelling that it had been him who forced her to kill Basil. In her rage, she pounded the back of her head into Fergus' face and tried to claw at the hands that bound her.

Kicking Fergus in the shin, she moved away from Harrison as he tried to grab her legs but didn't duck in time as she whipped the fork across his forehead, narrowly missing his eyes.

Her wrists and fingers were bleeding by this time and the guard was finally able to subdue the flailing arms and jerk the fork from her cuffed hands.

Harrison came up from behind and shoved her into a chair, allowing the two guards to bind her hands and legs.

"I hate you," she screamed at Ramsey.

Ramsey's nose was bleeding, and he held part of the sheet to it. "I thought you loved me?"

She spat at him, reminding Tamsin of an asp striking to kill.

Her hyperventilating affected her speech. "I...I caught him...by...surprise."

Fergus barked, "Who did ye catch by surprise?"

"Basil." Her wind hadn't evened out yet, and she dug deep for a breath. "I usually crept in after...after midnight when I needed extra cash. And there...Basil sat...He...he...always drank a glass of something, whiskey, brandy in the evening. He'd been ingesting small amounts of arsenic for weeks without knowing it."

The room quieted. You could hear her panting. "He never asked for the key I was given when we married. On occasion, I went in and out of the house at night when my funds grew low. He always put extra money in his bottom drawer.

"I planned to surprise Desmond with Basil's death." She took a deep breath and glared at Ramsey. "But, with Desmond's engagement to that bitch reported in *The Daily*, everything changed for me.

"That last night, I went to Basil for the purpose of reuniting. I suggested we begin again. He laughed when I put forward the proposal that we try to make our marriage work. I begged him and pled with him. But he'd have none of it."

She had regained much of her composure at this point and continued on. "When he declared he'd have nothing to do with me, I made the decision to finish him off. I drained a vial of arsenic in his drink."

"Yecame prepared to poison him?" Fergus noted her glance slanted to him with a mysterious challenge swimming in those dark eyes.

"I'm sick of men dictating what I can and can't do." Her

lip snarled and her hands twisted together. Clearly, she was psychotic and more than likely grasping her doomed future.

Her testimony was interrupted by three nurses rushing into the room. They carried surgical dressings, a bottle of carbolic acid, rolls of gauze, and shooed everyone from the small room.

Their efficiency tending to the patient was instant as they began washing blood from his face and arms. A doctor saw to the sling that held his leg. It had loosened and his leg was bent, and what was left of the bindings on his knee were soaked in blood as was the mattress.

In the hallway, a guard, holding a cool cloth to his cheek where he'd been slashed by a fork, stood next to Mrs. Reynolds-Walker as Fergus urged her to continue. She appeared calm and relieved to tell her story as if a great weight lifted from her. He could hardly fathom her disconnection from the real world.

The doctor and two nurses charged into the room and listened in fascination as Mrs. Reynolds-Walker described her hatred of the man in the sling. She followed that up with admitting how Basil died.

"I stood on the opposite side of the desk from him pretending to sip the drink he'd poured. I watched him die, and soon Hilldale would be mine. And when Desmond came around, I'd have the upper hand, wouldn't I?

The small group of hospital workers listened in amazement. Mrs. Reynolds-Walker appeared to be enthralled with her narration and audience.

"I hated Basil's refusal and hated Desmond for replacing me with that stupid little mouse, Horwrath." Such was her vexation, she took a deep breath, and her chin lowered as she glanced at her cuffed hands. No one had offered to tend to her bloody injuries.

A nurse had given Fergus a damp cloth to hold to his nose as it bled, and his left eye as it turned red.

Tamsin grabbed Harrison by the arm and moved them to a corner of the room. Tears streamed down her cheeks.

Her raspy voice quizzed, "Did you hear her? She admitted to Uncle Basil's murder." She drew her wrist across her eyes, wiping away hot tears.

Harrison put his arms around her and held her close as she sobbed, her whole body shaking with emotion. The burden she'd been shouldering finally culminated in the release of heart-breaking pain at the discovery of how her beloved uncle died.

All these weeks, deep inside, she had known it was Mrs. Reynolds-Walker. The pain of knowledge did little to help her in the moment. She would never see her beloved uncle again, never again hear his deep, comforting voice.

Two nurses who had trailed the doctor into the room of the injured Ramsey immediately began cleansing the battle-weary Mrs. Reynolds-Walker and prepared her for transport.

Responding to a pill the nurse gave him, Ramsey began to nod off. The fork cuts and bite marks had been washed and treated, and the doctor was completing the new bandage on the knee.

After Mrs. Reynolds-Walker belted him with her cuffed hands, Harrison wasn't sure if Ramsey heard her confession. He seemed a bit woozy from her attack. Harrison had it in mind that Ramsey was as much a part of Basil's death as was Mrs. Reynolds-Walker. His outlaw instincts caused extreme suffering and death.

Relief swept over the hospital room as the patient, nursing staff, and guards saw the last of the distraught and bitter murderer. She was escorted by four guards on her way to Newgate Prison.

An hour later, Barrister Fergus, Tamsin, and Harrison arrived at Metro to tie up a few loose ends. One of greatest importance, getting a written statement from Mrs. Reynolds-Walker. Fergus felt that Tamsin should celebrate the woman's admission. Since Tamsin had discovered Basil's body, her diligence never wavered in the belief Mrs. Reynolds-Walker was his killer.

In less than five minutes, Mrs. Reynolds-Walker wrote out her confession, witnessed by Fergus and Tamsin and safely tucked in his breast pocket. Then Fergus asked the woman several questions that still lingered.

"Who took the body out of the cellar? And what was done with it?"

Her glassy eyes darted to him. He saw her conversion from exterminator to submissive prisoner. "Can't you leave me alone now?" In her wild frenzy, she'd injured herself attempting to kill Ramsey. Bedraggled and exhausted, her keen eyes sagged with the realization it was over.

Fergus warned her. "If ye have one decent bone in your body, you owe it to Miss Morgan to tell her the whereabouts of Basil's remains. She's left grieving over the loss of her beloved uncle."

She glanced across the room at Tamsin and snorted. "Garrity left his remains at a teaching school under the name Thaddius McFee. The doctor he chose was in charge of a small school, and their funds were scarce. Garrity mentioned Mr. Besaw said he would keep the heart in case the family changed their mind to have a memorial."

"Have ye a name for the medical school?"

She sighed. "St. George's, I think."

Fergus was curious. "How is it Basil never meant

anything to ye? He was very well thought of, and one of The Queen's favorites."

She shrugged and turned her face away from him. Her largely self-centered life left no room for remorse about the lives she'd ruined and the people she'd hurt. Her journey now was going to be the courts and a sentence that might well lead to the hangman's knot.

The prisoner was taken from the room under guard and transferred to a more secure part of The Metro to await trial.

Meanwhile, Garrity was brought into the interrogation room.

Tamsin turned her back on him and stood at the filthy window, dead cockroaches scattered on the sill. She could barely see down into the yard where prisoners exercised. The sky was chalky with mist and a chilling wind. Oddly, the helplessness she'd been weighed down with seemed to have declined in these last several hours.

Fergus was the first to speak. "Seeing as how I'm in charge of Basil's murder investigation it's a wonder I don't have yer name on the list." He glanced at Garrity, obviously dissatisfied with what he saw.

Garrity straightened his shoulders in an attempt to gain a semblance of propriety. "I've been involved in an undercover operation, sir. Nothing I can speak of right now." Garrity lifted a narrowed gaze at the barrister. "I'm certain you understand the error of cuffing me and bringing me in for investigation."

The Scot knew the scum was lying. "Ye've been canned. Davis & Fenway washed their hands of ye long ago. And, lucky me, I get ta lock ye up and await trial for the murder of a dear friend of mine."

Garrity shot out of his chair overturning it, and two guards stepped forward grabbing him by his upper arms.

"What the hell." Garrity backed up. In his struggle he

shoved the table a few inches as he tried to get free of the guards.

Fergus ordered, "Lock him up until further notice."

Garrity's chin jutted as he yelled, "You can't keep me. I didn't kill that man." He struggled to shrug off the guards. "Get your hands off me. Or else..."

"Or else what? Seems ta me, ye've locked in yer future by the company ye keep. By the by, ye'll be needing a good lawyer."

His voice croaked and his eyes bulged. "Hold on. That bitch was the mastermind."

The guards glanced at the barrister, who beckoned them to wait a moment.

Garrity growled, "Lock her up and you'll do us all a favor." The guards kept hold of his arms. Beefy as he was, a chair tipped over as he squirmed to be let go. "I'm not your problem. It's Reynolds-Walker. She planned his murder and doing away with the corpse."

His voice scattered against the rock-solid walls. At a nod from Fergus the guards shoved Garrity out of the room and down the hall to a cell.

Fergus always took satisfaction in the part of detective work where one malefactor revealed all the dirty little secrets of another.

Chapter Thirty-Four

Saturday, 3:45 p.m.
8 October 1870

arrison assisted Tamsin into the carriage and then leaned back against the horsehair bolster. When they arrived at her home, he followed her into the house where Mrs. T waited for them. Tamsin noted a distinct, almost superior look on the housekeeper's face. "Has something happened?"

Mrs. T handed her an engraved missive. "This came for you soon after you left this morning."

Tamsin glanced at the folded letter and flipped it over, noting the royal red wax seal on the vellum where The Queen's Coat of Arms was embedded. Both Mrs. T and Harrison glanced at The Queen's signature stamp and then at Tamsin.

"Well, do something. Open it!" gasped Mrs. T.

She broke the red wax seal, unfolded the page, and read its contents. "I've been invited to tea with The Queen."

Mrs. T took the letter from her and read it. "Oh, my. What an honor."

Harrison said, "Not to be confused with high tea. We are expected at three. Fergus informed me this morning of the summons."

A long silence followed with Tamsin quirking her head. "I've nothing proper to wear."

Her nothing-proper was solved with Mrs. T's supervision. She transformed a black felt hat with a three-inch brim, and a mix of very dark pheasant and barn-fowl feathers, into a delight. Mrs. T had matched her skirt with a dark gray jacket in Tamsin's closet that she'd barely worn, forgotten about in fact. Knowing The Queen still wore mourning, and Tamsin mourning her uncle, she thought her choice was appropriate.

She looked in the mirror startled by what she saw and wondered if she might be the image of her mother. It rather pleased her that the possibility existed. Even though she was quite young when her mother died, Uncle Basil often spoke of his sister's attributes. He would smile at Tamsin on those occasions as if he could see his sibling in her. The pleasure she noted in his eyes always sent a tingle through her as if her mother was somehow at hand.

Sunday, 3:00 p.m.
9 October 1870

Fergus, Harrison, and Tamsin arrived at Buckingham Palace in Fergus' carriage. A footman escorted them along a corridor with portraits covering the walls and dark blue and gold runners covered the marble floors. Footmen in red and gold livery with white wigs opened the double doors to a room flooded with sunshine from a bank of windows looking out over the gardens onto a large pond with a huge water fountain, and an intriguing maze beyond.

Her Majesty stood at the end of the room with Scotland Yard Commissioner Thomas Merryweather.

Though she'd seen The Queen at a distance twice before, Tamsin was up close now and realized how tiny she was.

Presented to Her Majesty, Tamsin curtsied as a footman gave her name, then Harrison bowed, followed by the barrister.

They were led to a table covered in fine linen with pink roses and bluebirds. Gold rims on the bone China enlightened the table, and golden dinnerware was imprinted with The Royal Seal.

She sat at the head of the table, allowing each of her guests to take their own places as indicated by the footmen.

Her Majesty turned once more to Tamsin. "Miss Morgan, I wish to give you my condolences on the passing of your uncle. He was a favorite of The Crown. Many afternoon teas were enjoyed together. Is it difficult getting on by yourself?"

"At first, Your Majesty, yes it was. I owe a debt of gratitude to Barrister Fergus and Mr. Harrison Spenser for their compassion and investigation into his death."

The Queen turned to the men. "You have caught the villain?"

Fergus said, "Yes, ma'am. We will have our day in court with her for certain. And her accomplices."

"Are you saying it was the wife, after all?"

"Yes, ma'am. Miss Tamsin never wavered in her thoughts

that Mrs. Reynolds-Walker was guilty. It seems all of our evidence points to that fact most clearly."

The Queen glanced at Tamsin, who quickly set her cranberry scone on the plate and gave her attention to their hostess. "What made you suspect Mrs. Reynolds-Walker?"

"She married my uncle under false pretense. And her lack of sensitivity toward him was obvious. Whenever she came to the house, it was always to ask for an increase in her purse. And then there were rumors of her behavior over the years."

The Queen held Tamsin's eye for a long second, then said, "I admit, my reluctance toward divorce may have kept my dear Basil from releasing himself from such a one as Mrs. Reynolds-Walker."

All eyes were on their sovereign as she glanced about the table. It appeared as though she regretted her influence in the matter.

After a long moment, The Queen inquired, "Fergus, "What has been done about our dear Basil's burial?"

"We have a confession from the murderer and are ready to proceed with a burial." He glanced at Tamsin. "Why don't you tell Her Majesty what you are planning?"

She set her cup in the saucer. "He had many friends and colleagues, so I think something graveside with a closed casket would be appropriate. I would very much appreciate your thoughts, ma'am. You knew him in a much different way than I."

Her Majesty looked somber. "My dear, he is your beloved uncle. His funeral should be as you desire and don't let anyone tell you otherwise. I would, however, ask if I might be able to privately pay my respects."

Emotions stung Tamsin. It was difficult to keep from crying, but she did her best. "He will be honored. Yes, ma'am. I will inform the funeral parlor of your wishes."

"No need. My equerry will take care of the details. I wanted your approval first."

Tamsin's composure almost melted. Her beloved uncle would have the honors accorded him despite the ruination Henrietta caused.

The Queen questioned Tamsin if she had taken time to think of her own future.

"I am in mourning, of course. For a time, I would like to concentrate on my uncle's papers and put them in order. Did you know he wrote short stories through the years?"

"I recall him entertaining me with a reading once. A young boy who lost his mother if I remember correctly."

Tamsin nodded with a smile. "Yes, at the time he wrote it, he considered it was his best."

The Queen nodded to a footman, and he pulled her chair out as she stood. It was time to leave and everyone at the table followed suit. Her Majesty thanked Tamsin holding her hands for a moment telling her to send a note if ever she felt in need of a visit.

It was one of the sweetest moments of Tamsin's life and she had to blink her eyes to keep from allowing tears to fall.

The next morning Harrison finally had a moment to read the paper before he began his day and was not surprised to see Harvey Ramsey's arrest spread across the first page with Henrietta Reynolds-Walker's and Mickey Garrity's names tagged as accomplices.

Tamsin, at own home and having just finished breakfast, read the front page, and rejoiced. She then turned to the society news. And a picture of Miss Allison Horwrath was front and center at the banner, stating she was no longer associated with Mr. Desmond De la Croix. That little item choked out a laugh that was surprisingly refreshing.

To no one in particular, Tamsin said, "She certainly had been eager to wed a wealthy connected man, until she discovered he wasn't what he pretended to be."

Done with the newsprint, Tamsin set out on a brisk walk to Mr. Fowkes pharmacy. Her intention was to set the record straight with the obliging pharmacist.

"It's been a while since your last call Miss Morgan. I hope all is well."

She set her reticule on the counter. "It is, and I've come to apologize and to enlighten you about false information I imparted."

"Since I've not had anyone die of arsenic poisoning, except perhaps rats, I'll listen." His bushy gray brow lifted in question.

"First of all, I am not an author. I pretended because I needed information about arsenic poisoning. And not for a plot."

"And not for rats, either I'm suspecting." He leaned against the counter, arms folded as though he had the entire day to converse, though his brows crunched into a frown. "I'm sorry you are not a writer. You impressed me as someone filled with imagination and creativity."

Flustered, she didn't know if she should thank him or not. "My uncle's death will be in the news soon enough. He was poisoned. And the killer has been found."

"I read *The Daily* this morning. I would say you've been extremely active in your pursuit of solving a horrendous crime. Though I saw him rarely, I do know your uncle was a grand gentleman, and so proud of you. I'm sorry for his passing. You are far too young and lovely to suffer his loss. Please accept my condolences."

She drew in a breath, hoping to keep her composure. "You were quite helpful. I believe you were suspicious of me being involved in mischief of some kind. I just wanted to let you know what I was about, and that it has been solved, thanks to a very wise barrister, and a soon-to-be-lawyer."

Gathered up her reticule and he came from behind the counter to open the door for her. "Please stop by on occasion so that I may be assured of your health and wellbeing."

She turned from the door and looked at his pleasant, grandfatherly countenance. "At the beginning of this horror, when I found my dear uncle dead in his chair, it was you I came to for answers. I'll be forever grateful for your assistance even though you weren't aware how much you helped me. But you were so very willing, and I am grateful."

Stepping out on to Upper George Street, she turned around. He was looking out the window at her and she waved at the kindly gentleman.

Two Weeks Later
Monday, 1:00 p.m.
23 October 1870

Tamsin never had an occasion to go to Barrister Fergus' chamber, though she had accompanied Uncle Basil on occasion to Lincoln Inn. She was made aware that for the last fifteen years, the barrister had handled legalities for her uncle. She was meeting with him today to go over the estate so that she would be familiar with the financials now in her name.

A daunting task, but she was eager to have the barrister understand she felt capable and willing to be the keeper of her uncle's estate.

Barrister Fergus' family shield hung on the wall, showing his ancestry was of the Argyll clan in Stracher until the beginning of the 19th century, then joined with the Fergussons of Kilkerran who were active in affairs of state and among the ablest of lawyers of their time. Of course, she didn't have to read his family shield to know he was highly intelligent.

Once Fergus acquainted her with all the accounts, Tamsin began to feel somewhat familiar with the arrangements her uncle had made. He certainly had thought of her welfare.

Fergus also arranged for Tamsin and Harrison to visit St. George's Medical School. It had been one of the first teaching schools in London, dating back to 1733 and located near Hyde Park.

Mr. Steinhart was the medical doctor in charge of teaching, and the man to whom Mrs. Reynolds-Walker confessed to giving Basil's remains, under the assumed name of Thaddius McFee.

Once Fergus was able to prove the remains given to Mr. Steinhart were Basil's, Tamsin was able to receive his heart.

She was grateful Mrs. Reynolds-Walker had a pinch of consciousness regarding her uncle's remains. Or possibly, the woman may have thought her sentence might be lightened if she proved to be helpful. Though her actions revealed her to be a thoughtless, narcissistic, and completely dreadful woman.

In any event, Tamsin, joined by Fergus and Harrison, arrived at St. George's to retrieve her uncle's heart. Some might have thought the action to be decadent or ghoulish.

Tamsin, far more pragmatic than most women her age, was trying to hold back deep-seated emotions.

Mr. Steinhart greeted them and suggested they go to his office. Upon entering the large room, all eyes went to the shelving filled with skeletal human bones, and jars of human organs. A skeleton frame hung from a metal rod in the corner of the room.

Tamsin noted a jar filled with an organ sitting on his desk along with tomes and charts and more human bones.

She stepped close to the desk, her eyes fixed on the jar. Papers strewn about the desktop nearly hid it from view.

Harrison noted a look of surprise on Mr. Steinhart's face. He was obviously disconcerted when Tamsin stepped over to his desk and picked up the jar reading the label. Her hands circled it, and she held it against her as she whispered words before returning it to the desktop.

In muted tones, Harrison asked, "Are you alright?"

"I am. It is my understanding now we can have a fitting burial for him." She glanced at Mr. Steinhart waiting for confirmation.

He quickly composed himself and said, "Yes, Miss Morgan you are correct. You will need to purchase a site of your choosing at one of the several cemeteries in the area. I've addresses for you to visit."

Fergus, who had stayed back, asked, "We will need the names of the people in charge of the cemeteries."

"Yes, sir. It's in order, and all you need do is stop by the cemetery you choose and ask to be shown lots that are available. You may take the jar with you or leave it here until you've decided on a mortician."

She glanced at Harrison. "I will take my uncle with me."

Friday, 11:30 a.m.
20 October 1870

The day of Uncle Basil's burial was simple and beautiful, with many accolades, and lovely flowers from so many of his friends. The casket, of course, was closed.

Mrs. Thistlewaite, Charlie, and the two maids Evie and Sally, sat on the left in the first row of Christ Church. Across the aisle, in the first row sat Tamsin, Commissioner Merryweather, Barrister Fergus, and Harrison.

The Queen required a private visit earlier in the morning before the funeral home opened to the public. Tamsin had met her at that time and was proud of the honor it afforded her uncle. Though the casket was closed, Queen Victoria had come to say goodbye to one of her own special detectives. It was humbling to see The Queen care so much for one of her own.

Tamsin endeavored to stay composed. All was lost when Her Majesty took hold of her hand patting it and saying, "He meant a lot to me. I want you to know how much he will be missed." The Queen pulled an embroidered handkerchief from her reticule and put it in Tamsin's hand curling her fingers around it. "I dare say you might have need of this."

At the cemetery Reverend Jamesworth conducted the final goodbye. The burial was a touching tribute to the man she loved. She hoped there was truth to the saying about the ever after. She really hoped he was enjoying his friends who had gone before him. She assumed her own parents would be among them, and her twin brother.

Reverend Jamesworth mentioned her uncle's goodness, his years of working for The Queen, and his dedication to goodwill toward humankind. A brilliant sun beam shot out from behind a huge dark cloud just as the Reverend finished with his homily.

Not one to miss the astonishing symbolism, the Reverand dramatically spread his arms wide and almost shouted, "St. Peter is waiting for you, Basil Walker."

Six Months Later
Monday, 17 April 1871

Henrietta Reynolds-Walker was accused of murder and sentenced to hang. The poisoning of a husband was generally thought to be at the hands of a greedy, lusty, or mentally unbalanced wife; more so than a man who murdered his wife. And as was customary to send letters begging for a reprieve for the prisoner, none arrived in time to save her. Should that have happened, she would likely have been sent to a penal colony to live out her days.

The judge and jury sentenced Henrietta Reynolds-Walker to death by hanging. As hangings were no longer conducted publicly, Henrietta was privately escorted to the gallows and hung by the notorious executioner William Calcraft inside Newgate Prison.

Harvey Ramsey was accused of aiding and abetting Henrietta Reynolds-Walker. The sentence was dependent upon the circumstances of the case and the discretion of the judge and jury. Ramsey was liable for the same punishment as Henrietta Reynolds-Walker, unless he could validate that he was coerced, ignorant, or otherwise not responsible for his actions (which he could not prove). However, the judge and jury sentenced Harvey Ramsey to be transported to Australia where he would work as a forced laborer for the rest of his life.

Mickey Garrity was accused of aiding and abetting Harvey Ramsey's plan to dispose of the remains of Basil Walker. In illegally doing so, the judge and jury exiled him to the penal colony at Van Diemen's Land (Tasmania). The offender's exile meant he had to leave his home country and work as a convict in a remote and harsh land. The judge and jury sentenced Mickey Garrity to no longer than twenty years and not less than ten years dependent upon his behavior.

Tamsin Morgan was reprimanded by the judge for not disclosing Basil Walker's death immediately. Harrison, as her accomplice, was ignored for the most part because his intention was to protect Miss Morgan from the same people who murdered her uncle. The court was fully in agreement considering she spent her energy investigating his death. She had willingly turned over all her investigation to the courts. The fact that she hid his body was never made known to the judge or jury.

Tuesday, 18 April 1871

Harrison arranged to collect Tamsin at four o'clock, and it was a quarter to the hour. He'd said he wanted to show her something, and whatever that something was, he seemed inordinately excited about it.

Within minutes of Tamsin's arrival home, Harrison knocked, and she met him at the door ready for their adventure. "You've certainly roused my curiosity. What's it about, anyway?"

"You, Miss Impatient, will just have to wait. It won't be a surprise if I tell you."

A half hour later, he pulled the carriage to a stop at the corner of Regency and Argyle and helped Tamsin down to the pavement. He deliberately stood facing a building and looked upward. She followed suit and took note of words chiseled on the lintel above the double doors of the building.

Basil W. Walker Gym for Youth was etched in marble in large broad letters.

Speechless, she managed to ask, "What is this? How did this happen?" She turned to him, grabbing his arm.

He had the most delightful twinkle in his eyes watching her discover the memorial to her uncle. "I wanted to honor a man to whom I am greatly indebted. He did many grand things for others, and certainly for me over the years." He took her hand, and they walked up a few steps as he drew a key out of his pocket. Once inside, he turned on a gas light.

"The workers have only just begun inside. Another two months or so, I'm told. But this is for young lads. Your uncle is the main reason. But Joshua Zillig was also my inspiration."

She stood on her toes and wrapped her arms around Harrison kissing him on his cheek. When she pulled back, a lovely smile grew on his face.

His eyes twinkled. "I take it you are pleased with the idea of a gym?"

"He would be so proud. And so thankful for your friendship."

Handing her a kerchief, Harrison directed her down a hall where he explained what the several smaller rooms would be used for. There was a kitchen, a water closet, and a small infirmary should the need arise.

"I'm overwhelmed with your kindness toward Uncle Basil. He would be, too. But I must ask, wherever did you get the funds to do this?"

He chuckled. "It's always about the pound with you. I have savings from my grandmother who told me to spend it wisely, and it's been sitting in the bank for quite a while waiting for inspiration. I've already been approached by the school board who are willing to subsidize the effort. Barrister Fergus also donated funds along with several of Basil's friends with whom he worked on cases for The Queen. We've formed a committee of sorts to firm up a plan of operation."

She squeezed his hand, shaking her head. "You've been exceedingly busy solving a murder. However, did you find time?" She dabbed at an errant tear.

"For some things you just make time."

"To be sure, my uncle is smiling down on you."

"Let's get in the carriage. It looks like another wet blow. The gym is far enough along that I hope you can envision what it's going to look like. I've wanted to tell you, but until lately it's been a pile of dust and confusion. It's just in the last week that it's begun to take shape."

She chortled. "As if our lives haven't been filled with important things." She slipped her hand into the crook of his arm as they walked down the steps. "I'm grateful that you and Fergus have sorted it all out."

"There are a few unanswered questions, but knowing the Scot, he'll get to the bottom of every last detail."

Harrison added, "Over the years, I was able to occasionally catch a few conversations between Basil and Fergus. They were a pair, and an opportunity for me to understand the vagaries of law. The Ferguson Heraldry is on the wall in his chamber. I'll point it out to you next time you come around."

Thrilled that a memorial for her uncle was in the making, she was clearly overwhelmed. It was gratifying to know his memory would live on and benefit others.

She'd never get over losing him, but the idea of a building where youth could gather in his name softened the deprivation. And having spent a little time with Joshua Zillig, she felt even more so about him spending time in Uncle Basil's gym.

Arriving home, Tamsin stepped into a quiet foyer calling out for Mrs. T, when she remembered the housekeeper had taken Cook Ames, Sally, and Evie to the theater and wouldn't be home until dinner. Cook had it all prepared for when they returned.

Feeling a bit hungry, Tamsin looked in the cooler and lifted the linen covering a platter with slices of ham. She also pulled out a pitcher of milk, got a glass down from the shelf and drew out a chair to sit.

Suddenly, it seemed as if her uncle faced her with a smile. She shook her head of the nonsensical vision. Dazed, her pounding heart, and feeling weak-kneed, she fell into the chair trying to get a grip on herself.

She closed her eyes trying to keep the image of him. But whatever it had been, it was no longer.

She noticed a bottle of Cook's sherry used for marinating beef. And poured half a glass of the sherry instead of the milk.

Sipping the drink, she considered how things would change for all of them. Mrs. T was a stalwart soul and would never leave her, but she wasn't young anymore and that saddened Tamsin to the point where she washed down a large swallow of the dry wine and comforted herself as best she could, by tipping more of the liquid contents into her glass.

She dwelled on her future and family and friends who had always loved her for as long as she could remember. Except for Evie, who arrived six years ago, and Sally more like ten years ago when she became part of the household.

She hoped Charlie would stay on. What would they do without a man on the property, for heaven's sake.

She burped and giggled then glanced at the bottle and poured a bit more into her glass. Pulling another chair close, she rested her legs on the seat.

The feeling of a secure home, the dear staff almost like family, and friends caused tears to spill. She swiped them with her wrist and sipped her glass.

Thinking of the security of home and the comforts of the dear staff, almost like family, tears began to spill from her eyes. She swiped them with her wrist and sipped her sherry.

Oh, my. She was relieved to have had such a lovely burial for her beloved uncle. More tears slipped down her cheeks. She sipped again and was relieved that he had been put to rest with a lovely goodbye and a beautiful, engraved stone that was to be added.

She even thought of Mr. Fowkes and how kind he was to her. She thought she'd pulled the wool over his eyes about the poison. And giggled at the look on his face when he thought she was planning to murder someone.

She was sitting length wise against the table, her legs comfortable, her left arm on the table clutching the sherry, and began a soliloquy honoring her uncle. She raised her glass and realized it was empty and filled it, nearly emptying the bottle.

Dearest Uncle: I am most grateful you took me in when I was a little girl. You are dearly missed...I promise to care for our home...and do the best I can to honor you.

She nearly drained the glass and propped her head on her arms as they draped across the tabletop, mumbling to herself of loving him, resolving never to dishonor him, and hoped the vision of his smile would come back to her.

The hall clock chimed the full Westminster Quarters and stroked the sixth hour. Mrs. T and Cook chattered as they walked down the hall toward the kitchen.

Upon entering the pantry, they were stunned to see Tamsin softly snoring, her head on the table, an empty bottle of cooking sherry, and a pitcher of lukewarm milk untouched.

"That was my last bit of cooking sherry," said Cook.

Mrs. T was clearly baffled. "She drank the whole jug?"

"It looks so."

Harrison entered the room saying, "I wondered where..."

Tamsin lifted her head as lengths of curls came undone on the side she slept on. She yawned as Mrs. T, Cook, and Harrison stared at her.

"My, my, missy, what have we here?" inquired Mrs. T.

Harrison grinned from ear to ear but said nothing as he stuck his hands in his pockets and appeared to roll on the balls of his shoes.

Cook Ames picked up the empty sherry bottle. Tamsin didn't miss the look she shared with Mrs. T.

Her eyes fluttered as she cupped her hand over her mouth before burping.

Monday, 1 May 1871

Tamsin received a letter from Fergus, who in turn had received it from The Queen. Taking a deep breath, she sat in her uncle's chair and read it.

Fergus:

I did not authorize my Detective Lieutenant Basil Walker to reveal any of the particulars of his gathering of facts in what he referred to as his "Blackbeard" file.

My having met with Miss Tamsin and your soon-to-be Barrister Harrison Spenser, I do believe they should know more of the facts than they have been given.

Such as, Basil knew all along who Harvey Ramsey, i.e., Desmond De la Croix was. He had also arranged a fictional marriage without Henrietta's knowledge. It was a deception in order to garner facts from Harvey Ramsey through her. The Crown despises divorce thus the 'marriage' was handled this way and without her knowledge. The deception was meant for appearances sake to appear real and to do away with any suspicions that might occur. Basil's duty to The Crown knew no bounds.

Will you please see that Miss Tamsin Morgan reads this letter before you dispose of it.

Victoria R.

THANK YOU FOR READING

Don't miss out on your next favorite book!

Join the Satin Romance mailing list
www.satinromance.com/mail.html

Did you enjoy this book?

We invite you to leave a review at your favorite book site,
such as Goodreads, Amazon, Barnes & Noble, etc.

DID YOU KNOW THAT LEAVING A REVIEW...

- Helps other readers find books they may enjoy.
- Gives you a chance to let your voice be heard.
- Gives authors recognition for their hard work.
- Doesn't have to be long. A sentence or two about why you liked the book will do.

About the Author

Karen Dean Benson's passion for history was ignited through travels across diverse cultures. A prolific reader since childhood, she found solace and inspiration in the pages of historical narratives, nurturing her love for research and the intricate stories of complex lives.

Rich with plot twists that captivate and intrigue, her plots transport readers to thrilling and stimulating bygone eras. From an early age Karen discovered the enchantment of creative historical writing, relishing the creation of characters and the weaving of their exploits onto the page.

Born and raised in Detroit, her formative years were shaped by the teaching of nuns; her education culminated at Northwood University. Amid the tranquil surroundings of Northern Michigan's AuSable River, she raised six high-spirited children.

Currently residing in Southwest Florida, karen and husband Charlie enjoy the ambiance of their golf course community where she continues to craft stories that transport readers through time and space.

www.karendeanbenson.com
http://freshfiction.com/author.php?id=40966

facebook.com/Author-page-for-Karen-Dean-Benson-141512154210494I

goodreads.com/karendeanbenson

bookbub.com/authors/karen-dean-benson

amazon.com/Karen-Dean-Benson/e/Bo16PMAZRE

Prickly Hawthorn Village Series
Historical Romance

Delightful stories of the 1800s Ireland

A charming mixture of Irish perversity, puzzlement, and prankishness sprinkled with endearing affection